THE COUNT

OF

AMARANTH MOOR

OR,

MEMOIRS OF A MODERN VAMPIRE

IN FOUR VOLUMES

VOL. I

YORK:
PRINTED FOR
PIPISTRELLE & THRUSH

1852

And gazing on thee, sullen tree,
Sick for thy stubborn hardihood,
I seem to fail from out my blood
And grow incorporate into thee.

—*Lord Alfred Tennyson*

PART ONE

THE FALL

CHAPTER I

A coach wound its way through the forest road, proceeding with some trouble.

The fault laid not with the horses; they were well-kept, though fed perhaps too generously, and could face a gentle uphill climb without difficulty. The hour of day, too, proved no obstacle. Though it was nighttime, two lanterns blazed by the sides of the carriage, illuminating the coachman's way. Rather, the problem laid with the road.

The path had been smooth when leaving town, passable as the journey into the forest began, but troublesome after a fork. The further this second road split from its more fortunate companion, the more the coach jostled its sole occupant quite miserably.

This sole occupant, unfortunately, was I. It was upon that coach that I found myself on this warm summer's evening, tired and somewhat despondent, gazing out through the window with dull eyes.

I will never forget how the trees looked that evening, the way their branches twisted towards each other overhead, black against the dusk sky. They might have seemed inviting in the open light of day; but in that moment, they seemed to me like a set of empty ribs.

Disturbed, I leaned back from the window. I was upset with myself for entertaining such thoughts, but it was to be expected. After all, I was preoccupied with the unsettled feeling that is common to anyone who travels frequently for their profession: the mingled anxiety and tedium of coming to a previously unknown home, and the melancholy of that strange intermediary time, which mocks any stability once assumed and invariably invites the pondering of death.

I pulled my attention from the gloom and gazed down towards my knees. For a few moments, I stared vacantly.

Then, slowly, I lifted my gaze to the window once more.

"Avery!" Henry, the coachman—he was a stout and cheerful fellow, who I had known for many years—called merrily from the reins, over the din of wheels and hooves. "You're awfully quiet! Is something the matter?"

His voice surprised me and I jerked, causing a portmanteau, which had already been precariously positioned beside me, to clatter noisily to the floor.

"What was that?" he called again. "Has something fallen, or have you leapt from the door to evade my question?"

"Not yet," I sighed, and reached down for the case. "Am I quiet?"

"Barely a word since you greeted me!"

"I'm sorry for my manners, Henry. I think I'm tired."

"It's grown rather late!"

"It has," I said. I pulled the portmanteau back up between my legs and glanced up, towards the place where I knew he was perched outside, and raised my voice to better address him. "I must thank you again for taking me at this hour; I know I gave you little notice."

"It's no problem, my friend! No problem at all."

There was a long and uneasy silence.

In truth, I felt little inclined to engage in conversation; but Henry was an old friend of mine, and I did not wish to bore him when he had done me a favour, so I cleared my throat and called out again:

"Say, what's the matter with this road?"

"A good question!" he replied. "I cannot say; I've not travelled here often at all."

"What about the other path, perhaps half a mile back?"

"That one leads beyond a little old church on the moor, nothing else besides. Not much to find down this way."

"I see."

Falling silent once more, I leaned back in my seat. For a few moments, I fixed my gaze upon the flicker of the lamp bolted just outside the window. The murmur of the flame stirred the shadows inside the coach; but there was very little wind, and the musk of old leather darkened the air.

Surely, this time at last!—I thought with particular despondence—I was traveling to the very ends of my world. For certainly not the first time over the past months, I felt terribly hollow, as though the night wind could blow through me and find no sliver of spirit to impede it.

Indeed, the night wind blew, but the only result was a tightening in my chest and my throat. Recognizing that ill-received sign, I took my handkerchief and pressed it to my mouth, only then letting myself cough with abandon. They were throaty sounds, hoarse and catarrhal, which I had hoped that Henry would not hear.

Unfortunately, I had no such luck. He rapped on the roof with his knuckles. "Are you quite all right?"

"Fine," I rasped, checking the handkerchief before tucking it away. "I have a cold."

"But summer only just ended, how unusual! I have never known you to have a weak constitution."

"No, I simply—never mind that, anyway." I ran my hand through my hair. "I slipped and fell into the river."

"Ho! Don't joke, my boy!"

"I mean it, I did."

Henry hummed knowingly. "A bad omen. You see, the end of your employment with the Crawfords did have a herald."

I remained silent, a little sourly.

"Say," Henry began then, with some caution. "Would you mind a question?"

"That depends on the question."

"I was curious as to why you chose this place for your employment."

"And why is that?"

"Such a lonely place! Just one man in the entire manor, from what I have heard."

"Well, there is a housekeeper—"

"And that is all! Why would you choose such a place?"

"I didn't quite choose it," I replied; I was well past regretting having begun the conversation. "I was offered the position—at nearly double the rate I had with the Crawfords, which I would be a fool to refuse."

"My goodness! By whom? I have never met the owner of the

manor, only that old housekeeper. I thought perhaps the owner lived elsewhere, leaving this as some summer residence.”

“No, the owner does reside here.”

“Who?”

“His name is Count—”

The wheels had grown noisy as the road worsened, and Henry shouted: “What?”

“Beaumont!” I called back, raising my voice. “Count Alistair Beaumont!” The name felt uneasy on my tongue, and all the more so from having shouted it.

Henry was silent for a moment. “...Beaumont! Yes, that was it.”

“Though I only corresponded with the housekeeper, Miss Goode.”

“I have met her. What a character!”

I hesitated. “But *he* never wrote directly to me.”

The coach rounded a bend in the path, smoother now that the worst of the roots had cleared away.

“And do you not find that odd?” Henry mused. “After all, it seems that only two people live in this manor. Would it have been so difficult for him to write to you himself? Surely a count would like a formal meeting to select his new manservant.”

“I don’t think it’s so strange—”

“And the name!” he went on. “A count...surely you mean an earl? There are no counts in England.”

“No, he is definitely a count. Miss Goode referred to him as one in writing.”

“Is he foreign?”

“His name certainly seems so. I’ll ask him when I see him.”

Uncomfortable silence crept between us once more, and I raised my eyes up. I could tell that one of his questions remained unasked, a more sensitive subject, and I cleared my throat before saying reluctantly:

"What do you really want to know? I swear not to leap from the carriage unless it is a truly horrible question."

"Ha! You're just as sharp as ever!"

"Well?"

"Do pardon me for asking, but I was wondering why the Crawfords really let you go."

"Ah." I stared glumly out the window. "Well, *you* know the reason for that."

"I know they were losing a great deal of money, even after I left—but I was always certain that *you* would be the last to be dismissed."

Having been under the same impression myself, I could only give a pathetic answer, and so I remained in silence.

Despite this, he barreled on. "Why would Mr. Crawford remove you? You were exemplary! Did you do something, Avery? I am *certain* you didn't steal, and equally *certain* that your work cannot have faltered; so why—"

"He wouldn't say!" I cried out suddenly. "He only called me to his study, gave me a month to find a new employment, and delivered the reference from Miss Goode! He seemed so regretful that I even preempted with a decrease in my pay, but he only—"

"Whoa!" Henry cried out suddenly, and snapped the reins. The coach stopped so quickly that I nearly toppled forward.

Once I had recovered, I scrambled back up to my seat and leaned out the window. "What is it? What happened?"

"These deer! They'll be the death of me one day, I know it."

"Deer?" Curious, I leaned further out the window. "Where?"

No sooner had I spoken than I saw one.

It stood by the side of the path, its bowed legs frozen still; and though it was shrouded in shadow, the light from the coach lamp lit its eyes.

I stared into those great and luminous pupils, quite shocked. They were enormous; swollen dark and huge by the light, they seemed like twin moons, staring into some unknown distance beyond me.

I swallowed.

"Off with you!" Henry called; and I heard the other deer scamper away, but the one nearest to me remained.

The coach began to move again, and my heart was loud in my ears as the window approached the animal, then passed it, then finally left it behind. When I turned to look back, it was still staring after us, until its eyes were mere pinpricks in the dark.

I shuddered, but I was not afraid. An unfathomable sadness had come over me. It was a sorrow that hollowed me completely.

But Henry was jovial. "Curious creatures, aren't they? I do say! I find them curious."

"Oh?" I said distantly. "How so?"

"They're so very beautiful—even in the dark like this, sinister as ghosts. The world is full of such lovely creatures! I wonder why any man would think to take a rifle to them."

I had long known Henry to be prone to flights of fancy, so I quipped in return: "They hurled themselves in front of your coach."

"Out of mere curiosity, out of innocence!" Henry cried out. "Perhaps they were trying to help us! It is only the darkness that makes us condemn it as sabotage."

"How on earth would you know their intentions?"

"Unlike you, I like to assume the best in others, my dear boy."

"Well, if you ask me, regardless of their intention, they seem to be a nuisance. Perhaps a few sporting hunters would do us all well."

"How could you say such a thing?" Henry cried out. "Lovely creatures that they are! With blood down their fur—even to think of it hurts me!"

"It's a painful thing," I admitted, "But with fewer numbers, they will have more food."

Henry sighed unhappily. "Oh, but the dear little fawns, oh! Are we God, with the right to crush such delicate and frightened things in cruel hands—to coldly reason out their fates and tear the young from their mothers?"

"Nature is no kinder to them than we are."

"Is that it, then? Are we doomed to blindly destroy what is beautiful and good?"

I leaned my head on my palm. "Are you deliberately dampening my mood, Henry?"

"Now, now! Cheer up, old pal. Perhaps the deer were simply trying to warn you away from this old manor. Ho!"

At that, I managed a laugh. "Perhaps."

Closing my eyes, I forced down the strange feeling; I forced down everything, the odd sadness that had pursued me from the town, formless and aimless. Then, I opened my eyes and gazed on emptily.

"Perhaps."

I am not sure what to make of it all now, whether it was the beginning of the beginning or the beginning of the end. I suppose it all remains a matter of perspective; but regardless it was the first time I entered the night, and thus I begin with it now.

CHAPTER II

After a few more minutes along the mangled old path, I saw something up ahead. Leaning my head out the window, I recognized the decrepit remains of an open gate, by which a stone monolith stood crookedly. So somber did this object stand that I first mistook it for a tomb; but as we drew near, I saw that the faded engravings, nearly illegible from wear and moss, read:

Amaranth Moor Manor

Then it rushed by the window and was gone, and the road opened up into open space.

The coach emerged from the thick of the forest, and the trees grew sparser and sparser, until I looked up and saw before me the bare landscape of the vast moors lit by moonlight.

Here the hills rolled on towards the horizon, which even at dusk showed their colours; the swaths of greenery were brushed over with brass and gold where grasses mingled, and grown over here and there with patches of trees, which in the far distance drew together to form a shadowed forest. Yet, the details of the land were barely visible in the nearly extinguished light of evening, except the nearer trees looming starkly over the desolation.

It was upon the rise of one particular low hill, which our seldom-tended road jostled us towards without mercy, that there rested an enormous manor.

I could tell immediately that it was old, terribly old; the stone was dark, nearly grey-green, showing centuries of wind and dirt and changing seasons. I recognized the pointed windows and daunting heights of the gothic style, which I knew from manors I had seen newly built in such a fashion; but seldom had I seen a building which seemed to come directly from the age in which that tenebrous style was first conceived. There was something about it entirely distinct from any building in Helmsley, even the very oldest I had visited—as though the entire town had left it and created itself anew a mile or two away, leaving the ancient thing desolate; and it did seem lonely, as far as stone can seem lonely, utterly friendless there among the grasses.

I was speechless, and my heart was in my throat. For a soul in any state of suffering, to see a thing so dark and forgotten is to find a companion; and what a thrill went through me, when I imagined what waited within! For a moment, I forgot my miseries, and the fresh scent of the moor filled me.

"Henry," I said, after a pause of wonder, "Do you know why this is named—"

"What?" he called. The road had grown so uneven that the groans and clatters of the coach wheels drowned out my voice.

I spoke louder. "Do you know why this place is named Amaranth Moor?"

"Well, does it grow amaranth?"

"I don't know!"

"Suppose that's it," Henry replied. He seemed uneasy.

I tore my gaze from the window. "Henry?"

Indeed, my instincts proved correct. Before the coach could wind its way to the entrance, I heard the pull of the reins and felt us slow. The dreadful noise died down, leaving only restless hooves and howling wind.

Henry hesitated. "Avery, old friend, I have known you for many years."

"And?"

"And if you would prefer we turn back and return to town, I would be more than glad, and not charge you a penny for it."

"Why would I?"

He cleared his throat. "This manor here, well, it looks rather…"

"It looks fine!" I insisted. "Have you never seen an old manor like this? They have an ancient charm to them, I'd say."

"Ho! But you'd truly like to live in it?"

"Yes," I said. Then, I cleared my throat. "But I *am* grateful for the offer."

"I concede, then, if that is truly your wish!" Henry sped the coach again, guiding it into the courtyard, where the grasses at last receded into tended civility. "Write to me if you are still alive in a week!"

"Oh, for God's sake," I scolded. "This is only temporary. I will find another place soon enough."

He chuckled. "If it makes you feel better to say it—"

"Very well!" As the coach stopped, I opened the door and clambered down, then pulled my trunk and my portmanteau along with me. "Thank you again, Henry. Don't come down, I'm quite able to take these on my own; you ought to go while there's still some light, and I shouldn't keep Miss Goode waiting."

"If I must!" Henry sighed, then gazed down at me for a moment longer. There was an inscrutable look in his eye.

I glanced up at him, then adjusted my hat. "What is it, Henry?"

"You *will* write to me, won't you, my boy?"

Amused at this, I watched him. "Of course—I promise."

He settled back. "Excellent! I know you would never forsake a vow like that. Farewell, then, farewell!"

We exchanged a few final words of parting, until the coach rode off. I watched it go for some time before turning to the manor, and at last found my footing on the old and unfamiliar earth.

After a deep breath of the fresh air, which I hoped might do me some good, I dragged my trunk up to the entrance.

The trees whispered and tossed, murmuring amongst themselves, and the sounds of various night-creatures echoed in the distance. A loud churring nearby startled me; I turned to find a hideous dark bird, which I first mistook for a frog, calling noisily from a nearby branch. Shuddering, I turned from it and faced the enormous manor doors; they were engraved with all manner of branches and animals, which in the dark dripped with shadows like black tar.

All at once, the gloomy visions that had seemed enticing before now gave me pause. Melancholy had given me too much confidence over darkness; it only now occurred to me that I might encounter histories more gruesome than my own.

The wind gusted again, now somewhat more forcefully; I felt my hair toss in disarray, and was returned to my senses. I rummaged in my pocket for my comb and fixed it down, but had to stop, for the effort had set off a fit of coughing.

Again, the wretched coughing! I gnashed my teeth in frustration, but I knew it could not be helped. When such fits started, as they had for the past month, they would not stop except by their own volition; so it was only once it subsided, and I regained my breath, that I arranged myself and managed to heave my trunk up to the door.

There were two lamps on either side, but they had not been lit. It took me a few moments to find the knocker—it had clearly borne a design perhaps a century prior, but was now weathered to the point of obscurity, though I could very clearly discern a face lost in vines—which I struck twice.

There was no reply for at least five minutes. I opened my pocket watch and counted to ensure the proper timing before raising my hand to the knocker once more, determined to strike louder; but in the instant that my hand reached it, it swung back.

Startled, I pulled my hand away and looked into the newly open doorway.

There, with a lantern lit in her hand, stood a woman of about sixty by my estimation. Despite her age, there was yet a rigid strength to the way she stood, and her expression was weathered and alert, nearly angry. My first thought was that she looked distinctly like a witch; she had grey hair pulled back into her cap, with just an edge of wisps escaping, and the lace trim cast odd shadows across her face.

"Good evening!" I said, once I had settled my surprise. "It is a pleasure to meet you; thank you for receiving me so late. I presume you to be Miss Goode?"

She stared at me fixedly, in a manner that I found uncomfortable. Then, in a strong but aged voice, she replied:

"You may call me Josephine."

There was no warmth in her voice. I smiled cautiously. "Miss Josephine, then. I appreciated your generosity in offering me this position—"

"It was not I," she interrupted flatly. "The Count requested that I write to you."

I stared, bewildered. She glowered in return.

My silence seemed to irritate her further; she gave a deliberate sigh, as though it was all one great annoyance. "But you're here now, so that's over with." Stepping forward, she pushed her lantern into my hands and lifted my trunk entire. "I will show you to your room."

"Oh, I wouldn't dream of troubling you with those—" I tried to smile again, this time with less confidence, and stepped forward to take the trunk from her. "Please, let me help! It's quite heavy."

She ignored my words entirely, turning instead and beginning to walk back inside. "Follow me."

By now, I was shocked to my core. What had gone wrong? I traced all that I had said and done, but could not fathom what had prompted such profound dislike towards me. She had not seemed to despise me in the two or three letters we had exchanged, so what was this? Had I *knocked* in some offensive manner?

So great was my surprise that I could scarcely muster indignation. Instead, I followed her mutely into the great hall.

Though the initial excitement of my arrival to the manor had been thoroughly dampened, I consoled myself with the opportunity to see the interior—and indeed, what an interior it was! When my sight adjusted, and I was able to observe the place by the light of Miss Josephine's lantern, I was stunned. The main hall had a ceiling rising high overhead, upon which, in the dim light, I could barely make out the forms of a vast painting. Towards the back of the main hall, there soared two grand staircases, which reached up to the gallery of the second floor.

The most odd and wonderful sight, however, were the other paintings. There were an unbelievable number of works of all shapes and sizes, crowding the walls between the arched windows of the hall, and even painted directly upon the surfaces of the walls themselves. I looked up as I walked, and stared in awe at this vast collection; most depicted natural scenes and ruins, but among them there were various paintings of human figures, who by their flowing robes and artful movements seemed drawn from mythical tales.

There were other details in the hall—trinkets arranged on tables, statues perched on ledges, and candelabras which cast spidery shadows as Josephine's light came across them—but by this point, the uncomfortable silence between Miss Josephine and I had become unbearable to me, so I cleared my throat.

"This seems a beautiful place," I ventured.

I had meant it as a compliment to thaw her strange affect; but without looking back at me, she answered. "You will grow tired of it soon enough."

Now indignation came to me at last, and slowed my pace. How utterly rude and unpleasant! I had tried to be patient, but my patience had limits. Would I truly have to spend every day with such a disagreeable person?

It was then I decided to bear the absurdity of the situation no longer, and paused in my step. She noticed after a few seconds, and turned back to face me with dry threat in her expression.

"Miss Josephine," I said, with as earnest a voice as I could muster. "Excuse me—if I have done anything to offend you, anything at all, I apologize; but you *must* tell me what it is that

I have done! It will be more pleasant for both of us to work here together if we are cordial and honest with each other. I truly don't wish to take your place, but rather to learn from you, and help you in any way I can."

She gave me a stern look that made me feel terribly small. "And what makes you think I was offended?"

"I…" For a moment, I doubted my own perceptions. "Why, you seemed to be…"

"To be what?"

She had me trapped. I could not continue speaking without giving her a true reason to be insulted, so instead I shook my head.

"Nothing in particular," I said glumly. "I only wished to be sure. My apologies."

"Hmph." She turned away and continued down the corridor. I had no choice but to follow her.

We made our way past the bottom of the right staircase, and into the corridor beyond it. After a few strides down this length, Miss Josephine turned sharply into the right wing of the manor.

By now I was certain beyond all doubt that something was bothering her, and tried to discern the reason.

"How long have you worked here?" I asked.

My voice echoed hollowly. She waited an entire, painful minute before responding.

"How old are you?"

"What?"

"I asked your age."

"My age?" So startled was I that it took me a moment to remember. "Well, I am twenty-three, but why does that matter?"

She scoffed. "You were but a child when I began my employment here."

My God! Was she set to turn every topic of conversation against me? I began to feel distinct annoyance, but struggled to maintain a friendly voice. "You must have a great deal of experience."

She did not reply. In fact, she spoke not a single word until the corridor grew narrower, where she stopped at a door and turned.

"This is your room," she said, setting down my trunk. Then, she pointed at the door directly across the hall from mine. "And that is mine."

"Right." I nodded. "Thank you—"

"Do you see that?" She pointed at a small hook by the side of my door. "When the Count wishes to communicate something to you, or give you your pay, you will find a note here. If you wish to reply, you will take his note and place yours in its place. I have a hook as well. He passes to collect our notes about once a day, during the night. I have placed paper in your desk."

Perhaps it would not have seemed so odd to me, were the manor filled with servants and the business of a family. In my previous employment with Mr. Crawford, I was often passed messages. But why would the Count correspond through notes when he was only one man with two servants?

"Miss Josephine," I asked, as she took her lantern back from my hand, "When shall I meet the Count?"

She watched me blankly. The lantern's light illuminated her from below, casting ghastly shadows up her face.

"You shall not."

"Then when will I have the chance to introduce myself?"

"You haven't understood." She turned away and opened the door to my room. "You will likely never meet him."

"What? How is that possible? I thought—"

"The Count likes his privacy."

"But surely he doesn't remain in his room all day? Surely he requests that things be brought to him, and—I—" The very idea was ridiculous; I simply could not fathom it, and stared flabbergasted straight through her. "Why—I am a butler!"

"And I am a housekeeper," she mocked, "And he is the master, so if he chooses not to show himself, then that is how it is."

"Have you seen him, then?"

"Yes," she said. "But if you don't mind, Mr. Bedford, I would very much like to go to bed."

"Oh—my apologies." I lifted my trunk and followed her quickly into my room.

It was evidently a servant's room, but spacious enough to be comfortable, perhaps where a proper butler might ordinarily have resided. The furniture, however, was far finer than I would expect, which led me to suspect it had been brought from another room. An armoire in the corner was tall and decorated with swirling inlays; near it was a chest of drawers with a locking cupboard, whose doors were carved with great detail; a fairly sizeable mirror on a washstand; and an impressive desk with clawed feet—all of these admittedly impressed me, but more so what I found on the walls. Here, too, there was no lack of paintings, just as those in the main hall.

Before I could ponder further, Miss Josephine interjected. "Here." She thrust forward a paper in her hand. It was folded with a wax seal, which had clearly already been opened and pressed carelessly down afterwards. "This is the letter the Count left for your arrival. Now, if you will excuse me, I am going to bed. We will meet again tomorrow morning at seven in the main hall."

"Wonderful." I took the letter. "Thank you—"

"Mr. Bedford."

I paused, apprehensive; her voice had lost its dry contempt. "Yes?"

"A word of advice."

"Of course."

"The manor is very large," she said, "And there are many entrances. There has been theft in the past. It would be most unfortunate if you were roused from your sleep by an intruder."

She looked directly into my eyes, wearing a look of warning so fierce that I nearly stepped back.

"When night falls, lock your door."

The look faded, and without another word she left.

*　　*　　*

I did not arrange a thing when Miss Josephine departed. Instead, I stood in the centre of the room, dumbfounded.

My first thought was that it was imperative to begin searching for new employment post-haste.

Yet, even as that thought took form, a contrary one rose to meet it. The enormous manor, Miss Josephine's coldness, and above all else, the mystery of the Count who never showed his face, filled me with a sense of intrigue that I had not felt for an eternity. What a story it all sang with—what untouched, unexplored intrigue! There was a dark, romantic air and a thrill of repulsion, which mingled to create horrified curiosity. It was so potent that, for at least an instant, it made me forget my despondency; so I reasoned that it would not be so terrible to stay for some time.

I must admit, I knew that I was getting carried away with a

flight of fancy, but it was the first spark of interest that I had felt in a terribly long time. In the midst of a desert of bleak disappointment, a glimmer seemed to wink in the distance. A sunken heart is well-soothed by a story; and surely—here was a magnificent story!

Or, at the very least, an entertaining mirage.

It was then that I realized that I still held the Count's letter in my hand, which was doubtless real. This caused me such a flurry of emotion that my heart grew fast, to the point where I sat on my trunk for fear of inviting my cough again. Settling myself, I unrolled the letter with clammy hands.

The first thing I noticed was the handwriting. There was no question: I was faced with the most beautifully written script that I had ever seen. The letters were so artful and evenly spaced that they could have put a printing press to shame, and my mind could scarcely believe them to have been scribed by human hands.

I began to read.

July 22, 1822

Dear and Esteemed Mr. Bedford,

As master of the estate, I bid you a warm welcome to the manor, and hope that all has gone well in your arrival thus far.

I regret that I am unable to greet you in person. Unfortunately, I doubt that you shall ever see me, and for this I offer my sincerest apologies. I bear a rare illness which prevents me from engaging in ordinary life; but insofar as I inhabit this manor, I wish that you should feel the presence of my welcome.

I have informed Josephine of all that I would like conveyed to you concerning your work here, and I trust that she will pass the

His name was written in such a beautiful manner all of its own that I stared at it for an entire minute.

"Where on earth is Lerin?" I said aloud.

Then, I looked up to ponder.

I will admit, the thrill of the mystery had given me lofty expectations for the contents of the letter, which were not altogether met. There was indeed a flutter of disappointment. Yet, the longer that I thought upon it, as I stood and paced, the more I realized that the letter, in fact, made the situation more mysterious. Its air of normalcy was almost desperate—but no, not desperate; rather, it was sly, nearly coaxing as it explained its own mundanity, until that final line where some of the oddity came through.

Above all, the surge of intrigue was mingled with pity and

curiosity towards the author of the letter. It bothered me that I knew nothing of what he looked like; but since he had mentioned his being ill, and did not seem to have living family in the house, I pictured him as an older man with an unkempt beard, trailing a ragged banyan behind him as he walked along.

I placed the letter upon my bedside table.

I had wanted to inspect the paintings in my room, but by then, I was far too weary to lend them my attention. I was also feeling ill once more; the ever-present tightness in my chest was mounting, and worsened when I breathed, as it often happened near nighttime; so I arranged only the essential items that I had brought and went immediately to bed.

As I pulled the bedcovers over my shoulder, I felt the atmosphere of the manor settle around me. Somehow comforted, I closed my eyes in the dark and drifted into sleep.

CHAPTER III

I woke gasping in the early morning from a dream that I was drowning.

For an entire minute, I was convinced that I was still submerged—I held my neck, and was not satisfied no matter how much I breathed!—but then I managed to break into a fit of coughing, clearing my throat at last. Once it all subsided, all that remained was a sharp ache inside my chest.

I leaned forward, exhausted. Before me, my knees rose unsteadily beneath the covers. The nightmares were not unusual, but this one had been particularly vivid.

In any case, I had not slept well; but I decided not to dwell on it, and scolded myself for the great wave of reluctance I felt upon realizing that I would have to leave the bed.

I cleaned and dressed myself, shaving my face but for the side-whiskers as I was accustomed, then proceeded to comb my hair and fix my cravat. However, I was feeling unusually despondent, and avoided my own eyes. Though I cheered myself by remembering the mystery, it seemed far less enticing in the reality of morning than in the romantic air of night.

Then, I left to meet Miss Josephine.

*   *   *

It was a vividly uncomfortable experience. A night's sleep had not dulled Miss Josephine's apparent distaste for me, and she reminded me at every opportunity how much she wished I had not come.

But even though she was unpleasant, she showed me each of the important rooms inside the manor—the kitchen, the piano room, the reading room, countless others whose purpose I forgot as soon as the door had been shut—and above all, an enormous library, which stunned me speechless as soon as I entered.

What a library it was! There were two floors, occupying a majority of the right wing of the manor, a labyrinth of bookshelves inhabited by the musk of old paper. Sofas and chairs were gathered near tables here and there, all apparently of different styles and ages. The broad windows along the walls streamed with light, painting the entire place an ethereal golden-brown.

"Mr. Bedford," Miss Josephine called, for the second time.

I was pulled from my awe, and turned to follow. Now, however, curiosity overtook my discomfort, and I cleared my throat. "The Count, does he spend much time in the library?"

"Hmph," she muttered. "I think so."

"You think so? But do you not see him during the day, as you go about your work?"

"No; and neither will you."

"Do you mean to imply that he sits in his room all day, alone?" I stopped, and gathered my courage. "If so, then that is simply terrible! You have said nothing about making food for him, or tea, or—why, anything else!"

She turned to me. "Mr.—"

"And all the more terrible, if his illness is what confines him. What have we been hired for, if not to aid him? Even had we not been hired—"

"Mr. Bedford, he—"

"I cannot stand by while someone withers away with loneliness!"

"He is not withering away!" she snapped, with a sudden ferocity that silenced me. "You have crafted an image of him in your mind, but the reality is far from it. It is the Count himself who has demanded complete privacy."

"But..." I faltered. "If we could only..."

"Do not seek him." Her eyes were like stone. "Keep away. He is not a man whose wrath you want to invite."

"His *wrath*? We speak of a sickly old man, utterly alone and helpless—"

"Ha!" she barked. "Helpless, you say? He is not *helpless*."

"Do you not—"

"Understand?" Her voice blazed with contempt. "Of course I understand. You are young and foolish. You feel the need to do work that means something to you; you want to help someone, because you think that if you do something righteous, then you can continue to persuade yourself of your goodness. That is precisely why you ought not have come here. He neither needs nor wants your help. Nothing that you do here will ever matter in the slightest; you have reached the end of the world."

But my blood boiled at that, and I stepped forward. "How

could you *possibly* know that? You know absolutely nothing about me! From the minute we met, you decided for yourself what I am—whatever that decision was, I *truly* have no idea—and what does it matter to you, in any case, if I am trying to do my work properly? Why, after all, if the Count *did* become cross with me for my intrusions, then he would cast me out! Is that not what you desire?"

"I do desire it," she countered, with plain candour. "Leave."

My response came more out of abject confusion than conviction. "No."

"Don't bother to give any notice. Pack your trunk and go."

"My goodness, what is the *matter* with you?" I cried out.

At that, at last, a strange look crossed her face. I daresay that she was impressed, if a little grudgingly, by my refusal to let her rattle me. In any case, she turned away. "Then stay!" she barked. "But I have told you what this place is, and what your duties are. Fail at them at your own leisure."

*   *   *

When that eternity of a day ended, and I returned to my room, I could hardly believe that such a terrible experience could bestow upon me such a sweet mercy as its ending.

I paced my room for some time, brewing in my frustration with Miss Josephine, creating arguments in my head against her. The circumstances were clear to me: surely she had found a way to waste the days away being paid for doing nothing, passing it off as work. Naturally, seeing the arrival of someone determined to do their work properly would make her fearful of being dismissed, or at the least of being held to a higher standard.

Finding this theory quite convincing, I settled on a goal just as quickly: I would do my best to provide aid and company to this ailing Count, despite Miss Josephine's efforts. Just as soon as I came to my decision, however, my excitement dimmed. I sat upon the bed; my energy had left me.

Outside, I could hear the howl of wind, and sat still. A feeling was coming upon me, the familiar dread of existence, which grew thick in the isolation of the manor.

Just how often had I decided on plans, simply for them to fail or lead to nothing? And how often had my successes left me no less empty?

Those strange words that Miss Josephine had said echoed in my mind: *you have reached the end of the world*, she had said. In that, I thought dryly, she had been correct; but I had reached the end long before coming to the manor, and I supposed there was still more to see of it. To live in an addendum might not so terrible. Without direction, without meaning, I could do as I pleased.

Contrary to what I had hoped, this thought did not console me. Indeed, it had the opposite effect, and even prompted a sigh so harsh that it nearly brought on a coughing fit.

Seeing no recourse but to distract myself, I realized that I had yet to peruse the paintings in the room. Curious, I approached the largest of the three.

This first painting was a colourful scene which I took for a ball, or some other dance; it depicted many figures as seen from a distance in a great hall. It took me a moment to recognize the place as the main hall of the manor. In this depiction, the walls were covered in rich tapestries rather than paintings.

Intrigued, I moved to the second painting. The majority of it was grassy moorland at dusk. In the distance, however, there loomed a small church with a light in the window.

It was the third that I understood the least. Whereas the first two showed reality, this one seemed fantastical; against a night sky, a great building, which almost seemed to be the manor, roared with flames, and an enormous winged creature soared overhead through clouds of ash.

The latter baffled me most of all, and I stared for a good long while, wondering what error of taste had led the Count to consider it fitting for my room. It was then, however, that I was distracted by another realization. None of the paintings were signed. Furthermore, the style of the three was not dissimilar; there could only be one explanation.

"He painted them!" I exclaimed aloud. "That is why the entire manor is covered…"

The words surprised me even as I spoke them, but as soon as I did, I knew that I was correct. Every painting in the manor was the work of the Count himself!

In a daze, I stepped back and thought of the sheer number of paintings in the manor, the decorated ceilings and walls, and faltered. Such a collection could be the life's work of several artists, not to mention one; how long had the Count lived here alone?

At that thought, my fate was sealed. There was no question; I needed to write to him.

After much fretting and pacing, I managed to organize my thoughts and sit at the desk. An ornate inkwell had been left there, cast bronze sculpted with several proud nereids and mischievous puttos; I had meant to exchange it for another, being embarrassed to use such a gaudy thing, but now I hastily prepared it instead, then procured a paper and quill.

Greetings Sir, I wrote:

Thank you for your warm welcome. It is an honour to be in your service. Please inform me of anything that you may need or desire, and it will be my pleasure to be of assistance.

I paused to think, brushing the soft end of the quill-feather across my lips. Then, I dipped it again and continued.

The paintings in the manor are exquisite. Pardon the question, but are they your work? I am curious to hear about the subjects of the three in my room.
Your humble servant,
A. Bedford

I opened the door and pushed the note gently through the hook upon the wall. Then, I readied myself for sleep.

*   *   *

I had a restless sleep that night, and found myself constantly waking in the dark, desperately tired, but burdened with a cough that made me unable to comfortably return to slumber. Yet, despite the terrible night, when morning came, the first matter to come to my awareness was the note.

Going quickly to the door, I paused to make sure that I did not hear Miss Josephine outside. Then, I pushed it open and looked to the hook with bated breath—and how childishly excitement seized me, when I saw that the note had been exchanged!

In my haste I even forgot my weariness. I ripped the new letter from its place and shut the door to my room very softly. Then, I sat down to read.

Good morning, Mr. Bedford, it began, in handwriting so beautiful that it was nearly ridiculous.

Thank you. You are correct; the majority of the paintings in the manor are my work. I no longer recall the precise subjects or meanings of many of them, but they come either from life or from dreams. You are welcome to exchange the ones I have placed in your room for any others you find. They are not in any particular arrangement.

Regards,
Alistair Beaumont

It took me a few moments to realize that the note ended there, and that nothing else followed. The anticipation in my chest, which had burned so hot previously, dwindled to sheepish disappointment. After all, I reasoned, what had I expected? What could he have answered that would have excited me? I felt foolish for having taken up his time.

Perhaps, I thought, Miss Josephine had been correct. Perhaps the Count did not want to be disturbed, and there was no mystery here, only a manor owned by an ill man who enjoyed painting alone, and a very disagreeable housekeeper—but the first letter! Had he not said that he was bored?

There was nothing wrong with a short answer, I decided. I knew that my conviction could be the product of my own ennui, but I was nonetheless certain that something was amiss, and that I could play a part in interrogating it.

CHAPTER IV

The first two weeks passed without much incident, and balmy July waned to gentler August. I worked, Miss Josephine missed no opportunity to scold me, and the Count did not appear.

He did exist; that much I knew. I noticed things moving day to day, particularly in the library.

How he subsisted, however, I could not say. The Count never requested food; he sometimes requested water, but only in buckets to be left out for bathing and washing. There was no evidence that he drank anything but the occasional glass of wine, which I knew from keeping a careful eye on the cellar. His preference seemed to be for red wine; a bottle would vanish every few days, only to reappear empty in some other location in the manor. Miss Josephine collected them without much care, barely glancing at them as she picked them up.

Indeed, it seemed that Miss Josephine was very familiar with the Count's habits, and so the notes that he wrote with requests all went to her. Such requests always held us at a distance. Books were to be left by the desk in the library; ink, in a certain cabinet; sheets, in the room beside his quarters. The Count's clothing was all Miss Josephine's business, so I was uncertain of what he wore, and she always sent me to town when it was a laundering day.

Of course, since Miss Josephine was responsible for delegating our tasks, only the most uninteresting of menial labor was left to me. I found myself in roles that I had long since left behind at my last household—sweeping, dishes, and dragging buckets back and forth from the well outside. In short, I felt like an errand boy; I was quite ready to resent Miss Josephine endlessly for it, were it not for her mature age, and for the fact that these tasks took so little time that I was left alone for the majority of the day.

In order to keep myself entertained, I created explanations for the eccentricity of it all. In one such idea, the Count was a recluse with a beard down to his knees, crouched in his room among piles of books and filth and the bones of rats he had eaten. In another, he was deformed to the point where he had been shunned by all the world. In yet another, I imagined him as an eccentric painter who simply despised people more than he could bear.

But the explanation that I dwelt upon most, and eventually began to consider seriously, was that the Count was a wealthy old man, too ill to manage his own affairs, and that Miss Josephine had recognized this, now holding him as a captive of sorts, waiting for his death in order to somehow reap his fortune. It explained a great deal, from her struggle to keep me from meeting him to his apparent dearth of need for food.

By the end of the second week, I was convinced that I was

correct. The only question that remained was what to do.

There was a dullness within me that begged me to do nothing. Perhaps many years ago, my instinct would have been otherwise; back then, I had flourished as a creature of hope, and believed that every effort could be a brick in a foundation upon which I would build great future deeds. To be a fine servant had once been my greatest pride, and to become a butler my greatest triumph. My fervent dream had only been to find what good I could do from my position, and how to reach the next step from which I could better the world.

There had been no single event that shattered that illusion, only the creeping melancholy that laid bare my stagnation and the futility of my struggles.

Such things, however, are premature to discuss. After all, there are parts of dreams that never quite disappear even when shattered, bound up in habit and nostalgic sentiment; and so when I looked out through the window of the manor library as the light faded from the sky, I felt a familiar surge of stubbornness that no amount of despair had managed to quell.

I would not leave this matter alone—I would see what on earth this all was, or die trying!

*   *   *

Despite the great lengths to which I went in order to keep my first effort secret—purchasing supplies with my own funds, glancing into the kitchen before entering to ensure Miss Josephine was not there—she found me as I left the kitchen with plate in hand.

I feigned not to notice her, continuing along the hall without stopping; but she followed me, seething with frustration.

"Mr. Bedford, I *told* you—"

"You told me nothing of this," I said curtly, and continued on. "Stop!"

But not even the devil himself could have made me stop; hearing her steps behind me, I lifted my platter of biscuits beyond her reach. "What am I to stop?"

"Whatever foolish plan you've—"

"Plan! What plan? The Count said I could use any tool in the house as I wished, and so I did. He has a fine kitchen."

With a speed that far outpaced her age, she came around me and blocked my way forward. "You know full well what I mean."

I stopped, giving her a look; I felt righteous and angry with her. "If you refuse to make him any proper food, then I will."

She stared no less furiously. "He did not request it."

"Fine! Then I am doing something kind for him, a concept which seems rather unfamiliar to you."

"Are you listening to me? He did not request it—"

"Well, precisely! It would not be a kindness if it was requested by him. Then, it would be an order; there would be no point."

"I am warning you, he will be irritated. You do *not* understand him."

"And you do?" I held the platter more surely and weaved past her. "I doubt that."

She made no effort to follow me, but still stood bitterly there, her eyes narrowed, and still called after me—"It is not a kindness if it is forced upon him from nowhere!"

"I am not forcing anything upon him," I replied coolly. "I am simply giving him the biscuits and, why, he could do with them whatever he chooses."

For the briefest instant, something like fear and desperation were heard in her voice, which were soon concealed by her usual gruffness. "It is a waste, an utter waste! He neither needs nor wants your food. Come back and put that down."

I paused before turning the corner of the hallway, curious at her tone, and looked back at her. "Whether or not he needs the food, I believe he needs the kindness."

She watched me, and seemed to hesitate. In the end, however, she shook her head and turned away.

More certain than ever that Miss Josephine was keeping the Count weak and starved for her purposes, I grew stronger in my resolve.

I left the platter on the small table by the Count's bedroom, with a small note upon it, which read:

Please enjoy. —A. Bedford

*   *   *

I spent the afternoon lingering along the top floor, dusting things that had no need for me, to ensure that Miss Josephine did not lay waste to my endeavor. Once or twice, I saw her draw near; but when she did, I cleared my throat or walked noisily to make my presence known, and she withdrew. It was not until she returned to her room for the night that my vigil ended, and I went down to sleep.

It was a difficult night. The weather was growing cooler, and with it my cough grew in obstinacy and soreness. I tried a few drops of medicine, which did not help, then a lozenge, which did; and I fell asleep sprawled across my bed, straining to listen and ensure that that Miss Josephine's door remained shut.

When I opened my eyes again, it was morning.

Standing stiffly, I made my way to the door and opened it, unsure of what I would find—but there it was! A note hung from my hook.

I tore it and quickly drew back inside, shut the door behind me, and read:

Mr. Bedford,

I was most touched by the kind gesture you directed towards me yesterday. I felt in it every generous and thoughtful intention of your heart.

However, because I prefer to arrange my own meals, I am afraid that I cannot partake of it properly. I regret that your laudable efforts are thus wasted. In the future, you may share what you make with Josephine.

—Alistair Beaumont

I felt deep, embarrassed disappointment sink through me. Despite his praise for my action, it seemed overly cordial, and crushed my intentions with a stiff formality that sent a chill through me. What was this? Had he been annoyed by it, or neutral towards the action, or had Miss Josephine somehow forced him to write the note in such a way?

However, the consequences from the deed did not end there.

In the afternoon of the following day, I was cleaning the kitchen as Miss Josephine cooked our supper when I suddenly heard a faint scratching. It was so faint that I first assumed I was imagining it, and returned to my work.

But a few seconds later, the noise returned, louder, and Miss Josephine scoffed. "Terrible. It is the rats again. They always—Mr. Bedford, what on earth are you doing?"

I had crouched down, straining to hear, and tapped on the wood of the counter. "I can hear it—"

Behind me, I heard Miss Josephine say something else; but abruptly, as I gave a particularly hard tap, a rat darted out from behind the counter. Something else skidded out as well, but I dove for the rat; and just as it was about to escape behind a pot, I lunged after it and caught it by its tail.

I held it out far from me and got to my feet. It dangled squirming from my grasp, a mass of matted black fur and ghoulish teeth; but before I could do anything else, Miss Josephine snapped at me. "What are you doing, picking up that dirty thing? Get it out at once!"

And so I did, walking quickly to the door and letting it loose outside on the ground. It laid frozen for a moment before it scuttled into the grass and disappeared.

When I made my way back to the kitchen, Miss Josephine threw me a scathing look of disgust. "Clean your hands immediately."

"My apologies," I muttered, stung by the injustice of it—I had caught it!—but did as she said. Yet, just as I was resuming my work, my gaze caught something on the ground.

It was then that I remembered something had skidded out with the rat. Had it been holding something? Furrowing my brow, I leaned over for a closer look.

I heard Miss Josephine speak. "Mr. Bedford, if you would like to play with vermin—"

"No, it isn't another one," I said. I moved the small object nearer with my shoe. "It is no animal at all. In fact, it looks like…"

Suddenly, there came the shock of recognition. The crumbling texture, the pale yellow colour, the circular shape distorted by little bites—it was a biscuit from the ones I had made for the Count.

"By *God!*" I cried out. "He fed them to the *rats!*"

*   *   *

Inevitably, at first, I suspected Miss Josephine; perhaps the biscuits had never reached the Count at all. Yet, her reaction to the rat made this notion unconvincing. She had not been pleased; it was not the demeanor of someone who would feed one. Perhaps she had simply dumped the plate outside into the grass, or perhaps the rest of the biscuits were still with the Count, and it just so happened that a mischievous rat had made off with one of them.

But for the following week, I continued to find biscuit pieces here and there in the crevices where the rats roamed, and it became undeniable that someone—whether Miss Josephine or not—had at the very least thrown them all away; and I could not dispel the conviction that it had been done with the full knowledge and intention that it be for the benefit of those vicious, ugly little mouths that roamed the shadows.

However, by now I had other worries to keep me occupied.

The light illness I had brought with me to the manor worsened. One night, for the first time, I fevered. The unnatural feeling woke me, and I felt hot and then bitterly cold in turn; I shivered in the dark for hours, taking sips of water as best I could, until I was able to return to sleep.

From that night on, I would awaken drenched in sweat. My heart pounded in my chest, and I was fatigued no matter how much I slept; but I loathed the idea of withering away in my bed, and was determined to go on with my work regardless.

What I could not ignore, however, was Miss Josephine.

I began to lose my appetite, which she noticed. She would

typically make supper for the both of us, and we would eat together in thoroughly uncomfortable silence at the plain wooden table in the kitchen; but now, the silence became even more unbearable, with her watching me in suspicion as I pushed the food about my plate and stared morosely at it.

I could not bear the thought of food being wasted—but neither could I eat!

So I would remain there, sullen, as she finished her own meal and then stood up in a way clearly indicating that she was offended. On the first few instances, she left me alone, but by the third supper that passed in such a way, she confronted me. "What is it, Mr. Bedford? Is there something wrong with the food I make?"

I sighed. "I'm not hungry."

"Do you believe I would poison you?"

"No." I could no longer feign sincerity, and replied with the full weight of my soul. "I have simply lost my appetite."

This gave her pause. She stared at me in suspicion for a few moments, then seemed to look me all over, as if searching for something.

This stare quite unsettled me, and I stood, drained of patience. "Fine! Then I am ill; are you happy? Good night, Miss—"

"What do you mean, ill?" she interrupted oddly. "In what sense?"

Had I been in possession of a clearer mind, I would have thought more of the anxiety seeping into her reply; but I was too weary. "In the sense of being ill. Good night."

There was a twitch through her face, as though she had suppressed something severe. In the end, however, she only dusted her hands down her dress and turned away without a word.

CHAPTER V

My daily activities passed rather like that for some time. It was all rather mundane at first. The weeks passed, Miss Josephine bristled, and the moor was very beautiful, even as it dulled in anticipation of autumn; but the mundanity would not last much longer.

If I had to choose a single instant, a length of time no longer than a second or a breath that changed my fate irrevocably, it would be when I opened my eyes one night. A month had passed since my arrival at the manor; the heat of summer had waned entirely at last, allowing my room to cool somewhat during the night, which improved my sleep despite my cough.

It was that fateful night, that very moment! When I first stirred in the dark, finding myself on the brink of wakefulness, I could have returned to sleep. Indeed, it would have been the more reasonable choice; how rare it was, to have a truly restful sleep! How delicious it would have felt, to escape my world once more and return to slumber—how peaceful!

But I was curious. I wished to know what had woken me, and why I felt such ease; so I opened my eyes in the dark, and immediately felt a chill.

Somebody was playing the piano.

I stared up towards the ceiling for a few seconds, blinking in the dark. Then, as the faint strains of music coming through the walls became undeniable, I sat up. My hands were unsteady as they gripped my sheets.

Somebody was playing the piano!

But it was pitch-black, and Miss Josephine was surely asleep, and in any case I doubted that she could play it, so there remained only one possibility.

It was the Count.

A few moments passed as I strained to listen. I could barely make out the notes—in part because it was so distant, and in part because my heart pounded in my ears. Once I caught the melody of it, however, a thrill crept up through me and made me shiver.

I could not understand why it excited me to such a degree. There was nothing necessarily unusual about it. I already knew that the Count walked about at night, and I had always noticed sheet music changing on the piano every so often. All of this was true; but to hear it!

Over the past weeks, I had ceased to ponder the mystery of the Count. The weariness of many months had come with me to the manor, and though it had lightened when I had something new to see, it had quickly reclaimed me upon my failure. Just like before, I had the sense of being on a straight and simple path towards nothing.

But here! Here was a detour into something unknown, and

somehow terrifying.

From then on, I moved as though possessed. The need to hear the music clearly overwhelmed all else.

Once I had come to my senses, I fumbled for the candelabrum on the bedside table, a huge and ornate thing that I had taken out of curiosity as decoration. Now, I lit it blindly, flinching from the sparks when I struck my flint. An ominous orange light licked at the darkness of the room, and I bore the cold and heavy bronze into the air.

My steps were quiet; I was wearing no shoes, nothing except for my nightshirt, and it was strange to feel a cold draft about my ankles. When I reached the door, however, I stopped.

Miss Josephine had warned me ceaselessly not to leave the room at night. I did hesitate. What would she do, were she to find me outside?

But it was late, and there was the dreamlike feeling of night all around me. It coaxed me forward, cast a pall over reality; my hand eased onto the doorknob and turned it.

The glow of the candles seeped onto the walls of the servants' hall as I opened the door. Once the creak of the hinges had quieted, I paused to listen.

There it was still—the sound of the piano! I could hear it more clearly now, but it was too muffled to discern. I had to move nearer.

The floor was cold beneath my feet as I stepped out of my room and began to walk. I moved as though in a trance, and the flames of the candles pulled back against my stride.

I had no sense of what I was searching for, nor why.

The hem of my nightshirt brushed about my legs, pushed by an errant breeze here and there, but I did not shiver; and as I reached the end of the servants' hall, I forgot even that, for now

I could make out the music. I stopped walking, and the faint smell of smoke from the candles came to linger around me as I listened.

It was a beautiful piece, the sort that wrenches the heart—not rhythmic music, not a waltz to dance to, but rather a rich and varied melody, like a singing voice with something dark rolling beneath it. Indeed, it was sad, magnificently sad, sad to the point where it was terrifying; but it was haunting as well. It weaved down and down into grief, then climbed up unexpectedly, as though beckoning—then twisted my heart along with it as it plunged back down. In the loneliness of night, it was nearly unbearable to listen to.

What *music!*

I had begun to tremble. Still, I had to move nearer.

Reaching the great hall of the manor, I turned and started down towards the piano room.

It filled me, it tore into me—what music, what sorrow! It carried the same feeling that had inflamed me, when I first beheld the moor and the soaring sight of the manor. I had the sense of being soothed and understood. Such is the effect of music, making misery glorious, even noble!

In an instant, my ardour for the mystery of the Count was rekindled. I had to know: who on earth was this man, and what could have inspired such torturous feelings? I could not abandon somebody who understood such resonant feelings as this, which I too had carried within my breast. Lowering my candelabrum, I turned finally into the corridor where the piano room was.

But all except the light that I carried was deathly black, and I saw not even a single flicker from the door of the piano room, which hung slightly ajar. Was he playing with no light? Was it possible?

Here, now, the music was so near that I began to feel genuine trepidation. My better senses returned to me, and I realized that at any moment he could be alerted to my presence. It was my last opportunity to turn back. If Miss Josephine had not lied, then he would be upset to find me so near; it would be a disruption of his privacy. Perhaps this had been foolish. It was lovely music, but who was I to intrude?

Unsure, I took a single step back—and heard the single most horrifying sound possible.

The floorboards creaked beneath my foot.

The music stopped at once.

My heart rushed into my throat. Too late to run—too late to hide! My God, what had I done? In a piercing flash of reason, I blew sharply to extinguished all my candles.

I was left in impenetrable dark.

My idea had been simple: if I could not see anything, then neither could he. Still, how long would I have to wait? Utterly frozen, I listened for the sound of steps and heard only silence for a few long moments. My heart pounded, and I struggled to quiet my breathing.

Yet, just as it seemed to me that perhaps it was safe to leave, something changed abruptly.

I could still see nothing, absolutely nothing, but one by one the hairs on my arms began to rise.

A prickling crept up my skin; my eyes were wide in the blackness. What was it—what was it? I only knew one thing: that my body was sensing something which my eyes could not. The prickling crept up my shoulders, and reached the nape of my neck. I held my breath and eased back, but then my back met the wall at the end of the corridor. My palms tingled with sweat, the bronze grew slippery in my hand, and I swallowed, struggling with my breath—but the feeling only grew and grew, until I was locked in a silent panic.

I shut my eyes tightly and pressed my lips together to block any breath, setting my jaw, but the feeling remained; and so, as slowly as I could bear, I edged around the corner, into the hallway I had come from. Then, I opened my eyes, and saw—

Blue. A shockingly clear blue, set in a penetrating stare within a mad crisscross of wrinkled lines in skin, like lightning.

I fell back with a shout and landed hard on the floor. The candelabra slipped from my hand and struck the ground with a tremendous crash.

Miss Josephine was staring down at me. There was a candlestick in her hand, which was the source of the light illuminating the blue of her eyes so strangely.

"Mr. Bedford," she said sharply, "What are you doing here?"

"Oh—Miss Josephine!" I cried out. At first, I was relieved, but then knew not what to say to her. "I thought I heard the piano."

Her stare was indecipherable. "I told you not to leave your room at night."

I pulled myself meekly to my feet, retrieving my candelabrum from the floor. The candles had all broken off. "I know."

"So why did you disobey?"

I could not fathom any way to explain, so I shook my head. "I was distracted. I'll return to my room in a moment, but first, the candles—"

"Leave them where they are." Her voice was tense. "You can clean tomorrow. Come."

"But the wax will—"

"Oh, will you listen to me, for once in your life?" she snapped. "Come!"

Defeated, I left it. "Very well. Tomorrow, then."

For a moment, something like relief washed over her expression. Yet, then her eyes hardened, and she looked over my shoulder and into the other pitch-black corridor—coldly, furiously, as though she was warning the dark.

*   *   *

I was unable to return to sleep that night. Once it became clear that my mind would not rest, I left my bed and wrote the Count a note.

Sir Beaumont,

I happened to hear someone playing the piano last night. It was a lovely piece. Was it you who was playing?

Please do let me know if there is anything else you would like me to do for you.

—A. Bedford

That night, I placed the note upon my hook.

The following morning, I received a reply.

Dear Mr. Bedford,

Yes, that was I. Thank you for your kind words. I am glad that you enjoyed the music.

More importantly, are you ill? Please use any funds that you require to purchase medicine. Avoid calomel and arsenic, as these poison the blood. I have some experience with apothecary arts, and would feel much reassured if you would inform me of the medicine you are using.

—Alistair Beaumont

I was stunned by his response for one simple reason: how had he known that I was ill? After some thought, I realized that perhaps I been keeping him awake with my cough during the day. At that, my face grew hot, and despite my rationality—it had been a very simple letter—I felt chastised, like a child, and desperately lonely. How I loathed to be a burden!

But then, another thought came to my mind: had Miss Josephine written to him that I was ill?

The thought made me terribly bitter, and I resolved that I would see what else there was to discover about the situation.

The following evening, sitting at my writing desk, I hastily wiped the sweat from my hands before laying out a small piece of paper. After perhaps half an hour of abusing the end of my quill with my teeth, I dipped it in my inkwell and bent over to write:

Good evening Sir,

Thank you for concern, but please trouble yourself not. I have plenty of good medicine, and my health is improving swiftly.

I did not know you were trained in a profession. Are you an apothecary, or a physician, or some other sort of natural philosopher?

—A. Bedford

To this, he left a reply the following day:

Mr. Bedford,

Forgive me for insisting, but I truly do beg that you at least tell me the names of the medicines you are using. It will be useful to both of us; you will gain advice by it, and I will be interested to see what poison is being passed off as medicine as of late.

I have no formal profession, only knowledge and experience.

—Alistair Beaumont

I was frustrated at this short reply. In the evening after receiving the letter, I asked Miss Josephine as I helped her hang up linens outside:

"Say, does the Count have a profession?"

"Being a nuisance," she replied curtly, and would say nothing more.

I deliberated for some time on whether to tell the Count the names of the medicines I had brought. I had no specific attachment to them; I had purchased them at random the week prior to my arrival at the manor. Rather, my reluctance was two-fold: firstly, that I felt I was sacrificing leverage to find a way to see him. Secondly, that there was a part of me which loathed to cause anybody trouble over a problem that was my own— particularly when it was a problem I very much wished to ignore.

But I knew that to refuse his kindness, which he had offered so genuinely as to beg for my compliance, would be terribly rude; so I gathered all the bottles that I had and left them beneath the hook outside my door.

That night, I tried to lie awake and listen for the clinking of glass outside. My exhaustion overwhelmed me, however, and so it was only upon my awakening that I discovered what had been done.

Out of the three bottles, two had been taken away and one had been added. This unfamiliar bottle was small, and contained a dense red liquid which smelled strongly of copper.

His note read:

Mr. Bedford,

Two of the three were poisonous, and may indeed have been prolonging your illness. I have taken the liberty of disposing of them and given you an additional medicine. Please forgive the taste, but rest assured that it is important.

—Alistair Beaumont

I propped my elbows on my writing desk and held the little vial to the light, turning it to and fro, watching the liquid cling to the sides. Unlike the bottles from the apothecary, it had no label, and yet there was a familiar quality to the substance that I could not quite place.

For a few moments, I pondered whether to drink it. The decision could only depend on belief; if I trusted my own judgment in this affair, then I would drink without hesitation. If I allowed for any doubt, then I would not.

The Count was correct. The taste was abhorrent.

CHAPTER VI

For the days that followed, as August waned at last to September, I was consumed by restlessness. Though my condition was no better, what I had heard that night in the hallway instilled within me an energy that not even my health could affect. Now more than ever, I suspected that Miss Josephine was somehow responsible for the Count's seclusion, and I was newly determined to understand it all.

It became almost an obsession, I must admit. When I had served at my previous employment at the Crawford household, I had prided myself on my dignity; I would never have thought to pry. I wished to be trusted naturally.

But the gardens of that great house had been prim and well-kept, whereas here, the moor was wild. There was a primordial sun that rose over the landscape every dawn, and an endless mess of grasses and vines that threatened to consume the grounds of the manor entirely; purple heather had bloomed for the season, and dyed the hills like blood. Such sights inspire no duty to civilization; rather, they invoke the gut-feeling of primitive man, which is apt to loosen even the most principled dispositions.

Perhaps that was why I dared to act as I did.

At first, I did nothing but ponder it. There was time, plenty of time, often great stretches of hours where I had no task to keep me occupied. The Count did not ask for much, so after the essential duties were finished—cleaning, dusting, preparing food for ourselves, drawing water from the well, and twice a week buying what was necessary from the town, which Miss Josephine and I took turns at—there was little more to do.

With these hours, I explored the manor for information. It was full of interesting objects and trinkets of all sorts, some whose use even I could not identify; enormous paintings to puzzle over; and of course, the library, which was so extensive as to stun me. Many of the books, especially those so old that the pages crumbled away in my hands, did prove to be nearly incomprehensible. Some were in Latin, or an English too unfamiliar to read easily; many others were written in what I came to realize was Spanish. From this, I surmised that my Count must be a *Conde*.

Whenever I exhausted my curiosity for the day, I took long walks to gather my thoughts. When I was too tired for walks, I read; indeed, I borrowed a novel from the circulating library in town, and finished it all in a few days—a thrilling story about a monster, which the affable owner Mr. Parker had recommended to me himself. In short, I had all the time in the world.

At my previous employment, I had scarcely found the chance for such leisure, unless I had been tasked with shepherding the younger members of the family on a stroll. Here, however, I was entirely alone and without distractions. Both the expansive moor and the time I had to explore it were entirely mine. My only common interruptions came from the few bats I found perched around the manor, who I chased out with brooms at first, but soon ceased to pay them mind.

Rarely in my life had I had such opportunities to think. In some ways, I did not like it. I knew well that I was prone to extremes when my thoughts turned inward.

Luckily, the mystery of the Count was enough to occupy my mind, and I was happy to let it do so. Thus my curiosity grew and grew, perhaps on the wings of newfound freedom and many days among the wild grasses, and I grew bolder. If I could not extract answers from Miss Josephine by speaking with her, I decided, I would obtain them through other means.

My chance came a few days after my encounter with the Count's music at night. Miss Josephine had left for town early one afternoon to run errands, and I knew I would have no better opportunity to seek the truth. As soon as I saw her disappear into the foggy distance from an upstairs window, I tore away and hurried downstairs.

I entered her room slowly, cautiously, my heart beating with great force. I knew that I had crossed a terrible line, which could easily put a swift end to my employment, or condemn me to worse; but my curiosity was more powerful than my fear. Whether from terror or excitement, my hands shook. By God, I would find an answer!

Her room was similar to mine, only considerably more cluttered. It was evident that she had indeed lived here for some time. Unlike in my room, however, there were no paintings here; there were only hooks on the walls, where paintings had clearly once been hung. The most prominent decorations, apart from embroidery, were two large birdcages which both sat empty and ajar.

Quickly, I set myself to the task of carefully digging through her belongings. I was not certain what I was looking for; I opened drawers, searched in her closet and behind the furniture, searched for something—anything!—that could tell me what her hold over the Count was. Despite my annoyances with her, it felt terrible to invade her privacy so directly, even as my conviction that she hid some dark secret bore me onward.

Yet, after around a half hour, even that feeling began to wane. I stood in the centre of the room, feeling lost. I had done something horrible and deviant for no reason.

Once again, I found myself questioning my judgment. Could it be that I had imagined the entire mystery for entertainment? Was I simply twisting the ordinary to find answers that did not exist?

Doubt consumed me in an instant, and I felt a hot swell of embarrassment. Searching through another servant's drawers, wandering in the dark, creating strange fantasies in my mind— had I become a madman?

At the very least, if I was not a madman, I was certain that I was a terrible butler. Perhaps the Crawford family had been right to rid themselves of me.

With that thought, I was crushed. I gave one final, hurried look around to make sure I had left everything in its correct place, then went to the door and opened it. Yet, just as I was closing it behind me, I stopped. It occurred to me that I had missed something.

I knew that Miss Josephine burned her correspondences; I had watched her toss them to the kitchen fire once or twice, in small bundles. Could it be that the latest bundle yet survived?

At once, I had an idea. After a moment's hesitation, I entered the room again and sank to my knees, lifting the covers at the edge of the bed. It was there that, beside a chamber pot, I found a beaten old bedwarmer.

I grasped for its handle and dragged it out, then opened it and felt a great shock run through me.

There, tossed in with the extinguished coals, was a bundle of letters wrapped in twine!

Nearly trembling with excitement, I pried the twine away, keeping the knot intact so as not to arouse suspicion when I replaced it. Then, turning the letters to begin with the oldest, I began to read.

Immediately, I recognized the Count's handwriting. These were the notes that he and Miss Josephine exchanged from the hook outside her door for the past week.

The first one was simple, though the handwriting was beautiful as always.

Please purchase two bottles of black ink. You may leave them on the desk in the library.

"How strange," I mumbled to myself. There was no opening and no closing to the letter; it was only the message itself. It certainly did not seem very cordial.

Miss Josephine's reply, which I found on the opposite side, was simple.

Monday

I went to the next one.

Please borrow two books of any kind.

Her reply was the same.

Monday

Thus far, nothing seemed out of the ordinary. Once more, I doubted; perhaps there was nothing to find here after all.

With a sigh, I put that one aside and looked to the next one—

and my eyes grew wide.

Is Mr. Bedford well?

I could not believe it! The Count had asked after my health? With bated breath, I turned to Miss Josephine's reply.

No he has always been pale and sickly not a rugged sort and not suited for this type of employment at all so you should find another servant presently

Oh, how my blood boiled! I stared at her words, open-mouthed. What had I done to offend her so terribly? I looked to the Count's reply.

Please make sure Mr. Bedford is taking his meals.

I felt a warmth in my chest, and turned to the next one.

It is useless he barly eats a morsel and I do think he is full of diseese

That upset me, as the previous one had; but it was upon turning to the next one that matters became strange, and my ire was forgotten.

I know. He looks especially pale today. Please make sure that he is taking his meals.

I paused upon reading the words, and furrowed my brow.

When had the Count seen me?

It was impossible—I had never seen him! What was this? His words seemed to imply that he had seen me more than once, and that he was watching me with some regularity.

I looked all around, feeling somewhat nervous. Something was unusual was afoot; but I had to see what Miss Josephine had replied, and put the previous note beneath the others to read the next.

He is sickly and will never be well I promise he is useless to you. Let him go

Now, my instinct was warning me. Something was wrong, I was sure of it; but I read on.

I know not what you imply. I am only trying to ensure that Mr. Bedford is in good health.

I swallowed, then turned to the next one.

Let him go

Only one note remained. I was almost too afraid to read it, but with a deep breath turned it over and lifted it up.

A powerful chill travelled up my spine.

Careful, Josephine.

*   *   *

When she returned, I almost confessed my deed.

I was torn. There seemed to be an obvious story behind what I had found: that Miss Josephine despised me, and that the Count—who cared for my well-being, and had caught a glimpse of me!—was warning her to be careful and calm her dislike, lest he dismiss her. Certainly, it no longer seemed to me that she held any control over him, and so that idea was laid to rest forever.

But some elements still fit my theory poorly. Why did the Count conceal himself from me, even while he presumably watched me without my knowledge? Why did Miss Josephine want me gone so desperately?

I almost asked her directly, as we sat eating supper; the courage was welling up inside me, but it was she who spoke first.

"Starving yourself again tonight?"

I sighed. Every notion I had of our finding common ground left me at once. "No, Miss Josephine."

"Then why not discard it?" she scoffed. "If you have no intention of eating it, throw it away."

I leaned my forehead onto my hand. "I do intend to eat."

"Go on, discard it. Why wait?"

I felt that I was about to burst. "Please, would you—"

"You always—"

"Miss Josephine!" I shouted, throwing my hand down, "For God's sake, will you let me be! You don't understand anything at all! Why are you—?"

But then, my voice cut off; I could suddenly feel a burn in my eyes, and knew that to speak further would betray my emotions. Instead, I stopped and put my head in my hands.

There was utter silence.

I burned with shame, afraid to look up. Now that the righteous fury of the moment had passed, I felt foolish for losing control; and so, I spoke in a whisper. "I apologize. I didn't mean to shout."

There was silence for a few moments more, but then, I heard her voice. This time, there was no contempt. Her voice was weary but clear.

"You were poor, weren't you?"

I glanced up at her, finding a strange expression, then looked away with some shame. "Well, I certainly wasn't wealthy."

"No, you were poor."

I was silent and uneasy, and pondered whether to lie to her; but she interrupted my thoughts.

"No-one who has lived comfortably would catch a rat with bare hands, nor lose their wits over wasting food."

"Very well, then," I said quietly, and sighed. "Yes, I was poor. But a great many of us were; or were you born into some fine house? It makes no difference—"

"You were different," Miss Josephine interrupted. "You were not merely poor, you were desperately poor, wanting for food. Were you not?"

I stared into my plate, and did not say anything. What could I have responded to that?

But Miss Josephine was behaving peculiarly now. "Where were you raised?"

"York," I replied.

"The city?"

"Yes."

"What did your father do?"

I said nothing.

"Did you know him?"

"That is quite enough," I said quietly. Suddenly, I was very tired, and I stood. "It has been a long day. Good night, Miss—"

"When I tell you that you should leave," she said, in a strange and forced tone, "It is for your own benefit, not mine."

I stared at her. I was tired and confused, and together the two feelings made me annoyed. Could she not cease to be cryptic, and speak to me directly? "Miss Josephine," I said wearily, "I'm sorry, but I don't understand what you mean."

"This place is wrong for you. You shouldn't be here."

She almost seemed lost, standing there at the table, and I almost pitied her; but then I remembered her scathing letters to the Count, and my pity dwindled. Perhaps this strange behaviour was a farce as well.

I shook my head and went to the door. "I'm sorry, I don't understand," I told her. "Good night."

*　　*　　*

The exchange left me restless, and I did not return to my room. There was still some weak light over the horizon, and I could see without the help of a candle, so I went to the library.

I did not know why I went; I suppose I had grown to find it comforting. When I was in my room by myself, my life was a river that I drowned in; but amidst towering shelves of books, filled with the words of authors across the centuries, my being and my miseries were but a speck.

When I arrived, I selected a thick and imposing book from a shelf at random. Placing it down on the small table in the centre of the library, I drew up a chair and sat down.

I could not understand the words, but it was elaborately illuminated and exceedingly old. The pages crackled threateningly as I turned them, and the smell of old paper made me cough.

It was comfortable and quiet in the library, and after a few minutes I found that I felt drowsy. I realized suddenly how tired and sore I felt, how eager to let my worries leave me; and so I resolved to close my eyes for a minute, folding my arms into a nest on the table and resting my head inside them.

The stillness of the room soothed me, and I closed my eyes.

*   *   *

Slowly, I became aware of a bothersome light. At first, I tried to block it with an arm, squinting miserably; however, I soon realized the strange position I was in, and opened my eyes with a start.

It took me a moment to remember where I was; I had fallen asleep on the table! The very first rays of sun were beginning to seep through the windows, falling straight across me. I blinked groggily and straightened up.

Upon this movement, however, I became aware of an unusual

ache in one hand. When I looked down at it, I stared; somehow, I had slept in such a strange position as to inflict a scrape onto the back of my hand, around which a small bruise blossomed. Perhaps it had been pressed against the corner of the table, or the sharp edge of a page. What a way to have spent the night!— though oddly, I had slept through it all, something I could no longer do reliably in my bed.

Suddenly, however, as I began to sit up, I felt something rush down my back.

With a pang of alarm, I gasped in surprise and turned, scrambling back and nearly toppling off my chair, just in time to see a heavy red blanket slide off of me and fold down.

I stared at it for a few moments in shock. Then, I picked it up slowly and with intense guilt. "Miss Josephine," I muttered. I had not felt her drape the blanket over me. Perhaps I had been too quick to judge her intentions.

After a few moments had passed, I sighed and stood to gather the fabric in my arms. It was unexpectedly heavy and thick, the sort of thing that would be a burden to drag anywhere. A mild scent of spices clung to it, which I breathed in deeply and wondered at.

There was a trill of birdsong outside. I felt the warmth of the blanket in my arms and was peaceful for a moment, before taking it with me to Miss Josephine's room.

I hesitated outside her door, wondering whether she was awake. Yet, just then the door opened, and she looked up at me.

"Miss Josephine," I said, with warmth and apology. "Thank you for the blanket."

She furrowed her brow and stared. "What blanket?"

I blinked. "The one you left."

"What are you talking about?"

"I thought…" I looked down at the blanket in my arms. "Was it not you who…?"

At once the revelation hit me, with a shock so powerful that I froze!

"Mr. Bedford." Now her look was alarmed, and she stepped forward. "Explain yourself."

"It is nothing." I stepped back, towards my room. "I was simply confused, I apologize. I must have had a vivid dream."

"What were you going to tell me?" She looked down at the blanket. "Where did you get that?"

"This? Oh, this is nothing, I found it in the library. Excuse me, I am going to my room."

She tried to interrupt. "Wait! Come and—"

But I did not hear her finish the sentence, for I had entered my room and closed the door behind me.

I stood there for a moment, bewildered. Then, I leaned my back against the door.

The Count had draped a blanket over me as I slept in the library. He had not woken me; he had not left me any note reprimanding me for my trespass onto the hours of night during which he roamed. He had simply found me and covered me.

Being so startled by the act of kindness, and in general so unused to such gestures, I was at a loss for how to respond. An apology would be appropriate, but I had the odd sense that he would not expect one, and the even odder sense that he would be disappointed to receive one.

The notion of expressing gratitude, however, unsettled me even more. It would be akin to meeting his gaze, almost an invitation. Somehow, it frightened me.

But after some deliberation, my sense returned to me in a rush, and I felt ridiculous. I was a servant, and I had made an embarrassing mistake, and the Count had done something kind for me; I had to conduct myself with proper dignity and thank him at the very least. This decision settled my unease, and I was even amused. How strange my thoughts had turned! Perhaps I was truly falling ill.

CHAPTER VII

As if by prophecy, my reasoning came true. Even before I could sit and write out any letter, I began to feel terribly ill in the afternoon. I was flushed with heat and shaken by chills in turn, until I had not even the strength to take my supper. I retired early, nearly collapsing into bed and falling into a stupor.

I returned to consciousness briefly when Miss Josephine knocked, asking sharply whether I would take supper. Through a groggy haze, I told her to eat without me, and immediately fell back into sleep.

Yet, this was not a peaceful slumber. I tossed to and fro beneath the covers, sweating miserably. The air seemed exceedingly thin and hot, and yet I shivered.

On the following day I awoke in a worsened state, barely able to open my eyes. Determined to do my work, I arranged myself and managed to reach the kitchen before I had to sit down.

When Miss Josephine entered to find me, she gave a flat look of disapproval.

"You look terrible."

"I am fine," I said hoarsely.

"Go back to your room and rest."

"I can work!" I insisted. "If I work, I will feel better—"

"That was not a suggestion, Mr. Bedford. Go back to your room."

And so, reluctantly, I did. I fell back into my bed, and sleep claimed me almost immediately.

I awoke in a mess of damp bedcovers sometime around noon, rising from among a sea of bizarre and terrifying dreams. At first I was wildly disoriented, and barely realized where I was. Even when I gained my bearings and extracted myself from the mess of the bed, there was still a feverish chatter within my mind. I heard words and phrases repeated endlessly, and could not stop thinking about my mother, seeing her sick in bed over and over. What a cacophony! I felt half-mad!

Yet, after a long drink of water and a couple of minutes sitting, I began to feel slightly better. There, on the edge of my bed, I remained for some time feeling pity for myself. Had Miss Josephine been correct to tell the Count that I was too sickly to work?

How I despised to be a burden!

Bitter at this thought, I compelled myself to leave my room and pick up a duster, which I could scarcely use without setting off a terrific coughing fit. This soon alerted Miss Josephine to my presence, and she sent me away sternly once more.

That night, I was so exhausted that I could not fathom the thought of eating. When I informed Miss Josephine of this, she quite nearly forced me to have at least a portion of bread and cheese, which I choked down miserably. I was too tired to ponder her apparent goodwill until much later; in that moment, I was simply exhausted. Indeed, in the instant that she released me, I went quickly to the servants' hallway, opened the door from my room, and closed the distance between my bed and I in mere seconds.

What debility, as though my body had turned entirely to lead! I neither changed into my nightclothes, nor washed my face, nor my hands. I simply collapsed onto the covers and closed my eyes in dizzy relief. I daresay that even if I knew death awaited me on the opposite shore of my slumber, I would have gone all the same. I did not think of the Count, nor Miss Josephine, nor anyone.

I did not lock my door.

*　　*　　*

I awoke abruptly in the middle of the night and opened my eyes in the dark.

The awakening had been too sudden to be natural. Moreover, my heart was beating quickly; I felt as though I had been startled.

There was no sign of what had awoken me; it was pitch-black in the room. Yet, an odd feeling hung in the air, a tingling at the back of my neck and a pang of fear. It was quite unusual; I had never been one to be frightened of the dark.

I felt a desperation to return to sleep, the sickly weariness that sets in after midnight, intensified by illness; but even in such a state, I felt a flicker of interest in my heart.

I sat upright slowly, listening closely for music from afar. One thought came to me vividly: I wished to hear the piano. I had heard it occasionally after that first night when I was nearly discovered, and though I had never left my bed to pursue it again, I had grown to depend upon the sound for companionship. Tonight I felt especially lonely, and yearned for it dearly.

Hearing nothing, I sighed. Still, the odd sense around me lingered.

Feeling uneasy all of a sudden, I felt compelled to light a candle and dispel the sensation. Clumsily, I fumbled to reach the candelabrum on the bedside table; but after a few moments of groping blindly across every inch of the surface, I paused.

It was missing.

Had I forgotten to place it there, in my haste to sleep? Where else could I have left it?

I relented and edged slowly back into the bedsheets, confused and disoriented. After a few moments, I decided there was nothing to do except return to sleep.

Gathering the covers around me, I tried to ignore the eerie stillness and closed my eyes.

*   *   *

The morning swam in and out of my awareness for a long time, but what finally roused me was the feeling of thirst.

Once I became aware of it, it was impossible to ignore. My clothes were drenched with sweat, and when I pulled myself from the bed, half the bedcovers came with me in a great mess. As I loosened them from me, however, I tripped over the candelabrum—which was on the floor, for some reason—and staggered to the ground.

From there, I did not stand, but rather crawled until I found water from the day before. It was in a bucket, but I was too parched to mind; I tried to lift the entire thing to my lips.

In the instant that I did, however, I let it fall again; I had felt an ache shoot through my arm—a mild pain, but still one that made me wince. Loosening my grasp, I drew back my hand to see.

Somehow, perhaps while fumbling for the candelabra, I had injured my wrist. There was a distinct puncture healed over with crusted blood, and a bruise darkening messily around it.

Though I puzzled over it for a moment, I soon remembered my thirst. Miserably, I ducked into the bucket and drank rather like an animal. It was only once I was satisfied that I felt embarrassed, and wiped away the water with my hand. At the very least, Miss Josephine had not witnessed it.

But this thought prompted one far more sheepish: I had forgotten about Miss Josephine! There was bright light from outside behind the curtains, and realized I had slept for far too long. The subsequent pang of alarm woke me instantly. I changed my clothing quickly, washing myself with almost violent vigour, and knotted my cravat by the looking glass. Then, I opened the door and stepped out.

Immediately, I saw Miss Josephine at the door of her room. She seemed to have been pacing, wringing her hands, and muttering under her breath. In the instant I appeared, she looked up in terror, stood wide-eyed for a moment, and then rushed towards me.

"What happened?" she barked. "Why were you late?"

I froze in surprise, then became confused. "I'm sorry, Miss Josephine. Though it's no excuse, I have been ill—"

"I thought you were dead!"

"I only…" I furrowed my brow, slowly realizing what she had said. "Why—dead? Why on earth would I be dead?"

"You never listen to me—I *tell* you these things, I break my back trying to make sure you—"

"My goodness, are you all right?"

"Yes, of course I'm all right!" she snapped. "But you never listen to me, and it is going to *kill* you one day!"

I stared, baffled. "Because I was late?"

"What—*late?*—of course not!"

"Then?"

She looked straight into my eyes, and spoke in a terrible voice: "Lock your door!"

I stared at her for a few moments, and she stared in return. It was only then that I noticed the dark circles beneath her eyes. She looked as though she had barely slept.

I was at a loss. I did not understand at all, but I did realize that whatever I was failing to understand was important. Making my voice gentler, I tried for an explanation.

"Miss Josephine," I asked slowly, "Why, precisely, is it so important that I keep the door locked? And how did you know that I forgot?"

Somehow, that insulted her. She scoffed and seethed, then turned to shuffle down the hallway. "Do whatever you want, oh, do whatever you want!"

I watched her go, utterly at a loss. After a moment, I called after her: "All right, then! I will lock my door."

"Like hell you will!"

Seeing that I would get no more answers on the subject, I turned to practicality. "In any case, forget it. We have business to discuss; it is my turn to go into town tomorrow. Do you have the shopping list ready?"

"No," she barked, "And I shan't!"

"Miss Josephine!" I called after her, growing frustrated.

By then, however, she had turned the corner and disappeared.

I threw up my arms. "Fine! Then I will leave the door wide-open, until the devil himself comes to have a bloody visit! Are you satisfied?"

It took a few moments for me to realize I had let profanity slip, and I balked. I seldom spoke so crudely, and in fact took my purity of speech as a point of pride. There could be no more doubt: either by fault of Miss Josephine's character or my own fever, I was losing my head!

CHAPTER VIII

Though I felt somewhat better that day, and found myself quite able to work, Miss Josephine's strange affect impeded me at every turn. She chased me away from every task; when I insisted, she became so irate that I left, if not for my own good, then out of concern for her health.

Her conduct seemed wholly nonsensical to me. If her intentions were indeed malicious, then would she not burden me to work until I collapsed from fatigue? And yet, if her intentions were good, then why could she not tell me directly?

Unable to do work, I became restless and consumed with guilt. In essence, I was being paid for doing nothing; and no prospect terrified me so deeply as becoming useless. Despite the improvement in my condition, my heart sank, and I was consumed with melancholy.

Surely, there was no worse indignity than to be a leech!

I tried to lift my spirits by noting the improvement in my

health, and taking a full supper so that I would have the strength to do the following day's shopping in town; but to my great dismay, Miss Josephine refused to give me the list. She insisted that she would go in my stead, and after a short-lived battle of words, I surrendered.

When I left Miss Josephine that night, she had a strange gleam in her eyes. If she were some brash young man, I might have even thought it murderous. This furious intent, however, did not seem to be directed towards me; she was gazing down at her folded hands at the table in the kitchen, as though pondering some terrible and nameless deed that had to be done.

I spoke to her with some caution. "Well—good night, then."

"Good night," she replied, low and tired, before adding: "Mr. Bedford."

I paused at the door. "Yes?"

"Remember to lock your door; and this time, no matter what you hear during the night, in any form—stay precisely where you are until morning."

At a loss for words, I nodded mutely before departing.

That night, as I took my medicine and laid down to sleep, I felt uneasy. No matter how much I tried to persuade myself that Miss Josephine was simply being superstitious, or had been driven half-mad by decades of working in a solitary place, I found myself questioning every noise I heard in the dark. At some point, I thought I heard the creak of footsteps outside the door. It took some time to fall asleep.

Yet, it was the following day that a most curious change took place.

When I went to the kitchen to take breakfast, I stopped the instant that I stepped through the door. I was greeted by a strange sight: at the place on the table where I ordinarily sat was a full meal, arranged neatly. Ordinarily I had bread and butter with tea in the morning, and thought that to be quite enough. Here, however, somebody had laid out a hearty portion of meat and cheese, and even an egg seated neatly its cup.

Miss Josephine was busy at a cabinet, though she turned quickly when I arrived. This shook me from my startled state, and I addressed her.

"Good morning," I said haltingly. "Is the Count joining us for breakfast today?"

She gave a start. "What? Has he said something to you?"

"No, I only assumed from the table…"

She quickly came forward, pulling out the chair, and seemed nervous. "No, no. This has nothing to do with him. Sit."

I stared at her in abject confusion. "Why—do you mean to say that this is for me?"

"You have been ill," she said at once. At no point did she meet my eyes. "Don't trouble yourself. You will get well very soon, and sooner still if you eat."

So startled was I that I continued to stare, unable to help myself, until at last she became cross.

"I made it, so eat!"

There was the Josephine that I recognized! I relaxed, though I still gave her a quizzical look as I sat. "Pardon me. Thank you—I was only curious as to why you would go to the trouble of preparing all of this."

"Perhaps I am tired of doing your share of the work," she snapped, but her words had no bite. Her nervous expression remained, and she constantly glanced back towards me. "How are you feeling, then? Have you taken your medicine?"

I was at a loss, staring at the meal before me. Seldom had anyone shown me such a gesture, and I was unused to it; I politely tapped a spoon against the top of the egg, before responding with a lie. "I am much better today, I think. As for the medicine, the Count left one more vial this morning…"

"Have you taken it?"

"Not yet. I have caused him too much trouble thus far; I thought perhaps I might save it."

Miss Josephine's words took on an edge of urgency. "You ought to take it. The sooner, the better."

That made me pause, and I regarded her strangely. "Miss Josephine, forgive the question, but is everything…?"

"I must go into town today," she said sharply, sweeping past me. "Stay here. Rest, and don't do anything foolish."

"What foolish things would I do?" I said, baffled, but no longer received an answer. She was gone.

Once I was alone, I stared at the meal before me and wondered whether it had been poisoned. The thought of wasting it was unspeakable to me, however, so I took my chances.

After I ate, I was exhausted; merely the effort of eating had drained me. I returned to my room and laid in bed for some time. After two hours I began to feel profoundly ill, and sweated profusely through all of my clothes.

At this point, I became so frustrated that I nearly shed tears. I fought a bout of dizziness to sit, deciding in my muddled state to write a letter. I would tell the Count that I had been unable to work for the past few days, and that he ought to withhold the corresponding wages. To this end, I crawled halfway to my desk when I felt a horrible swell in my stomach, and barely made it to my chamber pot before being violently sick.

After that, though my physical state was improved, a hollowness settled in my chest. Once I had finished washing my face, I stared down emptily into my basin.

I had become so useless that I could not even work, nor even take a meal without wasting what I had eaten. In the truest sense of the word, I had become worthless.

There was a terrible bitterness in my heart. I knew this feeling all too well, and knew that to indulge in it was perilous; but even so, I could not help but let it swell up in my chest, until a great desolation had claimed me in that small room. It was beneath the influence of this feeling that I decided to take a walk outside.

*   *   *

Though it was not late in the day, the sky was grey and the moor was dark. A light rain had started up, barely enough to wet the ground, and the damp scent of newly sodden earth was beginning to rise among the grasses.

I set off from the door to the servant's hall, and began trudging aimlessly from there.

It may be of use here to describe the arrangement of the estate. The manor itself was settled on a broad hill, which overlooked the winding road leading up to it from town. To the east of the building was a great expanse of grasses, only sparsely interrupted by trees. When I took leisurely walks, it was here that I tended to go; the grass was easy to traverse, and very beautiful. It was in this direction that, when the day was clear and bright, one could glimpse the moorland church from the manor's tallest windows.

Behind the manor, however, was something entirely different. Beyond an old well and the few old ruins of a garden around it around it, there began an old and tangled forest, which stretched out over rolling land and into the horizon—from there, spanning such a distance that the difference between a hill and a mountain became difficult to distinguish.

At first, I chose the open moorland in the direction of the church, and wandered along lost in thought. The memories of my previous employment returned to me, and I imagined that I might turn around and find my usual routine waiting. Perhaps I had not moved to such a desolate place as this; perhaps I had only been sent just now to deliver a message, and would presently return to the Crawford house. Once I returned, I would serve the afternoon tea. Then, I might count the silver, and ensure that all the candlesticks were in their proper places. As the family conversed into the night, it would come time for the children to sleep; I would entertain them to give the nurse respite, before ushering them to their bedrooms and calling her back to help. Then, I might confer with the housekeeper…

At the thought of the housekeeper, I slowed my step and felt terrible guilt. Our farewell had been under circumstances that I wished dearly to forget.

The ill feeling of that memory brought me out of my thoughts, leaving me only with the weakness of my body and the rain dampening my clothing. In the chill that it brought, the dampness seemed even colder. I slowed my step and stopped.

It was then that I heard something curious.

Nearby, somewhere in the forest along the edge of the grass, there was a river. It rushed along rather loudly, as though swollen from the beginning of the rain. Upon hearing the sound, I remembered: I had indeed seen a river or a beck on a map in the library, though thus far I had not searched for it. Surely it laid somewhere beyond the boundary of the more forested area, where the sparse trees turned gnarled and thick.

For a long moment, gazing towards this darker and more shadowed place, I hesitated.

Then, as though possessed, I headed towards it.

Yet, despite being so near, I never made it past a few steps. Just as I had reached what might be considered the edge, I heard a sound behind me and turned—then startled at once!

A pair of deer were standing behind me, deathly still and silent.

I took a step back before realizing that it might send them into a panic, and quickly froze. Soon, however, I realized that neither of them had moved an inch. To this, I gave a quizzical look and waved a hand to scare them off, which did not work. Then, I called out:

"Go, go! Go on, now!"

This produced no effect, neither the tensing of muscle nor even the flutter of an eyelash. The pair stood in the very same uncanny stillness.

After a moment, I hesitated and felt quite strange about it all. There was a chill traveling up my neck, and I wished to prove to myself that nothing was wrong.

"What's the matter?" I said aimlessly.

At that, the deer finally moved. They turned their heads in tandem, gazing back through the misty rain towards the manor that rose up behind them.

Then, slowly, they turned back and fixed their gazes upon me once more.

My heart leapt into my throat and began to hammer. Feeling quite ill, I took a step back and spoke hoarsely. "What do you want?"

As I stepped back, the deer both stepped forward.

With that, I had reached the end of my wits. I backed away further, then tore my gaze away and ran.

I knew that it was a terribly childish thing to do, but I could not help myself; I simply felt that I had to get away from those oddly-behaving animals as fast as I could, though I could find no explanation for it.

In my haste, I forgot about the river; I went off in some unfamiliar direction, nearly tripping over tree roots and great masses of weeds. Here and there, I paused to look over my shoulder, and to my relief found no strange animal pursuing me. It was only after several of these glances that I could persuade myself to slow my step, and stopped to catch my breath.

Such exertion naturally came with a price; as soon as I leaned against a tree and lowered my head, I was consumed with a fit of coughing so loud that it would surely have frightened off even the most preternaturally calm animal.

This was, at least, my belief. Yet, in the moment that I finally fell silent and closed my eyes to rest in the peace of the forest— expecting only to hear the light rain overhead, or perhaps the rushing of that long-forgotten river—I was instead met with something far more startling.

What I had taken to be the rustling of leaves had in fact been another sound entirely.

When I raised my head, no less than ten deer were silently gazing back at me.

*　　*　　*

I woke with a terrific shout!

Seldom in my life had I experienced such a violent awakening; I had the sense of wrenching myself away not from the precipice of sleep, but from death itself. Gasping for air, I sat up and clambered to the edge of the bed, where I remained for several minutes. My heart thrummed so loud as to obscure my own thoughts.

I had experienced far worse nightmares, I thought to myself, but this had certainly been the most vivid.

As it often occurs to one after a dream of such unusual intensity, I thought I might reassure myself by recalling the events that had led to such a difficult night. It was then, however, that I became confused.

What, indeed, had become of the day?

It was late afternoon; I could tell as much by the light fading at my window. Yet, I could only remember taking breakfast, noting Miss Josephine's curious change of manners, and then starting on my walk. Furthermore, I was nearly fully dressed; I must have fallen asleep instead of leaving.

But surely I would remember having removed my shoes to lie down?

After a moment's hesitation I decided to have a look at them, in hopes that the sight might restore my muddled memory. Standing from my bed, I walked to the door and found them there, neatly paired.

The sight of them did nothing to amend my memories, and only confused me further. Absentmindedly, I picked one up—and almost instantly dropped it in abject terror.

Mud! There was mud, still damp, on the bottom of that shoe!

There could be no other explanation: I had lost my head, I had gone mad—that, or I was still lost in a dream.

In an instant, my heart began pounding anew, and my throat was dry. I staggered back and clutched at the edge of the bed. All of a sudden, I could not trust myself to distinguish reality from dreams; what a terrifying feeling that was!

Closing my eyes, I willed myself to invent a story: perhaps I had indeed departed for my walk, but fainted from illness and had some wretched nightmare about deer. I must have laid in the grass until someone had carried me back.

And in such a case, who could have done so other than the Count?

Contrary to my hopes, however, this thought brought me no comfort. I was suddenly deathly afraid, though I knew not of what, and I came to a vital conclusion.

I had to flee the manor at once!

When I had arrived, I had been enchanted by the mystery of the place; now, I was purely terrified. I had discovered something new about myself: that I was far more cowardly than I knew, far more suited for humility or pleasantries than whatever wild darkness laid beneath the stone of this place. To be a simple servant, stifling as it had become, was better than being a lone soul being tossed to and fro in the terror of the unknown. I had found something that frightened me more than oblivion.

Gathering my wits, I decided to cross the hallway and wake Miss Josephine, and inform her that her wish had come true: that I would leave, and never return.

In the moment that I rejected the manor, I felt as though it rejected me in turn; my room felt hostile to me, so I hurried for the door and threw it open. Yet, I had scarcely taken a step before I stopped. I had seen something from the corner of my eye.

The Count had left a note upon the hook by my door. Beneath the hook, on the floor, was a very small vial.

For an entire minute, I paused and stared.

Then, I knelt down and picked up the vial, recognizing the coppery medicine that the Count left me every so often. With it in hand, I gently unfastened the note and returned to my room, going to the window to read beneath the last rays of sunset.

I hope that you are feeling better. Josephine informed me that you delayed in taking the last dose of the medicine that I left you. Rest assured that making this medicine presents no trouble for me, and furthermore, as it spoils easily, it must be used soon after it is made. I have provided another dose, which I do urge you to take as soon as you receive it.

Once you have taken it, please come to my quarters at your earliest convenience. Kindly knock before you enter. I will be waiting within.

With apologies for the late notice,

Alistair Beaumont

My stomach dropped and a thrill passed up my spine, though it was followed instantly by dread.

The Count had asked to meet me?

Only a moment before, I had been ready to leave forever. Now that I was on the verge of seeing the very centre of the mystery itself—how could I go?

Wiping the sweat from my hands, I sat upon my bed and gave myself a moment to ponder clearly, past the terror and confusion and excitement, trying to think of any reason that the Count would ask to meet me.

The first, and most rational, was that the Count wished to evaluate my health in person and see whether his medicine was having the intended effect. The second was that he had noticed how little work I was doing, and had decided to send me away—either for my own health or the health of his purse. The third was that Miss Josephine had devised some plan to rid herself of me that I had yet to understand.

Beyond that, the only options that remained were fantastical ideas conjured by fear.

I knew in that moment that I could leave it all behind me in an instant. The door was open, and nothing was impeding my flight. Never again would I have to wonder about this mystery; it would remain in my past forever, some strange creature that I had never quite understood, and in the monotony of my life even that curious memory would fade.

I would return to that other world, where nothing awaited me but the very same river of tedium that had first driven me away from it.

For a moment, I stared emptily across the room, which had now grown dark. Night had fallen.

Then, I swiftly uncorked the vial still held in my clammy hands, tipped it back, and drank it in one swallow, before snatching up my tinderbox from the bedside table and lighting a simple candlestick. Taking it in hand, I hurried to the mirror and arranged my cravat and my hair, setting everything in order. In the firelight, the reflection of my eyes seemed to glow.

To hell with it all! Whatever there was to find, whatever sense or meaning remained to discover in the world, I would find it!

CHAPTER IX

The stairs creaked beneath my shoes as I reached the warm gloom of the upper floor. The sound gave no echo; rather, it faded stiffly, absorbed by the uneasy silence of the walls.

I was trying to move quietly, knowing that waking Miss Josephine might cause me trouble. Despite the way her behaviour had changed in the morning, I had no doubt that to venture out in the nighttime would still draw her ire, and so I had not so much as breathed as I passed her door.

Pausing halfway up the grand staircase, I glanced over my shoulder to make sure I saw no sign of her. Satisfied to find no movement but that of shadows by candlelight, I went on and reached the upper level of the manor.

The Count's main quarters were on the left side of the upper level, which was divided into three rooms as far as Miss Josephine had told me: a bedroom, a dressing room, and a final room which I assumed to be a study. Having never ventured into any of them, I was not certain which of the doors was which. As I went along, however, I suddenly stopped and shuddered in surprise.

For the first time since I had first seen it, the central door—the largest and most ornate of the three—was slightly ajar, with a faint and flickering shaft of candlelight leaking across the carpet. Nothing else was visible; the door was not open far enough to permit any glimpse of the room inside.

My God, what a moment that was! I even forgot my fear in my excitement, and could scarcely hold myself back from rushing forward; but I was not so moved as to forget my place, and quickly took on the disposition of a servant once more. Even if this would sate my curiosity once and for all, it could still be the most ordinary of meetings, and to behave foolishly would be an embarrassment.

Holding my candlestick aloft, I walked up to his door and stopped beneath the ominous heights of the hall. There, I hesitated one last time.

Then, I lifted my hand to knock.

But in the instant before my knuckles could touch the wood, a deep and sonorous voice sounded from within:

"Do enter," it said calmly.

I nearly leapt out of my skin; I was awash with surprise. It was his voice—and what a voice it was! It would not have startled me so to hear an elderly voice, nor the bright and arrogant tone of a wealthy young man; but this voice held an imposing character that I could not place, mellow and resonant, far deeper than I had expected.

Yet, a voice alone would not satisfy my curiosity, and with a deep breath I gathered my courage. In one firm movement, I slid my hand over the doorknob and pushed, entering the Count's quarters.

The first thing that met me was the redolence of the place, a sweet smell of old books and polished wood. As I stepped in, I glanced at my surroundings and understood: this was the study. There was ornate furniture with gilded handles and clawed feet, covered in all types of books; two high and decorated cabinets; and a large desk nearly as aged and magnificent as some fine ancient mariner's ship. Yet, as I closed the door behind me, something else caught my attention.

As I turned from the door and took a step in, I froze. I had found the Count.

He stood statue-like in stillness, remarkably tall, facing a broad window. The first feature of his I noticed was his hair; it was dark and unusually long, spilling down over the curves of his shoulders. These shoulders were finely dressed with a long and dusky coat, which was cinched at his waist. In the dim light, I could make out little else.

I had to force my voice to leave me, but at last gathered my wits.

"Good evening, Sir," I said, with as much cordiality as I could. "It is a pleasure to meet you."

"The pleasure is mine," he said immediately in return.

Though the exchange was brief, the very fact that we had exchanged words made me excited, and then bold. I steadied myself, then took another step forward.

"I apologize for any trouble I might have caused you; I—"

"Mr. Bedford," he interrupted, without facing me. "Before you speak any further, please sit."

For a moment, I paused in surprise, then glanced at the nearest armchair. How odd, I thought, that he would propose that I sit while he yet stood; but I was determined to play my part well, so I strode forward and settled into the seat, placing my candlestick aside. Yet, before I could thank him, he spoke again.

"I must ask that you tell me something."

I fell silent in surprise, and stammered. "Why…certainly."

"I left you a new vial of medicine. Did you drink it?"

"Yes," I answered slowly. "I did."

It was an odd start to the conversation, which made it difficult to know what to say next. There was an uneasy feeling in the air, which I tried to dispel by showing a servile disposition. "You must forgive my delay in taking the previous dose," I said sincerely. "I am only a humble servant, you see, and so when I come across something valuable—"

Without warning, the Count turned to face me.

His eyes were a dark and vibrant brown, and they flashed dangerously upon catching the candlelight; but his face! Before, I had been curious for him to turn to me, but now I regretted it.

The Count had fine and elegant features, perhaps the finest I had ever seen on a man. Arched brows and dark lashes gave his expression a dignified air, which was sharpened by the line of his nose. Though there was a gentle curve to his face which might have suggested softness, it was all undone by an icy expression that could have made even the most phlegmatic disposition cower.

This was a face that could have been called truly beautiful if graced by a smile, but now it was a visage of savage night that was terrifying to behold!

Though his features struck fear into me, what truly startled me were his clothes. Though he was well-dressed, the style was strikingly dated. His breeches might have passed as modern if worn as livery, or as the evening wear of an older gentleman; but the coat, with its loose and ruffled sleeves, was at least a century out of date by any standard. The generous ruffles tucked into his collar were likewise not far behind.

In short, I was suddenly unsure of who I was facing, and my voice faded to nothing. Absently I noticed that he was holding a stemmed glass, half-full with red wine; and for some reason that I could not identify, the sight of it brought a cold sweat to my forehead.

The Count watched me for a moment, as though waiting to see whether my look of surprise would yield anything further. Then, his proud lips parted, and barely moved as he spoke.

"No apology is needed," he said coolly. "A bitter remedy is readily delayed."

"That it is," I said politely, though I had no sense of what he meant by it.

To my horror, a cruel and humorless smile curled his lips.

But then, I remembered my dignity and my purpose—after all, was this not merely an ordinary conversation with the man who had employed me for some time now?—so I straightened in my armchair, meeting that chilling gaze with the most gracious expression that I could muster. "I must thank you, then, for your kind attentions. You have been singularly hospitable, and I am pleased to be at your service."

Then, realizing that I still did not know why I had been called, I hesitated.

"In that regard, if there is any reason in particular that you wrote to me tonight—is there anything that I can do for you?"

At first, he did not move. Then, at last, he tilted his head.

"Yes," he said. With a smooth movement of his arm, he turned his gaze and set his wine glass onto the table beside him with a faint *clink*. "I believe there is."

"And what is that, then?"

He faced me abruptly and spoke, with a sharp look that made my breath catch.

"Answer one question for me."

"Certainly—"

"Do you value your life?"

My heart was pounding in my ears. Perhaps he was only playing the part of a philosopher, I thought to myself; perhaps this was his strange manner of conversation, and so I would go along with it. His question in itself was not a simple one to me, but I gave a hoarse and clumsy reply.

"Well, I would like to."

I would come to know this as the final ordinary moment of my life.

For in the next instant, the Count's eyes flared and his lips pulled back; and before my shocked and disbelieving eyes, his canine teeth appeared to lengthen in an instant, sliding over his lips—they were fangs, they had turned into fangs!

With a surge of horror, I shrank back into my chair; but I would not remain there for long.

"Then fight for it," the Count thundered, took a step forward—then *pounced!*

With a shout of surprise, I threw myself aside so violently that I tripped and fell. There was a tremendous crash behind me; when I looked in terror over my shoulder, I saw that he had collided with an armchair where I had been sitting an instant earlier.

I was so shocked that I barely breathed. What on earth was happening? Was I still lost in a nightmare? I could not understand a single thing that I had seen; why would the Count attack me?

Then, slowly, he rose from the ground where the chair now laid toppled, pulling his cloak from the wreckage, and turned smoothly back towards me.

And in that moment—dear God!—I realized that I was not lost in any nightmare, that the fangs were no illusion, and that the Count was not merely trying to attack me. He was trying to kill me.

I scrambled to my feet; my knees barely held steady. "Wait!" I exclaimed, holding up a hand. "Please, there must be some sort of misunderstanding—"

He started towards me again.

I was beside myself with panic and confusion, but I had yet to exhaust my final hope to find some resolution. As he advanced, I stepped back and continued to beg him. "Wait, wait, wait—"

His boots sounded sharply against the floor, his steps slow but firm, until at last I exclaimed with force:

"For God's sake, *stop!*"

This last shout was so loud that he obliged.

Seeing him halt, I was relieved to the point where my legs quivered, and I thought I would fall to my knees. Yet, then, he met my gaze directly.

"I bear no ill will towards you," he said quietly, in a voice so dangerous that my blood ran cold. "Surrender now, and you will suffer no more."

I was livid. "What do you mean, suffer no more? What do you mean by that?"

He stared, as though waiting for me to understand.

"Have you mistaken me for somebody else?" I cried out. "Have I done something? Speak, at least say something!"

At that, he finally replied:

"Words will not save you, Mr. Bedford."

To hear him speak so cruelly in that smooth and resonant voice, I was overcome with dread. Knowing now that there would be no easy resolution, I steeled myself and barked out a question.

"What are you?"

It was pointless, of course. I had known what the Count was since the moment I had seen his fangs, and realized why his clothing was a century out of date; but to hear him say it would silence my doubts forever.

He gave me no such satisfaction. Instead, he began to move towards me again.

I was going to die—I was going to die—I was going to be consumed! The world was sharp around me, and my heart hammered painfully. His words echoed inside my mind, and for an instant, I suddenly considered them.

When he had offered me a peaceful surrender, he had seemed sincere. Here was the opportunity for a swift end to all my troubles, an end to fretting over my purpose, an end to regretting my place in the world. What more was left for me now, after all I had done, other than to face my judgment? And if this itself was my judgment, my punishment, then surely—surely!—there might be hope for my salvation.

Perhaps to sacrifice myself in the name of my mother would be a noble deed.

A sick hope claimed me. There, in the shadow of my impending death, I was filled suddenly with an overwhelming feeling of love.

But a strange and different hope gripped me then, a loud and fiery thing, and tore the peace of surrender from me.

I could not die.

I could not die!

I have no idea what struck me; I cannot put it to words. It was one of the most powerful feelings that I had ever experienced, a warrior's frenzy, a wild hope that there still remained something to be experienced, or healed, or fixed—I could not die, not yet!

All of these thoughts passed through my head in an instant. With their culmination, terror came; and so, as the Count approached, I backed away.

The Count saw my action, and sighed very slowly.

I watched him, tense like a cornered animal, and wondered whether he would speak; but he did not speak.

Instead, he tore off his cloak and threw himself towards me.

With a shout, I dodged him, and tripped my way to the door. When I reached it, I took the knob and yanked it back—but it would not turn! The door had locked! How was it possible?

It was then that I realized that my hope might have been futile, and that I was trapped and about to die at the very moment of the realization that I wished to live. This thought made me wild; what a shock of terror went through me, what trembling shook my very bones! In a panic I began to pound at the door with my fists, and wrenched at the doorknob like a madman.

"MISS JOSEPHINE!" I shouted. "Help, Miss Josephine— *HELP!* It is a demon! It is the *devil!* Miss—!"

But upon hearing steps approach me, I quickly ran to the other side of the room, only then turning to face the Count again.

He watched me and said smoothly: "You can save your breath. She will not come."

My vision blurred. I was beginning to feel sick; my heart was beating quickly, and I resorted to begging. "Please, then…please, let us be civilized about this—"

He swept towards me.

I gasped and stumbled back, but then struck a table; I was trapped, and he was moving closer.

What a surge of power filled me then! I was suddenly a savage, an animal with the sole purpose of survival. This finely-dressed man, who had for so long played the part of a welcoming host, had been toying with me all along. Now, there was no need for such pretence; his movements were graceful but brutal. Every gesture he made told me that I was beneath him in every possible manner, that he had no reason to care for what I said or did. My life was less than nothing to him, a mere hindrance to his satisfaction.

Indeed, in that regard, he was no different than every villain that I had met in my life.

I was filled with rage and disgust. It must have inflamed my expression, for he paused in his stride.

This gave me my chance, and I took it; I flew to the fireplace, where I seized the poker. Then, I turned to him and gripped it tightly, feeling the weight and cold of the iron in my hands, shaking with fear and hatred all the while.

The Count held still for a few moments, glancing at the poker. After a pause, he frowned, and his lashes lowered as looked down to reach for his side.

Then, out of the sheath on his belt, he pulled up. With a flash of candlelight against metal, a gleaming rapier sword emerged.

I felt my face lose its colour. It was a miracle that I did not fall, though my vision blurred and my ears rang. I could not restrain a pathetic gasp, nor the burn of desperation gathering in my eyes.

One of us had to die—I had to kill him!

After that, it all happened very fast. He moved towards me,

and I moved back; but I reached the wall, and he was suddenly before me, towering with his sword. I tried to swing the poker at him, and brought it down with such force that it rang, but he moved aside easily and seized it with one hand.

No matter how hard I pulled, straining until my face flushed with exertion, I could not free my weapon; but all of a sudden, I realized I did not have to. Instead, I wrenched it to the side, and lunged forward with a shout until his hand slipped—and stabbed the iron straight into his side!

At first, I was filled with elation; I had wounded him! But to my horror, with barely a pause, he seized it again and wrenched it out of himself, and threw it viciously aside with narrowed eyes. It landed with a dreadful clang.

I tried to flee, I did! He grabbed for me, and I, anticipating at any moment the run of a sword through my stomach, fought him with every ounce of strength. I shouted and kicked and clawed, and managed to tear from his grasp and stumble to the window. There, I clambered onto the sill and tried to ram my elbow through the glass—but alas! It was far too thick and latticed, and would not give. Nonetheless, I readied myself to try again, but was suddenly pulled kicking and struggling from the window; the Count had seized me!

But I would not go easily. I screamed and writhed like a wild animal in his grasp until it loosened, and managed to wrench myself free. Then, I stumbled, dove to where the poker had fallen, and turned to hold it in front of me again.

Now, his calm was gone. He was thoroughly disheveled, his clothes torn and bloodstained where I had stabbed him. Even though he moved gracefully, his breathing had become strained.

In that moment, I realized that I could fight him—I could win!

Yet, an instant later, the unthinkable happened.

My exertion caught up with me, and it was suddenly difficult to draw breath. I strained for a moment as my throat tightened. Then, I began to cough.

"No," I begged my body aloud. "Not now—"

But the coughing only worsened, and a feverish heat rose to my forehead. My limbs became rigid, and I shook uncontrollably.

The Count watched me as I tried to regain my breath. Now, the calm returned. He gave me a look that was almost understanding.

Then, he lowered his sword, sheathed it, and began to walk towards me.

My legs finally betrayed me. I dropped the poker and fell to the ground, first to my knees and then my side, coughing and gasping for air. Tears streamed down my cheeks; I was helpless!

As I watched in terror from the ground, my face hot with fever, his boots stopped in front of me. Then, he knelt carefully at my side.

I pulled weakly away, but he took my arms behind me and pushed me onto my front.

Now I began to weep in earnest. "Please," I begged. "Please, we can strike a bargain! I would—" I coughed, and struggled to breathe. "I would do anything, anything, please, I cannot die yet—!"

"Quiet," he said softly. "Settle your breathing."

I gulped in air, but cursed him. "You devil, let me go!"

"Waste not your breath cursing me in this state, Mr. Bedford. You will have plenty of time for that later."

"After you kill me?!"

"Quiet. I wish to preserve your dignity, so listen to me

carefully. Nod if you understand."

I was weeping too stormily to comprehend him.

"Nod if you understand."

I did not.

"Mr. Bedford," he said. "Nod."

"My *dignity?*" I cried out. "How dare you speak of dignity, when you have me trapped like this? Let me live! By God, what have I done to you? Let me live!"

"I am giving you a choice."

"What bloody choice?!"

"You can choose to do as I say, or to die."

"That is not a choice, that is a threat!"

"It is not. Do you wish to die painfully?"

"No—no, please—"

"You would do anything to prevent it."

"Yes!" My voice shook with terror. "Have mercy, anything!"

"Anything."

"I already said anything, you beast! Oh, God help me!"

"Then do as I say, and you will live," he said. "Tell me whether you truly drank the last vial I left you. If you lie, you will be dead shortly."

At once, a dreadful shock went through me.

Blood! It had been blood all along, it had been *his* blood that he had left for me to drink!

I dissolved into weeping once again. "Why, why are you doing this to me? What is this torture, what have I done? Oh God, what have I done? Mercy, mercy, mercy…!"

At that, finally, there was a long silence.

Then his voice came again, with a tone that was almost gentle. "You will live," he said quietly. "You will live. I will make that promise to you. Tell me the truth, and you will live."

And I surrendered to him. I did not understand, but was too weary now to ask, and fever was claiming my judgment. "Yes," I said hoarsely. "I drank it."

"Good," he murmured.

I waited with bated breath, and wondered whether he would set me free. As soon as that hope crossed my mind, however, it was swiftly extinguished. I froze in terror.

I could feel my collar being folded down from my neck.

At once, I began to struggle again, and my mind went white with panic; the hairs along the back of my neck stood on end, and I cried out. "Why, you—!"

But I was too late. I heard the part of his lips, and his sharp intake of breath—and then, there it was, the hideous wrench and sting of pain, as he sank his teeth into my neck!

I choked on a gasp of betrayal. He had bitten me, he had me by the throat—what a terrible moment it was! I knew that I was done for, and yet, I still struggled. My heart was so swollen with terror, which flowed out like ice and consumed me, that I barely felt the pain. How I fought him, how I fought for my life! I struggled and wailed against him:

"You promised I would live! You promised, you beast! Oh, let me go, let me go, stop! Damn me for believing the devil! You promised, you promised…"

But with horror, I realized that he had begun to drink, and no amount of thrashing would stop him. My neck was crushed in his maw, and I knew that to struggle would be to rip out my throat; I could only cry out in anguish as I felt him drain my life steadily away. What futile rage and hopelessness, to hear it swallowed so meaninglessly!

At first, there was only the pain at my neck, the soreness of my shouting, the rush of fear through my veins. Then, I was overcome by weakness; a cold sweat rose up all over my body, over my forehead, pricking at my palms, accompanied by a deathly and unnatural dizziness. My shouts grew feeble, dwindling to soft cries, before the weakness invaded me in full force. My hands and feet were like ice; I could feel my life fading, and seeing no other option, continued to beg.

"Please…" I pleaded, unmoving now. A wave of nausea overcame me. "I feel so cold, I am dizzy…you must stop, you are killing me, stop…you promised me I would live, oh…!"

I was beginning to lose my sight. Seeing my pleas fail, I cried out with the last of my strength.

"Please, I cannot die yet…I…"

The world became a tunnel; all pain vanished, and all strength left my limbs. For a moment, I felt comfortable and well, and an overwhelming peace was all around; in this peace, I sensed another presence. Slowly, I opened my eyes.

My mother was there, watching me with a smile. A white light bathed me in a feeling of pure love; all was well.

"Mama," I whispered with numb lips. "How I have missed you!"

The hold on my neck loosened.

Then there was a deafening rush and a ringing, and the world around me vanished.

PART TWO

THE DANCE

CHAPTER I

I opened my eyes and bolted upright with a start, my hand flying to my neck.

At first, all I could do was gasp; I panted with the desperate thirst of a fish placed back in water, soothed only by the pulse that I felt beneath my hand. I was faintly aware of a blanket sliding off my chest and collapsing limply into my lap.

Initially my limbs felt wooden, heavy as though I had slept for an entire day. Confused, I looked down and realized that I had been sleeping on a daybed.

Where was I?

But all of a sudden my memories flooded back, and I flushed with shock as I gripped the blanket.

"I'm alive!" I whispered in awe.

It took a moment to grasp the enormity of it. Then I was overwhelmed in an instant; I put my face in my hands and wept. It was all I could manage, trembling violently as I clung to the feeling of life. How sweet it was to be alive, to breathe—how beautiful! Some time passed before I managed to regain my composure and my senses.

It was then that I realized I could hear the sound of the piano.

The notes were muffled and warm through the walls, but unmistakable. The melody was pleasant, but the memory that came with it was anything but.

Of course! I seized with cold terror as I recalled the events that had led to—what, precisely? All I knew was that I had been in the Count's study, and he had become terrifying; but I remembered him killing me, and yet I had lived.

I raised my hand to my neck once more, and pressed down where I remembered his killing bite vividly. To my surprise, I felt no mark.

Though I was indeed rattled, I gathered my wits and tried to think rationally; I acknowledged in that moment that I knew nothing of my situation, and that no amount of pondering would bring me closer to the truth. The only answers would come in the direction of the music.

Despite the stiffness in my limbs, I managed to turn and lower my feet to the floor. With a wince as I stood, I reached out and steadied myself on the arm of the sofa. Then, I hesitated. If I went to the Count, would I be sacrificing my final chance to escape? It was possible, but to escape would bring me no answers. In a situation that was pure madness, only madness would resolve it; I would go to him!

Though my chest was tight with fear, I made my way to the door that led to the piano room. I swallowed once to relieve the dryness in my throat, and with a deep breath, seized the cool metal of the doorknob and pushed.

As soon as I opened the door, the music was fully exposed; a haunting melody, mellow and graceful, made me pause. Transfixed by the sound, I wavered. Then, my eyes found the piano across the room, and subsequently, the elegant figure playing it.

It was the Count!

There it was, the unholy thing which had tried to consume me! Panic choked me anew, and I stepped back. At that, the music stopped.

The Count paused, then looked up.

We met eyes, him and I, across the tense space of the room. His fiery-brown gaze was piercing against the horrified pall of mine.

"Good evening, Mr. Bedford," he said at last, in the same deep and noble voice that I remembered. He tilted his head slightly. "You are early. Did you have a pleasant sleep?"

Though I could not pull my gaze away, I managed to gather the courage to speak. "What have you done to me?"

He stood up smoothly, straightening his clothing. From the small table beside his instrument, he lifted a wine glass. Through the spider-like hold of his hand, I caught a glimpse of red.

But he said nothing. Instead he closed his eyes briefly, breaking the gaze, and swept a length of dark hair over his shoulder.

I spoke again, beginning to tremble. "What did you do?"

"Calm down," he said smoothly.

"Calm *down?*" I exclaimed with temper. "How could I calm down? You attacked me! You…"

Yet, all of a sudden, I perceived that something had changed within my mouth. Though I had been faintly aware of it since I awoke, it was only upon speaking that I noticed it clearly. I paused, confused.

It came to my attention that my two canine teeth felt different than I was accustomed to. Then, my tongue found the sharp point of one, and I blanched. A gust of wild anguish soared up into me, and a cold sweat drenched my forehead. At last, I roared at him in disbelief:

"What have you turned me into?!"

His voice remained level, as swirled his glass. "If you calm down, I will explain."

"What have you *done?*" Though I was terrified, I could no longer stem the furious flow of my words; a hum of panic rang in my ears. "Answer me! What in the devil have you done to me?"

"Mr. Bedford."

"No!" I had transcended fury by this point, and my whole body shook. "I will not be calm until you explain, you fiend!"

"Then at least do not shout. Am I being uncivil to you?"

"*Uncivil?*" I cried out, raising my hands to my head. "Who are you, to speak of civil manners? You attacked me!"

"Yes, yes, I know; will you lower your voice?"

A mighty rush through my veins compelled me to shout; my heart shuddered with the desire to raise my voice until it ripped my throat! Yet, shouts and pleas had proven useless against him thus far, so with momentous effort and clenched teeth I restrained myself. "Then explain."

"Very well," he said. With a slight and measured sigh, then, he stepped out from behind the piano. "Firstly, as for what you are, I assume you already know."

"Don't give me such vague answers! What have you turned me into?"

"I don't know. What am I, Mr. Bedford?"

"A demon! Some awful vampire!"

"Then that is your lot as well."

"*What?*"

The Count watched me, and seemed to wait for me to understand.

"What do you mean? What do you mean by that?" I stepped forward again, clenching my fists. A desperate burn rose to my eyes. "Do you mean to say that I am forever the sort of demon that you are?"

"I do."

"That I am cursed with an eternal life, feeding from blood?"

"Whether you are cursed, I cannot say. The rest is true."

"Change me back!"

"I cannot."

"You must! You absolutely must!"

"No need to ask of me what is impossible." Then, pressing his fingers against his temple, he closed his eyes slightly. "Don't shout."

"Why shouldn't I?!" I roared. The storm of my anger still found its way to my lips. "You are lying, you must be—and *stop* swirling that glass, it makes you look like the devil!"

At that, he gave a slight smile. "If the devil has a taste for wine, then I might find him a kindred soul."

"Don't mock me!" I cried out. Yet, an awful suspicion occurred to me then, and my eyes returned to the wine-glass. "Oh, God in heaven, is that...?"

"No, Mr. Bedford," he said dryly. "It is not blood."

My thoughts were a terrible mess as I took another step back, remembering the presence of the wine within the house, remembering Miss Josephine carefully selecting the bottles from the shelf. My mouth went dry as sand. "Miss Josephine, is she also...?"

The Count shook his head. "She is not."

"Then why am I? How could you?" My knees quivered, and a white, feverish haze rose past my forehead. "How could you make me into this? I had a life! It was miserable, but it was mine!"

"Calm down."

"How could I *ever* calm down?!" I shouted, beginning to tremble. "I can never live normally again, and all you can do is swirl your sickening glass of blood!"

"It is not blood."

"Liar! You are lying! Why should I trust the words of a demon? I am done, I am finished!"

"This is wine." The Count's voice had developed an edge of exasperation. "Wine."

"Blood, it is blood! Oh, my soul is doomed! Let me go, let me go—"

"Mr. Bedford," the Count said, his voice dangerously soft. He met my gaze.

I fell silent in terror.

When he noticed my silence, he paused and glanced away. There was a quiet moment as he tapped his fingers lightly on the piano.

"I will help you," he said finally. He set the wine glass on a table, and began to come towards me.

I was confounded; I shrank back. "Help me?"

"Yes." He approached slowly, his steps echoing in the room. "I will teach you all that you must know about your being; I will show you how to live in this body. However…"

He stopped in front of me. The presence of him was enormous, so overwhelming to me that I could barely breathe.

"You are not trapped here." His speech was quieter now. "You are not my prisoner. You are free to come and go as you please, and if you wish to go, I will not stop you."

I stared at him in shock for a few moments. Then, my fury roared back ten-fold.

"Then *why on earth did you turn me into this?*" I cried out. It was a cry of my entire soul, of my entire being! "Why did you *do* this to me? If not to make me a slave, if not to make me a servant, then why? How *dare* you pretend it is nothing, how dare you say that you will *teach* me? Explain to me why you did this! Explain it!"

The Count looked at me for a long moment, and for an instant, I saw something odd cross his eyes. Yet, to my horror, he gave a humorless smile.

"A whim."

I felt my heart plunge. "What?!"

"I was curious to see whether I could. I have long toiled to understand the various elements of my nature, the different powers that the vampire exhibits. The creation of a fellow vampire was yet unstudied. If purpose is what you desire, you can consider yourself made for this aim."

Speechless, I stared at him. All at once I formed the idea that I was gazing straight into the face of evil, of true and eternal evil, the type of evil that had neither beginning nor end, that sought destruction and chaos for its own sake. I looked into that cruel face and saw nothing that could ever resemble me, nothing that I could ever understand or that could understand me; and I felt so terribly lost and alone at this thought that I could do nothing but sink to my knees, letting my face fall to my hands.

"What have I done?" I wept bitterly. "What have I done to deserve such a thing? I have taken such care—I have done no wrong! All of my life, what have I done wrong? Oh God, have mercy…!"

I heard his measured footsteps approach, until he stood directly before me. For a few moments, he said nothing, though I could feel him gazing down. Then, his voice came again.

"Rest assured, this has nothing to do with you. This is no personal grudge, nor holy punishment; it was my doing alone."

I took a rest from my anguish to snarl at him. "I hate you."

"I expected that you would," he replied smoothly. "It is of no consequence to me. Hate me to your heart's content, but know this: it is in your interest to tolerate me until I have taught you your nature. After that, you may do as you please."

I could speak no longer, nearly folding over myself on the floor. As I did, the Count went on.

"I understand that you need time. I will give you this time. Return to me before midnight, when you are prepared to learn what I must teach you."

"It isn't real! It cannot be real, it is all a nightmare, it must be…!"

The Count looked down at me with a mixture of contempt and quiet that was the closest thing to pity he had offered. For a moment, he was still, and I believed that he would say something more; but instead he turned away, and left me to my misery.

*　　*　　*

Once I had been left alone, I remained listless on the floor for some time. Eventually, I dragged myself up and retired to the safety and silence of my room; yet, even there, my emotions raged. Several times, I tried to wake myself from what I had decided must surely be a nightmare; I gouged scratches into my arms, then tried to sleep, then went in a daze to my looking glass.

Here, I paused and hesitated. Then I cautiously opened my mouth, and beheld my greatest fear: the change barely noticeable to the plain eye—my two canine teeth had sharpened slightly. Yet, as I opened my mouth wider to inspect them, I felt a new sensation, as though I could clench my jaw without gritting my teeth. I bore down against this feeling—and immediately leapt back in horror!

My canine teeth had descended into fangs, giving a savage and demonic appearance to my face!

At once I gasped in terror, and tried to push them back to their places with trembling fingers, which proved impossible. It was only once I calmed myself and loosened the musculature of my features, closing my eyes and leaning feebly against the counter, that I felt them slowly ease back into their places.

The shock of that moment left me with weakened knees and a restlessly pounding heart. I stumbled back, nearly upending a chair; with numb practicality I caught it and righted it quickly, knowing that noise would be likely to wake Miss Josephine.

Miss Josephine!

I had remembered her out of habit, but at the thought of her, a fresh shock coursed through me. All of a sudden, I had the perspective with which to understand her actions. It was never out of hatred or prejudice that she had tried to drive me from the manor. How could I have been so blind?

In every word and action, likely at great peril to her own life, Miss Josephine had been trying to protect me.

This realization plunged me into such despair that I gave a helpless cry and collapsed to the bed, weeping frantically. I was furious with the Count, but towards myself I held the greatest antipathy; for if only I had tried to understand Miss Josephine's intentions, if only I had looked past my own notions and seen the obvious—I would yet have my whole life ahead of me, if not for my petty pride!

Now, all was lost. I knew of vampires only what I had read in books, which varied considerably, but I had read enough to know one truth for certain: that I was now condemned to live an eternity of darkness, and that nothing but merciful death could remove from me this curse.

At the thought, I gave a groan of anguish. I searched within myself and could not fathom why any of it had happened, what sin I had committed to be cruelly dispatched to this horror; I refused to accept it. After some time I managed to go to my drawers, and clutched the small wooden crucifix I had brought with me. Contrary to legend, I realized, it did not burn; and so, I clasped it like a dying man and cast myself prostrate onto the floor. I begged God to reverse my sentence, cried out from the deepest wells of my soul to be woken from a nightmare. My view of my cross was blurred by hot tears, and I curled my fist around it.

"I beg of you!" I pleaded at one point. "I would take any sorrow but this! How will I live forever in this manner? How will I feed from the blood of the living? I cannot take this; I don't wish to sin, nor lose the human essence of my being, as the Count has!" I gripped the cross tighter still. "Am I destined to become a terrifying beast as he is, over hundreds of solitary years? Oh God, save me from this darkness, I would rather die, I would rather die!"

I wept until I was but a shell filled with sorrow, until the waves of misery had hollowed me completely. Exhaustion filled me, and hours passed without meaning.

But after a considerable length of time I regained some focus, and my eyes found the drawer that I had fumbled open for the crucifix. Slowly, I raised myself up and went to it, and opened a particular box that I had brought with me.

Two flintlock pistols—a parting gift and payment from my employment with the Crawfords—gleamed in their box.

All of a sudden, a rush of ghastly inspiration came to me.

Perhaps this had not been a punishment, but rather a new purpose. I had inadvertently stumbled across an awful secret and a demonic being; but thus far I had not lost myself, nor my moral core. To become a vampire had not been my choice, but what I did with my condition would define me.

Did I have the courage to kill the Count?

This thought brought a cold sweat to my forehead. I quickly closed the lid over the pistols and pushed in the drawer, but the idea remained, and so I pondered it. There was no question that ridding the world of such an evil being would be an absolute good, the sole good that remained to be done with my life; and yet, the thought of killing willfully—how it terrified!

Still, I considered it carefully; it would not necessarily be a bloody affair. I did not yet know the true weaknesses of the vampire. Vanquishing the Count could be as simple as dousing him in holy water, or burning him with silver. To think of these violent scenes still made me shake with dread, but I forced myself to remain calm. After all, until I knew how to defeat him, I would not know whether I was capable of carrying out the deed.

Furthermore, if I was to know the weaknesses of the vampire, I would need to learn them from the fiend himself.

Though the prospect of returning to him was enough to make me feel ill, I drew courage from my new purpose. In order to learn what I could, I had to play my part well, and so I could not look like a savage; I retied my cravat and combed through my hair and side-whiskers, until I looked respectable enough.

Yet, even when I gave myself a sharp look in the mirror and stood up straight, I could not conceal the weary panic in my eyes; for what could my useless look do against the towering blaze of the Count's poise? Mercy! Just the thought of him made me quiver, the thought of the frigid look in his eyes, devoid of any warmth or compassion—oh, God!

I splayed my hands over the wash stand and lowered my head. How *desperately* I feared to face him! But I still remembered the wrath with which I had fought for my life in my final moments as a human being, that mighty passion which I had not known myself capable of. If I was capable of reaching such heights, then perhaps I could traverse these depths.

I had to struggle onward; I had to face the Count. There simply was no other choice, and so I quit the room.

CHAPTER II

I climbed the stairs in the darkness, losing bravery with every step.

To ponder a matter in privacy is to kindle it in the safety of the mind; to keep that flame alight upon leaving is a far more difficult task. The manor at nighttime felt endlessly dark and tenebrous, and made me doubtful of my own purpose. It occurred to me that I was accepting my terrible fate far too easily; was I paving my own path into darkness with excuses?

The most fearful realization on this walk, however, was shortly to come.

As I passed several tall windows along the upper floor, I stopped abruptly. I had realized something peculiar: in my haste, I had forgotten to bring a candle!

But it had not been haste, I realized, that had led to my forgetting. Rather, the reality was far more terrifying.

With a sinking heart, I hurried to one of the windows. A

dense sea of darkness smothered the glass, pierced only by the faraway glow of the moon; but the window was thick, and only opening it would answer my question. With trembling hands, I unlatched it and pushed, receiving a cool gust of night air. Where this air might ordinarily have soothed me, however, here it drew a sharp gasp; for my realization laid plain before me.

The night was as clear and detailed to me as day!

It lacked some colour and the warm gaiety of sun, but the definition of the grass rolling over the moor, and the craggy surfaces of trees, were as obvious to me as though I perceived them in the light of morning.

Though initially I was struck with wonder, my curiosity turned swiftly to despair, and as I staggered back from the window I suppressed a desolate wail; for now more than ever, I understood that I was viewing the world through the eyes of a creature meant for darkness!

"Oh, devil take me!" I choked out, and rushed to close the window.

Shaken from my discovery, I tore my gaze away and continued to walk. Yet, I was fleeing one darkness in order to face another; soon, I came to stand before the door of the Count's study.

What madness I felt, to return to the place where such a pitiable event had befallen me!

I clung to a final moment of peace as I raised my hand to knock—but before I could, even that peace was taken from me.

"Enter, Mr. Bedford."

I jumped at the sudden voice, but steadied myself. Then, I closed my eyes to fight a wave of dread before pushing open the door.

The Count stood from his desk and set a book down. No

candles had been lit; he had been reading lightlessly, and the locks of hair spilled about his shoulders made his face stand out vividly against the dark.

With a dim but peaceful gaze, he watched me for a moment before speaking.

"Good evening."

I was unsure of how to express myself. Before, I had been compelled by my despair to shout and rage. How was I to address him when uneasy cunning had replaced fury? And if to converse normally was to invite him to reciprocate, then would I be accepting some part of his evil?

But in the end, I elected to speak normally; I was far too weary to take any other path. "I would say that it is night, not evening." I said cautiously, not daring to meet his gaze. "How do you sense my presence before I knock?"

He paused, as if curious at the question, before responding simply. "To live in silence for many years begets a sensitive ear."

I responded with an uneasy nod, as I fixed my stare upon the ground.

All of a sudden, I heard his steps begin to clip across the floor towards me. With an involuntary shudder of horror, I stilled. Mercy! Had I done something wrong?

But the deep voice that followed had a quality that was almost amusement.

"Furthermore, you swore loudly just across the hall."

I nearly apologized for my profanity before remembering that he deserved no such politeness, and instead clenched my jaw and said nothing. Noting my silence, he went on.

"Tell me: what did you find so objectionable?"

At that, I could not suppress my resentment any longer, and replied poisonously. "What wouldn't I?"

"I suppose we shall find out."

I tightened a fist, quelling a wild urge to strike him. "I suppose."

Though I did not look up, I heard his steps draw nearer. I turned my head, not knowing what expression to face him with, until he stopped before me and spoke quietly.

"You are allowed to look at me, Mr. Bedford."

For a moment, I continued to gaze stubbornly upon the ground; but I knew that I had something to prove to him, and so I relented. Slowly, I forced myself to lift my gaze, past the smoothly rippled cloth of his jabot to the villainous glint of his eyes.

He was taller than me, and I had to crane my neck slightly to meet his gaze. I did so with a nervous defiance; he returned the look with the sharp, piercing search of his stare.

His gaze seemed to study mine, and I suppressed my trembling as I waited for one of his awful comments.

"You have interesting eyes," he mused finally.

This confounded and angered me, and my reply was fierce. "Do I?"

"Indeed. Quite animated." Then, he tilted his head. "I suppose you are ready?"

The question caught me off-guard. "Ready for what?"

"I assumed it would be obvious."

All at once, the reality of the situation came rushing back to me. I drew in a sharp breath and seized with tension. "You cannot mean—"

"But I can."

My heart pounded, and at last I could restrain myself no longer. My composure crumbled as I stepped back and regarded him furiously.

"Don't be so flippant!" I seethed. "I came because I have no choice, but my compliance has limits. Taunt me, if you dare to test how far my patience spares you, but know this: where evil is concerned, I will never compromise. I will never hurt nor kill a fellow-being; I will *not* do it, I would rather die!"

The Count watched me with a steady but unusual look. From the tension in his features, I could tell that the volume of my voice had irritated him; once I fell silent, he simply sighed.

"Are you finished?"

"Quite," I spat.

"I don't recall implying murder," he said at last, with a raise of his brows. "The blood of the dead does as well as that of the living. There is a church across the moor, and a chapel behind it which is well-occupied."

This information calmed me somewhat, and I swallowed my panic. However, a chasm of despair soon followed. What creature of death would I be, to feed off corpses? How repulsive!

The Count noticed my despondency, and gave me a cool look. "I can see that you are troubled," he said, "But I assure you that it will come very naturally once you learn."

Cold-blooded creature, I thought bitterly towards him; for that which he meant as comfort was the very reason for my despair! Yet, I forced myself to nod.

Satisfied, the Count took his cloak and wrapped it around his shoulders, sweeping past me. "Then walk with me, and I will explain more along the way." He opened the door and gestured smoothly. "Shall we?"

*　　*　　*

The Count led me through the manor, walking on ahead.

His shoes were heeled, and echoed hollowly whenever they struck. This made me shiver, and the heaviness of my own stride redoubled; for how reluctant I was, to follow him any further down the hall! Indeed, to see him traverse the familiar places where I had worked and rested every day, oblivious to the horror concealed so near, made me feel such bitterness that I could have choked. Would that I had never fallen into such a gilded trap!

He did not lead me to the main entrance; instead, we went through the door at the end of the servant's hall, and I followed him outside onto the wild growth of the moor.

The air was cool and empty, devoid of the trill of birds. There was a sea of stars, and a desolate howl of wind through the trees; the wild grasses bowed and trembled supple in this breeze, protruding at uneven angles from the tumultuous roil of the earth.

I reached my arms around each other, and shivered with the chill of the wind. Oh, how the frigid sweeps of it so mirrored my own despair, I glumly thought! Yet, all the while, the Count's stride did not falter. He gave no flinch with the gusts, walking on ahead of me despite the flutter of his cloak. It was suitable, I thought resentfully, that one as cold and emotionless as he would flourish in such conditions. Still, I followed him.

We went in silence for some time, farther than I had gone myself before. The landscape grew different as we walked, and the trees gathered more closely. Tangled branches, mottled grey-green with age, snared together against the faint light of the sky, while wispy roots twisted from the ground.

My thoughts scattered, and it struck me how the trees stood in attention to the moon, to the endless seas of stars. Such woeful participants in the night! How they bowed as wizened apostles, in solemn attention to the soft howls of the wind, to the ruinous black of the sky! It suddenly struck me as a beautiful sight; I had rarely been outside at such an hour, and stared in distracted wonder at the boughs.

"Mr. Bedford," I heard the Count say suddenly, and I glanced towards him. He had paused in a patch of ferns. "Do catch up; I have information to dispense to you."

I had no choice but to oblige. When I reached him, he matched my stride and began to speak.

"Are you listening?"

I answered reluctantly. "Yes."

"Tell me what you know about vampires."

"They drink blood," I said flatly.

He gave a quiet laugh.

"What?" I pinned him with a vicious look. "They drink blood, I said!"

"Other than that, Mr. Bedford."

I swallowed my pride. "Fine. They have sharp teeth, which can be brought out." I hesitated. "And they can see in the dark."

"Good. What else?"

It was then that I remembered the new purpose I had fashioned, and pretended to think for a moment before mentioning, as though disinterested:

"They have particular weaknesses."

"Do name some," he replied. "It always amuses me to read what humans have imagined."

Hearing him refer to humans as something other than us, I could have collapsed with anguish. For the sake of my goal, I managed to keep my wits, though my voice shook with my answer.

"A stake through the chest," I said weakly. "Beheading."

He was quiet for a moment as we walked. Then, he shrugged

lightly. "Perhaps."

I was baffled. "Perhaps?!"

"Your first lesson is this," he said, turning slightly to catch my gaze. "My knowledge is incomplete. So, too, will yours be. What is unproven will remain in mystery." He gave a small, dry smile. "And certainly, I have never had the opportunity to try death upon myself, nor upon any other vampire."

Remembering that he had already experimented with me once, I looked away and suppressed a bolt of fear.

But he seemed to sense as much, and went on: "Neither will I try it on you. It would be far too difficult, as you will soon understand."

"Marvelous," I said poisonously.

"The marvels are yet to come," he replied. "There are strengths to this form, just as there are weaknesses. Listen carefully."

With no other choice, I listened.

"Where killing is concerned, some books describe the methods you name. Others describe burning, dismemberment, falls from great heights…" He paused with some amusement. "Now, Mr. Bedford, why that look of horror?"

I steadied my expression and gave a disgusted scoff, but said nothing.

"Remember," he added smoothly, "Humans maim and slaughter each other in one thousand more terrible ways. Most of these methods can no longer harm you."

I had no patience for his pithy speech, and interrupted. "Then what can we survive, that you are certain of?"

"Most arrows," he replied, "As far as I can tell. Most firearms. As long as there is no beheading or stake through the heart, most swords, or similar weapons…a fireplace poker, for instance.

Kindly don't do that again, by the way."

"You were attacking me!"

"I understand. What I asked was that you not do it *again*."

I was awash with frustration towards his casual tone. "Well!" I said sharply. "If you attack me again, I must."

"I will not attack you unless you attack me. Would you like me to continue?"

Falling silent, I looked away once more in disgust. He waited for a few moments before continuing.

"Though we may not know how to die, there are those among humans who do know how to kill us, or weaken us with a number of tools. These are vampire hunters. To meet a truly skilled vampire hunter will be the most terrifying experience you ever weather."

This gave me pause, and I could not help but ask: "Have you…?"

"Only once," he said. "So heed what I tell you. Here is the most important matter."

He raised his hand and gestured towards the church growing near in the dark.

"While you drink from the dead, your body is at its most defensible. You are static; you cannot be changed. Corpse blood will give you no benefits beyond slaking your thirst, and you will retain only vestiges of the special powers of the vampire; but neither will you be susceptible to any weakening trinkets flung your way—garlic, silver, and so on."

Garlic and silver, I repeated to myself. I had found two weaknesses that could hurt him.

The Count continued. "Therefore, consider your feedings a contract of sorts. When you drink only corpse blood, you are safe from most of these weakening tools. Yet, should you drink living blood, though you would gain powers beyond your understanding…"

The Count gave a sly look from the corner of his eye.

"You would be susceptible."

Indignant, I faced away from him. "Well, I would never do such a thing, so speak no more of it!"

"These abilities are not trivial, Mr. Bedford. These are powers over nature, and powers of mind; strength to defend yourself, and swift healing for your wounds."

"Speak no more of it, I said!"

"How will ignorance help you?"

I replied scathingly. "Just as much as knowledge would hurt others."

"You can feed from the living without killing a soul."

"Just as you did with me?"

"Very well," he said smoothly. "If it upsets you, I will speak no more of it. Only be forewarned that it is not knowledge itself, but rather its use, which matters most. That is your second lesson: henceforth, you always have a choice."

I fell silent. I was beginning to feel overwhelmed by it all, but said nothing.

He continued. "No matter what blood you take, the sun will not harm you, but you may find that you prefer night. I prefer it. However, your powers of living blood will always be strongest beneath the moon."

After that, he continued to explain, but by then I was lost. All of this talk, of vampire hunters and contracts, of blood and strange powers—by God! I only wished to be human again. A lump formed in my throat, and my eyes began to water, but I blinked quickly so that the urge would go.

"You will heal normally, but faster with plenty of corpse

blood, and faster still with living blood. You can eat human food, but only in small quantities, for otherwise you will become ill. You look unwell, Mr. Bedford."

Hearing my name, I startled. "What?"

He paused for a moment, then gave a quiet hum. "Perhaps that is enough for now, unless you have any questions."

I had many questions, but hesitated at asking him. To accept his teaching felt akin to accepting what he had done to me, and the thought was abhorrent; but what choice did I have?

"Do we sleep?" I managed hoarsely.

"Yes. That is the same."

We continued on, and the grasses rushed softly as they tossed around us. I tried to forget my thoughts by throwing them out towards the majesty of the scene, but they only returned to me, imbued with the gloom of the distance.

I had thought that the Count had finished, but his voice rose up smoothly once more. "In dire situations," said he, "A vampire may embark upon a hibernation of sorts. They are difficult to induce, but once begun, can last for decades."

I glanced towards him with trepidation. "Have you?"

"Yes."

"Why?"

He did not answer for a long time, glancing towards me with an unreadable expression. Finally, however, he turned towards the distance and answered without much import. "It was simply the prudent thing to do at the time."

The answer did not satisfy me, but I hesitated to question him further, and so we walked on in silence.

*   *   *

Soon enough, I beheld a small shape in the distance, and as we approached I was able to distinguish a church. It was a small, weathered thing, with a sinking ceiling and a lone blunt steeple which barely surpassed the scraggly heights of the trees. A row of arched windows nestled beneath brow-like stones, glinting gentle with moonlight in the dark; and behind the building a peaceful area hid, where I could make out the somber shapes of graves protruding lopsided over the earth.

I suddenly remembered the few tales I had heard of vampires, and looked cautiously towards the Count. Were vampires not banished from treading upon hallowed ground? A terrible image rose to my mind of bursting into flames upon stepping in, and I shuddered with fear.

Yet, we entered the grounds without any issue; and when the Count started towards the churchyard, I remembered my purpose there and grew sick with horror once more. How would I ever live joyfully again, bound to such a gruesome task? To think that this would be my life!

Unbothered, as though he had done it thousands of times before, the Count weaved through a number of graves until he reached the chapel; this was an old stone building, set some distance behind the church. Upon reaching the wooden door, he lowered his head and waited.

Sickened with anxiety, I choked out a question: "What are you—?"

"Hush. We listen first."

A few moments passed, silent but for the sounds of insects all around. An enormous pale-yellow moth held still on the doorway, as though waiting and listening with us.

Then, the Count nodded and gestured.

"Come."

With a small push, he took the latch and opened the door. I was surprised to see that there was no key, and looked towards him.

He was watching me, and noticed the expression; but he put his finger to his lips and spoke quietly. "Enter first."

With a final glance back towards the church, I steadied myself, scaled the two steps up to the entrance, and crossed the threshold after him.

At once, I could see the interior. It was humble but well-kept; a few rows of slabs were laid out in the darkness. Upon a select few, unmistakably long shapes laid in repose, wrapped in their shrouds; but at the ends, the sorry shapes of feet pointed upwards and slightly askew left no doubt of what laid within.

"The corpses of the destitute are brought here," the Count said quietly. "This parish gives them a proper burial, as an act of charity. It is their long tradition, which has been of great use to me."

My throat was dry and my limbs were numb; a chill rose up over my head. To see such a place brought back terrible memories indeed—and worse still, knowing what I had come here to do!

Yet, just as soon as this terror seized me, a sensation came with the opposite effect. To my surprise, the chapel seemed to carry a pleasant scent. It was difficult to identify, rich and sweet, but it stirred feelings of warmth and agreeable hunger.

Then, I realized what it was, and went entirely pale; for only the devil himself would enjoy the fragrance of corpses!

I could not help but gasp in dismay, and covered my face with my sleeve before crying out: "What wretched instinct—!"

But the Count interrupted. "Speak quietly, or we shall have a guest soon enough."

"Let the priest come! I have had enough, I have had enough!"

"Mr. Bedford."

I took a step back, ready to flee. To feel a new instinct of hunger was an unmatched terror. Though it was within my control, just as ordinary human hunger would be, I had realized a terrible truth: that regardless of my ideals, a natural impulse like this would draw me endlessly to evil deeds until I justified them myself.

"Mr. Bedford," the Count said again, with an edge of frustration. "You have not even seen the act."

"Neither do I care to!"

"You will have to do the same yourself. Would you not prefer to do it correctly?"

Seized by a swelling panic, I shook my head and shut my eyes. "I will not watch you desecrate the dead. It is a sin!"

"You are being unreasonable."

"And you are being repulsive!"

"It is repulsive for creatures like us to desire survival?"

"Yes—yes! This is horrible!"

"You are not listening. Is the draining of a corpse any worse than the slaughter of an animal? Would you blame the vulture over the lion?"

I hesitated. I had indeed always felt sorry for animals, and though I was repulsed, I understood his meaning. "I don't know, but—!"

"Then watch, and then decide for yourself," the Count said, then suddenly swept forward between the slabs. "You may find it less alarming than you expect."

Though I backed away, I could not avert my gaze.

As I watched, he approached a particular form. With a delicate touch and an air of routine, he opened a shroud and brought it down, revealing the body within. This one belonged to an older man, feeble in repose.

All the while, the Count continued to explain. "If you have your choice of corpses, you will know by scent which is most suitable. You can feed either from fresh blood or from essence mingled with it; the presence of either will vary by the recency of the death. Furthermore—"

As he spoke, a few sprigs of herbs and flowers, loosely bound, dropped from the inside of the shroud. He caught them neatly, and tucked them back into their place.

"—furthermore, know that the manner of death will sometimes affect your ability to feed."

I watched him with mute horror, barely heeding his words; I had realized that he had brought out his fangs.

Meeting my gaze coolly, he waited for a moment, as though allowing for any questions. When none came, he leaned down swiftly over the body and sank his teeth into its throat.

I gave a shudder of dismay. The sight was awful to me: the Count's figure, in all the somber elegance of his clothes, hunched over the body of a human being—a fellow-being, who had once lived! This remnant of a person, surely mourned and beloved by someone, was reduced to mere object.

What a foul nature was that of a coffin fly! Oh, cruel fate!

In my shock, I must have made a sound; for when the Count completed his work, slowly rising from the body, his gaze moved to me. "There is no need to be upset, Mr. Bedford. It was painless to him. You will see for yourself shortly."

But I had come to a decision, and stood back with defiance. "I will do *no* such thing!"

The Count gave a thin sigh. "Excellent. Then let us hear your vital argument."

"This is evil. To intrude on the sanctity of death, of this man's death, you have disturbed his entire being, treating him as a mere *thing* for your consumption! He would never wish for such a fate, which is why you wait until he is dead; but it is a sin all the same." My voice grew harrowed, quavering out of my control as I spoke. "Humans *do* kill animals for sustenance, but this is no animal. This was a fellow-being, who had a will and a purpose! It doesn't matter that he is dead, it doesn't matter that they are all dead; I will not do it! I won't!"

The Count gave a cold laugh. "You claim that *I* am the one who treats humans as bodies for my use? Please, Mr. Bedford, how you amuse me. Do human beings not turn each other to mere *things* every day? Do they not kill each other, work each other as tools for a pittance—and let us not forget those dear fellow-beings of yours who remain property by law. If I am the devil to you, then what does that make your compatriots?"

"Such deeds are evil, but yours are no less so!"

The Count replied coolly. "Even you cannot believe that."

"It matters not; I would rather die!" My eyes blazed, and I was faintly aware of tears gathering. "I will not measure out my evil on my scales until it pleases me, I would rather slowly starve away—"

"Ah, but this is what you don't understand," the Count interjected, now with warning. "If what you fear is your own nature, then rest assured that denying it will be worse still. Have you any prospect of what would happen, should you resist the urge to feed?"

I clapped my hands over my ears, wild with the desire to shut out his voice. "I will not hear you, I will not listen! I will not drink blood!"

"But you *will!*" he proclaimed, loudly enough to breach my

defenses. "You will slowly grow weaker, succumb to pain and sickness, and then fever. Then, only then, when you are within a hair's breadth of your life, you will turn wild. You will lose your moral senses and attack anyone and anything in your way; and when you find a human alive, you will rip out their throat, and lick their blood from the street with none of your former guilt."

"You are *lying!*"

"Why would I *lie*, Mr. Bedford? Could you believe that I prefer to keep you here, so that you may yell your grievances loud enough to risk my sustenance?"

"I cannot—oh, why did you do this to me?" I backed against a wall, covering my face in torment. "I want to be human again!"

With that, I had exhausted my panic, and became weary. I fell silent as I struggled to hold tears at bay.

The Count regarded me silently for a moment, before looking off. "Remember your second lesson."

Trembling from the exertion of my energies, I raised my head and spoke hoarsely. "What bloody lesson?"

"You always have a choice. Just as you may choose between living blood and corpse blood, you may choose no blood— which, as I have told you, means eventual murder. I cannot force you to drink. It is your choice."

"But it was *never* my choice!" I cried out to him, furious. "You did this to me by *force!* Where was my choice then?"

"Hush. If the Father comes, we are finished."

"Then answer me!"

The Count thought for a moment, before reaching down to finish closing the shroud of the corpse before him.

"Your third lesson, then," he said quietly, "Is that you must forgive yourself for what was out of your control. Drink."

Despite my hatred for him, there was a quality to his voice

that did soothe. In that moment of relative tranquility, I realized that my decision was inevitable.

My mother, who I had loved more dearly than anybody, had always told me one phrase in the worst of our moments. There were only two reasons to live on, she had said: to defend what was good, or to defeat what was wicked.

If I wished to protect the lives of my fellow-beings from my own cruel nature, as well as defeat the wickedness of the Count, I would have to do what was abhorrent to me.

"I'll do it," I breathed, failing to steady the trembling in my voice. "But don't be mistaken. I am not taking on your wickedness, and I never shall. Don't mistake my compliance for agreement."

He leveled his gaze. "I seek not your agreement, Mr. Bedford. I am merely here to guide you."

"You will not guide me," I whispered. Then, I turned and walked among the slabs.

He was right; the scent of each corpse differed in its appeal. I paused at each, waiting to sense the redolence before moving along. There were few, and before long I had identified the most suitable one. It was not the one which the Count had taken, I noticed absently; he had fed from the second best.

With a sigh, I reached down and undid the shroud from the body before me. The face that met me was not old, only just past the spring of youth.

"I'm sorry." I said to her quietly. "May you rest peacefully."

Though I spoke very softly, the Count was clearly listening; I could tell by how motionless he stood.

Then, I drew out my fangs, and leaned down to sink them into the crook of the chilled shoulder before me.

Slowly, a sweetness filled my mouth. It seemed to have the

consistency of honey, thick and warming, and all of a sudden the vice-grip of instinct had claimed me. The next moments were amorphous and savage; I remember little but ravenous hunger.

After some time, the rush slowed, and I remembered myself and ceased. Once I dislodged my fangs and stumbled back, I was addled; I knew not how much time had passed, nor what precisely I had done.

This precious ignorance lasted little, until I looked down and realized with a pang of horror that I had damaged the skin of the body most grievously. This stood in stark contrast to the neat, twin punctures which the Count had left on his corpse's neck.

Looking up, I found that the Count was watching me with carefully measured surprise. "Well," he murmured. "For one who was so hesitant at first, you certainly settled."

I stared towards him for a few moments, still mired in disbelief. Yet, suddenly I perceived that there was something coming down my chin, and I reached up to touch my own face. It was blood, of course; and when I looked down, I saw that it had seeped into my cravat in gaping flowers of crimson.

An intense disgust rose in my throat, but I held it in, clenching my fists to restore my composure. Slipping the cravat from my throat, I cleaned away all the blood from my mouth. With the remaining sanity that I had, then, I tucked it away and closed the shroud.

"Is it finished?" I whispered.

The Count nodded silently, then turned to sweep towards the door

I followed him, leaving the silent chapel behind.

We walked out into the churchyard, then onto the moorland. It was the dead of night, perhaps three in the morning, and the moonlight overhead gave some colour to the land.

Despite this, my thoughts only grew darker as we went. I could not forget the residents of that chapel. They had departed from those bodies, and would surely soon pass on to heaven; but my own soul had been corrupted. If there had remained any doubt that the kingdom of God was out of my reach for the sins of my human life, then all hope was surely lost now. The rest of my pitiable life would take place within the confines of this demonic body, until I was killed and banished to hell.

Miserably, I wondered whether I would come to wish for that death after many years; for was this not hell already? Was it not hellish to live in the darkness, forever apart from the friendly faces of people? The thought made me swallow a sob, and my pace slowed.

Then the Count, who had thus far remained silent, spoke seemingly at random.

"As you can see, a feeding is nothing to fear."

I gave a look which I hoped expressed the profundity of my hatred of him, and said nothing.

After another few moments, he spoke again. "I have on occasion purchased blood from barbers and surgeons. Any bloodletter is eager to sell what they would otherwise discard."

I was too mired in my grief to take any meaning from his words, and kept on walking silently.

"But bloodletting is predicated on ignorance," he added, "And indeed worsens health. Thus, despite the grotesque nature of it, to feed from a corpse is the more defensible act."

Be quiet, I thought bitterly! Had he not prattled on enough?

As though he had sensed my thought, he spoke no more. In that silence, however, I slowly realized something.

Until I truly paid attention, I had not noticed one detail: the

Count's speech had an unusual cadence, along with a mild but noticeable accent. This accent was particular for his firm and striking "r," so sharp that it sometimes seemed foreign, or at least from a distant part of Yorkshire; but this quality had diminished the longer we spoke, and by this point, I had begun to suspect him of concealing it by mimicking my own manner of speech.

This accent, so familiar and yet so distinct, could only mean one of two possibilities. The first, that he had come to the moor from a distant place. The second, that this was his native land, and he had outlived his own manner of speech.

Indeed, I had forgotten altogether that the Count had once been human. Had he been as great a force of cruelty as this in life, I wondered, or was he simply some ordinary soul tarnished by evil? And if he had been tarnished by evil, would I suffer the same fate?

To know nothing about him was a weakness, I realized. If I intended to defeat him, I could not be blind. I pondered for a few minutes on the acquisition of such knowledge, and in the end settled on the bluntest path.

"Since when have you lived in this manner?"

The Count turned his head, and seemed subtly surprised. "The manner of…?"

"A vampire."

"Ah." The Count paused, as though remembering. "Since the summer of 1583."

This put quite a shock through me. I had not expected such a distant year, and stammered frankly: "Then—how old are you?"

He seemed to take no offense to the question, boorish though it was, and answered simply:

"Two hundred and sixty-five."

I swiftly did the arithmetic, and realized with a start that he had become a vampire at around twenty-six years of age. For some reason, I had believed him to be older, perhaps as a consequence of his stature and his resonant voice.

As the familiar rise of the manor's hill approached once more, the thoughts were still turning in my head. What could have driven such a young man in a distant time to choose a wicked path as this—if it had been chosen at all?

Having received answers to my questions thus far, I was overconfident. I braced myself and asked him.

"Was it your intention to become a vampire?"

In an instant, he shut closed like a heavy tome. "That does not concern you."

Frustrated at having my answer taken from me, I answered churlishly. "You responded to everything else."

He reached the manor's eastern door and opened it, now striding ahead of me. "Unfortunately."

But I was not satisfied; I suddenly felt something that I had seldom felt towards anyone. I wanted to hurt him deeply. "Is it too painful a question to answer, sir?"

The clip of his heels sounded sharply against the cold manor floor. "As I said, it does not concern you."

Seeing that I would not rattle him, I relented. In any case, we had nearly reached the main hall, and I presumed we would go our separate ways; but I was still confused, and spoke timidly.

"Wait."

"No more questions, Mr. Bedford."

"No—another matter; what am I meant to do now?"

He turned towards me, and the dim light caught on the cruel outlines of his face. "Why, anything you wish. While you remain at the manor, I will answer your questions. As I no longer employ you, what you do otherwise is not my concern."

The feeling that bloomed in response was something like abandonment. I almost wished to have been created for some purpose, for then I would have at least been useful and desired; but to create me, and then throw me aside like refuse, was a worse insult than any other! I was about to open my mouth to answer bitterly, when he suddenly seemed to have another thought, and turned back to me.

"But I don't recommend that you depart yet," he added. "If you can tolerate to remain for one month, I will be able to counsel you enough to survive in the world."

"I…" I gave him a lost and helpless stare. "But what then? What purpose is there for a thing like this?"

"That is not my concern, and neither will it be yours. Survival is our purpose. To this end, you must beware the desire to rejoin the human world." As he spoke, his voice became dangerously soft. "It will seem the same to you; but should they know your true nature, they will turn against you in an instant."

"But what is the purpose of survival?" I said tiredly, taking a step forward. "If I may never be part of society again, what does it matter?"

He gave a dark smile. "I have no idea. You must decide that for yourself." With that, he started up the curve of the grand staircase. "The sun will rise soon. Come to me once every day, before you sleep. Good-night."

"It is not night, it is morning," I muttered; but by the time the words had left my lips, the Count had already gone.

A great weariness made me tremble as I turned and walked back, down the darkened servant's hall. It seemed different to me now; I noticed the other doors lining it, and realized that they must have once served as housing to an entire fleet of servants. I wondered about them, those ghosts of three hundred years ago, without a doubt now dead.

When I entered my room, I caught sight of myself in the mirror and turned away at once; I could hardly face myself, after the terrible deed I had done. Adrift in grief, I sat on the bed and mourned for my previous life. If the Count was correct—and thus far, he had not seemed to mislead me—the life of a vampire was a life alone; but how could I live apart from the friendly faces of others?

The Count certainly did not seem troubled by his state. I almost envied him for his ease, but quickly guarded against such thoughts. This was what I had to brace my soul against, I reminded myself: against the temptation of evil, the lust to forfeit my humanity for the sake of easing my pain. I had to do so, at least until the Count had been defeated. It would do me no good to ponder my fate beyond that.

With a quiet sigh I changed into my nightshirt, which I had last worn as a human. Then, I fell to the bed, and let my lashes down as morning came.

My dreams that day were vivid and strange, as though I were watching a play. I was standing at the end of the great hall of the manor, gazing out over a sea of people laughing and making merriment; but despite the joy of the scene, I felt little. There was a sense of sadness deep in my breast, as though I had lost something that would never return. Yet, soon, there came a flash of foreboding.

In the centre of a crowd, a young woman in a black gable hood had turned and caught my gaze, then smiled sweetly.

CHAPTER III

Very slowly, in a manner so regular that it was nearly extraordinary, the trappings of routine reclaimed my days.

To my surprise and relief, true to his word, the Count did not disturb me. Indeed, I saw him very little, despite sharing his same schedule. It was only once a day, when I visited before morning's sleep came, that we would truly speak; and for the most part, he merely imparted information as I listened sullenly.

For instance, on the day following our journey to the church, he described the timing of a vampire's feedings.

"Once every week is ideal," he said to me, sitting at the desk in his study. "If you have a steady source, as I do, once every fortnight is sufficient. Once a month is tolerable, but very unpleasant. Any further, and you are courting disaster."

Though I was relieved to hear that my torment would not be a daily affair, his last statement chilled me. "How long would it take for disaster to come?"

"Two months," he replied, swirling his wine glass impassively. "But long before then, you would become too weak to hunt, and would be doomed to become a beast regardless."

I was confused. "But if I would become too weak to hunt, then how would disaster come?"

"Simple," he replied. "Upon reaching the crux of starvation, all of the powers of living blood are briefly restored, though you would be senseless while manipulating them."

I asked no more on this subject. The thought of supernatural abilities frightened me hellishly, and in any case, I had answered the question most vital to me: I could not kill him by simply draining his blood, lest he go mad with bloodlust. Though he was terrible even now, to face him in such a state would be far worse.

These conversations with him took up very little time. When I was not pondering ways to defeat him, I began to go to the library and read any book that caught my interest. There were many, and they filled my mind for some time. Among the darkness of those days, the words were a guiding light for me; for what a glorious thing of peace it was, to set aside my worries and lose myself in the thoughts of another!

The only interruptions to my sojourns in the library were the bats. They were more active in the night, and I was often startled by a shadow flitting past.

I no longer saw Miss Josephine, taking care to go to sleep before she awoke. How much did she know of what had happened to me, I wondered? I still felt guilty, and decided to ease her mind somewhat, so that she would know that I yet lived. To this end, I left a note upon her hook one day, which read:

Dear Miss Josephine,

She did not respond. I pondered it, as two days with no response became one week, but let it be.

Despite making peace with this, my turmoil over other matters was deepening.

During the shock of my first days as a vampire, I had been in extremis; all was chaos, and so to think of something like killing the Count was merely one more terrible possibility to add to many.

Yet, now that mundanity had returned, though it was uneasy, I was loath to lose it. After having survived so much madness and come out half-sane, it seemed a waste to sacrifice it all. I was furious with the Count, but my fundamental character had not changed; I was no murderer by nature. Indeed, I feared my own capacity for evil more than I had ever feared death, and so I began to worry: after all my hand-wringing over taking on the Count's wickedness, could the act of killing him be the start of my journey into the dark?

But how awful it would be, to leave him to ruin another servant!

One day in the library, I was gloomily contemplating this, when all of a sudden I looked down and flinched; a bat was resting by my hand. Its back rolled with the sharp movements of its wings, as it crawled further along the table.

I paused, expecting it to flee, but it did not. Slowly, I moved my hand away. Still, it remained.

Staring at the vile little creature, realizing it might be some vassal of vampirekind, I was swept through with measured rage. Before it could go, I brought my hand down and caught it!

It unleashed a shriek of panic, but held oddly still as I turned it over. Beneath my hold, I could feel how delicate its bones were, how soft the skin of its wings, how easily it might be crushed by any movement.

Holding it against the table, I looked down upon it coldly. With my other hand, I took the nearest book and lifted it up, suspending it over the creature's head.

The bat stared up with jerking wings. Within its gaping mouth, four sharp fangs were prominent, and gave it an appearance of frozen surprise.

I wavered for a moment longer. The book in my hand began to tremble, and the hand overlaying the creature began to sweat.

Then, unable to bear it any longer, I released the creature and barked at it fiercely:

"Go!"

It fled as though it had understood me, leaving me to put my head in my hand. Oh, to ponder the chasms I would have to cross in order to murder easily made me tremble for my soul!

Then, however, I was distracted. I saw that the book I had been about to use as a cudgel was a tome on plant varieties, which appeared to have been written beautifully by hand. Breathing out wearily, I settled down to read it.

With its guidance, in the following days I began to venture out onto the moor again. Though it was dark, my changed eyes could see quite clearly, and after some time I grew so accustomed to it that it was as natural as day. Taking advantage of my solitude, I brought a small notebook and a pencil to record the species that I came across. This notebook, which had prior been half-filled with lists of tasks, was now cluttered with my clumsy sketches.

Over those days, I came to recognize the wide varieties, to distinguish the thin, bushy bunches of juniper from the wider, browning leaves of bracken plants; and though the nearing of autumn had leached some of the colour and life of the moor, I was able to recognize the withered sprigs of bog-rosemary and heather which would bloom into great swaths of pink and purple come springtime.

There were the tall wavy-hair and cotton grasses, and the tangled masses of heath-bedstraw; but to my surprise, I could find no amaranth. It struck me as odd, especially as it was the namesake of the moor, though to my knowledge it was uncommon in the area; but I assumed, if it were present, that it might bloom in summer when I would already be long gone from the manor.

Thus time went on, and I often spent quite a long time sitting among the rushing plants. The moon glowed peacefully above me in the sky, and cool, fragrant mists sometimes snaked through the grasses near the earth. Every so often, I could close my eyes to ruminate on the rustling of plants and the chirping of insects; when I opened them again, the expanse would spread out before me, appearing painted against the heavens.

Eventually, this pursuit began to give way to other impulses. The farther I ventured across the heath, the nearer I drew to the church where we had fed; and eventually, consumed by a need for guidance, I summoned the courage to take a step further.

I timed my venture to take place in the very middle of the night. Under cover of dark, I began my walk across the moor.

This was more or less the same journey that the Count and I had taken to the church; yet, without his presence beside me, I was better able to appreciate the beauty of the land and the freshness of the night. After perhaps half an hour, which passed rather pleasantly, I sighted the steeple at last.

As I approached, I threw a glance towards the churchyard, knowing the place where I had committed my heinous deeds laid just around the corner. I did not go towards it, however; I went instead to the main door of the church. There were a few enormous moths, richly feathered and patterned, fluttering about the doorway; I waved them gently away before giving the door a push.

Though my touch was gentle, the door creaked open willingly. How quaint, that it should be unlocked! This was a true country parish, I thought to myself, with nothing precious to be stolen in the night besides a few moments of solitary peace.

Indeed, it was peaceful. Pews spread out across the room, draped in tapestries of shadow from the walls; and from the windows, silvery moonlight trickled through to illuminate motes of dust in the air.

I walked along between the benches, lightening my step to mute the echo. Here, even my faint breaths sounded clearly in the absolute silence. It was warmer than I expected, and the scent of sweet wood was thick in the air.

At last, I found what I was searching for. There was a weathered alms box at the front, which I slowly approached. In the gloom, I could see a long-faded inscription carved into the top, which could no longer be read.

I reached into my pocket, drew out a shilling, and released it into the slot. My heart eased somewhat, at the muffled thump of it against the deep inside. Here—at least here, I was capable of some good, however small it was! In the uncertainty that I lived in, it was a shaft of light through the darkness.

With that done, I glanced towards the benches, wondering whether it would quiet my spirit to pray. However, I was seized with an uneasy feeling at the thought, so I hurriedly left the church once more.

The wild, creeping tangles of the moor and the blanketing of stars soothed my soul, and allowed me to ponder the warm feeling I had earned. Perhaps I could subsist on simple actions such as these.

Once more, on the following night, I did the same; I thought I might go every day to give a small bit of charity, until my mind was clear and my decision on how to move forward was made. Yet, though I drew no closer to any decision, on the sixth day I encountered something very different.

When I awoke on that particular evening, I was feeling more restless than usual. On the night before, after a short and dreary lesson, the Count had reminded me that our next feeding would be in two days' time. How I dreaded it! Thus, even though there still remained some waning light of day, I decided to head for the church earlier than usual to calm my spirit.

It was dark by the time I arrived, but I still lingered for a few minutes before entering, listening carefully to ensure that I heard no sound. When I was satisfied, I pushed the door open.

Yet, just as soon as I stepped in, I became aware of a light. In the next instant, a voice sounded nearby.

"Good evening. Do you need anything?"

I was seized with a great fright, and startled! When I whirled to find the source, I found a priest, who was sitting and watching me with quiet curiosity.

His hair was grey and pulled back into a queue; his brows were bushy; his face was spotted here and there from age. Despite a wizened face, which often gives an air of sternness to members of the clergy, he yet retained a benevolent appearance. Despite the hour of night, he still wore his black cassock, over which two white preaching bands descended from his neck.

"Forgive me, sir," he added, seeing my look of shock. When he smiled, the wrinkles by his eyes deepened. "I did not mean to startle you. My name is Ferdinand Raleigh; I am the rector of this humble parish."

This, indeed, was the first living human I had encountered after becoming a vampire.

"Ah, Mr. Raleigh, do forgive me!" I said in alarm, once I had recovered from realization. "I never meant to disturb—"

"Please, worry not," he assured, with a voice of the warmest quality. "You have not disturbed a soul. I only noticed from the alms box that somebody was coming during the night, and wished to see who would give charity in such honourable obscurity." He paused, and gave a friendly smile. "Forgive me if my curiosity has robbed you of that. What is your name?"

Much calmed by his demeanor, I gave a smile in return—the first true smile that I had expressed, since that awful event that had befallen me. The world, in that moment, seemed open and convivial, and I felt my ills vanish in an instant.

"You have robbed me of nothing," I replied. "It is a pleasure to be in your company, more than you could know. I am Avery Bedford; I live nearby, though I have never..."

To say that I had never visited this church would be a lie, I realized.

"I have never attended a service here," I finished weakly.

Perhaps mistaking my tone for shame, he shook his head. "This is not a place of judgment, especially not towards someone with righteous intent."

I nearly laughed at that. If only he knew! What type of righteous man fed off corpses in the dark? But of course I revealed nothing, and simply nodded. "Thank you. You are very kind."

"Is there anything in particular you are giving in honour of, that I might pray for?"

"Oh! No, not precisely. I am only here to settle my mind."

He took his oil lamp from the pew, leaving a space. "If I could be of any use in settling it, do share your thoughts."

I felt a deep pang in my heart, yearning to pour out my soul, but still hesitated. "It's so late, I daren't trouble you longer…"

"Less still would I sleep without answers; do sit."

And so I relented, and settled on the pew beside him. "Very well; only tell me if you grow weary." I hesitated. "And you must pardon me, if I speak of strange and obscure things."

"Strange in what sense?"

"I must speak in vague terms of what has befallen me, for—"

"Speak as you would like, Mr. Bedford," said Mr. Raleigh, with some amusement. "As long as I am not kept in suspense."

I gave a small, helpless laugh. "Suspense is precisely the trouble. I have a terrible choice to make, and no way of making it."

He folded his hands in his lap. "Let us hear it, then."

Being able to speak with some honesty made me feel vulnerable, and I became nervous. It took a moment to determine how to describe the indescribable; I spoke haltingly.

"I am facing a great trouble—I would even call it a great evil," I said quietly. "It is an evil that spreads, that consumes others in its path."

"Something like an idea?" Mr. Raleigh said curiously.

"Worse. Something which can corrupt a life and a body entirely, and make return inevitable, like a sickness."

"I see," Mr. Raleigh murmured.

"But it has a source," I replied, with my voice now losing some steadiness. "A terrifying source, which is difficult to defeat—but that *can* be defeated. Yet, I am afraid that in doing so, I might sacrifice some essential part of myself; and if I do, then I fall prey to the very same evil that I was so intently resisting."

"Do you have any other option?"

"Fleeing from it," I said hoarsely, "But leaving it to do further harm."

In truth, I was afraid that Mr. Raleigh might think me mad; but he seemed to consider it seriously, then gave a solemn nod. "I am very sorry for your troubles. Rest assured that I will say a prayer for your well-being. Further than that, however, I do have thoughts to impart. Would you hear them?"

Curious, I nodded. "Gladly."

"You seem preoccupied that you will fall prey to evil, but you seem like a fine young man. Why would you doubt yourself so deeply?"

At that, I felt a pang of guilt, and hesitated. "Though it may not be readily apparent, Mr. Raleigh, I must confess that I come from sullied roots. Furthermore, my consciousness bears a terrible stain, a most grievous sin which I committed even before I found the great trouble I face now. I believe it might have cost me my employment, and I cannot help but feel that I have been punished ever since."

"A grievous sin, you say?" said Mr. Raleigh, with a gentle smile. "By the expression which you make upon its mention, I can see all the sincerity of your regret, and every sign that you can distinguish right from wrong. If your employment was the only victim, then be at peace."

I gave a weak smile, grateful that he did not pry further. "I certainly try."

"But you still doubt in yourself," Mr. Raleigh went on. "For you ask the fundamental question. It is written that all human hearts are inclined to sin; but how does an ordinary being, who would otherwise follow a virtuous path, succumb to darkness?"

Lifting my head, I was suddenly struck with clarity. "Yes—yes, that is precisely it!"

He seemed surprised at my enthusiasm, but simply went on. "What is darkness?"

I was curious to be met with a question. "Darkness?"

"Yes; darkness, as in night. What makes darkness?"

"Why, when there is no light…"

"Indeed. Therein lies your answer. As a wise man once explained, if all that God has created is good, then evil has no positive nature; but the absence of good is named evil. Therefore, it cannot be fought directly."

"Cannot be fought!" I exclaimed, afraid. "Why, but surely it can, it must be! For instance, an evil person can be defeated."

"Are you certain?" he replied, with a twinkle in his eye. "Does a general sent against a tyrant not risk becoming a tyrant himself? Perhaps I take this too far, but this is my belief: evil, done in the service of good, has no use. Evil feeds upon good, you see. It cannot live on its own, cannot create as God can. It must feed from good like a leech gorges on blood, robs it from the body, consumes it and corrupts it for its own purpose."

My heart sank at this description, and I began to feel ill. "I…"

"That is how an ordinary man becomes truly evil. He warps good; he justifies. And so, the only thing that may counter it…"

He lifted his lamp from the floor, raising it up and illuminating the growing pallor in my expression.

"Is light." Then he paused, and his look grew concerned. "Are you quite well, Mr. Bedford?"

"Yes, and I must thank you," I said. I suspect that my face gave away my anguish at the answer, for he regarded me with some care. "Your words have made my decision clear to me."

"Have they?"

"Ah, indeed! You have described, without knowing it, the precise evil that I face. If it is allowed to continue on, then it will justify every sort of sin, and corrupt all the good in its path. It must be stopped at any cost." I stood from the pew, rather shaken. "So long as I can do it in a manner that does not corrupt me."

"I am glad to have given you clarity," Mr. Raleigh said kindly. "But don't overexert yourself. Remember: to keep your own flame lit is the surest way to spread light."

"I will," I said surely. "Thank you—I must go now."

"Don't hesitate to return, Avery," Mr. Raleigh replied. With his lamp still in his grasp, he stood and placed a hand upon my shoulder. "You are not lost; and even if you were, you would still be welcome here."

At that, I did feel a sting of bitterness. His hand was warm, but my body felt cold at his words.

You say that now, I wanted to cry out to him; but were you to know my true nature, what I did to the corpses in your parish, you would turn me away in an instant! You would call to your fellows, and they would beat me until I bled, hold me down as they rammed my body full of stakes—and you would watch with relief as I writhed! Oh, cruel, unhappy fate!

Worse still, if my fears were true, and the Count had once been an ordinary man, then perhaps in time I would come to deserve every stake that was driven through me. My only chance of salvation would be to end his corruption before it claimed my own soul.

"Thank you," I managed, and I left into the blessed cold and solitude of the outside once more. Once there, pondering the task that laid before me, I clenched my fists and did not want to feel anything; I simply wished to lose myself to the remainder of the night.

*   *   *

Even though I gained clarity after my conversation with the reverend, it came with a cost. Knowing what I would have to do, I felt ill with dread. An impulse towards good was a burden, I thought to myself; I understood at last what it might feel like, to wish to rid myself of it.

Such thoughts frightened me, and hardened my resolve. In the following days, I thought over all that I had seen and learned, trying to answer that most troubling question: how could I defeat the Count without becoming a beast, without changing myself irrevocably?

It was during these tumultuous days that my second feeding took place. I met the Count at his study at midnight, and he stood placidly.

"Are you ready?" he said, as he fastened his sword at his waist.

"I am," I replied, keeping a steady eye on it.

Our journey onto the moor was nearly identical to our first.

This time, however, far less was spoken. Furthermore, I was not entranced by the moorland at night, as I once had been; instead, I watched the Count's back, where his dark hair spilled long over his cloak.

To find some silver implement and cleave it in through his ribs would be simple, but bloody. No civilized soul could catch a man unaware and crudely stab him to death without tarnishing their own heart. It was too near to what the Count himself had done to me.

While I entertained this thought, my gaze drifted back down to his sword, which swung along with his leg with every step. It was then that I realized something crucial.

Despite his savagery, the Count had never used his sword. He had drawn it to distract me, but never employed it beyond that. Moreover, though the Count had indeed killed me by siphoning my blood, he had never spilled a drop with his blade, not even to defend himself when I wounded him.

Such a thing could be explained as his avoidance of wasting blood; but then, what of the time *after* my turning? During my first feeding, he had made it clear that I was threatening his sustenance by shouting. Still, he had made no physical threat.

Why would such a deadly and cold-blooded creature avoid his surest route of command? What cause would he have to avoid violence?

It occurred to me suddenly that the motive behind my creation might have been darker than I imagined. I had read many dreadful tales, fictions which I had never thought much of, where villains bathed in blood to retain their youth.

Perhaps I had been created to conserve the Count's blood, and therefore his youth; and if I were gravely wounded, he would be finished!

It was a far-fetched thought, but such a motive convinced me far better than the one he had claimed. He continually insisted that I learn to survive, and so my survival must lend him some benefit; there had to be some truth to the theory.

But if I could not ask, how would I test it?

This thought occupied me as we reached the chapel and entered to feed. This was done in grave solemnity, and lasted nearly nothing compared to the first feeding. Neither of us spoke to each other until we had quit the chapel, and walked back along the moor. It was the Count who broke the silence.

"It is the autumnal equinox," he mused, gazing up at the moon.

I did not trust myself to speak without revealing the anxiety of my thoughts, so I said nothing.

Despite this, he went on: "You are reserved today. Are you unwell?"

There it was again! Yes, there could be no more doubt; he was asking after the health of his vessel. To this, I issued a reply which I hoped would end the conversation entirely.

"What a question!" I spat bitterly, and meant it.

For the remainder of the walk, he made no further attempts to parley, and so I spent it devising my plan.

CHAPTER IV

That day, I barely slept. I tossed to and fro as though ill once more, scarcely gaining a moment's rest. Nevertheless, when I woke the next evening, my resolve was steady and my heart was set.

Today, I would test my theory soundly.

I dressed myself as usual, then went to my desk and opened a drawer. From here, I took a silver pen knife; this had been a gift from Henry, which he had more or less forced into my hand before I boarded his coach to the manor. For that, I now thanked him in silence, and thought wistfully: so long, old friend! Whatever fate I met in this struggle, I prayed that he might continue on.

Concealing this implement in my sleeve, I headed for the Count's quarters.

Ordinarily, I went to our meetings at the end of the night. I wondered if I might catch him by surprise, coming so early; but this hope was taken from me as soon as I stood at his door, just as my hand recoiled in hesitation to knock.

"Enter," he said smoothly, through the door.

A jolt of fear passed through me, but I dispelled it. Touching my sleeve, I ensured the position of the knife before pushing the door open and stepping inside.

The Count walked languidly to his desk; he had entered from the adjacent room, shutting the door behind him. There was a glass of red wine in his hand, evidently just poured, which he set down on the table before facing me. As he did, however, he paused.

"My," he said. "That is quite the determined look."

I grew tense; nothing escaped him. "It is."

"What could merit such an early visit, I wonder."

"I have a question for you," I said firmly; I met his gaze, and did my best to hold it steadily. "Something I must know."

"Ask, then."

I took a deep breath, and then demanded:

"Why did you turn me into a vampire?"

A certain tension hung in the air between us, a dreadful silence. For a few moments, he returned my gaze impassively.

"Ah," he said finally. With a haughty look, he sighed and reached for his wine glass. "I did already tell you, though perhaps you were too upset to understand. It was a whim—"

"Don't give me that answer!" I exclaimed with fervor, stepping forward. My voice shook with sudden frustration, and my eyes blazed. "You may be serene, but you lie. I can see the deceit written across your face!"

The Count's hand recoiled from his glass, and he turned to face me with an odd look. "Then you will believe nothing that I tell you, and we have nothing more to discuss."

"I agree," I hissed.

Then, with one fluid movement, I wrenched the pen knife from my sleeve and snapped it open!

In an instant, his demeanor changed. His eyes flashed coldly; he stepped back and reached for his waist, where his sword hung. "Put that down, Mr. Bedford."

My heart beat wildly, and the knife in my hand shook; but I did not point it towards him. Instead, I pulled up my sleeve and held the blade to my arm. "I shan't!"

To my shock, that produced the effect that merely drawing the knife had not! He lost his composure; his eyes flashed, and he released the hilt of his sword to step forward. "Bedford!"

"Sir."

He seemed taken aback by his own outburst, and restrained himself. "What are you doing?"

"There it is," I replied with triumph. "At last, I have uncovered the truth. I know why you did this to me—ah, to think I was almost fooled!"

"We can discuss this," the Count said tersely, with his eyes fixed upon the knife. "Release that first."

I was elated to have him beneath my thumb. "Why should I? I can speak just like this."

"Then speak, but move it not."

I gave a savage laugh. "It is as I thought! I have uncovered your fatal weakness: if I am wounded, you are finished. By turning me into this, you gained either youth or power from my being; and whatever it is, I will carve it out of myself!"

For a few moments, he gazed off strangely. Then, the tension in his shoulders lessened, and he sighed.

"Ah. Then don't bother."

"What?!"

"Waste not your blood. Your theory is wrong."

I was shaken. "Then why—"

"Why do I want you alive?" He gave a cold smile. "Because it suits me. Nothing more."

For some reason, it was this that turned me livid. Every extremity of my body buzzed with the fires of rage, perhaps the built-up ire of weeks, and made me break out into shouting.

"You *blackguard!*" I cried out. "You wretched leech! After everything, how dare you lie? Do you know what you have done to me? Have you no soul? Is there even a sliver of remorse left inside you, or has time burnt it away? Speak! Speak! Say something! Perhaps you will never fall into God's hands, and he will never judge you—but I will! Defend yourself!"

For the first time, he seemed openly startled. "I—"

"I am your judge! Speak!"

But he quickly settled himself, and interrupted in a voice so soft and dangerous that it terrified:

"Mr. Bedford."

I fell mute.

"I'm not lying," he said calmly. "Use your more rational instincts, if they yet exist. Even if I could preserve some power within another vampire, which to my knowledge I cannot, why would I place something of such value to me with somebody so inclined towards recklessness?"

But I was seized with rage, and tightened my grip on the knife. "Let us find out!"

His eyes sharpened, and he stepped forward. "If you move that any further, you will force my hand—"

I wrenched down my cravat and took the blade to my neck.

"BEDFORD!"

Far quicker than my mind could comprehend, my hand had

been seized and pulled aside. He had me by the wrist!

I tried to pull away, but his grip was like iron, so I could only shout. "Damn you!"

"Then damn me, but release your blade."

"Never!"

"Remember," he said, looming over me dreadfully. He was so near that his hair brushed the wrist he held trapped; I had never seen his face so close, and nearly froze in terror as he went on: "I have the strength of living blood—*your* living blood. If you had cared to ask on the subject, I would have told you that such powers persist for a month. You have no chance."

"Ah! Unhand me!"

"Unhand the knife first. I cannot touch it at present."

"Then I shall drive it into you, devil!"

With that, he seemed to lose his patience at last, and seized my other wrist before I could draw it away. "You think that you can kill me, Mr. Bedford?"

I was in a panic, struggling to free myself; but he neither tightened his grip, nor made any other move. Instead, he spoke with exasperated amusement.

"I knew that you would attempt something like this sooner or later. It is natural, and I blame you not; but you have neither the strength nor the experience to defeat me yet."

"How would you know?!"

"Because I know why you would choose a method like this." He leaned over me. "You have not yet grown fully into ruthlessness."

I seethed. "You will *not* drive me to barbaric acts. I will never take on your nature!"

He gave a dry look. "When have I suggested such a thing?"

"You have not," I said furiously, and remembered the

reverend's words. "But a general who rises against a tyrant risks becoming a tyrant himself; and I will not!"

"A general?" The Count gave a dark laugh, so cold and resonant that I felt it in my chest. "We are no *generals*. We are rats in the dark. Yet, I do understand."

"You understand nothing!"

"But I do. What you desire is civilized barbarity. You wish to murder as kings murder, sending soldiers from afar, never leaving the comfort of their own righteous thrones—"

I struggled to pull my wrists away again, growing clammy with mounting terror. He loosened his grip slightly, but continued.

"Yes; sending man against man to carve flesh, while remaining holy enough to wear the crowns that deem them chosen by God. Is that right?"

"No!"

"Listen to me. You wish to murder without extinguishing your natural pity, which you value so dearly."

"I value it because it is valuable; I will not heed your horrible ideas!"

"But you misunderstand me," he said evenly. "I'm not driving you towards anything. I only intend for you to fully understand what it would take to defeat something like me."

Then, to my shock, he pulled together both of my hands— which until then, he had still held trapped—and wrapped them around the knife handle that I refused to release, pointing the blade towards his own stomach!

I gave a wordless exclamation of shock, and felt my knees weaken at the sight.

Hearing this shout, he wore a mocking expression. "Why the fear? Killing has nothing to do with a vampire's nature.

Humanity and ruthlessness are happy bedfellows."

The sight of my own hands holding a knife to his stomach was too much to bear, and I cried out: "Wait!"

But he only leaned forward savagely, near enough that I could see my own horrified expression in his eyes. "If you still believe yourself human—yes, human enough that you need killing as your purpose—then kill. Drive the blade into me, feel the warmth of blood on your hands; only do not lie to yourself about the essence of the act."

"Wait, wait—"

"Let your keen knife see the wound it makes, Mr. Bedford," he exclaimed, and pressed the tip of the blade between two buttons of his doublet; his eyes were lit strangely. "You can neither blind yourself, nor hesitate, for either could spell death; so open your eyes—and *drive in your blade!*"

How his voice thundered!

I could take no more; with a gasp of terror, I released the pen knife. It slipped from both our hands and clattered to the floor.

Seeing this, the Count—whose expression had been fiery only a moment before—resumed his cool demeanor, though there was a faint but unmistakable trace of relief. He unceremoniously kicked the knife aside, then released my wrists.

I stumbled back, trembling and staring at him.

Leaving me to my shock, the Count drew out a handkerchief and serenely walked over to pick up the fallen weapon. Using the cloth to keep it separate from his palm, he regarded it with interest and mused to himself: "It was a failure, but a brave one."

Then, as I willed my knees not to betray me, he turned smoothly to me and asked:

"Is this knife of value to you?"

"Yes," I said hoarsely, once I had calmed enough to

understand his words.

"Then I will use the remainder of the powers of living blood still within me, until silver poses no threat. By tomorrow's night, I will return this knife to you." Wrapping it in his handkerchief, he tucked it into his pocket. "I hope that is an acceptable arrangement. For my part, I consider it generous."

I could not think of a single thing to say in response. Though I had assumed all along that the Count would not have allowed the knife to pierce him, the sight of it in my hands, poised to kill, had ignited my panic. With it, the worst of my memories from years past had returned; I was rendered nearly senseless with dread.

Noticing my silence, the Count tilted his head. "Ah. Have you any need for laudanum?"

"No," I said hoarsely.

"Wine, then."

I shook my head and turned, heading stiffly for the door; but all of a sudden, his presence was dark beside me, and I flinched away and burst out:

"Leave me be!"

"I am," he replied. "I only wish to know where you are going."

"My room," I said, after a moment.

He opened the door and gestured. "Then I shall walk with you; you seem unwell. Regardless, I planned to have a word with Josephine."

At that, my chest tightened, and a swell of anxiety made my head spin. By God! What did he want with her?

"Come," the Count called, beginning to stride along.

Without any choice, I followed.

Watching him as he walked, I was terrified; if he did something to Miss Josephine, I would have to impede him—but he had taken my knife! Would that I had kept it hidden, instead of showing it like a fool! If it came to blows, would I have time to snatch it from his pocket?

Before long, we had descended the stairs and reached the east wing, starting down the servant's hall. I could barely breathe as the Count came to stand before the closed door across from mine, and called pleasantly:

"Josephine."

For a few moments, there was silence.

Heaving a sigh, the Count raised his hand and knocked. "Josephine, I can hear you. Come."

With that, he inclined his head to listen. Then, seeming satisfied, he stood back.

The door cracked open just a hair's breadth, barely enough to give the occupant of the room a sliver of space through which to see.

"What do you want?" I heard Miss Josephine quaver.

"Only to give you a reminder," the Count replied, nonchalant. "Please ensure all the manor windows are closed before you rest. I found a bird at the edge of your water bucket today, quite ready to fall in."

There was silence from inside the room.

"Pardon me for disturbing you," the Count added. "I would have left you a note, but you would have been asleep."

"Fine," Miss Josephine said, sounding aggrieved, and began to close the door.

But as she did, the Count slotted his shoe into the opening and stopped it. "Ah, and one more matter. Somebody is here with me; would you like to greet him?"

Ah, how I hated that villain in that moment, how I hated him!

Yet, before I could say a word, the door paused.

Then it slowly swung back open, and Miss Josephine's face peered around the edge. The terror in her eyes was unmistakable, along with something else quivering and unidentifiable.

In the instant that my gaze met hers, I went pale. "Miss Josephine!" I said at once. "I wanted to tell you, I am so, so very—"

She retreated and shut the door, leaving me halfway through my sentence.

The Count made an exasperated sound. "Josephine, really."

"Miss Josephine!" I called out. "I—"

"Leave her be," the Count said, waving a hand. He turned to walk back along the hall. "There is no reasoning with her in this state. Go and rest."

*　　*　　*

I sat on the edge of my bed for a long while, trembling with some nameless and intolerable feeling.

Two things were evident to me: the first, that I would not be able to kill him easily. The second, that his useless little rendezvous with Miss Josephine had been more than a whim, and was perhaps a threat—whether towards me or towards her, I did not know. Above all, however, I knew that I could not remain any longer. If she was in danger, then the responsibility fell on my shoulders.

Though I had no inkling of where I would go, or where on earth I could travel where corpses were readily available to feed from, I reasoned I could find a barber who might sell me blood. I could stay in an inn for some time, and then find somewhere to stay for good; perhaps I could find employment at a church, or become the assistant to an undertaker. In any case, blood was the least of my worries.

I spent the rest of the night packing my portmanteau, resolving to leave my trunk with half my belongings, and carefully counted out my money in its box.

Yet, there remained one more matter to take care of. The Count had claimed that I could come and go as I pleased, but his word was worth less than nothing to me.

Once I regained the courage to leave my room once more, I crept out and went to the library. There, upon opening a drawer, I found what I had remembered vaguely: a silver candle snuffer, with sharp blades to trim a wick.

With sweat dampening on my brow, I concealed this instrument within my coat and returned to my room.

*　　*　　*

On the following night, I waited until the clock struck seven to seek the Count.

Though leaving in secret would have been infinitely preferable, I had decided to take my chances and inform him of my departure. An easy farewell would quell my anxieties; but if he meant to stop me, then I would rather have him reveal it sooner rather than later, and thus allow me time to better prepare for my escape.

My walk through the desolate manor corridors was slow and reluctant, but all too quickly the tall door to his room was before me. My heart pounded furiously within my chest; I forced my hand up to the wood, and knocked briskly.

The sombre sound echoed, and I shivered despite myself. Yet, as the seconds passed, I became confused.

There was no reply.

When I knocked again, I was met with the same silence.

Carefully, then, I pushed in the door and found it open. When I entered his study, it was empty; only his window was open, and a warm night air rustled papers here and there.

Standing there, baffled, I walked through and reached the door to the next room. This door, I opened slowly; but here, too, I found nothing but a desolate bedroom. A grand four-poster bed, richly draped and carved, stood empty with curtains fluttering in the breeze.

Still hesitant, I even checked the next room over, finding nothing but a neatly arranged dressing room. With that, I concluded surely that the Count was not in his quarters, and withdrew.

As I walked back past the windows of the second floor, I tried to assuage my fears. The Count could be in the library, or outside, or anywhere else. Surely he had not somehow learned of my departure, and taken some unexpected action—had he? It would be impossible; I had given no sign.

Nursing my anxiety, I reached the head of the staircase; but it was then that something startled me, and I spun—and cried out in terror!

A massive black shadow had passed over the windows!

I balked, falling back so suddenly that I struck the banister. There, I cowered with chattering teeth, willing it to have been an illusion.

But after a moment, there came the shadow again, this time with a ghastly fluttering, and I could lie to myself no longer. Some dark and massive creature was flying outside the manor.

And at last, cold sweat beaded on my brow, and my mind could take no more. A voice within me cried out—*enough!*

When the spirit is consumed by fear, reason falters. As I turned and ran down the stairs, the fog of horror allowed me to think only as far as this: that the thing outside the windows was my enemy; that I was in terrible danger; and that if the creature was destroyed, all would be well. I needed no more logic than that.

When I arrived at my room, I practically collapsed to the drawers. With wildly trembling hands, I tore one open and withdrew a box, which I placed on the floor and threw open.

Inside, the dueling pistols from the Crawfords glinted. The very sight inflamed me with a sense of power, which I had craved so desperately in the past helpless weeks; and when I lifted one out and cocked the hammer, this sensation only strengthened, silencing any doubt that yet remained.

I had little experience with flintlocks, only as much as I had learned from serving gentlemen on their hunts, but in my panic I found that I remembered it all vividly. Though I nearly spilled half my flask of gunpowder in pouring it down the barrel, then nearly spilled the other half in loading the frizzen, there remained enough to give me confidence.

At last, I rammed the bullet down into the barrel and stood. I left the other pistol untouched; I knew that I had to move quickly, lest my wits betray me.

Snatching the silver candle trimmer from my desk, I stuffed it into my pocket and swept out.

With the stock clenched in hand, now doused in sweat, I left the manor by the eastern door and crept along the wall, pressed so near that I skimmed the stone with my shoulder. I kept my eyes to the sky, and moved slowly; if I was caught by surprise, I knew that I was finished.

But I need not have worried. When I neared the front of the

manor, a sound met my ears and made me tremble.

What hideous flapping, accompanied by a shrill and crackling call, horrifically loud—much like a rat, if it were half the size of a carriage! Barely daring to breathe, I peered around the corner of the manor, and saw that my estimation of size had not been far from the truth.

A massive black bat, with a wingspan larger than a man, was flying across the courtyard. It dove down to gain speed before soaring up, flapping its wings so forcefully that the tips nearly joined above its head—that frantic natural movement of the bat, which strikes fear into any heart; and all the while, it continued to produce its strange and echoing cries.

I cursed in silence and shrank back against the wall, trembling wildly, as that most sickly sound of fluttering persisted above.

This was either the Count himself, or some dark vassal. Either way, if this creature was flying about in front of the manor entrance, I could only think of one reason: it was waiting for somebody to exit.

I clasped my pistol and tilted my head back, taking a deep breath of the cool night air. In my mind, I spoke a silent prayer.

Then, I crouched, edged around the corner, and raised my pistol.

The range of this firearm was short, I knew, and could very well have some delay. If my aim was anything but perfect—a likely event, given my inexperience—a swift death awaited me. Only the sharpness of the candle snuffer in my pocket gave me courage; but I knew patience would serve me better than courage, and so I waited for an advantageous moment. As I did, to calm my nerves, I recited my mother's old saying in my head.

There are only two reasons to live on, Avery.

I stared down the barrel of the pistol, moving it slowly to

follow the creature's flight.

To defend what is good, or to defeat what is wicked.

I tightened my finger on the trigger.

You must know which is which.

The creature fluttered to a wall, then clung to it—

And I *shot!*

All around me, the cool night air was transformed to acrid gunpowder. Coughing, I batted it away and looked up, only to behold a most shocking sight:

The creature froze where it was upon the wall—and then slowly slid down, scraping its claws down the stone as it went, until at last it fell spiraling to the ground!

I gasped as I watched it plummet, hardly believing my eyes; yet, it was only once it had hit the ground, producing a sound that made me flinch, that the most startling change occurred. There on the overgrown yard, the jumbled mass of black wings melted back and became a cloak, beneath which a familiar form regained its shape.

The Count, with his hair spilled about his head and his cloak draped over him, laid across the ground and held quite still.

Yet, at the very moment which should have given me a rush of triumph, something entirely different overtook me. All of a sudden, at that awful sight, I felt a rush of clarity that had hitherto eluded me.

I had made the wrong choice!

This was no conscious thought; it was a gut-feeling that had no rational source and no name. To see the form of a human being lying vanquished by my own hand was unbearable beyond words. Every doubt surged forward, and every fear was realized: in seeking safety, I had corrupted the safety of my very being!

Driven wild by this realization, I sprang up from my hiding

place and hurried forward.

As I drew near, I saw it all clearly. The Count laid curled over his midsection, staring ahead along the ground in somewhat of a daze; but as I drew nearer, he lifted his head sharply to the sound and caught sight of me.

In an instant, his eyes flashed and he drew back, half-dragging himself along the dirt.

Seeing this, I stopped at once and cried out: "Are you hurt badly?"

"Come no closer," he hissed, lifting himself with one hand. With his other, he held his middle tightly. "If you wish to live, stay back."

"Please—let me help you!"

At that, his face changed. He stared at me in disbelief.

I took another step. "I mean it, I'm sorry!"

"You're *sorry?*"

"Please," I begged. "You're wounded—"

He made a sound that was nearly a wild laugh. "You expect me to believe—"

"Look, I am unarmed, I have nothing!" I threw my pistol furiously aside, then reached into my coat and drew out the silver candle trimmer, which I too let fall.

At that, he almost choked in his disbelief. "You went looking for *more* silver?"

Realizing my mistake, I kicked it away. "It is gone now, look!"

He flinched as it skidded along the ground, and hissed: "Be *careful* with that, Bedford!"

"Please!" Desperation overtook me, and I clutched my chest in anguish. "Let me help you, I beg of you—"

"If your intent is to *help,*" said the Count, and seemed genuinely perplexed, "Then what is your bullet doing in my gut?"

"I didn't know what I was shooting at!"

He stared blankly for a moment, as though he could hardly believe what he was hearing. Then, he sank back to the ground, and muttered sullenly: "Nobody ever does."

"I would not hurt you in this state, I swear on my mother's grave, I swear it!"

"Then if your regret is sincere, keep your word and leave me alone," he said sharply. "This is not a mortal wound, and I have had worse."

"It matters not," I said vehemently. "For my sake, I *must* help you. If I don't, I will lose my head."

Letting out a harsh sigh, he closed his eyes for a moment and seemed to gather his patience. Then, his expression regained its aloofness, and he shook his head.

"Fine. Come."

I rushed forward, weak with guilty relief, and crouched beside him. "Where did it…?"

As though remembering his injury, the Count glanced down and moved the hand that was still held to his stomach. With it, there came a smear of dark red blood.

Though I could have cried out with despair, I pushed his hand back over it. "Hold it there!"

"I know, Mr. Bedford. If you would, please help me stand."

Without a word, I took his arm over my shoulder and gripped it tightly, then unfurled my legs. The Count was heavy, and his weight dragged me down severely; but I clenched my teeth and forced my knees to support him. At last, his legs gained purchase, though he favoured one over the other.

"Help me to my quarters," he said quietly. "I have tools there to aid me."

I nodded quickly; I could hardly believe that he could put any trust in me after what I had done, but I was determined not to betray it. In that moment, I felt none of the raging bitterness towards him which had dominated my mind for the past weeks; my fear over my deed had overwhelmed any fear of him.

I heaved him up the front steps of the manor, and guided him through the front door. Step by step, we traversed the great hall, towards the nearest staircase.

All the while, he said nothing, only held his wound and gave laboured breaths. His head was lowered, and I wondered whether he was in pain; but when I looked over, the expression on his face was despondent, as though what plagued him was something else.

"Does it hurt?" I said timidly, as I helped him up the first step.

This only seemed to deepen his misery. "Yes, Mr. Bedford. It hurts where you shot me."

"I'm sorry, I didn't mean to—" I realized that I was lying, and went pale. "Or, or rather, I didn't intend—"

"I know," he replied hoarsely.

This surprised me, and I blinked.

"I know you never meant to," he said again. Then, all of a sudden, the colour drained from his face, and his arm grew heavy on my shoulder.

Any surprise at this sight was overcome by the renewed burden. I winced as I strained to hold him upright, feeling my knees threaten to buckle. "Sir!"

"I never wanted…" he murmured, and seemed to bear his own weight for a moment; but then it all rushed down again, and I managed to catch him and hold him steady.

"What?" I stammered. "Whatever it is, forget it for now; I cannot hold you much longer—sir?"

His shoulders gave a soft and peculiar sort of jerk; and I realized, quite shocked, that what I had taken to be the convulsions of my own frantic heart were in fact not mine at all.

"Good lord! Are you trembling? Sir?"

I knew without having to ask. It was not a healthy movement of the body, but rather the sickly sort of shiver that comes with fever; and yet he suddenly gripped my arm with strength, and spoke in a strained voice that shook as though he were dying:

"Forgive me."

Then, before my very eyes, the last of his strength left him.

The entire huge, dark form of the Count pitched down heavily, the heft of his towering form collapsing over me in some final state of defeat. With a shout of surprise I caught him as he fell, and managed to prevent him from striking the ground; but I could not bear his full weight, and staggered down with him.

"Sir!" I cried out in wild panic, throwing aside his cloak. "You cannot be dead, can you? Please, God in heaven, tell me that I have not killed a man—or whatever you are—wake, wake! Sir!"

With trembling hands, I reached for his neck to feel his pulse. Upon finding it, and noticing that his chest still rose and fell, I nearly gasped in relief. He had merely swooned.

Very carefully, then, I eased him down to the floor. With that, I stared down at him and had not the slightest idea of what to do next.

The Count was a demon to me, a hateful being, and he was now entirely at my mercy. If I ran to retrieve the blade I had dropped outside the manor, I could cleave it through his heart and end the entire nightmare in one sure stroke.

But in the instant that the thought occurred to me, I recoiled from it with revulsion. Such an act would not return my humanity, and indeed would drive me further from it! No, I would not compromise my conscience any further. I had learned my lesson in that regard.

Yet, aside from that, as reluctant as I was to admit it, my loathing towards him also was hampered by worry. I realized with some bewilderment that I did not want him dead. Perhaps it was only a human reaction, to see someone in pain and to suffer in turn; and in any case—what had he meant by those strangled words, just before he fell?

Either way, my decision was made. I reached down and put his limp arm around my shoulder, then raised myself up and took my first step.

The journey up the staircase was so arduous that sweat rolled down my neck, and I had to stop at every effort. Once or twice, I nearly slipped, but grasped for the railing; and at last, I arrived at the upper floor.

It was then that I felt him stir, and anticipated that he would startle; so I raised my voice, and spoke clearly. "Only a few more steps, sir!"

He raised his head suddenly, and nearly pulled away; but I gripped him tightly, and reassured him. "We have almost reached your quarters, look!"

"Bedford," he muttered, and his senses seemed to return. He looked all around, though his face was still deathly pale, and at last held some of his weight.

Relieved, I pulled him along until we reached the door to his bedroom. "There, there, just a little further…"

But we had taken no more than a few steps inside the room when he stopped, bracing his hand against a bedpost. "Wait."

"What is it?"

"Go," he said, staring on ahead. "Fetch me water."

"Water? I will, but first—"

"I will prepare my tools here, but I need water."

Too wracked with guilt to argue with him, I unlaced his arm from my shoulder and stepped back. "Very well. I will return shortly."

With that, I turned and ran, my thoughts already occupied; but in the instant that I took two steps outside the room, there was a deafening sound, as though something had been thrown against the door. When I whirled to see, I saw that the door had been slammed shut, and the firm locking of a deadbolt sounded soon after.

"Sir!" I shouted in disbelief, and rushed back to the door. "Why?"

"You have done enough," I heard him say wearily from the other side. "If you are sincere, leave me now."

"But—!"

"You cannot expect me to rest if you are near. Go."

Dumbstruck, I stared at the door for a few moments before swallowing my complaints. Being responsible for the wound, I knew that I had no argument but the selfishness of my own conscience, and so I left without a word. Yet, all the while, I shook with the weight of my shame.

To have the mirror of fear held up to me, and know that I had become the type of person who could not be trusted with a wounded man—how it ached!

I headed past the hallway with my thoughts muddled, and reached the staircase. Yet, just as I had started down, I heard a voice speak dryly.

"Did you kill him?"

I gasped, then looked down with a start.

There, at the foot of the stairs, Miss Josephine stood gazing placidly up at me.

CHAPTER V

In the instant that I met eyes with Miss Josephine, it was as though several weeks' worth of frantic worry were released.

"Miss Josephine!" I exclaimed, in a voice that trembled wildly. "I'm sorry if I seem in a frightful state, but I have just done something which may have been some terrible mistake. I'm awfully confused, and certain of nothing; but—"

"Mr. Bedford, I only asked one question," she said flatly. "Is he dead."

"No! No, but he is wounded."

She scoffed a humorless laugh, then turned to walk back towards the servant's hall. "Huh! Perhaps that will teach him something."

Baffled by this reaction, I wavered for a moment before hurrying down the stairs after her. "Wait! Miss Josephine, if you could tell me anything, *anything* to help me make sense of this—"

"Follow me to the kitchen. We can speak there."

Endlessly relieved, I acquiesced.

We walked along in silence until we reached the kitchen. She gestured to the table, where I sat with unease; and when she stood across from me, I could not help but speak my mind.

"I must tell you first," I said hoarsely, "I understand now that you never meant me ill—"

"Forget that now," she said, as she settled heavily in her seat. Her voice was old and weary, devoid of the sharpness which I was accustomed to. "It will do you no good to dwell on it. It happened, so forget it."

I answered quietly. "Still, I wished to thank you…"

"Don't thank me," Miss Josephine interrupted. She avoided my eyes in favour of casting a weary gaze over the table. There was a difficult look in her expression, somewhere between defeat and regret. "If you have questions for me, ask them. That is all."

For a moment, I wavered, wondering how precisely to ask. The enormity of it all seemed out of the reach of a simple question. At last, I spoke with some hesitation.

"The Count—does he have you under any threat?"

"No," she said shortly.

"Then, do you have anything you hold over him?"

"No. He pays my wages, and I do as he asks. Nothing more."

I paused, pondering these answers, before venturing weakly:

"Miss Josephine, I must be honest; I have made so many judgments in this place, all of which were more or less mistaken, that I have little trust left in myself. Before arriving here, I thought myself to be a sufficiently good judge of character, and certainly thought that I knew right from wrong; but now, I can barely take a step without questioning what I'm doing." I hesitated. "In short, if I cannot follow my own compass, then I must borrow yours."

"Then borrow it and ask."

I straightened and sought out her gaze. "I would ask you this: what is your sense of the Count? What do you know of him?"

She let out a deep sigh, and shook her head. "I know little."

"Even after residing here for so many years?"

"Even so. He tries to keep it all hidden, as best he can."

"But you knew of his nature."

She snorted. "Only because his best efforts are still careless. It was not so from the start, of course; in the beginning, he was very cautious, and my arrival was much like yours. When the old housekeeper left, and I was alone in the manor, I was half-convinced that I was tending to the home of a ghost."

Having had the same sense myself, I listened attentively.

"Eventually, he does get tired of his little notes," she went on with some disdain. "At times, he did have to speak with me, though reluctantly. Whenever he summoned me, he never faced me as he spoke; he was always behind a door, or facing away, or concealing himself in clever ways. That was all I knew of him for many years, and all that I cared to know. Unlike you, Mr. Bedford, I am not the sort to pry."

Despite a throb of guilt, I gave a dry look. "Then how, pray tell, did you find out what he is?"

"It was his fault. The poor wretch left a book open in the library, where he had recorded his thoughts."

Hearing her refer to the Count in such a strange way, which seemed halfway to sympathy, I was curious. "What manner of thoughts?"

"Nothing less than the story of the bite that altered him."

This stunned me into silence; to think that she had the answer to the very question plaguing me for weeks did stir my interest!

I leaned forward, and asked my next question with some intensity. "Was it intentional?"

"No," she replied curtly. "He was murdered, and violently at that."

My chest tightened, and I was stunned. "How?"

"I would say I wish I recalled it more clearly, but in truth I don't. His writing described a scene so vicious and bloody that I could barely stand to read it. Suffice it to say, the creature that did it left him for dead."

I shuddered at the idea, and felt suddenly quite cold. "I see—but you took it for truth?"

"I suspected it to be truth for other reasons, but it was his reaction that made it obvious. He must have been upset upon realizing what I had seen. On the following morning, I found the book reduced to cinders in the fireplace. Good riddance to that, I suppose."

But I was preoccupied, and muttered to myself: "Then I understand even less."

"What is there to understand?"

"If he was wronged in such a way, then how did he become so wicked?"

Miss Josephine gave me a flat look. "Wicked, you say."

"Yes—wicked!" I said, with insistence. "It isn't only what he did to me, though that may be the worst of it. From the little that we have spoken, I can also tell that he holds great antipathy towards the world in his heart, and indeed hates humankind as the devil would."

"Hates humankind?" she said, and laughed darkly. "Oh, he holds no such thoughts. Perhaps he wishes he hated it, but he couldn't."

"How do you know?"

"It is impossible not to. He goes through his books and journals like a madman. One might even think they are worth more than blood to him." She sniffed. "It was I who persuaded Parker's library to increase the limit on our subscription—perhaps the only matter in which Alistair thanked me personally."

Hearing her refer to him so informally was a great surprise, and I had the sense that she knew him better than I. Curious for more, I prodded further. "That may be so, but it answers nothing of his opinion on humankind! Perhaps he is simply bored; someone may be entertained by something they hate."

"Not when he asks for ladies' magazines, and then spends weeks drawing the new fashions. His tastes are so varied that Mr. Parker once asked if there was some young wife at the manor."

This left me quite speechless. I could not imagine the Count reading anything of the sort.

Yet, then Miss Josephine paused, and added with more gravity:

"But of course, that isn't all. There remains the matter of the manor."

"What matter?"

Miss Josephine turned to her candlestick, cleaning off a pool of wax that had nearly spilled over. She occupied herself with this for some time, evidently gathering her thoughts.

"You haven't seen this yet," she said at last, "But there are times, in order to add to his finances, that he lets the manor as an assembly hall for events. I post the notice at the inn, and the great hall is hired for festivities—balls, wedding feasts, gatherings."

"Here?" I said, with some surprise. "In the great hall?"

"Oh, yes. You would hardly believe it to be the same old manor you know, from the way it looks when decorated properly."

"I thought the Count hates to be seen…"

"Indeed. On such occasions, he takes to his room."

Then Miss Josephine glanced up at me with a glint in her eye, and added slyly:

"But he leaves his door open."

I stared back at her, stunned.

"Whenever he did," she went on, "I would tread quietly and go have a look. I nearly always found him in the very same state—leaned unstirring over his desk, with his shoulders hunched, and that long hair of his splayed out." Her voice grew dark. "A most mournful coat of night, he wears."

I shivered. "What was he…"

"Listening to the music and the voices, naturally. Where else would he hear them?"

Miss Josephine adjusted her shawl, as though she herself had grown cold, and went on grimly.

"Then he goes to the pianoforte at night, and plays the very same songs he heard. Over and over again, he plays them—but that is not his most wretched state."

Almost terrified to hear what would come next, I swallowed.

"No," she said quietly. "That, I saw only once, during a ball. I had chosen a place near the upper floor, at the top of the grand flight, to gaze down; but just as the violins reached a fervent pitch, I heard steps."

"He emerged?" I burst out.

"Oh, yes. I turned and saw him, standing and watching nearby. He is so very tall, you see; he towered tremendously over the railing, with his hands curled onto the banister. Though the cloak gave him a look of mighty gloom, the glow of the ball covered him in light. Why, I could see the colour and movement of all the people reflected in his eyes. They danced like fire in his gaze."

Then Miss Josephine's eyes lit strangely from her candle, almost as though terror had entered them.

"And his countenance, Mr. Bedford, bore an expression that I had never seen in my life, and that I hope never to see again. Deathly pallor and agony, a grief so deep and empty that even the bleakness of the grave could not hope to rival it—enough to feel the howling loneliness of a man confined to solitude for centuries past, and for-ever hence."

With the last words, her voice had grown unsteady with some nameless horror. She paused and collected herself, then went on.

"For a moment I thought he might pitch himself over the brink of the railing, or sanity itself. Yet, instead he composed himself and drew back into his room. That is all that I have to tell you, and all that I care to know."

With that, Miss Josephine concluded her story in a sombre tone, and folded her wrinkled hands over her lap.

I had been listening in rapture, overwhelmed by her account of it all; but even then, pondering over it, I found that my most crucial question had not been answered.

"He is pitiable," I said quietly. "That, you have made clear! And yet, being pitiable is no excuse for wickedness. I simply cannot understand why a being in such agony as you describe would inflict his suffering upon another."

"That is for you to decide," Miss Josephine said, "But I think your question is another."

I leaned my head in my hand and sighed. "Perhaps."

"You want to know whether you were right to shoot him."

"More or less," I said, and nearly laughed with helplessness. "I want to know whether I should hate him. That is all."

"*That* is your question?" Miss Josephine said, with a dull look.

I replied earnestly: "It may seem naive to you—and I admit, perhaps it is—but to me, *that* is the question that matters most. In scripture, it is written that we ought to abhor that which is evil, and cleave to that which is good. If I try to understand him too profoundly, then I may cease to hate him; and if I cease to hate him, I may inadvertently become him."

"Then ask your books for their opinions," Miss Josephine said archly, and stood.

I twisted my hands in my lap. "Well—but what do *you* think? Is he wicked?"

"I think it is long past my bedtime." She picked up her candle and shuffled towards the door. "Good night, Mr. Bedford. Think carefully over what I told you."

Somewhat listless, I remained at the table for a few moments longer; but no sooner had she departed that I stood and rushed out after her, and called out:

"Wait!"

She paused.

"Perhaps you're right," I said in a hurry, "And there *is* something more to understand in all of this; but I have ruined any chance at civility, and the Count has locked his door. Should I wish to speak with him again, what could I do? How might I—"

Abruptly, Miss Josephine reached into her pocket and flung something out. This object flew glittering through the air, until I reached up and caught it; and upon checking my hand, I found a noble old key.

"Give him my worst regards," she smirked, and disappeared

into her room.

After the conversation with Miss Josephine, I was left with an endless number of thoughts. As I entertained them, I took care of the essential tasks remaining.

The first was retrieving the fallen pistol from the courtyard, and the candle trimmer lying beside it. These, I regarded with something like shame; but I brought them back with me, and stored them in my room.

Next, now under cover of night, I went out to the well and returned with a fresh bucket of water. This water, I set to boil in a kettle; and as it did, I crossed my arms and stared into the fire for a long while. Miss Josephine's story turned and turned in my head, plaguing me ceaselessly.

For a moment, I closed my eyes, and imagined a life lived entirely in solitude. I tried to paint the image she had described in my mind's eye, of the Count standing at the brink of insanity at the banister. I heard the wail of violins, and the sepulchral silence that would follow them; I imagined the cold emptiness of the manor for one year, then ten years, then one hundred. After so long, the shrill sounds of crickets must seem as loud as the violins, only muffled by a century of dust. I tried to envision what it might be like to only hear another human voice in books, the majority of them printed by hands long-dead.

When I was unable to bear the sensation any longer, I opened my eyes and blinked at the brightness of the fire. The water was boiling.

I took it off hurriedly and brought a tray from the cupboard. Upon this tray, I set a teapot and two teacups, then busied myself with the rest. Indeed, I had decided how to move forward; and if I was to succeed, I had to lend it my full effort.

CHAPTER VI

With tray in hand, I stole into the Count's study.

This was no easy task, despite having gained the means to enter; I knew that I had to move quietly, and go as far as I could without alerting him.

Stepping into the darkened room, I looked all around and did not see him. Satisfied, I moved as close I dared to the bedroom door, which was slightly ajar, and peered in.

Aside from a gentle breeze from an open window, which rippled curtains and wafted through the crack in the door, I perceived no movement. It was as I suspected; the Count was resting.

Drawing a deep breath, I closed my eyes and gave the door a gentle push. It moved with the faintest of creaks, which set my teeth on edge; but no other sound accompanied it, and so I entered the Count's bedroom.

There, the darkly ornate canopy bed that I had seen empty in the morning was now occupied. In the centre, between the four carved posts, the Count laid asleep.

He had divested his cloak and his coat, leaving them draped at the foot of the bed, and set his boots on the floor beside them. His shirt, faintly bloodstained though it was, he had kept on his person; but where it lifted to reveal his midsection, there was a well-done wrapping of bandages.

I must admit to have been astonished by the look of him. Despite his injury and his disheveled state, the manner of his repose was elegant; indeed, his features, which had so often seemed cruel to me in wakefulness, were rather more delicate at rest. A dim moonbeam spilled over from the window, illuminating the swath of inky hair beneath with a touch of silver. Had it not been for the rise and fall of his chest, I might have thought him to be some fine lady's doll.

Upon drawing near for a better look, however, I nearly ruined it all by stepping into a pail on the ground. I stopped in time and peered down, though the tray in my hands rattled threateningly with my balance; and there, inside it, I sighted a few surgeon's tools, as well as a round leaden ball. All were streaked with darkened blood.

The sight made my heart pound. I glanced away from it and regained my footing before setting my tray on the bedside table. This time, I made no effort to conceal the sound.

This method had the intended effect. In shortening intervals, the Count began to stir, languidly turning his head away; but over the edge of his cheek, I saw his lashes lift.

Suppressing a chill, I looked away and pretended to be busy with the tray. Nevertheless, after a few moments, I heard him speak quietly.

"How did you gain entrance?"

When I glanced back towards him, I found him entirely awake and open-eyed. He had turned his head towards me, and was watching me guardedly.

In reply, I lifted the key from the tray and dangled it. "Does this belong to you?"

"It is certainly not yours."

"Then I shall return it to you; here." I set it aside from the tray. "All right?"

The Count watched me for a long and uneasy moment; his gaze moved to the tray before returning to me. At last, with a profound sigh, he sat up.

"Mr. Bedford," he said, with a soft but commanding voice. "Whatever your intentions are at present, you have entered here unbidden after shooting me. While I would like to believe your penitence, as I have told you, I cannot rest while you are here. For now, I must ask you to quit the room."

Here it was, the moment of truth! I drew myself up, and turned to him fully.

"I understand that," I said, with as genuine a voice as I could muster. "Believe me, if you repeat your request, I will go in an instant! Still, I would like to speak to you, if only briefly."

He displayed a taciturn disposition, staring at the door across the room. "On what subject."

Though this look nearly made me waver, I steadied myself. "I wished to tell you that I realized what you were doing earlier, flying about outside. You were merely using the remainder of the powers of living blood, as you had told me you would, to return my knife."

He blinked slowly.

I went on nervously. "I had—"

Then his gaze moved to my face, and he met my eyes. What

sharp eyes he had! They made me lose my courage entirely, and I paused.

But he spoke quietly. "Go on."

And so, I steadied myself and continued:

"I had mistaken it for some other sinister act. That was why I shot you; I was frightened, and mistaken."

At my admission, his form did seem to loosen slightly. His gaze drifted away from mine, and his countenance revealed a touch of understanding. "I find that reasonable, and I believe you. You may rest assured that I did not blame you then, as I do not now. We can consider the matter resolved."

Seeing that he would not abandon his reserved demeanor, I steadied my voice.   "But it isn't resolved to me. I have more to tell you—if you would hear it, sir."

He was silent for a long moment, evidently considering whether to humour me. It was only after this that his guarded look faded; and at last, he sighed and beckoned.

"If you insist on it, then at least sit."

I had done it! Relieved, I took a chair from the corner of the room and drew it up, setting it by the head of the bed. There I settled, and spoke with all the sincerity that I contained.

"I will be entirely honest now, and I would hope that you give me the same courtesy."

Then I hesitated, still feeling a flutter of fear towards him. Nevertheless, I gathered my courage and pressed on.

"During the past few weeks, I must admit—"

"You were searching for a method to kill me," the Count said with ease. "That much was obvious, Mr. Bedford. As I told you from the start, I expected animosity from you, and took no personal offence."

"That isn't what I'm driving at!" I said, suddenly frustrated.

"You have a maddening habit of turning every inquiry upon me, as though I might only think of *myself* in every situation—as if what worries me most in wronging you is my own rude appearance. You either consider me a selfish nuisance, or you are trying to shield yourself, or both; but in the latter respect, you have failed. In trying to learn how to kill you, I have seen more, and learned a great many things about your character."

Seeing that he had made no move to interrupt me yet, I pressed on quickly.

"Namely, the following: that you have a cautious nature, and plan everything that you do to a fault; that you much prefer civility over force; that at times, you have implied your moral principles—so you *must* have them, though you have not revealed them clearly—and that, though centuries have passed, you still suffer when you think of the manner in which you were turned. You are still somewhat disposed to be humanlike—at least, Miss Josephine seems to think so. In short…"

Strengthening my voice and regarding him steadily, I came to my point.

"In short, I am convinced that you lied. There is nothing in your nature that would drive you turn me on a whim, for the purpose of an experiment—really, it is a laughable idea!—and I am quite *certain* there must have been another reason, which you have taken great pains to conceal. As for what it is—"

All of a sudden, the Count held up one dignified hand. Seeing this, I fell silent; I was anxious to hear his response.

"First," he began, in his calm and sonorous voice, "I must make one matter clear. I have never considered you a selfish nuisance, as you imply."

This was a startling thing to hear from him, and I stared.

"Second," he went on, with a tone considerably less charitable,

"Though I recognize the depth of thought which you have given to my motives and my situation—the latter of which was private, and I presume Josephine has divulged without permission—I regret to inform you that you have merely gazed deep into your own looking-glass. Everyone wishes to have been created for some purpose, vampire and human alike. If you are unsatisfied with the reason for your turning, then that is unfortunate but universal. Change need not have a purpose; sometimes, it merely is."

My frustration redoubled, and I leaned forward. "Sir, you are *not* conferring with me honestly! You have once again tried to sink me in the mire of my own doubts, without addressing a single word of what I have told you. Speak no more of me, and answer my questions on your own motives: how did you measure the risk, the bother, and the moral injury of turning me into a vampire, against the nebulous benefit of some personal curiosity?"

But his voice did not waver, and indeed only steadied in response to my growing frustration. "A whim is a whim precisely because it needs no justification."

I gave him an ornery look. "I suppose that was why you fainted into my arms and begged my forgiveness, on our way to the room?"

He stiffened with indignation. "Were you pleased with that?"

"You seemed about to weep."

"I have always been prone to fits of fainting, even in life. Whatever I may have said—"

Seeing no other recourse, I mocked him. "Ah, Mr. Bedford, forgive me! I am so sorry for what I have done—"

The Count's eyes flared, and gave me a look so powerful with warning that I nearly flinched. "Mind your tongue."

But I did not cower. Instead, I stood. "All right, then."

His eyes followed me up, and he was suddenly tense. "What?"

"If you wish me gone, then pardon the intrusion."

"Wait."

"Yes?"

He hesitated, then released a slow and weary sound. "Were you not going to speak further?"

"Yes, but I have neither the time nor the patience for your caprices! Be honest with me, and I shall return the favour. Hiss at me, bristle and be harsh if you wish; but do not lie to me."

The Count regarded me silently. He looked suddenly very tired.

Seeing that I may have pushed too far, I sat back down and tried earnestness. "I'm not trying to fight with you; I'm trying to speak with you—with the authentic *you*, who did this to me. I will settle for nothing less. As for *why* you did it…"

His expression remained vacant, which did not encourage me, but I went on regardless.

"I suspect," I said evenly, "That you did it out of loneliness. That, or some twisted desire to create—perhaps to avoid the terrible fate of being the only one of your kind."

To this, he replied tartly. "If you had avoided offence before, I am pleased to inform you—"

"Be as offended as you wish!" I declared. "I know that you will admit nothing, perhaps not even to yourself; but I know it was no careless whim that drove you to it, and that you are determined to keep your true reasons secret."

The Count paused for a moment.

Then, he lifted his hand. With a curious sort of motion, he pressed his fingers delicately to the centre of his forehead, and closed his eyes for a moment, as though he were only just waking up.

I waited.

Finally, he lowered his arm and folded both hands in his lap. With a weary countenance, he sighed.

"What do you want from me, Mr. Bedford?"

Knowing that this was the closest I would get to an admission, I straightened and addressed him with clarity. "I have a proposition."

"Go on."

I felt strange, unsteady in this position of addressing him as an equal. Even now, he gazed upon me with the look of some cruel prince, and it was overwhelming to stare him in the eye.

"I know I have much more to learn," I said firmly. "Both about the nature of the vampire, and about you. Therefore, if you will tolerate me, I would like to stay for a year—only a year, and no further, so that I may then go freely without regrets, and leave this part of my life behind forever."

He did not reject me immediately, which gave me hope, so I pressed on.

"During my stay, I promise to pry no answers from you about my turning; if I come to understand you well enough—which is my full intention—I assume that your motives will become obvious, or that you will come to trust me, and tell me honestly. Furthermore…"

Here was the most difficult part to say. Unable to face him while I spoke, I stood instead and turned to my tray, taking up the teapot.

"To learn is not my sole purpose in staying. I also intend to keep you company."

"To keep me company?" the Count said with incredulity.

I neatly poured the first cup of tea. "Just so."

His tone grew disdainful. "Out of pity, then."

"Perhaps it *is* out of pity! Does that insult you? Well, then; let it! If it softens the blow, you may see it as my amends for shooting you, though that isn't the truth of it."

"And what have I done, then, for you to deem me worthy of your company?"

"Why, nothing!" I exclaimed, as I steadily poured the second cup. "Nothing at all! Thus far, I can imagine no amount of misery that would excuse your actions, and I may never forgive you; but that doesn't stop me from pitying you. I cannot help but feel sympathy for such a sorry thing."

"You flatter me, Mr. Bedford," he dryly replied.

"You are what you are, sir. I am only telling you the truth." I hesitated. "And despite my pitying you, it is *not* out of scorn or hatred that I show kindness. Indeed, I will only stay if you allow it."

He remained quiet for a moment, clearly deliberating.

"Consider it," I coaxed. "You only stand to gain. If you somehow come to appreciate my company, then that would be grand; and if instead you are sickened of me by the end of my stay, you will breathe a sigh of relief when I am gone. Then, you will feel blessed to retire back to the pleasures of solitude, and cast off all desire for company for good."

"You truly believe yourself to be so irritating?"

"When I choose to be," I said, and suddenly could not stifle a very small smile.

The sight of my smile changed his entire demeanor. Yes—for an instant, he seemed surprised, and stared as though transfixed.

Nevertheless, I quickly suppressed this expression, not quite understanding why I had displayed it, and returned my attention to the tea tray. It was imperative that he not think me insincere,

I thought; and to a somber soul such as this, any levity could give that very impression.

But then, I heard a sound that made the hairs rise on the back of my neck.

The Count had laughed very softly.

When I turned at last, I found him wearing a very small and genuine smile of his own. I must admit that it dazzled me.

"One year is nothing to me, Mr. Bedford," he said. "Not after living nearly three centuries. Still, it is a pleasure to see you wear an expression that is neither *worry,* nor *dire worry.* For the sake of that alone, I am inclined to consider your offer."

Recovering from my shock, I managed a quip—"Take care, or you shall see those expressions soon enough!"—but I could sense a great relief between us, which both calmed and intrigued me. I found it curious how the Count's presence, overwhelming as it was, changed entirely when it was suffused with goodwill instead of intimidation, and filled the room with ease.

But I still had not addressed all that he had said, and regained some solemnity when I continued.

"I know that a year is but the blink of an eye when spent in solitude, but I will keep you well-occupied. The seasons will pass slowly. Autumn has just set in, and the leaves will soon begin to fall in earnest; I will stay in this manor while they bud again, then through the days when they flourish and wither. When autumn has waned, and the trees are bare, I will depart. By then, it will have seemed an age."

He pondered this quietly for some time.

Anxious to hear his answer, rather fearing that it would be a rejection, I interrupted with something else. "Do you take sugar?"

"Sugar?" the Count murmured.

"With your tea, sir."

"Tea was not common in my time," he replied absentmindedly, still gazing off. "I have no preference."

This left me flabbergasted; I could not imagine England without tea. "Have you never once tried it?"

"Tried it, yes. Only seldom."

"Then…" I wavered, trying to find a way forward. "Do you prefer sweet things?"

Evidently, his mind was still elsewhere; he was silent for a few long moments. Just when I assumed he had not heard me, however, he replied at last.

"I think so."

And so, I ladled sugar into both cups, and turned with the tray in hand. "Here, then. It's a bit cold now, but try it."

This returned his attention fully, and his eyes drifted down to it; but he glanced up at me with a somewhat wary look. "I should perhaps remind you that I recognize the taste of poison."

"Indeed!" I replied. "For that reason, I have brought two cups. Choose yours freely, and I shall drink the other."

He tilted his head in clear amusement, appearing not at all serious in his concern. "And if you have chosen to poison the both of us?"

"Well, I would consider that a hideous waste of tea."

His amusement blossomed further, until he was smiling outright. Once more, this enthralled me; what an effect he had!

Finally, he reached out and took one teacup on its saucer, and held it in a manner which indeed convinced me that he had scarcely held one in his life. For a few moments he only stared into the faint steam; but he soon brought the rim to his lips and had a taste.

How strange it was, to think that the throat that had once

swallowed my life now drank tea that I had served! But instead of bitterness, I felt strange curiosity; I waited with bated breath, and watched him

The Count blinked slowly, as he pondered the taste. Then, in a measured fashion, he waited a moment—a moment just long enough that it must have been deliberate—before raising the cup again, and taking a much longer drink.

I admit that I was smug. "How is it?"

He set it down. "Fine enough."

Clearly, he had liked it; I felt a flicker of triumph, and a strange sort of pride in the customs of my time which I was imparting to him. "I would use milk as well, but we have none. If you wish, I can arrange for deliveries."

"You have not had yours."

"Pardon?"

"You have not had your share of the poison."

Flustered, I looked down and realized that I was still holding the tray, having left my own portion of tea abandoned. Setting it all down, I then took the remaining saucer. "Ah, excuse me, I forgot—"

"I jest, Mr. Bedford." He swirled his own cup. "If this were an attempt at poisoning, it would be a poor one."

"Still, I said that I would, and so I shall!" I took an earnest drink, downing half my cup before setting it down. "I keep my promises quite seriously, you will find."

"I imagined as much." Looking back up to me, he addressed me now solemnly. "Your earlier offer was likewise made seriously, and I presume you wish to hear my answer."

I grew still, and my heart pounded. "Yes—I do."

And at last, he lowered his teacup to his lap and replied at length.

"You may stay, Mr. Bedford, if that is what you wish. Should you choose to leave at any time, as I have told you, you are free; I will not hold you to your promise of a year. Only know that the answers you seek may not come, and that you may grow frustrated and bored with me. I have not entertained a living soul for at least two centuries, and will need privacy more than most."

"Why, sir, you need not worry about such things!" I exclaimed. "I have held every sort of servant's profession, and thus faced every difficult character on this earth; a little reticence is nothing to me, and I don't expect to be entertained. Indeed, I will leave you be for the rest of the night, and return tomorrow at seven in the evening; how is that?"

This reassurance had the effect that I intended; he nodded, and seemed relieved. "I think that wise."

"Then good evening, sir. Rest well, and heal swiftly from—" Suddenly awkward, I stepped back and gave a stiff bow. "From our unfortunate misunderstanding. Farewell!"

I gave him no chance to reply, and promptly fled the room.

As soon as I closed the door behind me, I realized I had been so tense that my shoulders ached. With a heavy sigh of relief, I allowed myself to loosen. Oh, how glad I was to be out! For the first time, I could not believe my own courage. It had taken every last sliver of strength to keep from fleeing from him, and every last bit of compassion to keep from bursting out in fury. In both respects, I had to pretend that he and the event that had befallen me were entirely separate. Oddly, I found this easier than I had expected; he was certainly quite patient and civil when he chose to be. Yet, still, how terrifying he was!

Having survived the encounter, I could now reckon with the awful fact of it: I had sworn away a year to the most frightening man I had ever met.

I chose not to dwell on this, and returned to my room.

CHAPTER VII

On the following evening, I woke uneasily.

At first, the haze of rest lifted slowly—that is, until I remembered my task. Then, dread swelled up, and I opened my eyes to face the ceiling with a pounding heart.

After a few moments, I swallowed and sat upright, rubbing my eyes. A quick glance at my pocket watch confirmed that it was around six in the evening. Yet, for a long time, I simply sat there and ran a hand through my hair, quite nervous; for in all truth, despite all my lofty declarations, to see the Count again was the last thing I wanted in the world.

In the end, I sighed and shook the downcast look from my face. If I was to deal with this situation for a year, I would need to begin somewhere, I reasoned; and so I rose from bed, and arranged myself neatly before gathering all that I needed.

I had left a note for Miss Josephine the night before, asking her to arrange for milk. This, I was pleased to see that she had done; there was a small jug waiting in the kitchen. With this, I was able to prepare a decent cup of tea, and was glad for it.

It was a quarter to seven once I finished, and rushed up the stairs to his room with my tray clattering. With my elbow I pushed down the handle of his bedroom door, and edged inside.

Daylight was dwindling over the moor, and the few remaining rays trickled through the window onto the sleeping form of the Count. His hair flooded the pillow below his head, draping over his shoulders and his neck, and gave him a spectral quality. When I observed this, combined with the well-ruffled nightshirt he wore, I once again decided that he looked quite like a doll, innocent in repose; it was waking him that would ruin this illusion.

I set my tray down on the night table, lifting a small bell from it. Then, I took a deep breath and approached.

"Sir!" I called, giving the bell a ring. The sound was piercing but light, echoing crisply. "It is morning—or, rather, night; it is time to wake up, in either case."

The Count opened his eyes sharply. Evidently, he was not used to being woken; but when his gaze found me, he settled.

"Mr. Bedford," he said languidly.

A sickening chill went through me, and I endlessly regretted all of my decisions. Nevertheless, I greeted him. "Good evening, sir."

With a measured sigh, he sat upright, dragging his long hair up with him. "What type of torture is this?"

"Why—torture!" I said, offended. "It is a proper breakfast."

He regarded me with strange amusement. "We have no need for such a thing."

"Neither does man *need* to wear clothing, and yet he does." I took a cup on its saucer and extended it to him. "I added milk this time. Try it.”

With a peculiar expression, he took it and gazed down distantly. Then, he lowered his head and had a careful sip.

I glanced over. “Well?”

“Pleasant,” he replied.

I could tell that he liked it more than he was admitting, and so I took the chance to make a more daring offer. “Would you mind if I did something with your hair?”

At that, he paused, and glanced up towards me. “For what purpose?”

“None; I merely found a ribbon, and I thought I might arrange it for you.”

“No.”

“No as in you don’t mind, or—?”

“No as in no, Mr. Bedford. You are not to touch my hair.”

His tone surprised me. I sensed that I had made some mistake, and stammered. “But why?”

“I can fix it myself. You are not my servant.”

“I truly wouldn’t mind it; I am quite used to being a valet. You can consider it compensation for my lodging here.”

“Mr. Bedford,” he warned. “Once again, you are not my servant, and while I acknowledge your kindness in offering, there are decisions which I must ask you to respect.”

Reluctantly, I decided to relent. I suspected that he preferred not to be touched, and I feared losing his favour before ever winning it. “Well, then, don’t worry. Finish the tea.” I hesitated. “But shall I still help you dress?”

He paused before giving me a look which, though dryly amused, was also laced with threat.

I was quite chastised by that, and turned away. “Fine, then! Fine; dress yourself, and I shall return in a half hour.”

With this I left, closing the door behind me, and wandered slowly into the gallery before stopping and turning to look back at the door.

I stared at it for a moment, unmoving.

Then, I went to room down the hall, found a sofa, and sank into it slowly. For quite some time I waited there, desperately trying to quell a sense of dread, and stared at my pocket watch in the dark. Only when enough time had passed, and I could bear my nerves no longer, did I return and knock before entering.

There he was, once again; but now, he was standing by the bed fully dressed, except for his coat—and oh, how much more terrifying he seemed! His legs were long and straight like violin-bows, in dark breeches which fastened tightly with stockings at the knee; and he wore above them an olive waistcoat with embroidery in gold, which was scarce up by the width of his shoulder but grew intricate as it flared out below his waist. A matching coat was laid out on the bed.

The Count straightened his cuff and turned to me with a sharp click of his heels.

I found myself nearly frozen in terror; it was with tremendous effort that I cleared my throat and greeted him. Without thinking, I nearly moved forward to take his coat for him, before remembering what he had asked of me and standing back.

He noticed the motion, and let out a quiet sigh. "Do you really wish to be a good servant so ardently, Mr. Bedford?"

I was rather embarrassed by myself, but answered steadily. "It may seem trite to you, sir, but it is the only craft in which I excel."

The Count considered me for a moment, and I could have sworn that I saw a hint of pity; but at last, he gestured. "Then come."

Relieved, I swept forward and took the coat. He raised his arms smoothly, allowing me to slip the sleeves onto them with some effort; he was so tall that I could barely reach.

As he shrugged it on, I stepped in front of him before I could lose my courage. "Would you care to follow me, sir?"

He tilted his head. "Follow you where, precisely?"

"Miss Josephine showed me most of the manor, but only as far as necessities were concerned. If you're willing, I would appreciate a proper introduction—especially to the library, which I quite enjoyed."

"Very well."

"Then you will follow me?"

"If I must."

Inside my heart, I celebrated a quiet victory. There was half of me wishing that he had rejected me, and yet I felt an odd spark of enthusiasm; for, despite my enmity with the Count, the manor had always felt friendly to me, and I was interested to know more of it. Thus somewhat heartened, I straightened my coat and headed for the door.

*　　*　　*

The clip of heels sounded behind me as I led the Count out to the hall, towards the flight of stairs which led down to the first floor. This was an uneasy position to hold—I had the sense that I was leading a tiger on a leash!—but I cleared my mind and held my posture straight.

"Have you read all the books in the library?" I said as we walked, glancing over my shoulder at him.

I was surprised to find that his demeanor had eased. He was

following me with an easy gait, as he glided down the stairs behind me. "For the most part," he replied, trailing one long hand along the banister. "There are some that I have no interest in, and others that have long lost their relevance."

"I see," I said. As I faced forward again, however, I was suddenly filled with despair; for I had realized that this was the extent of conversation I had planned—and I was now condemned to hours with him! What on earth would I say now?

Luckily, he soon swept ahead of me. "Let us end with the library. The rest of the manor will not take long to introduce."

"Certainly," I replied with some relief, and followed him.

We forwent the servant's hall and the kitchen, which I already knew well. True to his word, the Count gave me a thorough explanation of the rest, pausing to comment here and there.

"This is the great hall," he said, as we passed it. "In my time, all events of import were held here. It was decorated grandly, and there were once tapestries all along the walls."

I looked up, trying to picture it. "What happened to them?"

"They rotted," he said pleasantly.

I shuddered, but followed him.

We passed the piano room along with the chamber beyond it, piled with instruments from long ago; a guests' lodging room, which had been converted to a workshop; and a room used for storage, whose original purpose had never been clear to me. This room was cluttered with furniture and boxes of varying sizes, in which his materials for painting were stored, surrounded by heaps of canvases both empty and used. Noticing that the walls seemed quite ornate despite the disarray within, I asked curiously: "Was this always used for storage?"

"Not at all," he replied, as he shut the door. "It was a nursery."

This made me turn rather pale, as I wondered who precisely

had been nursed within it; and despite my better judgment, I cleared my throat and asked.

"Pardon the question, but did you ever sire any…?"

"Not to my knowledge, Mr. Bedford," he said dryly. "Thrilling though I am certain it would have been."

Sensing that I may have crossed a boundary, I suppressed my more curious nature and merely nodded.

After pointing out some other features on the first level, he led me back up the stairs to the second. "You have already seen my quarters," he said as he went. "The only detail to add is that they were not mine originally; they were my mother's."

Though it should have been obvious that he had once had a family—and with it, a mother who was surely long dead—I found myself surprised at the prospect. Every reminder of his humanity gave me both solace and unease; I tried to picture him as a child, and could not.

Before long, we came to the second floor, arriving at the eastern side of the gallery.

"These were my father's quarters," the Count commented, as we arrived at one particular door. He opened it, revealing it to have been transformed into a sitting room. "Quite spacious, as you can see. It makes a pleasant place to read, or to paint."

When he closed the door and moved along, I paused at the next one, which had always appeared to be another storage room. "If that was the bedroom, was this the antechamber?"

"Indeed."

"I thought it seemed to be one," I said absentmindedly. "When I dusted there, it had the shape."

"Ah, you ought not have bothered dusting."

"Why?"

"I don't use it often," he said. Then, he added matter-offactly: "My father was murdered there."

I almost lost my head. "What?!"

But he had already kept on walking, and I had no choice but to follow. Still, as I did, I remembered my musings on his humanity; and as I caught up with him, I spoke gently.

"I'm sorry. Whatever the circumstances, it must have been difficult for you."

"Not really," the Count said with ease. "We never saw eye to eye."

This startled me, and struck trepidation into my heart; but he caught my look of horror, and gave the faintest smile.

"No, Mr. Bedford. It was not I who murdered him."

I was rather breathless with relief. "Well—I should hope not!"

To this, he gave an indecipherable look and did not reply.

We peered into a lavish parlour and an old maid's room, then came to a smaller and more wooded chamber, which had always been laid out with heavy tools that I scarcely recognized.

"A chapel," the Count said simply, as he opened the door.

I was suddenly heartened. "So *that* is what it is!"

"What it once was," he corrected. "If ever there resided any holy spirit here, it has long since departed."

I withered. "And what has replaced it?"

"On occasion, I have used this room for my studies."

"By studies, you mean…"

"Anatomical and otherwise," he answered cryptically.

I balked. "On whose anatomy?"

"Fear not," he said, as he closed the door. "Nothing living."

This statement, which was meant to assuage my worries, only increased them tenfold. Swallowing a bolt of anxiety, I choked: "Oh, good."

Appearing to have noticed my expression, the Count went on

pleasantly. "No blood was shed here. I merely used it as a copying room of sorts, where I could finish all the pages of my studies and arrange them into books."

"I see," I said, relieved.

"The dissections themselves, I performed in the pavilion which once stood in the old garden."

I promptly decided to suspend any further inquiries on the subject.

There was little more to see on the second level apart from the Count's quarters, and of course the upper floor of the library, which was later to come; so he led me back to the stairs, and up to the third level.

The gallery on this level was vast and bright, with windows all around. I had always liked it; the views of the moor were spectacular, and in the morning, light streamed like water over the floor. Now, in the nighttime, it was a ship amid a sea of stars.

"Come," said the Count, waving me onward as he walked. "The garden is clearest from this window."

He unlatched it and pushed it open, setting free an earthy breeze, then stepped aside as I drew near. When I gazed through it, I saw that he was correct; it was a perfect view. In truth, I had never considered the area behind the manor to be much of a garden, overrun with moor grasses as it was; but from this overlook, I could see that the sparse ruins had once served a purpose.

"There were once two pavilions," he explained, pointing gracefully. "One there, and one there—and of course, stables."

I squinted at the ruins, and tried to picture it all. "Were they large?"

"The first pavilion was quite large, a banqueting house that was seldom used. It burnt down just over two centuries ago."

"Burnt down!"

"Indeed. The blaze spread to the stables, and that was the end of them as well." He gestured to the other side. "The second pavilion remained far longer, and I used it for anything ill-suited to be done indoors; but when I woke from my second hibernation two centuries ago, it had been caved in by a tree, and overrun by nature. I had it demolished, but the door to the crypt beneath it remains."

I had endless questions concerning his explanation, but one in particular. "Your second hibernation—two hundred years ago, you said?"

"Less, now that I think on it."

Being familiar with the history of the region, particularly of York, to hear of this era gave me pause. "Pardon the question, but…"

He leaned comfortably against the window. "Go on."

"Was that during the great rebellion?"

"Very good, Mr. Bedford," he replied, and seemed sincere in his praise. "That was precisely the reason for it. The battles drew too near to the moor, and I decided that hibernation was my best option."

I hesitated. "But I wonder—would a vampire not thrive best in war? It is morbid to say it, but if one is searching for blood from the dead, the battlefield would provide a great deal."

At that, the Count gave a small, sardonic smile. "First, I must say that I find nothing remarkably morbid about your question. Remember, *we* are not the ones who sought that blood most eagerly, and gained the most from its spilling."

Once again, I noted his disdain for humankind, which he so often seemed to display; but now I was more inclined to listen, and only nodded.

"Certainly," the Count went on, with a faraway look. "War is any scavenger's feast; yet, with war comes disruption, and with disruption comes risk. I have no loyalties, but my lineage is unquestionably Spanish; I knew that if my manor were overrun by the roundheads, and I were interrogated and mistaken for a Catholic, I would have faced trouble. Wiser to sleep through it all."

Though I understood his reasoning, I watched him curiously. "But while you hibernated, who would care for the manor in your absence?"

"Simple," he replied, and pointed off into the distant night. "The moor church is on my land, and our ties were forged in their original charter."

"A chapel-of-ease?"

"Yes and no. The history of the arrangement is too long to explain now, but the result was this: though the parish knows nothing of my nature, they know me as their patron. I forgive their rent, so long as the parish cares for the destitute dead; and if I must leave on a long *journey* of many years, as I tell them, I grant them a temporary deed which names them as caretakers."

"And if they enter the manor, and find you in hibernation?"

He gestured smoothly back to the garden. "I lay myself in the crypt."

I was admittedly impressed. "You have considered everything."

"As any vampire must."

With that, he leaned forward to close the window before beckoning. Once more, I followed him.

On this level, most of the rooms were sparsely furnished. One of them held my interest, containing what appeared to be a very old and meticulously painted instrument, which I had scarcely noticed before. The beauty of it struck me vividly; it was decorated with landscapes and animals.

"What a peculiar pianoforte," I said out loud.

"A harpsichord," the Count corrected.

I was surprised, and then interested; I had seen few, and this one was very distinct. "Is it very old?"

"Very," the Count said with some amusement, and walked on past.

At last, we came to the final room on the upper level. Among all the other chambers in the manor, this one had always seemed the most abandoned. In particular, I remembered it for one detail.

"Ah, this room," I recalled. "You ought to know, there is an enormous ink stain beneath the rug, from the window to the cupboard, which would not come out no matter how much I cleaned."

The Count wore an indecipherable look. "I thought I told Miss Josephine that she needn't bother."

"She told me the same, but I thought I would give it a try. Even ink should come out with enough scrubbing."

"Blood."

I blinked. "Pardon?"

The Count gave a polite nod. "It isn't ink, but blood. This was once my bedroom."

I was mute and uncomprehending.

"My blood," he added calmly. "I died here."

I stared at him for a long while, at an absolute loss for words. Then, I turned to look at the stain, which was so massive that the rug could not cover it. Upon first having seen it, I had wondered whether someone had spilled an entire case of ink.

"All of that?" I said numbly.

He met my look of shock with a tranquil gaze, which hid behind it something far more complicated. In lieu of answering, however, he returned to the door and beckoned. "Come. I will show you the library."

Not daring to spare another look into the room, I followed him.

*   *   *

We walked in silence as we retraced our steps down to the first floor.

I could not fathom what to say to him, and pondered it all the while. To say nothing seemed to be his preference, and perhaps I should have been happy to oblige; but the revealed violence of that innocent room had left me shaken. Any sympathetic statement would be a knife in his gut, for he had done to me much the same as was done to him. Somehow, however, silence seemed just as much like an accusation.

In the end, I decided to follow his example and say nothing. In any case, we had reached the library.

This had been what I anticipated most, and I soon lost myself in it as he explained. As we walked among the shelves, he lectured at length, pulling out a book here and there as an example. There were endless rows of them, spanning many languages and nearly every subject that the imagination could grasp: geography, philosophy, plays, fiction, music, manuals, histories, and so many other categories that I felt dizzy merely counting them—and an entire set of Diderot's Encyclopedia, every volume well-worn. Though I had certainly explored the library before, I had never been aware that it held such vast repositories!

After I overcame my initial surprise, I began to pull books myself, and ask the Count of their origin. From this, I learned that he knew them all keenly; that he could read not only English and Spanish, but also French, German, Italian, and Latin; and that some passages, he even knew by memory.

On occasion, I noted a spark of recognition in his eyes, and he even interjected with his own opinions.

Of one, after plucking a reluctant spider off it: "A terribly boring affair."

Another: "Tedious."

Yet another: "A masterwork, though it took me a century to realize it."

One book, more of a pamphlet, was unmarked; but when I handed it to him, he seemed to recognize it well and shook his head.

"Better to burn it."

At that last comment, I gave him a look. "Come now, sir; all books have value to learn from."

"Then open it," he said smoothly.

At first I sighed, but then opened it and skimmed the page; yet, I had gone no further than a paragraph when I recognized a revoltingly detailed description of an act that I cannot write of in good conscience.

"Faith!" I exclaimed in horror, and closed it. "That is enough—dear God, I believe you!"

The Count smiled. "All books have value, you said."

Ignoring the look, I pushed the book back onto the shelf, shoving it as far in as it would go. "How repulsive! Why do you have such a thing?"

"Years ago, Josephine became very cross with me, and bought it instead of an ordinary book."

"Miss *Josephine* bought this?"

"Oh, yes," he said. "Now, when I am cross with her, I leave it in a place where she will have no choice but to find it in the morning. She returns the favour, and we battle in this manner until one of us is sick of it and shelves it again."

I could not believe the childishness of that, and frowned. "You ought to get rid of it."

"Really? I suppose I find her little games of revenge amusing rather than insulting." He gave a low laugh. "Dainty Mr. Bedford."

"I'm not—"

But he then raised his pitch from its usual timbre, and exaggerated my accent to absurdity. "How horrid—you should have burned the book at once, and along with it the vile woman who procured it!"

I turned on him in shock. "Sir!"

"Was it a fair impression?"

To my misfortune, it had been; but the glimpse of myself through his eyes made me awfully self-conscious, and a little flustered. I looked away. "No."

"Ah, I have upset you. Forgive me."

"I'm not *upset*."

"There is nothing wrong with your manner," he coaxed. "I much enjoyed overhearing your battles with Josephine while you worked."

Realizing that he was referring to the time when I had still been human, newly arrived to the manor and oblivious to his nature, I suddenly felt very oddly about it all. For most of the day, I had managed to think of the Count and his bite as separate. Now, remembering what he had done to me, I fell silent.

This did not go unnoticed. Seeing that I had slipped into a mood, the Count straightened and regained his usual demeanor. The air of mischief was gone, and a distant tranquility replaced it.

"You may continue to peruse the books," he replied. "Should you have any further questions, I would be glad to answer them."

With that, he moved off to another part of the shelves, giving me generous space to cool my frustration.

Though I was justified, I could not deny that I felt rather poorly about having been so blunt. Strange though it was, I had been enthralled with all that he had told me thus far, and had even enjoyed the growing comfort of his demeanor. For a moment, it had felt like genuinely congenial company.

If I was to spend time with him, I realized, I could not play the game of splitting him in two. The Count who had bitten me and the Count who was warm and amicable were one and the same; but among them, the second seemed to be his more authentic demeanor. Until the former could be reconciled with the latter, I would have to remember it, but otherwise set it aside.

Glancing over, I found him putting a shelf back in order. Though I was daunted, I took a book from nearby and approached him.

"What is this one?" I said.

He turned, seeming curious at my approach, and took it from my hands. Yet, he only gave it a glance before raising it up; and to my surprise, I felt a very light rap upon my head. The Count had tapped the book against me, almost playfully.

"You already asked me this one," he said with some amusement, as he lifted it away. "Remember?"

I cursed myself! "Ah, right."

"Perhaps it is best to retire for now."

I felt a twinge of alarm; he was slipping through my fingers, and all my hard work would go to waste! Determined to correct my error, I stepped forward. "I'm not tired yet, it was merely a lapse of attention. We can stay longer."

"Mr. Bedford," he said. His amusement mellowed, and was mingled with pity. "I do find your efforts commendable, but you ought to spare yourself."

"Spare myself from what?"

"You are terrified of me."

He was right, of course, but to hear it from him startled me into defensiveness. "I am not! Just now, I was only—"

"Not just now. Do you think me blind?" He paused, then gave a rather pained smile. "Or heartless, more likely? I would not blame you for either idea, nor for your fear; but I don't intend to torment you past the reasonable amount. You have spent the night treading on coals, and are surely exhausted."

I stared at him for a few moments in stricken silence, which he took as assent; yet, just as he tucked his book away and seemed poised to go, I steadied myself and answered.

"Very well! I will be candid," I declared. "You are right; on occasion, I *do* find you frightening."

He watched me curiously, waiting for me to go on.

I opened my mouth and closed it, struggling with my words, then swallowed and spoke again:

"But my fear has diminished, and with every word that we exchange, it dwindles further. I am prepared to set aside the one fearful, incomprehensible matter, in favour of what I *do* understand—which is that you have given me no reason to dread you, and every reason to continue in your company. Indeed!— by now, what you mistake for terror is mere apprehension."

After considering my words, the Count wore a quaint

expression. "I believed I was doing you a favour."

Heartened to see that he had not rejected my plea, I strengthened my cadence. "A better favour would be to answer my question: what I would ask you, sir, is whether *you* wish to remain in my company, knowing that I have always been skittish by nature, and may hold my worries longer than most."

He listened calmly, and finally replied with a shake of his head. "I don't find you skittish. You are only very forthright, and honest with your thoughts; but that is not a fault." His voice softened. "I would hope that you persist in the same manner."

"I doubt that I could do otherwise."

He seemed relieved, and gave a cordial nod in return. "Then I'm certain that I will continue to enjoy your company, as I have thus far."

Then, he paused, as though unsure whether it was wise to speak further, but at last said indecipherably:

"You are not alone in your pursuit of understanding. I have questions I seek to answer about you just as well."

I was startled. "What sort of questions?"

"I will tell you when I have answered them," he replied, cryptic as ever, and beckoned. "Come. We can go on to the library's second level."

Though I was surprised, I accepted, and the rest of the night was peaceful. From then on, I found it much easier to speak with him, and it was as though a fog had lifted from between us. When I approached him in conversation, I raised my gaze firmly to his and spoke in my more spirited tones; and when he gazed back towards me and answered, it was not with any snakelike civility, but rather with the inward interest of a watcher. With his guard thus lowered, I was better able to imagine the more delicate, private feelings of an exile.

We parted cordially at the end of the night, agreeing to carry on in the library on the following evening. I returned to the servant's hall just in time to see the first light of day give the dawn its cerulean glow, and heard the first movements of Miss Josephine stirring in her room.

Though it was too soon to sleep, I was exhausted, and quite nearly collapsed into bed as soon as I entered. The Count had been correct; I had drained all of my strength. Yet, I found that I regretted none of it, and even anticipated the following night with some eagerness.

Indeed, as I finally changed into my nightshirt and considered all that I had learned about the Count, I realized that a most curious change had occurred: I no longer found myself thinking of him in such terms. The cold and lofty title was forgotten; Alistair he was to me, and by this name I shall refer to him in writing henceforth.

CHAPTER VIII

On the second evening of our new arrangement, I woke comfortably, and for the first time in many months felt rather like my old self. When I rose from bed, it was not with any sense of dreadful obligation, but instead with a light enthusiasm which surprised me. I readied myself vigorously, washing myself and combing my hair as though introducing myself to a new household; the night seemed fresh and inviting, and I left for the kitchen early to make tea. When this task was finished, I took the tray—this time, far more willingly—and took two stairs at a time up to the second floor.

Alistair seemed to be in a deeper sleep this time, as though he too had finally managed to rest well; he laid so still and silent that he might as well have been porcelain, though his hair was tossed and tangled as the sea.

My intuition was correct; when I rang my bell and woke him this time, calling out—"Good evening, sir!"—he opened his eyes slightly, very much awake, but promptly closed them again and languished.

"Another half-hour, Mr. Bedford, have mercy."

I set my tray down and poured out a cup. "Another half-minute."

At that, he gave a sigh and sat upright, rubbing his temple. When he glanced at the tray, however, he paused. "You have only brought one cup again."

I busied myself with pouring it. "If you like it, I can always fix you another."

"And yours?"

This question surprised me, and I paused to give him an odd glance. "Why, I drank it downstairs, of course."

This made him level a look at me.

I frowned. "What is it?"

"You are not my servant, and even if you were, I find such customs loathsome. You may bring your cup with you, and we can take tea together."

I was rather astonished by this, and stared at him for a long while. During my stay at the Crawfords' home, I would never have dared to eat at their table, much less while one of them was present; and to serve myself a cup of their tea—why, it would have been so boorish that even the thought of it made me shudder!

Though I was not a servant for the moment, Alistair was surely nobler than I, and so I hesitated. "Are you certain?"

He regarded me with amused disbelief. "Lest you forget, Mr. Bedford, we have already shared two meals."

"I hardly think *that* counts, sir."

"It does to me," he said simply, and took his cup from me. "But it is your choice."

I thought it over, then had a cunning idea. Clearing my throat, I faced him again and gathered my courage.

"If I do, will you permit me to arrange your hair?"

Alistair sighed, though not earnestly. "Is it so hideous to you?"

"Oh, stop it! It is the opposite; I merely see a grand opportunity. At my last household, I showed my skills so deftly that their young daughter would let nobody else near her hair. It is an art to me, and I would like to practice it."

Hearing that, he relented. "Very well, Mr. Bedford; we have a pact. Bring your tea tomorrow, and you may do as you please with my hair—but know that you must not cut any part of it."

I was mildly surprised. "Why, I would never dream of ridding you of your locks, but would you agree to a trim in the front? I know a few styles that could frame your face nicely."

Alistair smiled pleasantly. "If you choose to bring shears, be prepared to meet them with a sword."

I needed no further persuasion than that.

After some discussion, we decided to spend the day in the library. Now that I knew broadly what it contained, I was curious to explore it in more detail, and so we went.

Miss Josephine had left two books newly borrowed from Parker's library on the desk; when we arrived, Alistair took one of them and tucked it beneath his arm, before going to a sumptuous chaise lounge. "Take as much time as you need, and ask whatever you wish," he said, as he settled languidly. "I am in no hurry."

Satisfied with that, I set off to continue my explorations. I decided to browse the section on poetry; this was an area that I had seldom explored, and which had always held my interest.

Yet, as I opened a book and tried to glance through it, I found myself distracted. The books were certainly interesting; but behind me, reading quietly, was a figure of even greater interest. Whenever I read any word on the pages before me, I could only think of Alistair having read it before, and wondered what he would have to say on it. Yet, I did not wish to interrupt him so quickly, and so I read on.

Before long, however, my reading was interrupted all the same. In the silence, I noticed a sound from the nearest bookcase.

It sounded to me like the scrabbling of rats at the topmost shelf, which horrified me; so I found a ladder, despite Alistair's half-hearted warnings. "You are going to fall, Mr. Bedford," he called lazily from his chaise lounge, as I propped the ladder against the shelves.

"Nonsense!"

"You are going to fall."

With a scoff, I began to scale it. "How can you be so certain?"

"I had Jacob's dream; I saw angels at a ladder, half of them descending."

"Then I am a devil."

"All the more reason for you to fall."

"Be earnest, now!"

"Earnestly, then: two hundred years of use have polished those rungs to a luster that a goldsmith would envy. If you are unused to it, you will fall."

"Well! Even so, are we not immutable? What have I to fear from a fall?"

"I'm not certain whether we can survive a broken neck."

"I don't see why not."

"Perhaps it won't kill you, then, Mr. Bedford, but it will put you through a great deal of pain."

No sooner had he say this that my foot slipped on a rung, and hot panic rushed through me. Alistair then called up again; he had laid down his book, and come to stand by the foot of the ladder.

"You are going to fall," he called languidly.

"Oh, hush," I retorted, as I reached the top. "It was your speech that distracted me, and nearly toppled me."

At first, as I peered into the dark space above the books on the last shelf, I saw nothing; but there it was again, the sound of scrabbling! My hands were clammy from the ladder's height, but my resolve held firm, and I forced myself to let go of one side. Keeping a sweat-dampened grip on the other, I reached into the space. "There's some sort of rat—"

Without warning, the sharp sting of a bite shot through my finger!

Though the pain was faint, the sensation of it was enough to make me pull the hand away in shock—but alas! Once that forceful movement had been executed, the whole of my balance sought to follow it backwards. My hand slipped, and a gasp flew from my lips; every nerve flooded with terror as my shoes lost their purchase on the rungs of the ladder. The air rushed past, and my stomach dropped as I plummeted down—I was lost!

Then I fell with unbelievable force into something that was not the floor, which enfolded me and sank down with the momentum before steadying.

My limbs were askew, but I was unharmed. Aware of a peculiar warmth around me, I opened my eyes.

Alistair had caught me in his arms. His face loomed above; the dark and flashing eyes bored into mine, so near in distance that I froze.

"Did you find anything?" he asked calmly.

I stared up for a few moments, completely startled, and

suddenly cognizant of a warm and spiced scent all around me.

My face grew warm with embarrassment as I regained my bearings. "My apologies."

Now he had every reason to taunt me for having fallen, and I braced for it; but to my surprise, he said nothing. Instead, he let me down with care, only releasing me once I stood steady. "She bit you, I presume."

This baffled me. "She?"

Alistair now gazed up the length of the ladder. "Indeed. I will introduce you."

"To who?"

"If you knew her, then she would need no introduction," he replied. By now, he had stepped up onto the first rung of the ladder, then the second; but when he reached the third, he paused.

"Still, I must say…"

He glanced over his shoulder at me, with the most smug and self-indulgent smile I had ever seen him wear.

"For someone with the habits of a cat, I would have expected you to land more gracefully."

Oh, how that set me off! I flushed anew, and called up after him: "A cat—why, I'll show you a cat! See if anybody catches you when you fall—"

"Good," said he, "For I don't intend to fall."

Before long, he had reached the very top. It was striking, the way he stood there, the enormous form of him clinging to the ladder as if it were a natural roost.

"Be careful," I called up after a pause, and moved to stand nearer. "I really can't catch you."

"Worry not," he said patiently. "Watch."

Then, he did something most curious. Alistair extended his

hand to the edge of that topmost shelf, holding it out daintily with the fingers splayed just so, as though he expected a ring to be slipped onto his finger. He clicked his tongue a few times, then waited.

With a mixture of horror and awe, I watched as there was a scrabbling and a fluttering from deep within the shelf; and presently a small, dark form emerged, in a slow but methodical scuttle, until it reached Alistair's hand and clung securely to it. Leathery black wings draped over it like a gentleman's cloak, and when I realized what it was I drew in a breath.

"A *bat!*" I cried out. I could scarcely believe that it had come to him so easily!

Alistair slowly came down the ladder, holding his hand delicately so as not to disturb the creature's roost. When he reached the bottom, he gazed at it for a moment, until there was a gleam of recognition in his eyes.

"It *is* her," he murmured, and ran a gentle finger down the fuzz of its back. "Dido. I have missed you for some time."

"You *named* them?" I exclaimed.

"Of course." He turned his hand slightly, as the bat crept up to reach the cuff of his sleeve. "How else am I to tell them apart?"

I shuddered, remembering the one whose head I had nearly dashed. "I would never think to name vermin."

"Vermin, Mr. Bedford, is a human concept." The bat fluttered as Alistair tugged it back down from his sleeve to his hand, then held still as he stroked it. "It is humanity, in its infinite arrogance, that crowns itself despot of the natural world; it gives no mercy to the most vulnerable of creatures, yet dares pray for mercy from the ravages of the earth, and fails to see the irony."

Despite understanding his meaning, I still watched him with some wariness. I had been determined to forget his deeds, but at this sight, my resentment stirred. How strange it was, to see him dote upon a living thing in such a manner, and speak so loftily; for if he could treat a dark and ugly thing as this with such mercy, then why had he been so cruel to me?

When Alistair looked up at me, therefore, and extended his hand—"You may touch her gently; she is harmless, and will not bite you now"—I frowned, and answered curtly.

"I won't touch *that* if there is no need,"

"Why not?"

"I simply—" I looked sullenly down at the thing. "No reason in particular."

He must have gleaned some part of my thoughts, as he regarded me for a long and quiet few moments. His silence was interrupted by the bat, however; it suddenly craned back its head and opened its mouth, inlaid with rows of minuscule teeth, to emit a high and crackling call.

"She calls out to you, Mr. Bedford."

"I have no wish to hear it."

He lifted the bat slightly and tilted his head, as though listening. "But she speaks, and I understand it."

I crossed my arms. "What would a bat have to say to me?"

"She expresses her apologies for biting you, and pleads that she never wished to cause you harm. She only felt trapped in a situation beyond her control, and knew not else to do."

As he spoke, I grew still, then slowly returned his gaze. His eyes were dark and inscrutable as always, but my gut-feeling told me he was not only speaking of the bat.

Though I wavered, I finally sighed and held out my hand. "Let me see."

With a cordial smile, he reached out; and carefully, tilting his hand, he let the bat crawl onto my hand.

At once, my worries over him were forgotten; for what a beautiful creature I held in my palm! Contrary to my previous encounter, this time I was moved by no sick hatred, and was able to appreciate it openly. She felt light as air, softer and far more delicate than I had expected, and her small, flat snout and wide-set eyes inflamed in me a feeling of endearment that I could never have anticipated. I was delighted when my stroking made her dark ears flatten, and her body nestled into my hand with pleasure.

So potent was my affection that I forgot Alistair's presence. Breaking into a wide smile, I laughed abruptly and without control. Upon remembering him, however, I flushed and composed myself.

He was watching me with a fixed and uncanny look, intensely interested, though he swiftly concealed it. "You find her charming."

"Why—yes," I said. Desperate to move the conversation away from my reaction, I spoke quickly. "You said her name is Dido?"

"That is what I named her, yes."

"From the Aeneid?"

There was a faint gleam of surprise. "You know Latin, Mr. Bedford?"

"Well—a little."

"You went to school?"

I hesitated. "A little."

After regarding me quietly for a few moments—realizing, I assume, that he would get no more information from me than that for the moment—he rewarded me with the slightest of smiles. "That is correct; it is Dido, Queen of Carthage, who I named her after. However, I took the inspiration not from the poem, but from an opera relating to the story."

"When have *you* last gone to an opera?"

"As Josephine might have told you, I sometimes let the great hall to be hired for festivities. On rare occasions, a school or family will set up a dais, and use it as a theatre."

"A theatre!" I exclaimed. "But they let you watch?"

Something about me seemed to amuse him, in that moment—perhaps it was my asking him questions while a bat still crawled over my hand—and he looked upon me with a smile that was almost fond. "There is a hidden stairwell from my room to the great hall. Near the bottom, there is a panel of wall with a hole large enough to gaze through."

Picturing it, I could not help but feel pity. "It must be difficult to grasp the full idea of it like that."

"Difficult, but not at all impossible," he said, and seemed wistful. "Opera, as you know it, had not formed fully in my time; the opportunity to experience any part of it is precious to me. I can imagine written compositions on the stage of my mind, but nothing compares to a performance."

I glanced down at the bat. "So this Dido is from…"

"Dido and Aeneas, by one Henry Purcell. Whether it was ever popular, I know not; but it is certainly my favourite."

After a pause, I dared to ask a more direct question. "Why do you like it so? I always found that story rather dour."

"I was never fond of the original story either, but the performance had more spirit to it." Alistair's eyes gleamed, as though he had remembered something invigorating. "It expressed the heart of it perfectly: budding love and peace, torn apart by the will of man, which all the while masquerades as the will of gods. If the whole of history has ever been more beautifully and succinctly described, I have not seen it."

I found myself pondering his meaning. "Well, I never thought about it that way. I should like to see such a performance.”

He paused, then gave me an indecipherable look. “You have, at least in part.”

“Have I?”

“I was playing an adaptation from that very opera,” said he, “On the pianoforte, upon one night you may remember.”

“A night…why, you cannot mean the first time I heard you play? You remember it?”

“Of course I do. It was a very amusing letter that you left me after.” His gaze caught mine. “And I was surprised by your courage.”

“What courage?”

“When you tried to feel through the dark to hear it nearer.”

“What!” I gave a start. “How did you know?”

A mirthful look touched his countenance. “I saw you.”

“Saw me? You couldn’t have—it was pitch black!”

He stared at me for a few seconds longer, until the answer dawned upon me.

“Pitch black…” I said, with mounting horror, “But your eyes could see through the dark?”

“And yours could not.”

“How close were you?”

“Close enough to scare the life out of you, had you managed to light those candles again.”

“Oh, God!”

He shook his head. “No need for alarm. You were in no danger.”

Before I could ask what precisely he meant by that, he went on.

“But to return to an earlier subject, I’m still curious: how much education have you had?”

In an instant, I was guarded; I loathed to speak of my past, and tried to describe it sparsely. "I had a few years of school. My hope was to attend university, but I never could."

"University?" Alistair mused.

This, I had seldom admitted to anybody, so I was startled to hear myself admit it to him. A servant who had once dreamed of such heights would ordinarily be regarded with mingled mockery and pity; but somehow, I felt that he might not scorn me.

To my relief, his countenance displayed no trace of such sentiments. There was only an intent curiosity. "Would you still like to, if you could?"

I fixed my regard on the bat in my hand, stroking it absentmindedly. "I don't suppose I could."

"That wasn't my question."

"Then, yes!" I exclaimed, with some frustration. "But it does no good to dwell on it."

Alistair thought for a moment, watching me closely. "I have a proposal."

"Do you?"

With a grand gesture, he spread his arms and gave a slight smile.

"There is more knowledge contained in this library than the typical idle young lord in Oxford will ever read in a lifetime. Whether I have the qualities of a decent tutor, I know not; but where the breadth of my knowledge is concerned, I have some confidence. Though I can give you no degree, I can easily create a broad course and help you learn it."

I was so stunned by this offer that I burst out in disbelief. "You cannot be serious!"

He was very amused at that, and his smile widened. "Serious

as the grave, Mr. Bedford."

"But I can give you nothing in return—"

"I need nothing in return. Consider it compensation for your company."

"That wouldn't come *close* to settling the bill."

"Then teach me in return."

This was the most ludicrous thing I had ever heard, and I cried out in disbelief: "Me! What could I possibly have to teach *you?*"

"More than you think," he said calmly. "I wish to know a great many things about your world, and magazines can only give me so much."

Still flabbergasted, I stared at him for a moment longer, then settled myself. "Well! If you are willing, then I would never refuse; but I will not force you. If you grow tired of it, or I'm no good, then—"

"No caveats," Alistair interrupted. "I will teach you, and you will learn. I hope I have given you no reason to doubt my patience."

He had not; and I grew so excited on the prospect of learning that I struggled to conceal it. "Then I will try to be just as patient, as best I can."

"Excellent," Alistair said smoothly. "We will need some materials beyond what I have here. I will send Josephine into town tomorrow to procure them, and we can begin on tomorrow's evening."

I felt a flutter of guilt. "There's no need for that; I can go in the morning myself."

Alistair paused, and his smile faded somewhat. "To Helmsley?"

"Naturally—why, what is it?"

After a moment's hesitation, he replied:

"I imagined you would want to rejoin the world, and I will not stop you. I must only warn you, with as much gravity as I can muster: you must exercise the utmost caution, and reveal your nature to nobody."

I was startled. "Of course; I intended to keep it hidden, but your worry is excessive. I'm on good terms with many in town."

"That won't stop them from turning against you," Alistair said quietly. "Fear and loathing can corrupt any heart, and they will regard you as no less vermin than the bat in your hand. If you believe nothing else that I tell you, believe that. Be careful."

Scarcely had he finished speaking when Dido fluttered in my hand, tightened her wings, and scrambled into flight. I winced in surprise at first, but steadied; and I watched with some regret, holding an empty palm still outstretched, as she reached the top bookshelf and burrowed back inside.

"All right," I said at last, returning my gaze to him. "I will be."

Satisfied, he took down the ladder. "Then give me some time to prepare a list for you and decide how to begin, and we shall meet again tomorrow."

Still addled, I agreed.

CHAPTER IX

When the night began turning to morning, I set out.

I was lucky to find a milkman with his wagon, trundling on towards the town from one of the distant farms; I called out to him and waved, and finally managed to stop him along his way. After a brief negotiation, I paid him and boarded his wagon, and thus had a pleasant ride into town.

The sky was lightening, and wispy clouds had begun to drift across the sharpening orange haze of dawn. Sharp birdsong trilled through the trees, and the peace of early morning was fresh and inviting. Though it was the end of my day rather than the beginning, and I yawned here and there along the way, I was invigorated by the thought of seeing the town again.

Indeed, when I did arrive, I felt a smile spring to my face. How joyful it felt, to be among people once more! The streets were still relatively empty, the shops only just opening; but it was more humanity than I had seen for a very long time, and I felt the warmth of returning to a familiar home.

As I walked along, I drew no particular notice. Though I had expected this, I still felt a great relief, for I knew surely now that I could hide my vampirism, and continue on as though I were human still.

My first order of business was not Alistair's errand, at least not the one he had sent me for. Instead, I found my way down the street to a particular building, and pushed the door open.

The man at the counter, with a ruddy and good-natured complexion, was idly arranging his counter when he heard the bell. Upon glancing up, he broke into a surprised look.

"Why, Avery!"

This man was Mr. Arthur McKinley, the owner of the shop. He was a rather good-natured haberdasher and linen-draper, who I had come to know rather well when I ran errands for the Crawfords. Above all, I knew him as a great gossip, with his wife as a willing accomplice, so I reminded myself to be prudent before approaching.

"Good morning," I said politely. "How have you been?"

He tossed down his rag. "Me? Forget me! It is Michaelmas tomorrow, and I haven't seen you since at *least* St. John's Day. Where have *you* been?"

"I took another position—"

"That, I knew. The old moor manor, isn't it?"

I sighed, realizing that I would not escape questioning. "It is."

"With old Josephine?"

"With Miss Goode, yes."

"Well, you would scarcely believe what she has brought here, or perhaps you would. The garments she has given the tailor to mend—I have scarcely seen such ancient things! These are no cheap theatre dressings either; tell me, what does that old earl use them for?"

"Not an earl," I corrected, before I could stop myself. "A count."

"Is he? But a count from—"

"Enough!" I cried out. "The Count likes his privacy, and I am afraid that I can divulge nothing. Whatever you have failed to pry from Miss Josephine is likewise not mine to share."

"But you have come for something today," Mr. McKinley said deviously, and leaned over the counter. "And that, I shall pry from you most gladly."

Steadying myself, I spoke as soberly as I could:

"I'm looking for hair ribbons."

"Oh? For what colour hair?"

"Black," I said. "Black, and very long."

After a moment's surprise, McKinley gave me a peevish smile. I sighed. "What is it?"

"And who, pray tell, is the raven-haired beauty who caught your attention?"

"If by that, you mean a man with dark hair," I said dryly, "And by 'caught my attention' you mean employed me, then yes, by all means."

He was taken aback. "No! You cannot mean—the Count? Long black hair?"

"Very long, past his shoulders."

McKinley mulled it over, then leaned further over the counter. "I see. Then I must confess something to you, my good Mr. Bedford."

"And that is?"

"I don't believe you."

"Arthur!"

"I don't believe you, but I will pretend to!" he said, brushing

236

his hands down his apron. "Whether I am right or wrong, I will do my best to satisfy either possibility. Wait here."

"You wait first! What on earth is the other possibility?"

He winked before walking off. "What do you think?"

I leaned over the counter, calling out after him. "Come back here, you scoundrel, I don't—!"

But he was gone, and I heaved a sigh, praying that his slander would not spread far. Then, I propped my chin in my hand and waited.

He returned shortly with a box in hand. "Now, Avery," he said. "Don't be so glum. I have something here that would satisfy both maiden and macaroni alike."

"He is neither—"

"Look," McKinley interrupted, and opened the box.

Inside, there was a set of ribbons and bandeaus in an assortment of colours. Along with them, there laid a few decorated combs and frontlets, and a pile of pins. In short, it was a perfect arrangement for any fine young lady's hair.

"Too much," I said at once.

"But I will give you a price that will dispatch every doubt."

"Too much!" I insisted, crossing my arms. "What will the Count think, if I return with something like this?"

"Well, naturally you don't give it to *him* all at once," McKinley said wickedly. "You present one piece, then another and another, whenever there is a special occasion—or whenever you find yourself in need of your darling's affection…"

"Affection!" I cried out. "You have lost your head. There is no darling, nor any other type of maiden."

But he did not relent. "Avery Bedford, I will see this through to the end; you can rely on me, I swear it."

I sighed, deciding to pursue my easiest route of escape.

"How much?"

I walked out the shop a little bit sullen, but with a finely-wrapped box under my arm, which was purchased for far less than it was worth—at least, without considering the added price of new gossip.

Next, I went down the street to Mr. Parker's library.

The bell over the door rang as I entered, and the mellow fragrance of books met me. Though it was too early for customers to arrive, the crowded shelves gave the place a lively appearance. The ones behind the counter, as usual, were filled with the most expensive of books, leather-bound and arranged in rows. The other shelves were populated by all sorts of different novels and pamphlets, packed tightly together.

Near the back, sweeping mellowly, was the owner's daughter. Florence Parker was unusually tall and grim for her age, and had been ever since I had first met her. Despite only sixteen years of age to make use of, her height exceeded mine. Being known to sometimes go out in men's clothing, she had often been the talk of the town; but today she had an ordinary dress, and wore her long black hair drawn up to the nape of her neck.

"Good morning," I said cheerily. "Is your father free?"

She gave a dull look up, then set her broom aside. "Wait here."

I was accustomed to this demeanor, and waited patiently by the counter as she went to the back room. Before long, another figure emerged in her place.

Noah Parker wore his silver-streaked hair combed neatly along his head, and pair of prodigious side-whiskers which matched a rather heavy pair of brows. Behind the two round, coin-like lenses of his glasses, his eyes twinkled as they caught sight of me.

"Good morning!" I called out. "It has been some time."

"Mr. Bedford!" Parker said in surprise, as he came to the counter. "I can hardly believe it; is that really you?"

"It is, and I must beg you to forgive me." I pulled a book from my satchel with some shame. "I will pay any late dues that I owe on this—"

"Rest assured, they are long-forgiven. I was actually rather worried for you." His eyes showed genuine concern. "You have never returned a book late. Is something the matter?"

"Nothing awful. I changed positions, and forgot about it entirely."

He gave a start. "You're no longer with the Crawfords?"

"Not for a few months," I said, as I pulled four more books from my satchel. "In fact, I have come to return these as well— on time, on behalf of the name Beaumont."

At once, Parker's demeanor changed. "It cannot be; you work for *him?*"

"I do. I know Miss Josephine ordinarily comes on his behalf, but I have a few special errands today."

Then I paused, and added curiously:

"Why? Is he such an unusual customer?"

"Unusual is not the word I would use," Parker said in wonder. "I have long been curious about your lord Beaumont; is it really only one man reading all of these books?"

"Just the one." I gave a helpless smile. "If it puts any strain on your service—"

"Oh no, Mr. Bedford, you misunderstand me! I don't mean to imply anything but my own admiration. Any scholar of history and philosophy, devoted to the preservation of the past glories of mankind as he appears to be, is not only a worthy customer but also an ally to me."

"An ally!"

"Indeed," Parker said with passion. "As a bookkeeper, I see myself as guardian of the wisdom of ages past; and if only everybody were so devoted to its study as your master is, perhaps England would not be so wretched today."

I laughed. "Could ancient wisdom truly fill such a bottomless hole?"

"I believe so," he replied good-naturedly, though his expression was grim. "What the youth have made of this place, I can hardly recognize."

Trying to brighten his spirits, I tried for a compliment. "Your daughter seems to be growing quickly. I'm certain that she will bring some good to it."

Parker sighed. "She grows in height, but in manners…"

"Let her be," I said gently. "Why, if I remember correctly, only a year has passed since her poor mother went with God. When I traversed the same, I was far worse for far longer."

Though there was a gleam of sadness in his eyes, Parker smiled. "Then, seeing your kind manners, I will hold onto some hope." He pushed aside a pile of books. "But that is enough about me. What does Lord Beaumont wish to read?"

I brought out the list Alistair had written for me, in that dazzling handwriting that could easily have been print, and read out a few particular volumes. Parker called out for his daughter to retrieve those he had at hand, while he wrote out those which he would need to order, and I left with my satchel considerably heavier.

By then, the weight of the day was catching up with me. People were beginning to fill the streets, eager to begin their morning in earnest, but I was starting to yawn; and I was glad to find a post coach about to set off, which I rode to a convenient point before climbing out and walking the rest of the way back to the manor.

*   *   *

That evening, our new plan was set in motion.

Just as Alistair had asked, I brought two cups of tea for the both of us. As we took them together, I told him he had earned quite the reputation in town despite his absence. McKinley's wonder at his clothing seemed to amuse him; but to my surprise, Parker's lavish praise made him sigh, and he dismissed it with a shake of his head.

"Today's bloodshed and farce will be tomorrow's great glory and wisdom," said he, as he set down his teacup. "Those who seek their gods in the past are damned to repeat their mistakes. Humanity has changed little in its essence."

I propped my cheek on my hand. "Since you hail from the past, I suppose I must believe you; but I must admit, whenever I see some old painting or book, I find it rather beautiful and wise."

"Such things are charming," Alistair said, with a slight smile. "And indeed, there is beauty of ages past which is now long-lost, and worthy to uncover; but it was the work of hands like ours, and from hence it draws its wonder. In elevating it to divinity, your friend Parker has lost sight of the humility which renders it so precious."

This was the closest to praise for humanity that I had ever heard him speak, and I was curious to hear him elaborate; but instead, he turned his gaze towards the tea tray, and caught sight of the small wooden box beside it.

"I presume you intend to collect on yesterday's promise."

"You presume correctly," I said, and reached for it.

I had rid the box of all excessive details, leaving only the few ribbons in different colours. Upon opening it, I sought to gain Alistair's favour by offering him the choice of any; he pondered them with mild interest before selecting one in a light brown colour.

I had him turn away from me, and settled myself on the edge of the bed just behind him; but before I could begin, he added a dry warning.

"Nothing ridiculous, Mr. Bedford. If a bat could make a roost of it—"

"Please, sir," I interjected with some offence. "At least trust my sense of taste."

"Taste is not a vampire's most discerning quality," Alistair said archly, but issued no further threat.

With that, I dared at last to reach forward and gather his hair, trying to gain a sense of its character. It was far softer than I had anticipated, even silk-like, though it had enough form to hold a few gentle waves. Indeed, it was finer than that of the young Lady Crawford, and I could not help but recall how she had loved to let others play with her tresses. I wondered whether this enigmatic man would desire the same.

It was not only the softness of it that surprised me, however. Now that I was so near, I noticed a pleasant scent, of which I could recognize at least cloves and cardamom, and perhaps nutmeg. I had on occasion perceived a warm and spiced redolence around him, particularly when he had caught me falling from the ladder the day before; but it had never occurred to me that he might intentionally perfume his hair.

Yet, just as I fanned through a few strands, curious to find some trace of oil or powder, Alistair gave a shiver so violent that

I paused.

"Sir?"

"Pardon me," he said quietly. "Carry on."

"But what is it?"

"Nothing grave; only that I have grown unused to deliberate touch."

This confession struck me, and then inflamed my sympathies. When I had spent time in a workhouse during my younger years, I had sometimes tended to orphans; and I found that many would revile any amicable touch, having been denied it for so long. Though Alistair was no workhouse orphan, I wondered what centuries of utter solitude would make of this instinct.

"Is it bearable?" I said. "You must be honest."

"Most bearable," he replied, with amusement in his voice, "And certainly far more pleasant than your bullet."

I answered dryly. "You are begging for a bat's roost, or a tonsure."

"Mercy, Mr. Bedford. I would rather take the bullet than that."

Having settled the matter, I devoted myself to my task. It did not take long; I gathered a portion of his hair into a tidy queue and tied a full bow with the ribbon. In this manner, he would look almost the same as before, only slightly neater; I did not intend to alter his appearance too drastically at first, lest he reject any future endeavors.

This method proved successful. When I handed him a mirror and held another behind him, he seemed lightly surprised, then curiously pleased; and when I left him to dress and returned, I found that he had chosen an outfit to match the colour of the ribbon.

Satisfied that I would be able to experiment further, I

considered my efforts well-spent. Alistair looked less frightening in this manner, I thought, slightly more like a refined aristocrat and slightly less like the devil—except, perhaps, for the sharp glint of his eyes. That quality was his alone.

We then went down to the library, and thus began our studies in earnest.

CHAPTER X

As promised, Alistair had selected a few materials. Before he began, however, he sought to understand just how far my education had gone; and though I was very embarrassed, I clumsily read out what I could of Latin and Greek, and described some literature that I had studied. Of arithmetic, I remembered almost nothing but the torment of trying to learn it, which I told him quite honestly. This phrase made him smile coyly, and remark:

"Then we shall begin with small torments before attempting the greater ones."

In history, I had slightly more confidence, for this had been among my favourite subjects; but the more I described what I knew to him, the more I flushed with shame, realizing that the entire proud sum of my knowledge would be a pittance compared to his.

When my words grew more halting, however, he stopped me

and addressed it patiently. "This is obviously your greatest interest, and yet you seem reticent to describe it."

"Why, naturally!" I replied, flustered. "I cannot help but remember that you have lived through much of it. This feels rather like describing someone's homeland to them."

He seemed amused, but only shook his head. "Forget me, Mr. Bedford. Be not ashamed; think of me as your book, which passes no judgment on you."

For reasons I could not quite understand, this made me flush darker still, but I stumbled on until I had settled.

Of natural philosophy and astronomy, I knew almost nothing. This did not seem to daunt him; he only reached for his quill, and wrote two more books onto his list. This was the first opportunity I had to see him write in his impeccable hand, and I was so distracted by it that I nearly missed his next question.

"What did you wish to study most in university?"

I paused, and hesitated before answering:

"Divinity."

He glanced up. "You intended to be a clergyman."

"I did."

"But you have said nothing on the subject thus far."

I was limited in what I could describe on my failures without being forced to divulge elements of my background, which I wished desperately to hide; but I managed a few words all the same.

"Well, I still have my faith, but…"

"I was not questioning your faith, Mr. Bedford."

"But I was," I burst out, before falling silent.

I had hoped he would carry on, but he instead set down his quill and watched me fixedly, inviting me to continue.

Yet, I could not go on at all, and instead asked haltingly: "Are you a Christian, sir?"

This seemed to amuse Alistair greatly, and he laid his cheek in his hand. "No, Mr. Bedford. I am a vampire."

I had suspected such an answer, and sighed. "Then what do you believe?"

"It is curious that you should ask," he said, "For it is the poets of your time who have drawn nearest to it. Let us add them to your list in place of divinity."

Feeling oddly about the exchange, I watched him note down a few more books and wondered absently: "Could there ever be a Christian vampire?"

"Why not?" Alistair said as he wrote, without looking up.

"To drink blood seems an unholy act..."

"Less holy than to spill it as a Crusader, or to burn it as an Inquisitor?"

I could give no good answer, and relented with a weary laugh. I had realized how awfully I had misplaced my initial fears on his alignment; the formerly terrifying Count, who I had once feared to be a servant of some demonic influence, was in fact only an incurable romantic.

Remembering his lineage, I glanced up, wavered for a moment, then summoned my courage to ask: "Were you baptized, sir?"

His amused smile grew wider and more lopsided, as he tried to suppress it. "Yes, Mr. Bedford. I was."

"Did you choose a saint's name for your confirmation?" I said curiously, then checked myself and added quickly: "I have heard it is a common custom in Catholic lands—it has long intrigued me."

"I did."

"Who?"

"Giles."

The thought of this formidable soul naming himself after such a gentle patron was endlessly intriguing to me, and I stared.

"Do *you* have one?" said he.

In an instant, I was flushed with anxiety. I had forgotten that my forays into his history could just as easily be reflected upon me.

"No," I said clumsily. "It isn't common."

He bowed his head in mocking politeness. "If you fear your first baptism was undone by vampyrism, and we consecrate you again, you may now choose one."

"Just in time for Michaelmas," I said dryly.

"Our goose awaits us at the chapel," Alistair devilishly replied.

The rest of our conversation took the entire night, and it was only upon the following evening that we managed to begin the studies themselves; but once we did, oh, how they consumed me!

Alistair was exceptional. He was the finest teacher who I had ever known, one of those rare storytellers with the power to make the world outside his voice disappear. When he lectured, I lost track of time entirely; and when he spoke on the subject of history in particular, I was so anxious to hear every word that I barely breathed. How I wished to be able to bottle his stories and take them with me!

Yes—there, among the books, and a few candles which we lit more for atmosphere than for light, we were not two vampires speaking in the dark; we lived in the worlds of kings and queens, philosophers and poets, generals and adventurers, monks and oracles, and witnessed the struggles of humankind as it fought its way out of the dark. Miss Josephine had been correct, I realized. Nobody who spoke with such reverence on humanity could ever pretend to revile it.

Whenever he finished a lecture, leaving me unsatisfied and secretly wishing for more, he would give me something to read; and then he would pour himself a cup of our late-night tea, and lounge to peruse a novel or a magazine while I did so. Afterwards, we would discuss the material together, and thus gain more value from it.

The days passed quickly. By the time our next feeding came, we spent the walk in discussion. I had become far more comfortable with Alistair, having better understood his character: I had come to know that he was far more inclined to be playful than cold; that his preference for levity came like an ache, which he longed to express; and that to some degree, the hard affect which I had known before had been a mask, which he had worn for reasons not entirely clear to me.

Regardless, it was evident that he, too, had eased his defenses as well. On that day when we crossed the moor to the chapel of rest, we argued about arithmetics the entire way.

"It makes no sense to me!" I exclaimed, running lightly to catch up with his grand strides. "If I add the two sides—"

He gave a long-suffering sigh. "I will explain it directly from the book when we return. Until then, think it over carefully."

"But I thought—"

"No, Mr. Bedford. Please; it is not the two sides added, but rather their *squares*."

"*What?*"

"Squares."

"But I speak of triangles, not squares!"

"Oh, Mr. Bedford."

"Explain it!"

"Hush," he cautioned. "Shall we alert the Father? Would you care to ask him as well? I am certain he would be pleased to explain."

"I'm sure he would! Mr. Raleigh is a very kind man."

Alistair gave me a look. "You met him. I suppose I shouldn't be surprised."

"I did meet him, and he was very kind."

"He will very *kindly* drive a stake through you, I'm sure."

"Perhaps," I said. "But if you call him a Father, you may get the stake first."

"Ah. I assume that form of address has fallen out of use."

"In England, most definitely," I replied. "Elsewhere, I don't know."

By then, we had reached the chapel, and quieted to avoid detection. We fed as usual, and walked back along the moor; when we returned, Alistair at last spared me from my ignorance of geometry, which I understood for perhaps the first time in my life.

After that first week, finding our efforts pleasant, we broadened in our studies further.

Autumn was withering away at the forest, making passable many parts which had previously been too thick with foliage and insects to be comfortably traversed. Therefore, after learning something of natural philosophy, we would set out on long walks. Here and there, as though the world was an encyclopedia of its own for him, Alistair would pause and point to some aspect of the natural world—whether a patch of flowers or mushrooms, or some animal burrowing away, or a tree stump—and comment on a detail I would never have thought to inquire on. His knowledge of botany was astounding, and I felt that a gulf of knowledge separated us, though by his patient narration he seemed to lead me through with stepping-stones.

By this time, however, I had begun to feel guilt. Though I

knew that he did not mind tutoring me, and indeed seemed glad to share his knowledge, I wished to fulfil my promise of teaching him something in return.

When I told Alistair as much, he was not offended. On the contrary, he seemed pleased, and confessed to have been waiting for my offer.

Thus, though I was still unsure of what he could possibly learn from me, I tried to find subjects as best I could. I described the world outside, of which even the most mundane details seemed to enchant him; I told him of him the shops in town, the modern manners of dress, and even the different carriage routes. I showed him how to make tea and chocolate, the latter of which was a marvel to him. I also taught him to sew neatly; his own sewing hand was graceful but foreign, for he had taught himself the skill and had a peculiar method all of his own. As a result, I had the curious sense of teaching a spider to sew.

Soon realizing that Alistair was in fact enjoying my small lessons, I grew bolder. I visited Parker's library in town again, this time returning with some of my favourite books that Alistair had not yet read. They delighted him, and we discussed these cheaper novels as though they were classics.

By the following week, I had become so daring as to occasionally teach him a ballad. I knew many of these songs by heart from my time in the workhouse; I taught him Rosemary Lane and The Young Man of Sheffield Park—both of which he loved—and The Drowned Lover, which he could not stand to hear.

I was reluctant to sing, being somewhat embarrassed by my voice; but when Alistair offered to accompany me with an instrument, we arrived at the subject of music.

Once discovered, this pursuit began to occupy much of our

time.

Alistair taught me the essential aspects of the pianoforte and the harpsichord. Though I liked the former, it was the latter which truly delighted me; this was an instrument from a distant time, whose sharp and silvery sound seemed to conjure images of ages past. My enthusiasm for it amused Alistair greatly, and he was an ever-patient teacher.

Yet, quite early in these lessons, he asked me plainly as we walked to the music room:

"Satisfy my curiosity on one matter, Mr. Bedford."

"What is it?"

"If you are familiar with musical notation, then you must know an instrument of your own."

I hesitated, and shook my head. "Not very well."

"Ah, but there is one."

"Two," I replied. "When I was a child, I sometimes played a flute—though that hardly counts."

We arrived at the music room, and Alistair opened the door for me before continuing: "And the other?"

I stepped in after him. "Well, when I was in school, I was given the option of taking lessons in one instrument. I chose the violin."

"Why?"

"I thought it practical," I answered, somewhat awkwardly. "A small instrument that I could take with me would be convenient; but after learning it—and not very well at that—I could scarcely afford one of my own, nor justify the cost."

Pausing in his step, Alistair thought for a moment. Then, he gestured for me to stay before striding off. "Wait here."

Confused, I stared aimlessly after him as he went to the adjacent room. I had my suspicions, but it was not until he emerged that I understood his intentions, and balked.

In his hand, he held a long wooden case, which he opened as he drew near; and within laid a violin, polished and in perfect condition, as though it had just left the artisan's table. Alongside it, there was a long and graceful bow.

This sight brightened my mood; yet, what truly left me flabbergasted was what followed.

"Teach me how to play it properly, and it is yours," Alistair said.

For a moment, I thought I had misheard him. Then, I looked up with a start. "What?!"

"Though I have read many a treatise on the subject, and observed violinists whenever the great hall was used, an instrument so dependent on posture was too difficult to learn without a tutor. I have not used it in years."

I grasped for words. "Well, of course I would be glad to teach you—but what was the second point you made?"

"That I would give it to you," Alistair repeated patiently.

"To play, you mean?"

"To take with you, upon your departure."

At that, I startled and took a step back. "Why, I couldn't possibly!"

"Why not?"

"Just from the look of it, I can see that it is terribly expensive. You will miss it when it is gone; I would much rather—"

"If you leave it," Alistair interrupted with a smile, "I will use it for firewood. What would you prefer?"

Without much other choice, I relented.

I took some time to regain my own practice, and then I taught him the little that I could. Though I needed a footstool to reach his height and correct his posture, he learned quickly enough that it was soon set aside; and what a natural talent for it he had! It was not only in the music itself; it was in the glide of his arm back and forth, the way the bow of the instrument dipped with each movement of his chin. His hair swung softly around him, an ease softening his brow, and I thought as I watched that I had seldom seen such an elegant thing.

Among his old instruments, Alistair also found one or two simple flutes for me to use. These were larger than the sort I was accustomed to, long and hollow, and quite cumbersome for hands unused to them. Yet, the sound that they made was mellow and sweet, and I played them enough to grow comfortable.

When we had grown tired of our lessons, Alistair and I often played together—usually with him on the pianoforte or the harpsichord, and me accompanying him on the flute or the violin—and brought life to the music of ages past. These sessions sometimes produced sounds so passionate and mournful that I forgot the entire world; and from the manner in which he gazed off as he played, with a softened brow and a look almost yearning, I fancied that he felt the same.

One month came and went so quickly, from that fateful day when we first made our deal, that I could barely believe it had passed. Despite the awful beginning of the entire ordeal, I found myself happier than I had been in years, and to realize this was so odd that I sometimes laid awake and questioned my own judgment.

There was no way to avoid the essential truth. I did not merely enjoy Alistair's company; I had come to treasure it. Given this, how was I meant to feel about what he had done to me? I was no closer to understanding his reasons; such questions now seemed so distant that they could have taken place in some novel that we had read together, and then forgotten.

Indeed, though we had taught each other much, we seldom told each other about our own selves at all. There seemed to be an unspoken agreement: we would divulge only what was necessary to aid our studies, and no more.

Consequently, it did not take long for my curiosity to turn ravenous. The more time I spent with him, the more I longed to know everything about him. To this end, I searched desperately for any occasion to ask more of his past without prompting him to ask the same of me.

The solution came to me towards the end of October, when Alistair introduced a new topic to our lessons. He first mentioned it on the occasion of our fourth feeding together, as we walked back beneath a particularly beautiful night:

"Say, Mr. Bedford," he mused. "Have you ever painted?"

*　　*　　*

What a marvel Alistair's painting was!

I had been so involved in the other subjects as to forget all about the matter that dominated the manor's walls; but once I was reminded of it, I was desperate to see it, and he obliged.

On our first attempt, he showed me how he painted the moor. We chose an opportune spot outside, beneath a tall willow near the manor, and brought stools and an easel out. Alistair then placed his canvas up, and raised his eyes over the roiling earth, across the tossing grasses that stretched towards the brink of the horizon; he lifted his chin lifted slightly as he considered the scene. The wind soared up, a cool autumn breeze that fluttered at the ribbon I had tied in his hair that morning—and then he painted.

Oh, how he painted!

It was immediately apparent that he was not only good, but brilliant. I had never seen the execution of such expressiveness, matched with such precise vision—not only in the art itself, but also in his poise, in the way he straightened his back and held his brush with his wrist tilted just so. In great swaths and petting lines, he shaped the world out of a mastery of colours, olive greens and dry golden-greys for the grasses, darker blues and silvers for the skies. He took what was ordinary and elevated it to sublime beauty, spun straw into gold, and made it seem nearly effortless—the slightest stroke of his brush seemed to instantly transform into its subject, as though he knew the very language of the earth by heart!

We conversed while he painted, perched there like two herons in the night. Alistair would half-sit on his stool as he described his methods to me; he spoke on the way colour and form came before detail, the way warmth and cold were more alive than simple light and dark, and the way that gesture triumphed over precision.

Once he had finished explaining, he handed me the brush and invited me to add to his composition. With the very first stroke, I felt that I had ruined it, and could have wept; but Alistair only took the brush back, laughing at my anguished expression, and easily turned the clumsy stroke I had made into a very reasonable tree.

"Look," he coaxed, as he traced out the branches. "You must learn that anything can be salvaged. To paint is not to rush to perfection; it is to converse with your subject, until you are certain you have seen it with clear eyes."

"But we saw the same tree," I said, rather dumbfounded. "Why does yours look so much more like it?"

Alistair glanced towards me and tilted his head. "What colour is it?"

"The tree? Brown."

"It is," he acknowledged, "But it is also grey, and red, and green, all in different places. Until you have struggled to paint it, you have not truly seen all of these colours. You must try again and again, until you do."

"But your painting is so beautiful! What if I ruin it?"

Alistair gave me a long look. Then, he turned to the painting, picked up his brush, and—despite my shout of dismay—painted an enormous, dripping bat on the beautiful moorland sky, even giving it a lopsided frown.

Then, he returned the brush to me and smiled graciously. "Now you cannot ruin it. Go on."

Despite feeling that my soul had been torn in two, I turned back to the canvas, and was now able to work far more freely.

Yet, on the following day, when our exercises on this canvas were nearly done, Alistair seemed to grow preoccupied by something else. Much to my growing dread, he glanced at me every so often before returning his gaze to his palette.

"What is it?" I said, once I could ignore it no longer.

He tilted his head. "I have had a thought."

"God help me."

"What a dispiriting attitude," he said, feigning offence. "What harm could I possibly have in mind?"

"Any of a wide variety of awful things."

"Then you will tell me whether you think it so awful. Very simply, I was considering that I have painted this landscape many times already."

"Yes?"

"And that a change in subject would be quite refreshing."

All at once, I caught his amused eye and understood immediately. "Why, you couldn't mean—!"

Alistair twirled a brush through his fingers. "Oh, but I could."

"That—" I felt horribly flustered. "Absolutely not. That is preposterous!"

He seemed surprised by the force of my reaction. "Is it truly?"

"Yes! You have the entire moor at your disposal; paint that! What could you possibly gain from wasting paint on me?"

"Why is the idea so loathsome to you?"

My reasons, though I would not confess them, were twofold. The first was that I found it embarrassing; how foolish I would feel, to see such a simple and inconsequential person as I painted by a hand better-suited to depicting royalty! Yet, it was also the process itself that irked me. The very thought of him watching me, trailing his eyes across me for hours, frayed my nerves from the mere consideration.

"I am too plain," I began, but was suddenly interrupted.

Alistair had reached out and taken my chin, tilting my head as though inspecting some fine thing, and said charmingly:

"You have such animated eyes, Mr. Bedford. I beg of you to let me paint them."

I was mute with shock.

Seeming to realize that he had rattled me, Alistair released my chin and gave a genteel smile. "Ah, but forgive my enthusiasm. Perhaps a unique visage must preserve its mystery."

Understanding that he was trying to dignify my refusal, I was quite embarrassed; but I was inclined to reward politeness, and wished to give him something in return.

Yet, just then, I had an idea.

"Very well," I said stiffly. "I will allow you to use me as your subject—on one condition."

He brightened. "Oh?"

I gathered my courage, and at last put forth my proposal:

"While you do, you must allow me to ask you anything I wish."

He tapped his paintbrush curiously. "Anything on what subject?"

"On yourself."

Alistair blinked, and seemed distantly surprised.

Nevertheless, I went on. "When I ask anything about your life, you answer vaguely. Nearly a month we have spent together, and what have I to show for it? What do I know of you? Nothing!"

"Ah."

"Is that assent?"

Gazing off over his canvas and into the distance, Alistair seemed to consider it carefully.

I waited with bated breath.

Finally, he faced me and gave a courteous smile. "It is."

I nearly choked with surprise. "Really?"

"While I paint, you may ask anything you choose, and I shall answer."

Suddenly suspicious, I wondered what his motive was. Alistair was sly, I had learned, and prescient much like a chess player; without question, he had glanced a few moves ahead and found this to give him some benefit.

But curiosity and excitement overwhelmed my suspicions. "Will you tell the truth?"

He raised a hand to his chest. "On my honour."

"And what honour is that?"

"Mr. Bedford, how cold of you. My honour is my life."

Believing that he spoke in earnest, I felt guilty, and mumbled:

"Fine, then! Though, you always say that you consider yourself dead…"

Then he smiled devilishly, and I realized that he had been taunting me. That set me off, and he laughed, and we remained outside for some time longer until the sky began to lighten with the first rays of sun over the horizon.

CHAPTER XI

"Could you straighten your back?" Alistair said, as he blended a few colours on his palette.

I loosened my shoulders and drew myself up in my seat. "Like this?"

"Precisely."

Alistair lifted his head, then, and affixed me with a deadly focus. I chose not to meet this frightening gaze; instead, I looked glumly out through a window into the night. Beyond the latticed glass, it seemed more ominous than usual; the darkness seemed a dead stare, and the shivering grasses were pulled into the distance by a high and whistling wind.

Unnerved, I averted my eyes back to the candled warmth of the room; and I was suddenly conscious of how Alistair's shadowed form, previously the source of my greatest fear, now instilled a strange comfort by virtue of its familiarity.

He had draped his coat over the back of his chair and

remained in a plain shirt, whose sleeves he had pushed up to his forearms. Over his lap, he had draped a broad sheet, which was already well-stained with the marks of other paintings; and against his chin, he tapped the wooden end of his brush as he thought.

I was sitting opposite him in a simple chair, by a table over which he had arranged a book, the violin, and a small globe. This globe, I spun idly here and there out of nervousness.

"Very well," Alistair said finally, leaning back. His gaze shifted to his canvas, and he waved a hand. "You may begin your interrogation."

There it was, my permission! My eagerness overwhelmed my worries, and my chest thrummed with excitement; I had lost sleep pondering my questions, though I knew not with which to begin. Finally, I settled on the simplest.

"I would like a proper introduction," I said, "As though we were meeting for the first time."

"For the very first time?"

"Indeed."

He gave a little smile towards his canvas, as though sharing some private joke with himself, but obliged.

"Then it is a pleasure to make your acquaintance. I am Alistair de Beaumont, fifth Count of Lerin, of the peerage of Spain. Lerin was in Navarre, which in turn was subject to the crown of Castille; but whether any of this yet holds true, or whether my title still exists at all, I don't know for certain."

Met with so much information, I quieted to think it through. "Very well," I said, after a moment. "A Spanish count. That, I knew; but how did you come to live in England?"

"I was born here. The title was inherited from my father."

Then, he stopped and continued to paint.

"And?" I urged.

His brush paused, and he glanced up. "And what?"

"What else?"

"What else would you like to know?"

"Sir," I chided. "You promised to answer my questions fully and truthfully, did you not? Speak! Say more! I have all the time in the world; you are never so reticent when you describe the lives of kings. Why are you so reluctant now?"

He sighed, dabbing his brush delicately in a pool of blue paint. "Is that your question?"

"It is now. Why do you avoid speaking of your past?"

When he answered, his voice was strange, as though it came from within some sepulchrous depth.

"You must understand that the matters you ask about are centuries old, Mr. Bedford. Everyone who I once knew is long-gone, and even the clothing that I wore then has mouldered. These are stories so lost to time that only I remember them; and as such, they might as well be dreams."

"But if you tell them to me, they live again!"

Alistair gave a sly glance from the corner of his eye, and answered ominously.

"Some histories are best left dead."

I swallowed, and fell silent for a few moments. Then, I reached up and spun the globe.

"Hold still," he murmured.

Lowering my hand back the table, I sighed. "To forget your history must give you a great sense of freedom; I understand that—believe me, I do!—but I must beg you to reveal it all the same. I know that it is selfish to ask, but you have spoiled me with your lectures."

Alistair smiled towards his canvas, this time with genuine

mirth. "Have I?"

"Quite irrevocably."

"Then I shall take responsibility," he said, and at last seemed to resign himself to his fate. "Let us start from the beginning. I was born in 1556. Do you recall who reigned over England then?"

"Why…oh, that must have been Queen Mary." All at once, I lifted my head and cried out: "I see—and she married Philip of Spain!"

"Very good, Mr. Bedford," Alistair said, as he painted. "This union was meant to restore Catholicism to England, and was quite unpopular, as you may know; but even so, my father—a rather minor figure in the Spanish nobility—decided to come to England in search of trade and diplomatic alliances."

"I see; so he believed the union would bring opportunity?"

"I suppose."

"But why Yorkshire, of all places?"

Alistair nodded. "A fine question. Yorkshire, at the time, was sympathetic to the Catholic cause; it was therefore hospitable to a Spaniard, even after Mary Tudor's execution. Indeed, the Northern Rebellion would take place when I was young, though my father was not so foolish as to join it."

I was rather impressed. "It seems a great risk for your father to have lived here."

"Indeed."

"Then why did he remain, even after the union of the kingdoms was no more? Was the trade so lucrative?"

"Not really," Alistair replied. "Not enough to justify the risk."

After a pause to clean a brush, he glanced towards me with an impish look.

"The trade was an excuse, for the true reason was another; and therein lies a tale of intrigues, murder and secrets, faith and revenge, that I am *certain* would thrill you to hear."

I held still in rapt attention. "And that is?"

"And that is a tale for another time."

"Oh, sir, for God's sake!"

"Ah—lean back again, you have changed your pose."

"You said that you would answer my questions!"

Alistair put a hand to his chest, giving a courtly bow. "Mr. Bedford, on my honour as a Spaniard, or a vampire, or whatever aspect of my character you trust the most, I promise that I will tell you the entire story one day. You must believe me, it is much too complicated to tell while I paint."

His earnestness embarrassed me, and I leaned back with a flushed face. "Fine, then; I won't let you forget it. Now, you were saying that your father…"

"He arrived here and sired me."

"Was your mother also a Spaniard?"

There was a pause, which almost seemed a hesitation; but at last, he returned to his painting and went on. "He brought her from Spain, yes. However, I never knew her well; she was confined to her quarters, and I was seldom allowed to see her. I was told that she was mad, and that her affliction could pass to me."

"Why—mad!" I exclaimed.

"That was the story. When I grew older, however, I would steal away to meet her, and I never thought her mad at all; she had a sharp wit and a wicked laugh, and seemed to understand me better than any other, though she was in her own way afflicted."

"You had to find her in secret?"

"Indeed."

"How awful," I said, and shuddered. "To be cleaved from a member of your own family who you love—that is the cruelest possible thing."

"Whether it was the cruelest, I know not," Alistair said, with a sardonic smile. "It may have been the least among the cruelties that took place here."

I hesitated. "Cruelties?"

"My father was the demanding sort."

Suspecting that this was a difficult subject, I cleared my throat and chose the roundabout path. "What did he want from you?"

Alistair answered placidly, as he dabbed at his palette. "A legacy was his obsession. His dream was eternal honour for his bloodline: a son who would be near to nobility, well-instructed, disciplined, whose connections would straddle kingdoms and create some great noble house in his name."

"What lofty expectations!"

"Too lofty for anyone, but most of all for me. I was weak-willed and prone to fainting, but this never deterred my father; it only welded shut the door of my opulent cage, and condemned me to the whims of his authority."

In the silence that followed, the bristles of his brush against the canvas were the only sound. I watched the roll of his shoulder as he leaned closer to the painting, and stayed pensive for a while before speaking.

"That seems intolerable."

"It was, for some time." He swirled his brush in its cup. "Then, when I was fifteen, my poor mother died; and I swore revenge against all that had held her prisoner, and burned every fetter that had impeded me. With nothing to lose, I turned wild."

I was breathless. "What did you do?"

266

"I threw myself into debauchery, wishing to bring every sort of shame on my family's name. Oh, Mr. Bedford; if you had known me then, you would be far less charitable. Drinking, gambling, havoc of any kind—and lust, of course. I lost count of the guests in my bed."

At his descriptions, particularly the last, I could not conceal my shock.

He laughed at the look upon my face. "There it is. Scandalous, was I not?"

"Quite—but why fall to that? Couldn't you escape instead?"

"Escape to where? Even if my infirmity could be overlooked, only poverty and death awaited me."

"But if you remained, would your father not punish you for your transgressions?"

"He tried." Alistair then raised his eyes flashing to mine. "And upon his last such attempt, he was murdered."

Thunder rumbled outside suddenly, as if on cue. He held my gaze a while, as though waiting to see my reaction.

"By whom?" I managed.

"Not by me," Alistair said, returning his attention calmly to his canvas, "And not on my direction, nor with my prior knowledge; so it was no patricide, and you can stop your anxious spinning of that globe. Hold still so that I may paint you properly."

I had not noticed that my hand had occupied itself in such a manner. Embarrassed, I let it fall away. "But if not you, then whom?"

"The details are a story for another time."

"All right," I said. "But tell me: how old were you?"

"Twenty-one, I believe."

"Then, at least after that, you must have been free."

"Yes, in a sense, but my most painful problem remained unsolved. Nothing helped, even as my debauchery ran its course after his death."

"What manner of problem?"

Something passed over his face, then, a steady type of ache that I recognized from experience. Somewhere behind the refined caution of those eyes, I caught sight of a hunger to speak and to be listened to. However, his answer was simple.

"I was lonely. Do raise your chin again, Mr. Bedford."

I was woken from my trance by the request. Lifting my head once more, I swallowed.

"I was lonely," he murmured. "And you can surely imagine that what followed didn't help."

"What happened?"

At that, he moved his eyes to me, amused, until I realized what he meant.

"Oh, when you were…"

With a nod, Alistair said nothing and returned to painting. For some time, he remained silent; it was I who spoke quietly.

"Would you tell me about that? I won't force it from you, but I would very much like to know how you became a vampire. I suppose it's the only thing we have in common, and I…well…"

I heard the light tapping of a brush being drawn out of water, but nothing else.

With a sigh, I sank back in my chair. "Either way, it's your choice. I only—"

"I intend to tell you, Mr. Bedford. I am only considering how best to describe it."

I lifted my gaze in surprise, and stared at him quite intently.

After a few moments, still fixed on his canvas, Alistair shrugged. "I can tell you what I know, but in truth there isn't much to tell. I know nothing of why it happened; I suspect I never will."

After having another glance at me, he scraped more paint onto his palette before continuing.

"It happened on the occasion of a great festivity here, at the manor. This event was held in midsummer; I was bored and hoping to entertain myself. Years had passed since the death of my father, and I had nobody left near me—no family, few friends, and few prospects; I had only the vulgar reputation I had made for myself, a few business alliances, and a title from a homeland that I barely knew."

Another groan of thunder sounded in the distance, and soon, the soft pattering of rain started against the windows. The sound softened Alistair's voice, and put me into a sort of trance as the story continued.

"I was determined not to pity myself. I knew that I had more than most, a respectable sum of money which would sustain me; but I was deathly lonely, and always seeking something to fill that scarcity. It just so happened that on that night, I was approached by—"

"A woman in a black hood?" I interrupted suddenly.

Alistair froze, and for the first time seemed veritably shocked.

"I had a dream," I said clumsily. "I saw her."

After a moment, Alistair lowered his brush and gave me a long look. "How odd. I must have inadvertently passed my dream to you; I was not aware that living blood had such an ability." He paused, and tilted his head. "How much did you see?"

"Only the woman approaching," I answered quickly. "Nothing more."

"Then that is for the best," Alistair said, and dabbed at his palette before returning to the canvas and continuing:

"The event, which I am glad you didn't have to suffer through in memory, came entirely by surprise. At first, the woman merely approached. She had distinct features, which I had never seen; I could not discern from whence she came, and this intrigued me. Perhaps knowing that my curiosity would gain her something, she came and bid me to show her something of interest in the manor."

"Something of interest?" I said, confused.

Alistair smiled pleasantly and leveled a look at me. "With tendencies like mine, you might imagine what this implied."

I quickly fell silent, and gave him a withering look.

"I'm only telling you the truth," Alistair said simply, and went on:

"I led her up the stairs, and showed her the view of the great hall from the gallery above. Here, we lingered for some time. Then, covering her mouth with one hand, as though shy, she smiled sweetly and asked for a private audience with me in a quieter room."

The rain outside gained force, and I shuddered in knowledge of what would come; but Alistair simply went on, as though he had recited this story often.

"With this request, there could be no more doubt of her intentions. I took her up to my room, and closed the door behind us. Yet, before even the first kiss, she gave a lovely smile and opened her mouth."

"Her fangs," I whispered.

"Sharp, and quite obviously inhuman," Alistair replied. "Once I saw them, I sprang up in alarm; but before I could reach the door, she grasped me with impossible strength and interred them in the flesh of my throat."

I was hushed and terrified. "She drank, then?"

"She meant to, but it was then that I made the decision that would condemn me: I managed to wrench myself free, and then sank my teeth into her neck until I tasted blood."

"So you fought!"

"Yes, Mr. Bedford, but by then I was as good as dead. In dislodging her bite, I had pulled away too forcefully, and she had torn my neck open in her fury. I could feel the warmth of all my life-blood spilling in a great river down my neck, and in a hopeless final moment, I mounted the only defense I could."

I waited with bated breath while he wiped his brush on a rag, then said plainly:

"I shoved her to an open window, and by some miracle managed to push her out."

"From the third floor," I realized in horror.

"And all the way down to the first, where the guests were waiting, and a cacophony of screams soon sounded."

Alistair paused for a moment, as though hearing these long-forgotten cries; but he soon shook his head.

"By then, I knew that I was nearing death; my sight was slipping into darkness, and weakness held me sunk in my pain. Knowing not that the blood I had tasted from her neck would resurrect me, I crawled to the cupboard with the last of my strength and closed the door. I still hoped to hide from her, and somehow save myself; but in my heart I knew that I would not survive, and that I would die alone, never to know the reason for my murder."

Hearing these hopeless words, I could not help but feel an ache within my chest. "And then?"

Alistair peered out from beside the canvas, lightening the mood with a smile. "And then I awoke."

"In the very same cupboard?!"

"Plastered in blood, but very much alive."

I was flabbergasted. "Nobody came to look for you in your own bedroom?"

"Nobody dared. As I would learn much later, the vampiress had transformed into a beast, a great white wolf, and gone madly into the crowd in search of blood. After killing two others and maiming a third, she fled into the night. The manor was abandoned—with the exception of one dear variety of guest."

"Oh?"

"Robbers," Alistair said, with amusement. "I'm certain they regretted ignoring the warnings when they saw me emerge from my room, matted in blood and starved to the point of madness. I was lucky to have my first drink of blood thus, and they were lucky to escape with their lives."

I was confused, and furrowed my brow. "But why were you starved to madness? When I awoke, I wasn't even thirsty."

"Because I fed you while you turned."

All at once, there was an uncomfortable air between us. We had returned to the subject of my own turning, which until now we had tactfully avoided.

"What?" I said weakly.

Seeming to have realized his mistake, Alistair spoke quietly, evidently wishing to avoid the subject. "You stirred and woke at intervals, murmuring senseless things. You would not rest again until I offered…"

He seemed to hesitate, searching for the most delicate way to describe it.

"Some libation, from the most obvious path through which it coursed."

I felt a chill of horror crawl up my spine, at the thought of my body senselessly feeding like a leech from Alistair's neck. It was at once uncanny and repulsively familiar.

Desperate to change the subject and forget that entire event, whose presence in my thoughts was now a nuisance and an interruption to me, I quickly returned to the prior subject. "When you awoke, did you understand what was happening?"

"Yes and no," Alistair replied, clearly relieved that the conversation had moved along. "At first, I thought myself a ghost, or a resurrected corpse. A *vampire* was not a well-known creature in my time, and would not be for perhaps another century. Instead, after realizing that I had the capacity for transformation, I instead thought myself a werewolf."

"A *werewolf!*" I cried out. "Do they also exist?"

"Whether they exist, or whether they are simply another human conception of a vampire, I know not. I have certainly never met one, nor any other type of preternatural creature. As far as I can tell, we are alone."

The finality of this statement, mingled with the steady drum of rain in the darkness, made hollowness settle in my chest. I wondered briefly once more, as I often had, whether Alistair had turned me in order to know another of his kind.

But I was roused from my thoughts by Alistair's mellow voice. "Well? Is the good Mr. Bedford satisfied with the answers I have provided?"

Deciding to spare him from more painful questioning, I sat back and exclaimed—"Not at all! I have much more to ask."

We continued to speak, and I asked him about simpler things: details of all kinds concerning his time, and the history that he witnessed. He answered me tirelessly that day until I was satisfied, and when I went to bed I could barely sleep from thinking about it.

He had been aloof and aloft once, I supposed; he had gazed down at the world, possessing both everything and nothing, and searched for meaning that would not come. In the passions of his apathy, he had stood at the edge of his narrow world and called out to it, daring it to answer him; and one night, it had.

Why he had chosen to inflict upon me the same catastrophe, I still did not understand. Oddly, however, I found that this question no longer plagued me. Alistair had never understood the reason for his turning; he had made his peace with this unknown, and lived for centuries alongside it. I wondered whether I could do the same.

*   *   *

The painting was not finished in one session, and he vehemently refused to reveal it until it was. Therefore, after giving it a day to dry, we returned to the same arrangement: once more, he gave his conciliatory smile, telling me with a wave of his hand to begin my questioning. Gladly, I obliged.

However, after some time on this second session, his answers were no longer satisfying me. The questions I truly meant to ask felt too sensitive, and remained in my heart. Somewhere within me, growing swiftly was a desire to understand him much further than his tidy explanations would allow. His words were devoid of any the melancholy I sensed him to contain, which begged to be unraveled.

Yet, before I could gather the courage to ask in a voice unclouded by hesitation, my own curiosity was turned upon me.

It was the third session of his work on the painting, and I was sitting in the very same chair in that room. From the dampness of the earth outside, the sweet musk of wood was diffused in the air with the acridity of paint.

My back had grown stiff with discomfort, and I had begun to let my shoulders down.

"Sit up straight," Alistair said, glancing up from the painting.

"I am already—"

"A little more."

"Look; quite straight!"

"Not yet. You only need to pull your shoulders back—"

"This much is enough!"

At that, he gave a very deliberate pause. Then, he held my gaze and tapped a brush against his chin. "Are you tired of this pose?"

"Slightly," I admitted.

A sly smile crept across his lips. "How interesting. I have just had an idea."

"Absolutely not! I have had enough of your ideas."

He laughed. "Why, but I think you may agree."

"I doubt it."

"It involves a far more comfortable pose."

I turned and watched him suspiciously.

"I was thinking," he went on, "That this painting is nearly finished, and that I ought to begin another. This time, I would like to have you recline."

I found myself at a loss, having expected something far more sinister. "Oh, that is actually—"

"*But,*" he added, with relish.

My face fell. "But what?"

To my dismay, he seemed to enjoy the reaction, giving an indulgent laugh before speaking again. "There *is* one condition."

"It is always conditions with you!"

"Would you like to hear it?"

"No!"

"Are you certain?"

I sighed and leaned back against the chair. "Fine. What is it?"

"While I paint, and you lie recumbent," he said, pointing the end of a brush towards me, "It is *your* turn to answer my questions."

For a few seconds, I was shocked, and stared at him uncomprehending. Then, with passionate force, I replied.

"Absolutely not! Never!"

He sighed. "Oh, Mr. Bedford."

"No!"

"Why not?"

"Simply because!" I exclaimed. "I have always kept my life private, and—oh! Is that why you agreed to my questions? To encourage me to answer yours?"

Alistair bowed his head. "It did, perhaps, occur to me."

"I'm sorry to inform you that you have wasted your time."

"You would not be compelled to answer anything you deemed too private. I would not intrude any farther than you allow me to."

I turned my head away and scoffed. "You say that, knowing full well—no, worse than that!—*intending* that I should feel compelled."

At that, Alistair gave a conciliatory smile, though he looked almost sad. "You read too much malice into my intentions, Mr. Bedford. I am only as curious to know your life as you were to know mine, and decided that a simple trade of interrogations would ease your misgivings."

What he said was reasonable, and I believed in the innocence of his curiosity; but in truth, I was rather afraid. My circumstances were unappetizing at best, and repulsive at worst.

Thus far, through hard work, I had upheld the illusion of dignity, and throughout our time together we had played the part of equals. How would he regard me, if I told him my pauper's tales?

Dejected and now violently embarrassed, I realized how ardently I had come to value his opinion of me. Whenever he praised me as we learned together, I had been so indulgent as to let it enter my heart. How foolish, to have thought myself fit to be some nobleman's companion!

With my face burning, I tried to deter him. "There is nothing I can tell you that will make you esteem me more, and indeed the opposite may occur."

"I doubt that."

"I was born into poverty, and my life was dreary and boring for a very long time. There! You have the entire story."

"Then you should have no qualms in telling it." Alistair coaxed. "You ought not be afraid. There is very little that would shock me, and less still that would repel me."

I was glum. "You will eat those words."

His expression blazed with defiance. "Then test my candour."

Hearing this confident promise, I wavered in my obstinacy. When others had asked of my history, it was always with morbid curiosity, which turned to discomfort once even the smallest of blemishes was divulged; but Alistair's eyes were lit with the sort of devouring curiosity that seemed far too true to falter. Seldom had anyone so earnestly asked to know more of me.

A soft feeling lulled me, and I was suddenly at a loss. "You really want to know?"

"I do."

"Then fine," I said with a sigh, and sank in my chair. "Only remember that I warned you."

Alistair's eyes brightened like stars; he was satisfied, and apparently ready to do anything in his power to prevent a reversal. Putting down his brush, he bowed. "You have my utmost gratitude, Mr. Bedford."

Still sore over the loss, I mumbled: "I sense that I will come to regret this."

"Hardly; but that is enough of that. Would you like to see the painting?"

This piqued my curiosity. "May I?"

"Come have a look."

I slipped off my seat, and walked over to stand behind the easel with him—and almost instantly, stepped back in surprise!

It was my form, of course, rendered uncannily accurate in the paint. Alistair had traced in every detail of my clothing: clay browns and greys for my waistcoat and cream-white for my cravat, all enveloped in the darkness of my jacket, which, far from being a simple black, seemed formed from various nightlike colours. These choices made my ordinary clothing take on a sheen of refinement, and doubly so with the somber arrangement of objects on the table by my elbow. Yet, this was not what startled me most.

I stared into my own face, which he had depicted with a softness and grace unlike anything I had ever seen in my looking-glass; but the eyes! These, he had drawn with a look of conviction so striking that it gave me a terrific chill.

"What do you think?" Alistair said, gazing upon it rather proudly.

Recovering from my mute shock, I shook my head. "It is wonderful."

He glanced towards me and tilted his head. "Be honest. Your expression tells another story."

"I was honest! It is wonderful—even though it isn't me."

Alistair seemed amused. "Why not?"

"Well, you made everything look very grand, and…"

Realizing that if I spoke the truth, I would be goading him to praise me, I suddenly flushed and redirected my thoughts.

"That is to say, sir, that this is the sort of painting that the owner of some luxurious home might hang in his study; and I can hardly imagine owning a place such as that, and therefore having a painting such as this."

But Alistair was awfully discerning, and gave me a sly look. "Is *that* what you meant, Mr. Bedford?"

"Why not," I said tartly, and went off to return the chair to its place.

CHAPTER XII

How I came to regret having agreed! I anticipated the questioning for all the following night, with a steadily growing sense of dread; and to my despair, Alistair, conversely, seemed to grow more and more eager. When I grew quiet and withdrew to my thoughts, I felt his cunning and inquisitive looks upon me, as though he was already in the process of deciphering.

I could only imagine that a mouse being chased by a cat would feel as I did!

It was near midnight when my reckoning came. Alistair had become suspiciously pleasant towards me by then, but I saw through his attempts to sweeten me to comfort and felt positively sick with dread. At last, however, he stood.

"Very well. I had intended to wait, but I can see that I am tormenting you. Shall we?"

I closed my book and sighed.

At least he had not lied about the position being comfortable.

The chaise lounge that he chose was pleasant enough; but oh, nothing could have given me comfort then! As I gazed up towards the ceiling, I could only hear the steady clip of his steps moving somewhere beyond my head as he prepared his work. Yes, I thought despondently—this was the dread of waiting for the surgeon as he arranged his instruments.

The ceiling was painted, I noticed, as I searched for something to steady my nerves. This room was a parlour on the second floor, where I had scarcely ever looked up. Only now did I see various figures in robes, lounging among artfully coloured clouds which drifted through a dawn sky. It was Alistair's work, and the wistful air which gave so much life to his work was fully present here.

All of a sudden, however, the sight was interrupted. His tall form loomed over me. "Are you comfortable?"

"No," I said, glumly.

He nearly laughed, but left it at a smile. "*Physically,* are you comfortable?"

"I suppose."

"Come now, Mr. Bedford, there's no need to be so gloomy. Do you remember what I told you?"

I shook my head, ever more despondent.

"You may refuse my questions," he reminded me, "And I would blame you not. You are beneath no obligation, even now, and you may stand to—"

"Oh, don't tempt me!" I cried out. "I have made my choice, and I have made it soundly; but every minute you dally, my nerves soar and my patience drains away. Ask while you still can."

He gave a look of mingled helplessness and amusement. "Mr. Bedford, these are a few questions about your life, not the guillotine.”

“Give me the guillotine.”

Laughing quietly, he turned and strode swiftly away. His hair, which I had tied with a blue ribbon that night, spun past my line of sight and disappeared. “We are going to have a pleasant chat. A *tête-à-tête*, if you will.”

“I don’t much like the sound of that.”

“Then you ought to have studied your French more carefully.” His steps stopped, and were followed by the creak of a seat. “Now, then, Mr. Bedford, will you tell me to do my worst?”

I turned my head towards him. “If until now you have been at anything but your worst, sir, I would rather not.”

He gave a deep and resonant laugh, which almost cheered me; but I soon remembered my fate, and sank back into morose thoughts.

At that moment, for the second consecutive night, a gentle rain began outside. It pattered against the windows, and as I turned my head to look, I was distracted. Like sheets waving in the grassy wind, the droplets shimmered and beaded in the dark.

I closed my eyes.

“May I begin?” Alistair asked.

There was a groan of thunder outside.

“Mr. Bedford?” he repeated.

I was jolted from my thoughts, and opened my eyes. “Why— yes.”

“Good,” he murmured. I heard the scrape of his palette, followed by his thoughtful murmur: “Then I would like…how did you say it? A proper introduction.”

Remembering what I had subjected him to, I sighed. “As though we were meeting for the first time?”

“Please.”

And so, I gave my first answer:

"It is a pleasure to be at your service," I said quietly. "I am Avery Bedford, and that is all. Beyond that, I have little else to introduce. I have no titles, no formal profession, nor any magnificent history embroiled with mine to add."

"That may be," Alistair replied, "But you must have been born somewhere."

"Well, of course."

"Where?"

"York. I was born in the city, and lived there for many years."

"With your family?"

I felt a plunge in my gut, and nearly faltered; but I was determined not to lose my courage early, especially when he was still far from the most ignominious detail.

"With my mother," I corrected quietly. "Bedford was my mother's name."

"Ah," Alistair said, with a touch of understanding.

Hearing his tone devoid of the scorn that usually accompanied such a revelation, I felt my heart soften, and ventured further. "Her name was Adelaide Bedford."

At that, I paused, surprised at myself. I had not spoken her name for many years.

"You mentioned that you were poor."

"Very much so."

"But your mother must have worked."

I felt myself grow pale, and answered quickly. "She was sometimes a seamstress."

To my relief, Alistair did not question that. He only hummed. "Not a lucrative trade, I presume."

"No," I replied, and pushed the subject along. "Whenever she lost her work, I begged on the street."

"The two of you were alone."

"Quite alone," I said softly.

"How did you come to be alone?"

I nearly swallowed my words, but gathered my courage. "Well, my mother came from a respectable family, but she was beguiled by a man. He promised marriage, but…"

I let the rest go unsaid. The details were much too crude for easy conversation.

"How cruel," Alistair said pensively. "And you…"

"The result of that brief and unhappy union."

Then, after a moment's hesitation, I added:

"And the cause for her poverty and isolation."

"How so?"

"She chose to flee from all that she knew, to spare me a life of miserable scorn, in a house which would only ever see me as a bastard. It was her greatest sacrifice."

Alistair was quiet for a moment, then replied gently: "That knowledge must have been a heavy burden for you to carry."

"It is," I whispered. "She didn't breathe a word of it until she was on her deathbed. I was twelve years of age when she passed."

"My condolences."

"Thank you," I mumbled.

He spared me a moment to ruminate my grief before continuing:

"Before you knew the truth, who did you think your father was?"

Once more, I grew pale, realizing that we drew near to the subject I wished to avoid most. Quickly, I came up with a half-answer. "I didn't know. I thought up stories, and questioned no further than that."

There was a long silence, and I felt my palms grow warm with sweat; but to my relief, he only went on.

"You said that you begged."

"On the street, yes. I played the flute during the day, or found some simple task that a child could do for a few coins."

"Was that all you did?"

I gazed up at the painting overhead. "Nearly all. In the early mornings, my mother taught me what she could. We had little to read, but she had some education."

"An impressive effort, then."

"It was!" I said, somewhat wistful. "She wished so terribly that I would rise above our situation somehow, and…"

I trailed off, but Alistair mused:

"I suppose there was no chance for any proper school."

"Actually, there was," I said, folding my hands over my chest. I was feeling rather comfortable speaking, which was unusual. "If we had gone to a workhouse, there might have been a small school—but this was no option for us, for we would have been separated there."

"Separated?"

"Workhouses are divided into wards, sir, parents separated from children; it was a terrifying thought to us! She worried that I would meet other boys and turn cruel, and I worried that she would have nobody by her side to help her."

My palms were suddenly clammy from memories of helplessness, and when I spoke next, my voice trembled:

"The world conspired to tear us apart—but we wouldn't have it!"

With that last word I lapsed into silence, embarrassed at the sudden flow of speech; yet he went on, calm as always.

"But you have mentioned that you once lived in a workhouse."

"I did, later on, when she died." A familiar misery ached

within my chest, and it was with effort that I went on. "It was an illness which came on suddenly."

His reply was of the sincerest nature, gentler than I had ever heard him speak. "She must have held great love for you."

"As I did for her. She was kind, and very brave!—sometimes harsh towards me, but only out of fear of my fate."

Nervous, I glanced towards Alistair—he was gazing thoughtfully at the painting which I could not see, for the easel was turned towards him—and wondered whether I was being overly familiar, and too open with my thoughts; but he was only patient and quiet, so I looked back up to the painted ceiling, fixing my gaze upon a cherub with dark wings.

"I was a terrible burden upon her."

"If she took such pains to remain with you, I can hardly believe it."

"She had no choice! Otherwise, she risked creating a monster."

"But you never became one."

I was troubled, and did not answer him. Perhaps sensing some conflict, he was silent a moment before continuing.

"So you went to a workhouse upon her passing. Is that where you found your brief education?"

I shook my head. "How could I, when I was sitting there at a table with ten boys, all of us cold, hungry and tired, doing some menial task? The guardians were cruel, and even beat us. There was little to do but to survive. By then, my dream was to be a clergyman—I saw such pain and misery in the world, and wished to give it hope!—but for *that* I would need to go to university, and for *that* I would need a patron, or some other way to prove myself. All seemed hopeless, and sometimes, I even thought that I…"

With that, I lapsed into silence, surprised by my own words. Rarely had I spoken with such candour, and I was suddenly aware that I was putting together a very gloomy story. Embarrassed, I thought to myself that Alistair must be regretting having asked for it. Those of a higher class often found it disagreeable to hear harsh tales of lower circumstances, at least when they were not prettily resolved by the end; and I feared that Alistair would be similarly moved.

Yet, when I turned my head to him, I found that he had removed his attention entirely from the painting and was watching me fixedly. His look was focused with such intensity that it was nearly suffocating; and I think I realized then that Alistair wished to dissect me to my very bones, and that the rules that had governed interactions with others born in high society would leave me lost with him.

This filled me with a terrified sort of weakness. Not for the first time in his presence, I felt like a mouse before a cat: it seemed clear that he would readily crush me in order to extract my story, and despite the far-fetched nature of the thought I went rather white.

But presently, when I met Alistair's eyes, he moved his gaze away and broke the stare, perhaps noticing my unease. "Then how did you find a school?"

Relieved, I settled back again. "That is the one bright spot in it all. I had a guardian angel: I made a friend in Henry—have I mentioned him?—he is a coachman now, but was a pauper then. He was older than I, and helped me; it was only under the warmth of his attention that I regained some hope. Were it not for him, I fear I may not have survived long enough to see the fateful day when a visitor arrived at the workhouse."

This had indeed been the beginning of the scarce light in my life, and I gave a small smile before continuing:

"It was the headmistress of a boarding school, who was prepared to take on one or two children for charity. I knew it was my only chance, and begged her."

"Begged her?" Alistair said, amused.

"I went on my knees and clasped my hands, and pleaded with all my heart, and—" There was a prickling in my cheeks that signaled a blush. "And even wept, as I recited anything that I could from memory."

"A difficult offer to refuse."

"I suppose it must have been, for she took me."

"So this school…"

"It was a small, lovely place, near the sea—very pleasant. There were fields of grass, and flowers, and small farms scattered nearby. The teachers were strict, and the food dismal; but they told us that they would provide for *one* of the pauper students, the very best, to go to university. The hope was enough to nourish me and redeem my pain."

"But you didn't go."

I sighed. "No."

"Were you not the best student?"

"Of course I was!" I said snappishly. "I worked harder than anyone else."

"Then what happened to the dream of being a clergyman, Mr. Bedford?"

I knew what had happened to it, of course; but the conversation was edging ever closer to the tainted edges of my history, and I became nervous.

"Nothing," I said quickly. "I lost interest in it."

There was a silence. Then, Alistair said very simply: "You may choose not to answer any question, Mr. Bedford, but I would prefer that you not lie."

I swallowed, feeling chastised. "I'm sorry."

"No need for any apology. I know that I'm prying." His voice picked up, inquisitive and searching. "Indeed, I have pondered this for some time. If you want something, I daresay you are likely to pursue it to the very ends of the earth. You would not abandon something unless you were kept from it."

I turned my face away from him, setting my jaw. "There are many reasons that—"

"Perhaps you broke a rule?"

"I would never," I said, indignant, "And that is that!"

"Or perhaps…"

"Sir, that is enough!" I exclaimed.

To my surprise, he surrendered without a fight. "Then it shall be enough," he said smoothly. "I will inquire no further on the subject."

Though I was desperate not to speak any further, I was touched that he had kept his promise despite his curiosity.

Before I quite knew what I was doing, I felt my lips move, and heard myself speak.

"It was the head of the school," I whispered. "A rector."

Alistair watched me intently, and said nothing.

Now resigned to my fate, I went on dully. "When I was deemed the best student, and went to meet him and receive my formal award, I met an unfortunate coincidence."

I swallowed, knowing that the following sentence would condemn me, but spoke anyway.

"He recognized me."

"Recognized you from where, Mr. Bedford?"

"From the room my mother and I shared, at the inn where we lived," I said hoarsely. "For, despite being a holy man, he had several times sought the services of…"

"Your mother," Alistair finished.

Forlorn and mute, I pressed my lips together.

"Did she—"

"She made her living as she had to," I finished for him. I did not wish to hear him say the word, whichever he chose—not in the usual tone of contempt that accompanied it. How terrible it would be, I thought, to hear the sound of his voice tainted with scorn—infused with the disgust that had followed me around every corner, from every crevice of moral society, for all of my life!

Alistair regarded me indecipherably.

With a forceful sigh, I steadied myself and went on. "Well, I was never ashamed of it, mind you—never! But when the rector saw me, perhaps remembering his own shame, he chose to trade his comfort for my dream, and dashed my hopes across the ground—claiming all the while that it was some sad inevitability—as if it made any difference, as if my mother had been anything but a saint, as if the Bible itself doesn't laud the kindness of a simple and virtuous prostitute!"

Now my voice came faster and faster, as I sought to bury that awful event.

"After that, I promised myself that I would find some other path to a righteous life. I would become a servant, and spend my days in moral order and cleanliness—some employment that my mother would have had pride in. Pitying me, the headmistress sent me out to be the deputy to a valet, and from there I became a valet myself. When the old butler left, I was his temporary replacement, and excelled so well at a lesser cost that I was allowed to remain in that position; but all the while, I knew that if I breathed a word of what my dear mother had done to feed me, and thus repulsed the members of this fine household, that I would scarcely have risen beyond the position of a footman!"

With that, I decided that I had said enough, and closed like a trap before finishing:

"There! That is the reward for your curiosity; are you satisfied with it, sir?"

It was there, as I waited in gloomy spirits for his answer, that I realized even more profoundly than before how much I had come to value his opinion of me. What had only seemed to be meaningless habits before—carefully straining the tea leaves from his cup, checking twice in the mirror to ensure my hair was well-arranged, taking care to stand straight in his presence—I now recognized as little pleas for his favour.

Few had ever made any effort to understand me as anything other than a servant or a pauper; I had had never stood a chance against the cunning interest that Alistair held. Through my carelessness, I had opened my heart to his hand, and with any word he was capable of tearing it from my chest. I had given him the power to break my spirit.

But when he spoke, there was no trace of revulsion.

"Oh, Mr. Bedford," he said with ease. "You thought I would scorn you for *that?*"

I glanced over in surprise, just in time to see him stand swiftly from his stool and sweep his hair back over his shoulder. Walking gracefully to me, he settled down onto the plush arm of the chaise-lounge, right by my head; and he looked down at me from there, like some amused raven on its perch.

Immediately, I began to scramble up to sit; but he waved his hand. "Lie back down."

"Sir!"

"Lie down."

Though I hesitated—it struck me as uncouth, to lounge about with him near—I forgave myself that, and laid back. The feeling of it quieted my nerves somewhat, though I still held stiff in anticipation of his words.

"What reason could I have given you to think that I would scorn you?" he said.

Unsure how to answer, I could barely meet his eyes. "To scorn me?"

"To believe that I would consider you contemptible," he said patiently, "After hearing of your struggles; that after spending the better part of—what has it been, two months?—indulging in your tea and your company, that I would throw you aside for a difficult past."

I gave a dry look. "A mongrel is a mongrel, no matter how much tea they serve—"

"Why would it make any difference to me?"

Troubled, I hesitated.

"Do you not believe me?" he said curiously, leaning over to meet my gaze with his. "There is no difference in taste between noble and common blood."

I was flustered to see his face loom above me. "That, I believe, but regardless of taste, surely you know that there remains a difference. Surely you understand that I inherited the spirit of a man inclined to cruelty, who I never met; that from a very young age I saw the very worst in the world, and that it *must* have left some impression; and that those experiences are part of me, and separate me such that I would never fit among nobler stock—"

"And you have emerged still thoughtful and kind," Alistair interrupted, "Which is made all the more impressive by your struggles. Besides, what makes you think that I would better esteem noble stock?"

He slipped off the side of the chaise-lounge and stood, walking to my side, and reached out. I flinched in surprise, as he took hold of my chin; he looked me sharply in the eyes before continuing.

"Have you forgotten what I was, Mr. Bedford? Do you think I would judge what you survived, when my indulgences made me infamous?" He paused, and something bright gleamed in his eye. "Yet, even if you were a devil, not even then would I recoil from you."

I stared in shock. "Why?"

"Because I am too fond of your company," he replied impishly. Then, he released my chin, turned swiftly away, and walked back to the canvas.

At first, I only laid there, startled. As his words echoed in my ears, I was filled with a strange, unrecognized feeling. There was a tightness in my chest, and a warmth that rose to the tips of my ears—something that I could only describe as half excitement and half longing.

In that moment, unwittingly, I gave him a rare thing. For an instant, I think I trusted him completely.

"And you make amusing expressions," he added then.

Immediately, the warmth was replaced by chagrin. "I don't!"

He settled back onto his stool. "But you do."

"I *don't*—"

"There it is now."

I averted my face, embarrassed. "Sir!"

Seeing that, he began to laugh. It was a deep and resounding laugh, which came from within his chest and shook his shoulders.

At first, I wanted no part in it, but his mirth was terribly infectious, and a quivering joy found its way up my throat. It was futile to suppress it, and I could not help but laugh—though it was a peculiar laugh, as though the slightest push could send it into tears.

Regardless, Alistair was visibly delighted, as he often was when he drew out any levity from me. When I finally steadied my breath, he gave a courteous smile and a flourish.

"Incidentally, would you like to see the painting?"

I gave him a curious look, for he rarely showed them so early. "Why, if you'd like to show me—"

But then, I stopped, frozen in shock; because he had taken it from the easel, and turned it around to reveal empty white. There was absolutely nothing on the canvas. It shone benignly in the candlelight.

For a few moments, I only stared in surprise. Then, I let out a startled cry of "*What?*"

"I used the last of my white paint during the last session, and without it the rest of my palette is useless. Could you purchase more when you go into town?"

I stared at him in disbelief.

"Oh," he mused, twirling a brush. "You thought I was *painting*."

"Well, of *course* I did!"

"Ah."

"What do you mean, 'ah'? What were you doing?"

"Why, listening. I only wanted to ask of your history. That was all."

"Then why was I lying down?"

Clearing his throat, he twirled the brush between his fingers. Finally, he answered. "I thought you would say more."

"*Sir!*"

"Am I a villain for making you comfortable?"

"No, but—" I gave a sigh of defeat. "My goodness, you're mad!"

"Perhaps," he admitted politely, then quoted: "But though this be madness, yet there is method in it."

From his intonation, I surmised it to be some line of literature. My curiosity overcame any ire over his mischief, and I could not help but smile. "And what is that from?"

Alistair opened his mouth, then paused and seemed to consider something. After considerable hesitation, he answered: "I can't recall."

"Yes you can!"

"Fine, then; it is from Shakespeare."

I could not fathom why he was behaving so strangely, and pressed on. "Well, don't be coy, which play?"

"Hamlet," Alistair said finally, as though someone had pried the word from him.

"Perhaps we should read—"

"No. I loathe it irretrievably."

"You *loathe* it?" I remarked in surprise. "Why, some works may be better than others, but *loathing?*"

"Indeed," Alistair said, and set down his brush with a smile. "But should you wish to read any other play, I would be glad to accompany you."

He paused then, and tilted his head.

"Say, Mr. Bedford: have you ever acted?"

*   *   *

From this innocent question, we discovered in the following days one of the more amusing pleasures in our studies: the practice of theatre.

Alistair and I would each assume the different characters—
sometimes it proved difficult, when there were more than two—
and act a scene, using any of the rooms in the manor that suited
our fancy.

At first, I was most unused to playing a character, and felt
embarrassed to the degree that my face was red for the entire
performance—something which seemed to stoke Alistair even
further into mischief. Yet, after some time I grew more
comfortable, and even came to enjoy it. Our performances were
never quite serious, always with an edge of jest; but still, how
strange it was for the both of us to act and speak with stormy
words and feelings, when we would never have spoken thus to
each other!

Certainly the strangest moments came whenever a play delved
into a romance, and we had to play the part of lovers. Despite
the humorous flair which Alistair brought to most of these
scenes, reading the lines made me quite nervous; but I attributed
it to my inexperience in romantic affairs, and left it at that.

Yet, when we were standing opposite each other in the garden
behind the manor—he, playing sly Titania, and I, the obstinate
Oberon—I could not help but feel strangely. In the light of the
lamp we had hung up on the ruins of the pavilion, he glowed
golden almost like the genuine fairy queen, and his pantomime
of teasing jealousy felt no less real.

Above all, every time he came near enough that I could see
myself reflected in his eye—when I saw the glint of candlelight
off his receded fangs, as he read his taunting lines with that sharp
and noble mouth of his—I could not forget what he had said to
me that day on the chaise lounge.

Because I am too fond of your company.

What had he meant by those words? Why had he told them

to me? What was I to make of the look in his eyes when he leaned over me and spoke them, the gleam of interest that was nearly a spell?

I was startled to find the strangest and most improbable of possibilities within me. Despite everything. I had begun to consider Alistair my friend.

This was no trivial matter to me. To be on good terms with Alistair, or even to enjoy his company, was not the same as being his genuine friend. The latter implied a level of trust and companionship which I had not experienced anew for many years, and which held the most serious significance in my soul. Loyalty had always been my heart's tendency, and the few friendships in my life had always carried that mark. It was no simple token that I gave away freely.

Then, there was also the matter of reciprocity. In general, Alistair was generous and patient with me, and certainly seemed to enjoy my company; but did he think of me as his friend, as I did him?

There was no way of knowing for certain without asking him directly, which would be too awkward to bear, or waiting for him to refer to me as such. Somehow, I found myself reluctant towards the latter; I preferred the ambiguous affinity that we had, which carried no particular obligation or definition that would restrict it from being the strange beast that it was.

The more I mulled it over, the stranger I felt about it all. I realized that I very much wanted him to consider me his friend, and it plagued me when I laid in bed at night and struggled to quiet my mind.

In the end, I decided that if there remained any barrier between us, it was the inequality of our exchange. He still gave me endlessly more than I gave him, and I wished to correct this and repay him—if not for his instruction and his patience, then at least for having accepted my past with no qualms.

But how could I give something truly valuable to him?

CHAPTER XIII

My answer came one day in the library, when Alistair began to show me something of human anatomy. He brought out several tomes, which had been scribed by hand; these were products of his dissections, he explained, which he had performed a century ago.

When I questioned where he had procured the bodies, he gave a rare look of shame. "In my hubris," he explained, "I thought my studies important enough to become a grave robber, and took the occasional body from the chapel to perform my work. This, I do regret; and if you wish to blame me for it, I would accept any judgment on your part."

Seeing his remorse, which showed every sign of being genuine, I offered no reproach. The sight of a repentant Alistair was so peculiar that it made me wonder what other regrets he had, and my curiosity pushed aside any judgment.

Yet, it was then that he first mentioned his studies on the

nature of the vampire. Over the years, he had subjected himself to different injuries and stresses, keeping careful notes of the results. I listened with great horror to his accounts of these gruesome acts, shuddering at his tale of severing a finger and gasping outright when he described worse.

Yet, it was here that a possibility arose: I wished to give him something in return, and here was something valuable to him which only I could provide! As the sole other vampire who he knew, I was an ideal subject, who could renew his studies to help him distinguish the variations among our kind.

But when I mentioned it to Alistair during a painting lesson, he vehemently refused, in a voice clearly intended to end all inquiry into the subject.

"That is an absolute no," he said, as he leaned over my shoulder to see my progress. "I must admit that I am stunned to hear you raise the idea."

His tone was chastising, and not in a cordial manner; but this only made me redouble my insistence, curious to see where it led.

"What stuns you about it? If you did it to yourself, what is so different here?"

"Because I hate the very idea, and you should speak no more of it. Ah—" He pointed. "Place a shadow here."

I ignored his suggestion. "What do you hate about it?" As I turned to him, I lowered the palette in my hand and gave him a steady look. "No real harm would come to me, and I would soon forget the pain. It would add to our scant knowledge of ourselves—there may never be an equal opportunity!"

"No."

"But why?"

He seemed exasperated, and finally spoke with a sharpness

that I had not heard for months:

"Because I would never forgive myself for harming you."

I was startled, and felt compelled to continue my argument. "You needn't do anything at all. I will gladly perform any—"

"That is *enough*, Mr. Bedford," he said, now absolutely unamused. "Don't try my hand. If I find you cutting yourself open, I will—"

He paused, seeing my look of surprise, and seemed to realize that he had taken on a frightening tone.

"Forgive me," he murmured. Seeing that I would not brush the idea away so easily, he straightened and sighed. "I understand your curiosity, for it was once my own, so you must forgive my hypocrisy; but…"

He lingered on the word, then went on quietly.

"Don't. Please, Mr. Bedford, don't. Can I ask that of you, as a favour?"

I suddenly remembered his reaction a month prior—though it seemed much longer in the past—when I had nearly slit my own throat to prove his weakness. Realizing that his refusal held some depth, I nodded.

"Of course you can!" I said earnestly. "And in return for your gracious manners, I would readily accept—but I wish to know why. That's all I ask."

Alistair gave a look of profound relief, and the tension left his shoulders. Perhaps this was why his reply was so unusual:

"Because I hate to see you suffer." With that, he placed a hand upon my head, and ruffled it slightly in a manner that he had never done before, which made me freeze with surprise. "Remind me not of such possibilities. Frankly, they put me in a terrible mood."

Instantly, I was regretful for having brought up the matter at all, which I had only raised in order to give him something of value. All the while, what I had been fighting had not been his stubbornness, but rather his compassion. How boorish of me!

Deciding to comfort him, I decided to do something just as unusual as what he had done. In reply to his touch, I returned the sentiment; I reached out and lightly pressed his arm.

"You are excelling in that regard," I said jovially. "I haven't suffered much this past month at all! For these weeks your only crime has been your failure to teach me how to paint, which I'm afraid I cannot forgive."

At first, I was afraid that I had crossed some line, for as I removed my hand from his arm, he stared at the place I had touched with an odd look, then directed this look towards me; but then, with a small and incredulous sort of smile, he plucked the brush from my hand.

"Then *listen* to me," he said, with a hint of playfulness, and leaned forward to correct my work.

I crossed my arms and watched him, as he pulled a shadow out from beneath the table that I had been painting. After a while, I responded at last.

"I am listening to you, and I have another proposal."

The movements of his brush paused. "Mr. Bedford…"

"Listen: how about a very mild study? Measure anything you would like, and evaluate anything that you wish without cleaving flesh or spilling blood. There must be something you can find."

He gave a reluctant tilt to his head. "Even so, I wouldn't wish for you to see yourself as some specimen which I use only for my benefit."

"I am a very willing specimen, you will find; and I can learn from the results as much as you."

Alistair considered it for a moment, gazing into the painting.

At last, then, he sighed and nodded.

"For our benefit, then. Very well."

*　　*　　*

On the following evening, we decided to move forward with this idea.

We went to the library as we typically did. This time, however, after opening an old notebook and rifling through it, Alistair gestured to the side without moving his gaze.

"Do sit on the table, over there."

I balked. "The table?!"

"A chair would be too short."

Though I stared at him a moment longer, quite baffled, I soon turned to the desk and pushed the books aside before hoisting myself up to sit. There, I folded my hands and watched him silently for some time.

"Spare me a moment," Alistair murmured, scratching something in with his quill. "An age has passed since last I added to this."

"I'm in no hurry," I replied absently. Though my position on the table felt strange, the view was compelling enough. Alistair's brows were at ease, as he reviewed his notes; but despite his serious look, when he turned his head, the black ribbon I had tied in his hair bobbed playfully. His outfit that day was also more recent than most in his wardrobe, with a dusky waistcoat that could almost be worn outside without drawing attention, were it not for the prodigious cravat; and so, in that moment, he truly seemed like an earnest and clever student.

Then he looked up, and the cool intensity of his eyes undid any illusion of youth.

"What was your date of birth?"

"The—fifteenth of February," I said haltingly, caught off-guard. "Seventeen ninety-nine."

He set the book down on the table beside me, and scratched something in with his quill. Then, he took up a small measuring stick and stepped in front of me, reaching out his hand. "Let me see your nails."

I raised my hand and placed carefully it in his. Though there had been brief instances of touch between us before this moment, somehow this one, warm and sustained, made me feel peculiar. He held my hand very gently in both of his, and I could feel the soft touch of his fingers as they carefully spread mine apart.

His skin was far smoother and less calloused than mine, and to feel such a delicate instrument maneuvering my own coarser hands was at once embarrassing and soothing. Unwittingly, I shivered.

Alistair paused. "Are you cold?"

"No."

A smile curled across his lips, and he glanced up. "Afraid that I will read your palm, then?"

I gave him a dry look. "If there ever was a fortune to find there, it is lost to even the most skillful of chiromancers."

With a look of mischief, Alistair turned my hand over and smoothed my palm with his thumb, holding it before candlelight as though truly inspecting it.

"Oh, stop it," I scolded, though I nearly shivered again. "You have seen nobody's hands but your own for the past two centuries; we both know it—"

But Alistair suddenly drew in a breath, as he traced one of the lines across my palm with his measuring stick. His brow furrowed.

I froze, and grew nervous. "What? What is it?"

"Mr. Bedford," he said in a hush.

"What?"

"I have seen something most unusual."

"For God's sake, what?!"

Then he looked up, and met my eyes before saying with an ominous air:

"A very long life."

Then he broke into dark laughter, and I wrenched my hand back with a flushed face and wounded pride. "Sir!"

He reached out. "Ah, don't remove it. I had truly meant to study something."

But I was still burning with embarrassment. "You've lost your chance."

"Please," Alistair said politely.

"Go on, beg! See where it gets you."

"You can read my tea leaves tomorrow, and find all manner of hideous fates in my future. I will not complain."

His tone was so earnest, and his long hands poised so elegantly so as to receive mine between them, that I hesitated. At last, I succumbed to my own weakness; his touch had been pleasantly calming, even when he was feigning divination, and I was curious to feel it again. To a mind as restless as mine, it had offered a rare sense of quietude.

"Thank you," Alistair said, when at last he received my hand between his own. This time, he played no tricks; he only took up his measuring stick and laid it across the nail of my ring finger.

Yet, despite his return to earnest study, I felt a mounting sense of nervousness. What was it?

"I will cut this nail," Alistair said, and lifted up a small pair of scissors. "Because you drink no living blood, it should grow back to precisely the same length and no more. For me, this would take three days' time. We shall see what it is for you."

"Right," I said, after a distracted pause.

He did as he said, and released my hand. My skin prickled strangely at the loss, and I folded my arm to myself as though stung. I was beginning to feel quite strange indeed.

After recording something in his notebook, he straightened back up and reached for my chin. "May I?"

I stared back at him, addled. "You want to…"

"I would look at your fangs, if you are willing."

"Why, of course," I said woodenly.

With that, he reached forward and took my chin gently with his hand. "Open your mouth, quite wide—can you put out your fangs?—there, good. Pardon me." He gently pushed up the corner of my upper lip as he measured, then made a curious hum before releasing me and scratching something into his notebook.

I closed my mouth and swallowed before speaking. "What is it?"

"I think they are longer than mine."

"Why?"

"That, I cannot know. Put your chin up again, let me see."

He repeated the measurement, though by now, the purpose of it was the furthest thing from my mind. For reasons that I could not quite understand, my heart had begun to pound.

"It was correct; how interesting." Alistair turned back to his notebook. "No need for any worry. It is likely nothing of importance."

"I'm not worried," I replied.

To that, he said nothing, which made me wince inwardly;

nothing escaped his notice!

I resolved to better hide my nerves, but this only served to agitate me further. By the time he turned back, I was nearly dying of dread.

"Now—" He took my chin again, and involuntarily I clenched my jaw—"Be at ease, Mr. Bedford, this is nothing painful. Look ahead, and I will make some measurements of your eye."

Woe to me! Though I tried to stare ahead and pay no heed to the nearness of his gaze, it was inescapable, overwhelming; and I was so anxious with a nameless feeling that when he blinked, my hand jumped.

"Be at ease," Alistair said quietly again, as he put his small measuring stick up again. Leaning even nearer, to the point where the black well of his eye was all I could see, he blinked again.

"Stay still…ah. How curious."

"What is?" I said, in a hoarse whisper. My gaze was fixed upon his; I could not move, I could not move!

"Nothing." He picked something up from the table. "Only…" The shadows shifted, as he raised a candle and held it near my eye, before waiting a minute and setting it down again.

At last, he laid aside the measuring-stick before leaning back and facing me plainly.

"Am I unnerving you?"

"What?" I started. "Not at all."

"Your pupils are obstinately large, even for a vampire."

I hesitated. "How strange!"

He watched me. "How strange indeed."

"Well, I told you I'm a skittish sort."

Alistair gave no answer. He had returned to writing his notes, and I looked away with embarrassment; but before long, he was taking my hand once more, and holding my wrist to find the pulse. Then, he reached up and pressed at the heartbeat in my neck. I was mortified when he spoke at last.

"Has your heartbeat always been so quick?"

At that, I could hold back no longer; I jerked my head from his grasp, and spilled out a mess of words. "Perhaps I am a little bit tired, and I *do* become rather nervous when I'm tired, and I'm not much used to this sort of thing!"

He seemed surprised. "You could have told me."

"Yes, well, but—there was no problem with it, none at all!" My frustration was mounting faster than I could suppress it. "I think I didn't sleep well last night, or had some nightmare which I have forgotten, or—you have a very sharp look—why, it is enough to make anyone anxious!"

Alistair stared at me with calm astonishment. His silence only served to irritate me further, and when I burst out again, my volume had exceeded any level that could be deemed polite.

"There, there it is! You always have that look in your eye, and you give that fixed stare—you are doing it on purpose, you must be—you must be trying to unnerve me to *death* with it!"

Alistair continued to regard me with mute surprise for a moment longer. Then, concern came over his expression.

"Mr. Bedford, are you well?"

At that, I finally came to my senses, and reddened so thoroughly that I felt sweat gather at the back of my neck. Why had I spoken so wildly?

But Alistair did not seem offended, nor even rattled. Instead, he closed his notebook and tried to bring a reassuring look to the deadly eyes. "Pardon me for my rudeness. If I ever seem to leer, it is only because I am used to being on my own, where I can stare with impunity. If I have caused you discomfort—"

I was instantly regretful, and shook my head. "No—it isn't that at all! I spoke without thinking. There is nothing wrong with your look, and you have very handsome eyes."

Alistair blinked.

Realizing that I had said rather more than I wished, I rushed to elaborate. "It was not your fault, but mine; I hadn't realized that I'm unaccustomed to being watched."

He tilted his head. "To being watched?"

"To be a servant is to strive for invisibility," I explained. "In my work, if someone was ever staring, I could be certain that I had done something wrong."

Alistair had nothing to say for a long moment, and held a distant look as though still distracted by something else; but soon enough, he nodded. "Then rest assured that you have done nothing wrong."

"Right," I said clumsily. Then, anxious to change the subject, I glanced over at his notebook. "So did you find anything new?"

"Not yet," Alistair said, closing it. "But we will measure the rate of your regeneration, and perhaps glean something from that."

I wavered for a moment as something occurred to me, though I was not certain of how to ask it. "Well…"

He turned to me. "Yes?"

"Oh, nothing, never mind."

But his attention remained. "You were set to say something."

"Nothing important."

"Evidently important enough that you began to say it, then were too reluctant to complete the thought."

"No! Well—" I sighed. "I was only pondering something on the nature of the vampire; but it is nothing that can be measured by a ruler."

There was a gleam of curiosity in Alistair's expression, and he crossed his arms, leaning against the table. "Pray tell."

I cleared my throat, and ventured forth with my question.

"Have you ever considered what it means, that we exist? The very notion that a vampire is something real?"

"I'm not sure I understand."

His attention was making me nervous again, and I knew that this only served to increase his curiosity, but I could not help my stammering. "What I mean to say is this: a vampire is something preternatural. A creature like this is surely above what our minds can comprehend."

At that, Alistair understood. He tilted his head. "So you would like to know whether this proves the existence of divinity."

I was surprised that he had realized my question so quickly, and I wondered whether he had pondered it before.

He searched my gaze for a few moments. Then, he smiled. "Well? Does it?"

"I'm not certain! That is why I'm asking you."

"I know very little more than you do, Mr. Bedford. True, I have been alive for far longer; but why would that mean that I am any nearer to an answer than you?"

"I was curious to know whether you have *thought* about it, that's all. It would seem to me that our existence is a miracle."

"When does something cease to be natural and enter the realm of miracles? It seems to me that we deem miraculous what we cannot explain."

I looked away from him, troubled.

Seeing me struggle, he was amused but apologetic. "Ah," he murmured. "What a brute I am. I have robbed you of the one comfort this could have given you."

"I don't blame you for it. It was an honest answer."

But to my surprise, he did not leave it there. Instead, he came forward and settled beside me on the table before continuing:

"I know that you are the type to search tirelessly for answers, and to never rest until you find them. You share this sentiment with the natural philosophers of your time, whom I admire; but you must remember that the unknown is not your enemy. Humankind, in its zeal to explain all that it can touch, is eager to crudely impose ideas upon that which they don't truly understand."

I gave a weary smile. "So why continue to study the vampire at all, if living in ignorance would be just as well?"

He shook his head. "Ah, but I didn't claim to prefer ignorance; I prefer reverence. I know why the river runs, why the flowers come up in spring, why the moon changes in the sky; but to me, these remain divine. Likewise, I have seen neither hobs nor fae, but I continue to search for them in the dark all the same. You can decide whether or not the vampire is miraculous to you, Mr. Bedford. Even what you see before your very eyes can be unknowable if you look deeply enough. The divine is not measurable, nor external to you; it is in your spirit, and gazes out."

This address, spoken so suddenly and with such gentle conviction, addled me and gave me pause.

But Alistair had not finished. He opened his notebook, and turned it to show me the page he had been writing. There, beneath my name, were his measurements and his observations, and even a small profile that he had drawn of my face.

"When I observe you," he said calmly, "I am neither searching for any fault, nor forming ugly ideas. I am content to understand everything that I can, and yet to accept that there will remain aspects that take more unraveling; but this does not disturb me. It is these mysteries which give you your particular character, which I so enjoy."

These words raised in me an unfathomable feeling, and I weakly pushed the book away with a reddened face. "You are flattering me, which can only mean that you are plotting trouble."

He took it back and closed it politely. "I am only returning the favour. You flattered me first."

I gave him a look. "When?"

With that, Alistair smiled playfully and leaned his cheek on his hand before saying with a sigh:

"Tell me, Mr. Bedford: do you truly think my eyes handsome?"

Oh, the devil!

"Leave that as one your *mysteries*," I muttered, as I slipped down from the table to the sound of his soft laughter behind me.

*　　*　　*

Alistair's methods had given me a great deal to ponder. As he had demonstrated, I tried to observe my vampire's nature with neither judgment nor scorn, and instead to understand it as it was. This was no easy task, and I cannot claim to have succeeded immediately; but I found that it lent me a sense of peace, which I did cherish.

On the following day, as I drew water in the early night, this feeling took shape into an idea. Before me, there passed a graceful string of deer, loping gingerly across the grass.

The deer, I realized, had blood within them. It was blood as mine was. Who was to say that such blood could not provide me sustenance as that of corpses?

In utter awe of this thought, I stood frozen for a moment. A wild and gripping hope had seized me. What if I did not need to leech from the dead? What if I could take from animals, as humans did? If it could be done, then a vampire might not be considered a vampire at all—but rather, a variety of human!

Gripped by this hope, I had an idea, which would involve a visit to Helmsley.

It was the first week of November, and the weather was beginning to descend into genuine cold. Indeed, it was the evening before Guy Fawkes night; I had asked Alistair whether he wanted to do a bonfire, to which he responded with a dry glance and a very flat "no."

"What about bonfire toffee?" I coaxed. "I plan to go into town tomorrow; perhaps I can find some."

He looked up from his book and raised his brows.

I gave an encouraging look. "Have you tried it?"

"I have not."

"It is customary, and quite popular. Why don't I…"

"Why not indeed?" Alistair said, ever more tartly.

Already knowing what he would say, I burst out: "Yes, yes, I know! I suppose this is a vile holiday to you, meant to stoke humans' hatred against each other; but is that the poor taffy's fault?"

At that, Alistair could not suppress a smile. "You contend that your sweets ought not suffer neglect due to the intent of their creators."

"Indeed," I said stoutly.

He sighed, and made a pantomime of thought. "Well, Mr. Bedford, that *is* a convincing argument…"

And so, when morning came, I set out towards town for the

toffee. In reality, however, my true aim was another.

The day hung on the edge of dawn, and the sky glowed a stark, moonlit blue with the light of approaching sun. It was a market morning, and I wished to visit as early as I could to avoid notice. When I arrived, I went directly to the butcher's stand.

When I returned to the manor, I had two new items in my hands. The first was a hearty package of sweets, which I placed in the kitchen for the coming night. The second was a tin of pig's blood.

I had considered making a proper blood pudding with it, but decided that my experiment would work best if I consumed it in its most natural state. Therefore, after stealing away to my room to avoid encountering Miss Josephine in the midst of my deed, I opened the tin and drank.

The taste was not quite like human blood; there was a marked bitterness on my tongue as I drew back, and though I felt full, I grimaced.

After finishing the entire tin, I went at last to bed. The mark of my success would be noticed when I awoke: if my theory was correct, then I would feel satisfied and refreshed, as I always did the night after a feeding at the chapel.

Eager to see the results of my venture, I drifted into an easy sleep.

CHAPTER XIV

I was woken the next morning by a terrible pain.

It began as a muted ache, which ebbed bluntly somewhere within my middle. The sensation brought me to a state of dim wakefulness, but I paid it little heed. Instead, I turned onto my side and returned to sleep.

Yet, soon the sensation rose up sharply; and at once, I opened my eyes wide, only to realize that I was in agony!

Gasping aloud, I tried to sit up, but could only shudder and hunch over myself. What an awful feeling! It was as though a burning rope pulled around my insides, pressing the life out of me and searing all in its path.

Just as soon as I sat upright, I was beset by a fit of coughing, which soon became miserable retching. Only once it had subsided, and I removed my arm from my mouth, did I see that I had expelled a dark substance onto the cloth. I stared in shock, but had no peace to think further. The taste of iron filled my mouth, and I shivered with nausea.

My experiment had failed—not merely failed, but resulted in dire illness!

I managed to stumble out of the bed, and draw out my chamber pot from beneath it, which for months now had gone unused; but oh, how the pain seemed to go on and on, forever! I could do nothing but cling to the handles. Worse still, an awful itching had spread all over my body; and when I looked down, I found that an enormous rash had erupted, raising red welts all over my skin.

After being sick a while longer, I managed to steady my stomach, but everything else remained—agony inside, and restless irritation outside; and so, after changing into a clean nightshirt, I returned to bed and slumped.

In a brief moment between waves of illness, I put my arm over my face and sighed, hardly believing what I had done. What a fool I had been! What idiocy had I committed, for the sake of such an ill-conceived hope? I had not made peace with vampirism at all; rather, it was my madness for reclaiming my humanity had led me to this suffering!

Hours passed. I was exhausted, and my eyes stung from lack of sleep, but my wretched body would not let me rest. I carried on in this manner until I grasped for my pocket watch with a feeble hand, and realized it was time to wake Alistair.

It was impossible! I could barely stand! There was no other choice; with a laboured breath, I raised my voice and called from the bed.

"Miss Josephine!"

No answer met my ears.

"Miss Josephine!"

I heard a door creak open outside, then a dim shuffling

followed by a gruff voice:

"Yes?"

"Could you tell the Count—" I took a moment to catch my breath. "Could you knock at his bedroom door, and tell him that I won't be waking him today? I am—"

My voice broke into retching, and I seized the handles of the pot as my stomach heaved.

Her voice came again, now tersely concerned. "What's the matter?"

"I'm fine!" I choked. "I'm only a little ill! Tell him—would you tell him for me?"

"How could you be ill, being what you are?"

"It was my fault, a mistake on my part, nothing to worry about besides; but I cannot spend the evening with the Count today. That is all."

Her steps began to shuffle away. "I will tell him."

"Thank you!"

I laid there pitifully for an eternity longer, curled over the rumpled covers. I felt rather guilty for making Miss Josephine climb all those steps at the end of her day, but the mere thought of standing made me ill.

After some time, I heard steps returning in the distance. The steady clip of shoes echoed in the hallway.

Three short knocks sounded against the door.

"Miss Josephine?" I said, lifting my head wearily from the pillow.

A deep, amused voice came instead. "Not at all, I'm afraid."

My heart leapt, and I let out a shout. "*Sir?*"

"Much better."

"What are you doing here?"

"Miss Josephine told me you were ill. May I come in?"

"Absolutely not!"

I heard an apologetic sigh. "Oh, Mr. Bedford."

"You ought not see me like this," I retorted; but a wicked twist in my gut forced sweat to my skin, and I let my head fall to my pillow.

"While that is certainly noble of you, there is nothing to be gained from hiding yourself away."

"Neither is there anything to be gained from granting you entrance!"

A smooth laugh. "Certain myths *do* claim that vampires cannot enter places without invitation."

I was suddenly curious at that, to the point that I forgot my illness for an instant. "Is it true?"

"Not on our diet," he replied, entertained. "But I am polite, so I will ask your permission again. May I enter?"

I grimaced. "You are exacerbating my illness by asking! I—"

Just then, however, the nausea wracked my body again, and I mouthed a curse before folding over myself.

Three more knocks sounded crisply. "May I enter?"

"Oh, forget it," I said finally, exhausted and annoyed. "Forget it! I am far too tired to argue with you. Do as you please."

"Much obliged," Alistair said.

The door was pushed ajar, and he stood in its frame. His form loomed darkly there for a moment, with his hair pouring over his shoulders, before he stepped into the room.

The image of him struck me vividly, surreal in the smallness of the space. He was wearing a long, dark blue coat with floral embroidery, which curled along flaring sleeves and a high collar. However, upon entering, he removed this coat and hooked it neatly by the door, revealing a pale waistcoat swirled throughout with matching designs. The sleeves of the shirt underneath it ruffled loosely around his arms like clouds, gathering at his wrists.

Immediately, I regretted my decision to grant him entry. He seemed woefully out of place, towering ornate and well-dressed between the humble walls. In contrast, I realized that I was terribly unkempt, still wearing my nightshirt, which scarcely covered past my knees. Mortified, I pulled up my covers and turned away.

As I did, I heard him stride neatly across the room and pull a chair to my bedside. "Good evening," said he, with a smile in his voice.

"What is it that you want?" I groaned, laying the back of my hand across my eyes. "What could possibly have compelled you so ardently to disturb my privacy?"

"Ah, but how could I desert my dear *mayordomo?*"

"We were just at war with the French," I said sourly.

"First of all, *we* are not at war with anyone." I heard the chair creak as he sat, and the rustle of him crossing one leg over the other. "Second, that was Spanish."

Irked, I turned back towards him. "Oh, for God's sake, what do you want from me?"

Upon doing so, I found that he had leaned forward, with an elbow on his knee and his chin propped on his hand. His gaze focused intently on me, glittering with interest.

I returned a humourless look. "What?"

"Nothing," he said, with a sly smile. "In your nightshirt, you look like a bashful ghost."

Then, his gaze moved to the rash along my skin, which had spread up from my collar onto my neck, and he mused:

"A bashful ghost who has fallen into a bed of stinging nettle."

I gave an indignant scoff and looked away.

"Now then," he said calmly, straightening his back. "May I guess the events that preceded this illness?"

From his tone, I realized suddenly that he knew precisely the cause. This made me quite cross. "Oh, pray tell!"

Alistair's smile turned pitying. "Guided by some misplaced sense of curiosity, or perhaps hope, you decided to seek out another source of nourishment. Am I correct?"

"Yes," I said sullenly.

"What animal was it?"

"Pig."

He gave a thoughtful nod. "A reasonable choice, I suppose."

I furrowed my brow as I regarded him; he clearly had not finished. "And?"

He closed his eyes for a moment, heaving a sigh. "Really, Mr. Bedford, I must admit to being slightly offended."

"By *what?*"

"Did you *truly* think that I had never considered this possibility?"

"Why—" I wavered. "Why, but—"

He waved a disdainful hand. "Oh, of course I did. Many times, in fact, and with a variety of different animals, keeping close record of the conditions under which I tried. In the end, it was all futile, of course, as you have no doubt learned; but I did try."

For a moment, I stared at him blankly, then placed both my hands over my face. "Could you not have *told* me that at some point?!"

Alistair regarded me with curiosity. "I must say, I never thought it necessary. How could I have imagined that you would try without asking me first?"

In truth, he was correct, and the thought of asking him had

crossed my mind; but I suppose I had been fearful of him telling me it was impossible, and losing that shred of hope.

I gave a glum stare. "Then you overestimated my judgment."

"Or I failed you as a tutor," Alistair said, rising gracefully from his chair. "In either case, I have not come to gloat. Wait here."

Looking over feebly, I watched him stride to the door. Opening it, he leaned down and took a bucket from the floor outside.

"Is that blood?" I said hoarsely, draping my forearm over my eyes. "Oh, no, I can't drink blood right now, I can't *look* at blood—"

"It certainly isn't blood." I heard his steps draw near again, and a faint sloshing along with them. "Move your arm."

Reluctantly, I let it sink down by my side, closing my eyes in apprehension; yet, as soon as I did, I felt a damp cloth touch my forehead. By the time my eyes had fluttered open in surprise, I found that he was leaning over the bucket again.

He had left a simple cloth, soaked in water, upon my forehead. To my surprise, the cool sensation quelled the ill sensations considerably. As tension eased away, I released a breath.

He straightened again, holding another dripping rag in his hands. "How is that?"

"Why, it actually does feel better," I said softly, lying very still. The sudden peace opened the door to my exhaustion once more, and I closed my eyes. "Much better. Thank you."

He nodded graciously. "You are most welcome. It was the only method that helped me, whenever my own experiments failed." Then he stood, looking around at my furniture. "It is a rather drab room you keep here."

Lost in muddled thoughts, I left my eyes open slightly and

directed a hesitant glance towards him, as he swept towards my desk. I wondered, as I often had, what could impel him to show gentleness towards me. He was fond of my company; that much, I knew. He was interested in my story, and in my physiology, and he enjoyed observing me; but was I merely his entertainment, or did he truly think of me as a companion?

His voice interrupted my thoughts, as he picked a thin vase from atop the cupboard. A wilting flower hung limp over the cusp.

"Is this a flower?" he said, obviously charmed. Lifting it slightly, he tilted his head and considered the browning petals. "What an unhappy plant."

"Thank you." I said archly. "That was precisely the intention, you see. I decorate with dying plants."

"Ah, did you take that personally?" he laughed. "That was not at all my intention, I assure you. It is the plant's transgression, not yours."

"The plant didn't place itself in the vase and leave itself there for too long."

"That is true." He put the vase down, but promptly opened a drawer.

I sighed wearily. "What are you doing, sir?"

Lifting a waistcoat from the drawer, he shook it open and held it up with great curiosity. "How tight," he mused. Briefly, he held it against his own chest. "I wonder how you breathe."

"*Sir!*"

"Not an insult," he said, folding it neatly. "Merely an observation." Placing it back in the drawer, he pushed it shut and walked back off to the desk.

As I stared over at the wilting flower, which seemed to sag further with the weight of insult, Alistair's voice came again.

"Were you writing to someone?"

It took me a moment to remember. "Yes, I was."

"To who?"

"Henry," I said. "The coachman I mentioned, who I have known since childhood. I haven't seen him for a while."

Alistair gazed down at the letter for a moment, somewhere between curiosity and something else. "Are you close with him?"

"He was like a father to me," I said. "I—"

All of a sudden, I felt a surge of illness overtake me. With a laboured gasp, I curled on the bed and retched violently.

At that, he came to my side. "My apologies," he murmured, removing the cloth from my forehead. "I let this warm too long."

"It's fine," I said hoarsely, as it was replaced by a fresh one. I could not help but sigh at the comfort it afforded, and closed my eyes to the cool drops streaking past my forehead. "Ah—thank you."

"Of course."

As he stood at the side of my bed, speaking no further, I felt the air grow ripe for questions.

"Sir, I have an idea," I said hoarsely. "Though, this time, I have no choice but to ask you first."

"Hm?"

"What about the hibernation you mentioned once? If I attempted that, could I sleep past this pain?"

He frowned. "How much have I explained of that?"

"Not much at all."

His usual serene expression disguised a twinge of caution. "You cannot hibernate for one day, nor even one year. The length of your sleep is unpredictable."

Now I was curious. "How *do* you make yourself hibernate, anyway?"

"I'm afraid I cannot tell you."

"Why not?" I exclaimed. "It is part of my nature, is it not? It is your obligation to tell me!"

His tone darkened; he was warning me, though not unkindly. "A hibernation is something that a vampire undertakes only in the direst of times. If you ever reach such a degree of distress as to open the doors to it—which I don't wish upon you—then instinct will lead you regardless. Until then, it is a terrible and dangerous escape, which leaves you vulnerable."

"You are being too ambiguous!"

"Simply put, if you have need to hibernate, your own nature will teach you."

"But why not experiment with it? Is there a way to end hibernation quickly?"

"I believe so," Alistair said, "But I have proven nothing; and if my theory were to fail, then I have your senseless body for the next three decades; and all of your friends—"

He gestured towards the letter on the desk, which I had been writing to Henry.

"—will either believe you to be dead, or be dead themselves, by the time you wake."

The thought made me shudder. "I wasn't *actually* intending to try; but could you at least tell me how it's done?"

Alistair paced back to the vase, and curled one finger beneath a withered petal of the dying flower. Then, he glanced back towards me. "Believe me, it is an act of a most unfortunate nature. I will consider telling you before you leave the manor, but not before. Please, Mr. Bedford."

After that, I felt guilty to press it further. "Fine! But I will bother you about it in the future."

He laughed lightly. "And I will happily reject such requests."

As he turned towards the looking-glass on my wash stand, the smile remained on his lips. "For now, endure thy curiosity."

This small phrase was enough to distract me wholly from the subject.

"*Thy* curiosity?" I cried out.

He blinked, then turned to me with amusement. "What is it?"

"It had never occurred to me—you used to converse in that manner, did you not?"

"I did, when the occasion suited it." He stared back at me. "Do there not remain those in England who use that form of address?"

"Few," I replied. I was in wonder at such a relic of the past! Though we had read plays together which used such language, I had never considered the fact that Alistair had once employed it in ordinary conversation.

My illness was forgotten as I urged him. "I have noticed you changing other aspects of your speech; you have corrected your accent to mine. Speak more in the native dialect of your age!"

At my excitement, a curious half-smile bloomed across his face. Despite it, he shook his head. "No."

"Sir!"

"After having taken such pains to speak in a more modern tongue? Of course not."

"Please, I want to hear!"

"You are so spoiled today," he said with mocking censure. "I come to do you one favour, and you ask for the kingdom."

"A few minutes," I begged. "You owe me. Look how sick I am, sir, how pitiable!"

I was surprised by the mischief of my own behaviour. Even in my younger years, others had called me grim; but between the feverishness of illness and the levity of Alistair's own conduct, I felt that some other long-lost nature had been drawn out, and could not help but express it.

Alistair crossed his arms and regarded me with playful sternness for a long moment.

I met his gaze with impunity.

Then he sighed, and swept to the door. "Wait here. I will only be a moment."

I began to sit up, confused. "Where are you going?"

But then he was gone, and the room was silent once more.

While I waited, I turned the cloth on my forehead to the cooler side and descended into my thoughts. The conversation had left me with a warm sensation, which prompted strange and nervous joy. I stared at the withered flowers across the room and puzzled over it all.

After perhaps a quarter hour, I suddenly heard Alistair's steps newly approaching. With a creak, the door opened, and he stepped back into the room.

In the instant that he entered, I looked over—and sat upright at once, prompting the damp cloth to fall to my lap!

In his short absence, Alistair had changed his outfit to an elegant black doublet. It was a stiffly fitted thing with a high collar up to his chin, lined with a small and delicate ruff that circled his neck entire; and the padded broadness of the shoulders gave him a lively old-fashioned charm, as though he had come from a storybook. This doublet was matched beneath by breeches and hose, such that his entire form down to his shoes was a graceful display of black velvet. Only the ruff, and matching delicate white ruffles at the ends of his sleeves, formed any interruption to this colour.

Yet, this was not the most startling sight; for in his hands, he held a polished wooden instrument, sleek and round-bellied, which until now I had only seen in pictures.

"A *lute!*" I cried out.

"A lute indeed," Alistair replied, as he strode on. "Hark, Mr. Bedford; your troubadour comes forth, from deep within the wells of history, to serenade you through your sickness."

At that, I flushed with excitement and gripped the covers—but not only from the sight of him; it was his voice! He had spoken in his full and genuine accent, which I had so wished to hear.

I was so overcome with good cheer that I was afraid to speak, lest I were to sound like a drunkard. At last, I settled on a question. "Is the clothing from your time, too?"

"It is," he replied as he settled back in his chair. "This is the outfit which has best survived the ravages of time, among those I wore as a human." He lifted the lute. "Likewise, this instrument, but for the strings, is no less genuine."

At that, I am afraid I lost all sense of propriety.

"Will you play it for me?" I cried out.

He tilted his head. "Have you never heard one?"

"They have all but vanished! I have heard the harp-lute, and the guitar, and perhaps some other similar instruments—but never something like this."

Seeing the ardour of my excitement, Alistair was so amused that he seemed to glow. He held out the instrument. "Hold it first, if it would please you."

"What if I break it?"

He clicked his tongue. "It isn't fragile. Do you think the craftsmen of my time so unskilled? Go on."

Needing no further encouragement, I reached forward and took it gingerly.

Yet, in the instant that I did, I had something like a vision.

Alistair's hands were holding out the lute alone; but I seemed to suddenly see many hands, eager and joyful, joining along with his. I thought of the craftsman who had made it, the shopkeeper who had sold it, and the people who had sat in their particular clothing and listened to its music, all of them clamoring to be heard; and all of a sudden, as I received the smooth wood in my hands, I was overcome with volatile emotion. So many people and their joys, forever long-lost! I wondered whether Alistair missed them.

"Mr. Bedford?" Alistair said in shock.

With the lute in my lap, I had begun to weep. My eyes welled with tears, which lingered briefly before overflowing.

Alistair leaned forward in concern, and seemed about to speak; but I interrupted, embarrassed, wiping tears away with my palm.

"I'm sorry," I managed, with a voice in ruins. "Why, I couldn't help but think of the age that this hails from, and all the people along with it—I don't know what has come over me, I really don't. Fever, perhaps."

Alistair's expression was inscrutable for a moment, then softened.

"I understand," he said at last, with a smile. "Ah, Mr. Bedford, I understand every part of what you feel; but I'm sorry to have saddened you."

I shook my head and spoke briskly. "It isn't sadness. I want to—I *must* hear you play it."

"Greet it first," Alistair replied. "It has waited a long time to meet you."

And so, I plucked a string or two at random, and fingered curiously at the neck to change the sound, until the focus had settled me and my tears had dried. With that, I finally handed it back, and he received it.

"Settle back," he murmured, as he placed it on his lap. "I only need a moment."

I laid back in bed, resting my cheek against the pillow, and watched him as he tuned the instrument. The sight of his fingers turning the pegs nimbly, and his brow furrowing as he listened for each note, somehow lulled me.

Finally, he glanced up. "Ready?"

I nodded.

"This is Dowland's finest work," Alistair said calmly. "His *Lachrimae.*"

Then, he steadied his hand against the wood and gave his first strum.

In an instant, at that silvery sound which was so much like a waterfall, the hairs on the back of my neck stood on end; but after the first stanza, my eyes widened, and I ceased to breathe entirely.

Alistair had begun to sing!

What a rich voice he had, dark and elegant, how fine! In these most resonant tones, he sang slow and mellow, drawing out every word with each strum of his lute:

> *Flow, my tears; fall from your springs!*
> *Exiled for-ever, let me mourn;*
> *Where night's black bird her sad infamy sings,*
> *There, let me live forlorn;*

I was finished! The sound of that lovely old instrument, mingled with words which Alistair sang as though he meant every part of them, made a great mess of emotion well up within me.

Yet, despite the melancholic timbre of his voice, Alistair did not weep. Indeed, he was smiling as he sang on:

Down, vain lights; shine you no more,
No nights are dark enough for those
That in despair, their last fortunes deplore,
Light doth but shame disclose!

It was not only the sound that moved me so, I realized. Yes, there was an art in the music; but it was also in the way he moved, the way his wrist turned, the way he dipped the neck of the instrument ever so slightly with each thrum of his voice. How beautiful and tragic was the sound, and even more so the one playing it!

This last thought passed so quickly that I nearly missed it, but caught it suddenly and felt a strange thrill.

It was the same sensation that had come when he had been measuring me, which ran like an undercurrent in my veins. I recognized it now, and found that the initial terror of it had passed, so I tried to pull apart its threads. It was a curious sort of longing, mingled with gratefulness—pride, fear, or warmth— what was it?

Yes!—I looked up towards Alistair, at the ease of his brow, at the way one toe of his shoe was pointed out just *so;* and though I did not understand what precisely I wanted from him, I understood that, in some form, it was him that I wanted.

I had never felt a desire for friendship quite so visceral, and found it startling.

As these thoughts came and went, Alistair had continued to sing, and soon reached the last lines of the song.

The last stanza, he repeated twice, and finally lingered on the final word with a tremolo that persisted long after the lute had fallen silent.

Then, his eyes—which had hitherto been half-shut—opened slowly, and settled upon me.

"Oh, Mr. Bedford," he said then, strumming a wayward note here and there on the lute, and gave something like a fond sigh. "I have made you shed tears again."

Wiping them away with my palm, I shook my head. "Would you play another?"

"I would not wish to trouble you."

"I am not unhappy—quite the opposite!" I exclaimed, rather desperate to hear more of his music. "I am awfully glad to have let you enter; you have made it pleasant to be ill, and even an ecstasy to weep."

With his lute frozen in his hands, Alistair's gaze suddenly seemed a bit dazed; but this only compelled me to speak further and wilder, until I could hardly believe what I was saying.

"Ah!—sometimes, against all my better judgment, I must confess—I even feel so very *happy* to have met you!"

At once, realizing what I had said, I fell silent and swallowed my words, not yet ready to understand what I had meant by them.

Alistair stared at me, and for an instant seemed entirely lost. He had the slowly dawning expression of someone who had encountered a realization equally extraordinary and terrible.

But in the next moment he recovered, though he still seemed to struggle for words. "If I knew you would enjoy it so, I would have told you to try the animal blood sooner."

I was feeling unusually bold. "If I knew you could play in such a manner, I would have done the same."

Alistair had ceased to look me in the eye. He fiddled with a peg, quite obviously pretending to tune it. "Then what would you like to hear?"

I was beginning to feel very amused. Throughout all the time I had known him, I had never seen Alistair nervous, and felt compelled to goad him:

"How should I know? Are you not the musician here?"

But this sentence was interrupted with a yawn. At last, with my abating sickness, the sleep I had lost was returning vengefully.

Hearing that, Alistair smiled at last and turned towards me. "Something to lull you to sleep, then."

"Fine," I said hoarsely, letting my eyes drift half-closed. I was suddenly exhausted. "Help me sleep."

For a long moment, Alistair gazed at me without playing. There was a softness in his expression and a sort of resignation, though it did not seem an unpleasant one.

Then, at last, he strummed at the strings and went on. I closed my eyes, equally comforted and uneasy, too tired to think of anything but the lilt of strings and Alistair's dark silhouette across from me. Before long, I had drifted into rest.

When I woke briefly, the music had stopped, and through a haze of sleep I could see Alistair sitting at my desk. He had his chin in his hand and was gazing down, reading my letter to Henry.

When I woke a final time, he was gone.

I sat up, noticing that I felt well, and rubbed my eyes. Yet, a strange colour then caught my attention. Glancing up, I found the source.

The withered flowers were gone from their vase. In their place, flamboyantly perched, two hawthorn branches rested with their berries draping peacefully over the cusp.

CHAPTER XV

We set out towards the church on the following night. Having failed at my experiment, I had sullied my reserve of blood; and without any way of knowing how much I had depleted, it was prudent to take another feeding promptly.

That night was unusually cold. Winter was growing near, the land was dry, and a blanketing of clouds dampened the moonlight. Yet, as we treaded our way towards the old church—Alistair dressed in a heavy cloak which flowed mightily behind him, and I with a far less dramatic one—I was met with a most curious feeling.

Upon encountering the brisk air, I felt none of the usual dread, fed by unpleasant memories, that the approach of cold usually brought. Instead, sentimental images came to me. I thought of the manor, of the fireplace in the library, of the bitter howls of wind sweetening the comfort within. Never before had I felt the childish excitement that others seemed to find with winter merrymaking; but now, as I looked towards Alistair, these rousing feelings were tight in my chest.

How wonderfully well he went with the winter scene, I thought! Yes—he would be a fitting ghost, if he so wished. Despite the bite of the wind, I felt brightness come into my eyes as I looked, for this fascinating figure would be my object of study for the winter, mine to converse with and gaze upon for as much time as I pleased; but as soon as the thought came to mind, I was disconcerted, and then quite flustered.

Having had some time to think over the events of the previous night, I could no longer deny that to have Alistair's friendship affirmed had become my most ardent wish. To desire such a friendship so desperately with anyone was already mortifying enough, but to feel it towards Alistair somehow felt even more profane. Though I knew that he shunned all human hierarchy, I could not help but feel myself inadequate. What claim could I possibly lay to any companionship with this ancient and dignified soul—who, I had to remind myself, had ended my life as I knew it?

My thoughts were interrupted by a magnificent sight, as we neared the church. Alistair had reached out a hand to stop me quietly, while lifting his other into the air; and after a moment, an enormous white barn owl swooped low from a tree, alighting on his wrist!

I gave a cry of surprise, and nearly fell back.

"Do you like it?" Alistair said calmly, as the creature folded its wings and watched me eerily from its perch. It regarded me coolly, with that particular visage of the barn owl, which so resembles a dryad's dead stare.

An excellent winter ghost indeed!

But this was not the most significant matter that night. No;

the night had just begun, and was yet to reach its darkest point.

Alistair and I had reached the churchyard, and were discussing some subject—something on the habits of owls, which he described from his observations. This brought us to discussion on the vampire's influence over animals, which he had mentioned here and there.

"It is one of my few abilities that lingers in the absence of living blood," Alistair said, lifting his wrist where the owl still perched. "I am glad for it. It is my favourite among the vampire's powers."

With that, he thrust his arm up; and the massive creature ducked forward, lifted its wings, and flew off with such wing-beats so forceful that the wind made Alistair's hair toss behind him. Yet, its flight was utterly silent as it soared off into the night.

I watched it go for some time, captivated, until Alistair beckoned for me to enter the chapel.

Following him in, I went to a body at random, though my mind was still otherwise occupied. At last, I spoke curiously:

"That's how you know the bats so well, I suppose."

"Indeed. They were often my sole companions."

Reaching for the shroud before me, I pondered. "Have you named many of them, apart from Dido?"

"Of course. Any Dido needs an Aeneas, no?"

"If my memory of *that* story serves me well, she would have done far better without him."

"But then we would have no story to tell. The opera 'Dido Rules Carthage with No Problem Whatsoever' would not sell a single seat."

I suppressed a laugh, at that—I did not wish to laugh before the dead—and responded haughtily. "*I* would gladly go see it."

"I have no doubt." Then, he gestured. "Go on."

With a nod, I looked down to the body before me, and pulled the shroud down.

To my great sadness, lying within, was a rather young woman. For a moment I bowed my head and closed my eyes in prayer, a habit that I had taken on to settle my misgivings, then leaned down to bite.

Alistair was gazing off into the distance, thoughtful. "I will show you more of the bats when we return. We have not yet studied the—Mr. *Bedford?*"

He had stopped short, sweeping forward; for though I had bitten, and taken my first few draws of blood, I had suddenly been met with a terribly bitter taste, and fell back from the body in a fit of coughing.

In an instant, Alistair had his hand on my shoulder. "Mr. Bedford?"

"Bitter," I managed to say, between coughing.

"Bitter?"

"The blood," I said hoarsely. Alistair's look was so concerned that I was sorry for having worried him. "I'm fine—"

But then I shuddered again, hurried out the door, and then at last was violently sick onto the earth, losing those few mouthfuls of blood I had gained.

I became aware of Alistair's hand on my back. He had followed me out, and waited calmly until I finished. Then, as I caught my breath, he murmured: "Are you well?"

"Yes! Yes—perhaps I *am* still ill, from the pig blood—" I panted, dabbing my handkerchief to my lips; but he shook his head, and gestured for me to follow him back inside.

"I suspect something else. Come, let me make sure of it."

Following him back inside, I entered just in time to see him lean over the very same body for brief taste.

Finally, Alistair straightened and turned to me. When he spoke, his dark eyes were unmoved, his voice practical; but there was a touch of gentleness, too.

"Arsenic."

I stared, confused. "Arsenic? Did she take medicine?"

Alistair had sometimes mentioned poisonous substances used in medicine, which gave blood a distinct and unpleasant taste; but he shook his head.

"Yes and no. This is indeed arsenic, but an amount so excessive that it could never be blamed on human ignorance."

For a few moments I said nothing as his meaning dawned on me. "She was—"

"Either by her own hand, or another's."

I took a step back. "You cannot mean—murdered!"

"Or a suicide, Mr. Bedford."

But my heart was already in motion. I fixed upon Alistair a fiery look of conviction, and pressed my handkerchief in hand as I stepped towards him.

"We must find out what happened to her!"

"No."

Startled at the speed of his reply, I grew frenzied. "Sir, we must! We have found her like this; it is our duty!"

Alistair shook his head. "It isn't our duty."

"How could you be so calm? We have found a human being who could have been murdered, and nobody might know!"

"She would not be the first I have found."

I was horrified. "So you feel nothing?"

"That is irrelevant here."

But my eyes burned, and passion gripped me. I stepped further up to him, defiant. "For a long time, I *did* think you heartless, and was glad to find myself mistaken; but now, I find renewed reason to doubt! Have you ever cared for something outside yourself, sir? Do you feel no impulse towards aiding the innocent?"

Alistair looked down at me with a chilling and expressionless gaze, which he had not worn since far darker times between us. "We are not going to chase a murderer."

He spoke in a voice so dead that I flushed with terror, but I pressed on. "So say it outright! You care nothing of justice for this woman?"

"There is no such thing as justice," Alistair said. He looked very tired.

"There is!" I exclaimed. "There is, if we create it! We must find who did this—" My soul seemed to flow up through me, and in a desperate frenzy to find any kindred feeling in him, I gripped the edge of his cloak. "You cannot be so cold!"

At that, finally, he plucked my hand from his cloak and held my wrist gently. "Listen to me."

"I prayed for her—I cannot leave her now!"

Alistair moved his hold from my wrist down to my hand, and laid his other hand on top of it. "Mr. Bedford, *listen* to me."

At this plea I finally fell silent, with my hand pressed warmly between his two, though my heart still beat within me like a drum.

"This woman is dead," Alistair said quietly, his eyes gleaming in the dark. "Nothing will return her. It isn't out of cold apathy that I have chosen to leave the human world; if we begin to involve ourselves in outside matters, we will be found out. No good can come of this."

"I'm not afraid!"

"You should be. There are fates worse than death. I am

begging you to be rational."

"And I am begging you to have a conscience!"

"Understand me, Mr. Bedford," Alistair said then, with an uncharacteristic swell of emotion. He pressed my hand tighter. "It pains me to know that my way of life makes you doubt my sympathies, but I must beg that you at least deem me cowardly rather than heartless. I, too, have seen unfairness in the world, and fallen prey to the notion that I had to involve myself; but I have paid a dire price for following such whims, and thus now find my only refuge in indifference."

These words did move me. For a moment I wavered, then felt ashamed. "I'm sorry. I spoke thoughtlessly. I consider you neither cowardly nor heartless; it was a cruel attempt to have your aid. If anyone could find what happened, you, with your mind and experience…!"

"Neither mind nor experience will suffice," he said. "You cannot help everyone. I have already told you once: I have come to know your character. I know that you are the type to take responsibility for all that you see, to think yourself in debt to the world, to take endless blame onto your shoulders and never forgive it; but guilt should not lead you blindly into ruin. Look past the blaze of your righteousness and understand me. I'm not telling you this because I feel nothing. I'm telling you this because I have felt *precisely* what you feel, and suffered for it."

My throat was dry. I swallowed, and looked into the urgent expression in his eyes, as the tide of ardent feeling subsided and left me with guilt instead.

"I know," I said quietly. His patience had calmed me. "I do understand you—I do! I never thought you unmoved, not really. I only…"

He seemed surprised that I had heeded him, and waited for

me to go on.

"But…" I looked up. "You said that you have seen unfairness that you wished to interfere with."

Alistair nodded.

"On such occasions, have you ever intervened?"

"I have."

With a stormy expression, I met his gaze. "Do you regret it?"

That gave him pause. After a few moments of silence—he gazed down at me distantly, as though he was suddenly far away—he shook his head. "I cannot be certain."

"If you could go back, would you do it again?"

"I would do it differently."

"But would you act?"

Releasing my hand, he gave a quiet sigh and tilted his head to think. After a moment's consideration, he suddenly gave a resigned smile.

"Yes," he replied. "I would."

"Then you understand why I must interrogate this matter," I said. Now that we had reached a mutual understanding, I was able to speak calmly. "Really, you ought not worry. I don't intend to go too far, and I will ensure that our nature is kept secret. Why, perhaps nothing will come of this at all! Your boredom is the result of excessive caution."

"Very well, Mr. Bedford," Alistair said. Before, he had seemed weary, but now a conciliatory smile lightened his countenance, and there was even a curious spark in his eye. "You have your mystery to solve. Only heed what I have told you: be careful. Don't drive yourself mad, but if you must, at least don't do it for the sake of your penance."

"I assume you will tell me, if I start down that road." I gave him a vibrant look. "And will you help me, sir?"

He returned the stare with playful condescension. "If only to keep you from trouble."

"Then let us see what we can infer," I said, and returned to the body.

Our poisoned lady was a young woman, surely no older than thirty, with umber hair that came in tight ringlets to her shoulders. There was a necklace at her throat, which bore a few red coral stones joining in a simple clasp.

I looked at her for a few moments.

Then, I turned, put my hand over my mouth, and was nearly sick once more. This time, it was not from the bitterness of the blood.

"Mr. Bedford," Alistair murmured. He came forward and placed a hand to my back. "Let us step outside."

"I'm fine," I gasped, putting my handkerchief over my mouth. "Oh, this has never happened before—it must have been the pig's blood still."

He seemed unconvinced, but said nothing of it. "We have seen what we needed to; we will remember her face. Close her shroud again, and we may go to the manor to discuss this. We will return here tomorrow, once your good appetite is restored."

I complied, though not without shame at my sudden weakness. After carefully replacing what I had altered, I followed him outside into the churchyard.

"We know nothing!" I mused, as I closed the door behind me. The cold air revived my spirits, and I followed him as we began our walk back. "How do you propose we go on without even her name?"

"Simple," Alistair said, as he strode along. "Do you remember what I told you about this church, and its duty to the dead?"

I caught up to him, tightening my cloak around myself. "You

mentioned something about the agreement between you and the church—that it cares for the destitute dead, in return for their place on your estate."

Alistair nodded. "Indeed. Thus, you know the background of your unfortunate victim."

"Then should I inquire among the destitute in town?"

"Not quite. Particularly not now, when the death is recent and suspicions may run high. There is one more part to this, which you may not have considered."

I frowned. "And what is that?"

"Consider it yourself. Who is most likely to have met this young woman, with whom you have already traded words?"

I thought and thought. Alistair gazed down at me as he walked; his calm expression was framed like a second moon by his hair and the blackened sky.

Then, at last, I cried out:

"The reverend!"

"Indeed."

"Do you suppose Mr. Raleigh does charity other than burials?"

"I don't suppose; I am certain of it. I have seen him bring gatherings together for meals on holidays—quite a bother when I am trying to feed at the mortuary in peace, but I wouldn't blame them for that."

He then gestured into the distance.

"The poor bring their dead a long way to reach this church, so it may be that he has never met her; but he might at least know who brought her, or from where, or even simply the circumstances of the death."

"Perhaps," I mused. "But how would I raise the subject? I can't tell him how we found her…"

"You need not," Alistair replied. Then, he waved me along to hurry, as a frigid wind picked up and whistled through the grasses. "Come, come. Let us at least ponder it by a fire."

*   *   *

Upon our return we kindled a fire in the library and gathered by it, sharing a heaping plate of toffee from town. After much discussion, we settled on a line of inquiry that satisfied us, and elected a time.

"This reverend of yours sleeps late," Alistair said, leaning forward to warm a piece of toffee over the fire. "Late enough that, on occasion, he has nearly interrupted my feedings. If you aim to find him alone, you ought to go in early night."

"Fine," I said, but then hesitated. "Wait! Then I cannot wake you."

"No matter. I will wake on my own, and meet you later."

I felt an odd twinge in my chest, and frowned. Up until now, we had shared tea on every evening's waking other than Sundays, which we usually spent apart. To miss our appointment needlessly in this manner felt strange. Had I always been such a creature of habit, I wondered?

"But we had planned to spend the early night studying history," I said hollowly.

"We can start tonight instead. What time is it now?"

"I hardly know."

Alistair gave a curious look. "You carry a pocket watch, Mr. Bedford."

"A cheap one," I said, staring into the fire. "It loses hours every day. After a full day, it is about as useful as a stone in my pocket."

With a gleam of interest in his eye, Alistair cleaned off his fingers with a handkerchief before extending his hand. "May I see this useful stone?"

With a sigh, I took it off its fob and passed it to him. He regarded it for a few moments before speaking:

"If I manage to pry it open, would you mind if I paint the dial for you? It will give me something to amuse myself with tomorrow."

I glanced at him. "You intend to tinker with it, don't you?"

"Perhaps," Alistair said mysteriously.

I smiled faintly. "Fine. It can't be made much worse, after all."

With that, he tucked it into his coat pocket, and we lingered at the fire for some time before gathering our studying materials. Yet, as Alistair was lifting his notebook, something fluttered out from between the pages and fell to the floor.

I furrowed my brow and bent over to pick up this object, but upon recognizing it, I balked. "How on earth—!"

It was the awful book which Alistair had shown me the first day in the library, which Miss Josephine had bought in vengeance!

Alistair took it from me and sighed. "Josephine, Josephine, why are you cross with me now?"

"She placed it there?!"

"As she does, when she is upset."

"We should ask her why," I ventured. "Perhaps she is cross over my brief illness yesterday, and thought you had a hand in it."

"It would be useless," Alistair said dryly. "She will deny everything. We can only make our move in turn."

And so, I followed him to the kitchen, where he placed the vulgar book between her boots for her to find.

"How childish," I mumbled, as I watched him.

"She began it," Alistair replied, dusting off his hands.

*　　*　　*

Though I felt the loss of my nightly appointment with Alistair with peculiar intensity, the pleasure of meeting the reverend again overcame this feeling. I found him in the church, sweeping quietly.

We chatted aimlessly at first, him and I. After a few minutes I took up a broom alongside him, and helped him with his task until he turned to me with a twinkle in his eye and a sheepish countenance.

"I must admit, I can withhold a question no longer. Tell me, for I was left so very curious after we spoke; did you ever find resolution to the troubles you described to me?"

"Somewhat," I replied amicably. "At least for now, though it isn't the sort of matter that can find clean resolution."

"Is that so?"

"Yes, unfortunately! But at the very least, I have gained a better understanding of it." I smiled gratefully towards Mr. Raleigh. "I must thank you for listening to me that night. Whether I followed your advice as you intended, I cannot know; but I was in dire need of a kind ear."

"It was no trouble at all, Mr. Bedford. You'll always find me glad to listen."

Here that I found my opening, and ventured forth with my question.

"I have the sense that you've heard many people's stories here."

"I have."

"Ah!—that does remind me—I wonder whether you know

one particular person's story, which has dearly strained my heart."

At once he stopped sweeping, and turned to me. "Who? I will do everything in my power to remember."

"Well, a baker in town was asking me about a young woman, wondering whether I had seen her. He wasn't sure whether she was a beggar, but she sometimes asked for bread. Yet, for a few days now, he hasn't seen her, and confessed he feared the worst. Perhaps you, in all your charity, have crossed paths with her."

"What is her name?"

I feigned thought. "This man never knew her name, but he described her to me: have you met any woman with dark hair in coils, and a red coral necklace?"

Mr. Raleigh stared at me with a spark of surprise.

I watched him with trepidation, fearful that I had made some mistake in my lie, but soon he blinked and regained himself.

"Nora," he said ruefully.

"You knew her?"

"Oh, yes," he replied, and set his broom aside to affix me with a compassionate look. "It saddens me that you will need to convey a sad message to your friend; dear Nora passed, and lies in the chapel just behind us."

"Does she, now!"

"God rest her soul."

"What happened? Do you know?"

"It is a terribly unfortunate story," Raleigh said sadly, "Of which I must admit I know little. She came to me asking for charity and penance, both of which I tried to provide. You ask what happened to her—in all honesty, I haven't any idea. The little she told me of her private life, I would never divulge, but there was no sign that she would perish so swiftly."

This he said with the gentlest voice imaginable, and all the gestures of sorrow that showed his spirit to be compassionate and kind; I was touched by this, and felt guilty to be lying to him. However, the thought of our poisoned lady in life, the understanding that she had been real and wanting for charity, inflamed my sympathies and overcame my doubts.

"Mr. Raleigh," I said, with a look of sorrow that was not unfelt, "That pains me very much to hear. Why, I myself know what it is to be hungry and unloved by the world, and it is a fate I would never wish upon anyone! Tell me, do you know anything of her family or her friends, anyone who she may have known in Helmsley? I wish to help them if I can."

"That is precisely the strangest thing. She never mentioned any family other than a sister." Mr. Raleigh hesitated, and then gave me a knowing look. "She was alone, I assume—because she was driven to the most unfortunate means of procuring a living."

I felt a pang in my chest so forceful that my very heart trembled. Nothing was feigned when I put a hand to my chest and stepped towards him.

"Please—if you know anything—!"

"Well, if there remains any chance of finding her family," Mr. Raleigh mused, "There is only one possibility. You might go and ask the only kind soul who she ever mentioned by name in her life: do you know the book-seller, Noah Parker?"

*　*　*

All of this I related to Alistair upon my return, who listened patiently and with careful attention, all the while carefully painting the dial of my pocket watch. The removed pieces of the mechanism were piled nearby.

When I finished explaining, he tilted his head. "Obviously you must speak to him, then. It is just as well; I am in need of a new novel or two."

"Wait—but first, I had an idea," I said. "Aren't we returning tonight to feed? Bring something to draw with; if we can commit her face to paper, we may have a better chance."

And so, that night, we returned to the chapel; but upon arriving I stopped short and gasped. Rushing to the empty table where she had been, I turned and looked to Alistair in dismay.

In response, he gave an easy shrug. "They must have taken her for burial."

Though I was dejected, Alistair assured me he remembered the face in his memory well enough, and drew it for me in charcoal. I thought it matched, and agreed. Then I went to another body and drank my fill, and at last had an adequate feeding.

As we walked back, Alistair was silent.

I glanced at him.

He had been acting slightly different that morning. His conduct was neither rude nor unkind; whenever I had questions for him, he responded readily, and gave his usual coy smiles. Yet, he seemed just slightly quieter. Further than that, he also seemed to be keeping an unusual distance; we usually walked shoulder to shoulder, but now there was at least a step between us.

"The weather is growing colder," I ventured. "We should have the first snow soon."

"Indeed."

There was silence for a few moments, but for the sound of our steps on frosted grass and the ripple of his cloak in the wind.

I cleared my throat. "Well, I'm glad you remembered her face."

"And I'm glad you had a successful feeding at last."

"Right," I said.

He seemed dim.

"Sir," I said finally, with caution, "You're quiet. Is something the matter?"

"Not at all."

"Are you certain?"

"Most assuredly."

I paused in my step. "Are you upset that I'm pursuing this?"

He stopped in turn, gazing down at me with some surprise. "The poisoning? Not at all. It has been interesting thus far, and you were right; it isn't so involved as to be dangerous."

"Then what are you upset with me for?"

With an amused look, he tilted his head. "Now, why would I be upset at you, Mr. Bedford?"

"That is what I'm trying to ascertain!"

"I'm not upset," he replied with ease, "Only tired. I slept poorly last night."

"And why is that?"

He began to walk again, now wearing a yielding smile. "Spare me the interrogation, *Señor*, I swear I have committed no heresy."

I followed at his heels. "That will not satisfy the tribunal!"

"Very well," Alistair sighed. "Then I will confess. It is in my character to be easily plagued by thoughts, and to experience excesses of the mind as maladies of the body. Thus, my sleep is easily disturbed when I have much to ponder."

"That's all?" I said in surprise. "Why, that isn't so unusual. What manner of thoughts were keeping you awake?"

Alistair opened his mouth to reply, then closed it again, and finally shrugged. "I think I'm simply unused to so much exercise of the mind. You ought not worry. Make haste, now; we have the remainder of the night ahead of us."

I eyed him curiously, not quite believing him, but decided to have mercy all the same. In any case, drawing attention to his behaviour seemed to loosen his affect, and he seemed reassured enough to return to his usual character.

We went to the parlour, where he had left my pocket watch to dry. Upon going to the table, he twirled a brush between his fingers.

"Your dial has put me in the mood for miniatures," he said, as he sat down. "Give me something to paint while you finish reading your treatise."

"Something to paint?" I pondered, and gazed off. "Then, how about…"

I looked all around the room, wondering what subject to recommend. After a moment, I suddenly had a thought, though to suggest it made me shy.

"Do you remember the outfit you wore, when you played for me two nights ago?"

The brush in Alistair's hand paused.

"Could you paint that?" I went on timidly. "I think it would make a compelling picture, you and the lute. Don't you think so?"

After a moment, Alistair nodded. "If you consider that a good subject, I can paint it." He stood. "Wait here, start on your reading. I will fetch my mirror."

He walked off, and returned a while later with both outfit and lute, as well as a mirror. After regarding himself with the lute for some time, testing various positions and moving the candle on the table to change the light, he sat down and began.

I had a treatise to read for our studies, but could not fix my attention on it. Instead, I kept staring at Alistair over the book. At last I surrendered and went to him, peering over his shoulder; from where I stood, the fragrance of cloves and cardamom from his hair was pleasantly near.

Alistair paused, glancing back at me with a strange smile. "Have you an interest in portraiture, Mr. Bedford?"

"I should like to try it sometime," I said without thinking. My mind was elsewhere.

"Then tomorrow, I can model for you."

This made me return to my senses and balk. "But my skills are nowhere near ready; I will waste your paint!"

"I can help you," Alistair said amicably. "Mistakes in oils are easily remedied. Regardless, you must remember that there would be no waste. These works are meant for our entertainment, and remain for our eyes alone."

Alistair paused, then smiled deviously.

"Indeed, I shall give you something entertaining to depict."

"And that is?"

He returned to his brush-strokes. "And that is my secret, until tomorrow comes. Return with new books from Parker's, and I will reward you with it."

CHAPTER XVI

At dawn, I walked the long way to town. I had hoped to find a coach along the way, but saw only the occasional red fox darting through the trees; and so, deciding not to wait long in the cold, I went on as quickly as I could.

Before going to Parker's library, I stopped first at the haberdasher. Mr. McKinley shared his shop with a tailor, and I needed a new pair of gloves; for, upon having seen the state of mine, Alistair had begged me to buy myself a new pair.

Indeed, Alistair had nearly sent me into a nervous shock by trying to press a ten pound note into my hand before I left. This made me grow panicked, as I wondered whether he had entirely lost his sense of currency over the centuries.

"What are you doing?!" I had cried out, pushing it back into his hand.

He had answered patiently. "Giving you money for gloves."

"Gloves are a few shillings at most! How are you still solvent?"

Alistair shrugged. "Miss Josephine manages my finances. She does her work well."

I hesitated. From the unusually lofty wages I had received during my brief employment, I had assumed Alistair to be quite wealthy. Now, however, I realized that I had no idea. "Sir, if you don't mind my asking—when you refer to your finances, what size a sum are we discussing?"

Alistair tilted his head. "Miss Josephine mentioned a recent figure of…three hundred a year?"

I cleared my throat. "Sir…"

"What? Too much or too little?"

"Modest," I said politely.

He showed no sign of caring. "I have more stored in gold and gems, which are more reliable in their value than bonds; but it is all sitting unused, and you need gloves."

"Not gloves made of gold, sir."

"Then use the rest for your own amusement. Remember: our meals are priceless."

Thus I relented and took the note, suspecting that he knew far more of currency than he was revealing, and in truth only wished for me to take it. There was no chance that someone otherwise so careful would turn a blind eye to this most important subject.

I knew that Alistair would take heed of the gloves' quality, having a discerning eye, so when I met Mr. McKinley I chose a fine pair. He helped me with it, but as I paid I could see a glimmer in his eye. He would not let me go without more than just my payment; and so, when we had completed our business, he gave a mischievous smile.

"Well?" he said. "How did the *Count* like the ribbons?"

I gave him a look. "You still don't believe me."

"Oh, no, no, goodness, that isn't so! I was only *asking*, that's all."

"Arthur…"

"Then again, if you *had*, by chance, stretched the truth, I wouldn't mind your modesty one bit, for I understand it well. It is a joyous secret to keep, having a lover. Your raven-haired darling—oh, don't give me that peevish look, Mr. Bedford! I can't recall any man in this town with his hair so long and dark; what have you to be ashamed of?"

"Do I seem like the type to keep a secret lover?"

"You have a glow about you lately, I know it. Look—Martha!"

His wife came out of a side-room, wiping her hands down on her dress. "Who is it, dear? What is all this about?"

She was a pleasantly portly woman, with an ever-present blush across her cheeks, and warm, friendly eyes which discerned gossip just as readily as her husband's. They made a fine pair in their mischief, much to my endless chagrin.

"My dear, look at this young man," McKinley said, "And tell me whether he has a lover."

She squinted at me and rubbed her chin, as I gazed on helplessly. Then, she asked:

"How are you finding the weather lately, Avery?"

"The—the weather? Nice enough, for November."

She crossed her arms. "Besotted."

"What?!"

"Oh, I knew it!" McKinley triumphed. "I'm very happy for you."

I was flustered. "It isn't true!"

"The testimony of two against one," Martha said, as she returned to the side-room. "The odds are against you."

"But my word decides it!"

"Avery Bedford," McKinley proclaimed, with a tremble of passion in his voice, "When the time comes, I will make you your wedding clothes."

"Stop it!" I laughed, as I slipped on the new gloves and turned to go. "Please believe me, I have no lover. I have only had a pleasant month, and you are mistaking my peace with other feelings. Farewell—"

"Wait!" McKinley cried out then, rummaging for something under the counter. "Avery, come back, I have something for you."

"There's no need—"

But before I could complain, he had pressed something into my hand. It was a glass decanter filled with a faintly coloured liquid.

I recognized it at once. "Is this *cologne*, Arthur? Are you mad? Take it back!"

Yet, even as I tried to return it, he had already disappeared into the back room, though not before calling airily:

"Good luck with your paramour, my dear friend!"

*　　*　　*

With that I left, flustered and distracted. For a while I walked aimlessly down the street, shaking my head at their antics and dreading the talk that would doubtless follow; but I sobered upon remembering my task. Thus I found myself at the door of Mr. Parker's library.

Yet, just before I could push the door open, the small bell over it tittered; and out of the shop there strode a tall form, dressed in straight trousers and a coat, with long dark hair swept into a braid.

For a moment, struck by familiarity, I startled and made a sound of surprise; but I swiftly realized it only was Florence Parker, dressed in men's clothing and heading out the door in a hurry.

"Why—good morning," I said, still recovering. "Forgive my shout, I mistook you for somebody else."

"Excuse me," she mumbled, obviously preoccupied by something else, and swept past me.

"Wait!" I called after her. "Florence, is your father in?"

But she neither looked back nor answered, and soon disappeared around a corner.

"My goodness!" I remarked, but let her go and pushed the door open.

To my luck, Mr. Parker was already at the counter. His countenance was ashen and drawn, but brightened at the sight of me. His eyes twinkled over the broad spread of his moustache, and he raised one hand in weary greeting. "Mr. Bedford," he said with pleasure. "Come in, you must be cold."

"Thank you—it *is* rather cold."

"And how are you?"

"Oh, just fine."

"And the Count?"

"Behaving strangely, but by now I should be accustomed to that. He enjoyed the books from last time."

"Good, I'm glad to hear it." Already he was turning to the shelf behind him. "I had one more that I was thinking—"

"Before that," I interrupted, timid at first, but steadier as I went. "I had another matter to discuss with you."

Slowly, he lowered his hands from the shelf. "Yes?"

"I was speaking with the reverend," I began, "At the old moor church—"

Parker's look sank into misery and torment so potent that I almost stopped and apologized; but he spoke first.

"Is this about Nora?" he said quietly.

At first I was surprised to hear the name; yet, after a moment's pause, I nodded. "I'm sorry to summon any recollection that might cause you suffering; but I was wondering—"

He shook his head. "Yes, Raleigh came to town last night to ask me, too. I still don't know what happened to her body."

Stopping short, I stared at him. "What?"

For a few moments, he stared back at me before faltering. "That *was* your question, wasn't it?"

It took me a moment to grapple with my response. In the end, I could only say in bewilderment: "What happened to her body?"

"Somebody stole it, it seems."

My heart was all in a commotion; surely, something was afoot! "You have no idea who it could have been?"

"None at all; Raleigh fears it was a resurrectionist."

I stepped forward, trying to show the sincerity of my question. "Mr. Parker, if you don't mind, could you tell me what more you know about her, or where I might inquire? A friend, who was terribly sad to learn her fate, asked me to discover what happened to her."

"I don't know. I only knew her because…" All of a sudden, he paused. His eyes grew damp and he leaned on his palms, his lips tightening as he collected himself.

"Pardon me," I said, more carefully, and felt some shame for having pushed him to such a state. "If it is too—"

"No, no, there is no apology needed," Parker said, as he dabbed at his eye with a handkerchief. "Forgive me; but it was I who found her, cold and unmoving—forgive me." He stopped once again.

"It's fine!" I said, all the more gently. "I'm sorry to remind you of your pain; but did you see what happened? Where was she?"

"I found her in an old den, where I knew she sometimes stayed."

Sensing that there was more of a story there, and wishing to bring him to better memories, I coaxed him: "How did you meet her?"

A sad, troubled look crossed his eyes, distant and yet fond. When he answered, his voice trembled.

"She wanted to learn how to read."

*　*　*

Wishing not to pain him further, I gave my condolences and departed, then made haste towards the church. When I arrived to ask the reverend about the body's disappearance, he acknowledged it, but said there was not much to be done. With the chapel door always unlocked to allow the bereaved to visit their dead, it sometimes happened that grave robbers stole what they could from the bodies, though less often the bodies entire to sell.

Though I lamented the thought of poor Nora being used for some experimental atrocity—how I shuddered at it!—there was nothing more that I could do.

By the time I returned to the manor, it was far later in the morning than I was accustomed to, and I fell instantly into a dead sleep.

This was a rest so profound that it had the effect of dampening my memory; and so, when I brought tea to Alistair upon evening's waking, I had forgotten his promise from the night before. It was he who reminded me of it, with an impish look that caught me off guard.

Setting his cup down after finishing, he stood. "When you finish your tea, go to the parlour. Arrange your paints and your canvas as I have taught you. I will meet you there; only know that I may take longer than usual."

I knew not what he meant by these cryptic words, and gave him an uneasy look that conveyed as much; but I did as he said, and left to prepare my work as best I could. I made a clumsy job of it, and was contemplating my lopsided canvas when I heard the door open.

"There you are," I said, setting down my palette. "I was just going to ask—oh my *word*, what on earth is that?!"

I was aghast and in shock; Alistair had entered in full woman's dress!

"I told you I would give you an interesting subject," said he, as went to the chaise lounge and alighted on it delicately. "This will teach you well how to use colour and light. What pose would you prefer?"

When he faced me, my shock only deepened; for he had not simply donned the outfit in jest, but rather made every effort to make his appearance genuinely fine. He had donned a rich satin dress in a golden, olive colour—far out of fashion, with its voluminous sleeves and tousled, romantic elegance—which was fastened securely over a ruffled chemise, giving a generous view of his bust. Though he had no rounded breast to accentuate it, the attention was instead drawn by a string of pearls curled around his throat; and the pale lustre of these, matched with a pair of earrings gleaming like tears, was striking against the darkness of his hair as it spilled over half-bared shoulders and shapely collarbones. If I was not mistaken, he had even dabbed rouge to his lips and his cheeks

In short, it all fit him so well that I could hardly believe it. Had I seen him on the street, I might have considered him some unusually tall and old-fashioned young woman—undeniably graceful, and very beautiful.

A raven-haired beauty, I heard McKinley say in my mind, and in an instant flushed so profusely that sweat gathered at my temples.

Seeing my surprise, Alistair smiled, bringing an effect to his features that was nearly ethereal. "Have I stunned you?"

I grasped for words. "Well—of course!"

"Why?"

"You already know why," I said haltingly. "Unless you've somehow forgotten that in human customs, it is quite unusual for a man to…"

"Unusual, perhaps," Alistair replied, opening a fan in his hand. It was decorated with gold leaf, which shimmered as he waved it languidly. "But I have long considered such customs wasteful. Why spurn half the fashions that may flatter you, simply for the fact that they were made with another form in mind?"

I hesitated. "But isn't it…"

"Unnatural?" Alistair said coyly. "Unchristian? These are human words, which hold no sway over us."

"Well," I said slowly. "Even setting such judgments aside, some men might find it degrading."

This made Alistair display a bright and incensed look, and he spoke with contempt:

"Ha! How tactless mankind is. To conquer woman, parading domination beneath the guise of love and protection—nature and faith—but to so obviously reveal truth of it thus. Tell me, Mr. Bedford: if man cherished woman so dearly, why would a dress be so profound a humiliation?"

I could not help but smile at his argument; I was always struck by the passion with which he issued such challenges to the human world. Though I had once feared him for it, wondering whether it came from some deep well of hatred, I had long since realized that it was among the rare times when he thought of bettering the world, and that this ardour came from long-lost hope.

Having once lived with lofty ideals as the kindling flame in my own breast, it was on these occasions that I truly felt him a kindred spirit. Wishing to hear from him further, I prodded him with another argument. "I suppose that some would think that everything has its place."

He caught my mischief, and turned my words against me: "What do *you* think?"

I watched him for a few moments, still quite addled by the heaps of silken fabric and the flash of his eyes, which, though softened by the gleam of pearls draped all around, had for an instant had seemed to hold a fiery measure of will.

After a moment, I sighed. "Oh, then at least let me arrange your hair."

Hearing this, Alistair smiled slyly. "Gladly, but you haven't answered my question—"

"I think everything looks in its proper place, and quite becoming on you!" I said all at once, and followed the admission with flustered quickness: "I must go fetch something—wait here!"

Before he could give any answer, I fled the parlour and went down to my room. There, from a drawer, I withdrew the box of ribbons that I brought to him every morning; and in a small pouch beside the box were all the ornaments that Mr. McKinley had needlessly included.

Placing these effects back in the box, I steadied myself and returned to the parlour.

Alistair was patient as I arranged his hair, sated and complacent now that he had received his compliment. Yet, he was even more pleased, and indeed surprised, when I added the detail of an ornament.

"This isn't from the manor," he mused. "Why do you have it?"

"It was a gift," I said as I fastened it, then realized what I had implied and hurried to correct myself. "From Mr. McKinley, who has a sordid imagination and is *convinced* I am involved in some tryst."

This amused Alistair greatly. "You ought to have a dress made to your size, and truly give him something to gossip about."

"What for?"

"It is a very freeing garment, Mr. Bedford. You ought to try it."

"Oh, stop it, sir. It wouldn't suit me as well as it does you. Furthermore, I still live among human society; and if I wore something like *that* about, some might think me a…"

I stammered to a stop. I had been about to say a molly, but realized suddenly that I knew not whether he was familiar with the term.

Having been raised as I was, I felt no prudish fear over frank discussions of human relations; but for reasons that I could not identify, the idea of explaining this particular term to Alistair made me awfully nervous.

But Alistair smiled benignly. "They might think you what, Mr. Bedford?"

I hesitated, then finished stiffly: "A strange fellow."

Despite my obvious reticence, I was surprised when Alistair

pried no further, and instead busied himself with his shawl.

I soon finished with his hair, and found the look of it pleasing; it formed ringlets nicely when doused, and matched the satin of the dress with its shine. Though I knew that I could never succeed in conveying, through my clumsily painted efforts, what precisely was so handsome about the sight before me, I was satisfied to try. After all, to spend a while gazing upon something fine would be a pleasant affair.

This final thought sat peculiarly in my throat, seeming a sentiment far too heavy to be spoken.

In an effort to distract myself from any confusion, I put my full efforts into my work; and though I was unsatisfied with my depiction, as I predicted, I found myself enjoying the attempt. As I painted, I chattered with Alistair about this and that, and eventually told him of my visit to the town. To this, he gave his thoughts plainly.

"She wanted to learn how to *read?*" he said, with a sardonic smile.

"A great many people don't know how to read, sir," I said, as I tried in vain to mix a shade to match the dress. "In fact, I had to teach Henry myself."

"That wasn't my meaning."

"Then what was?"

"If your charitable Mr. Parker wishes to call it *reading,* then that is his prerogative."

I lifted my eyes from the canvas and met him with a withering look. "Sir, don't be vulgar. Mr. Parker lost his wife a year ago, and…"

"And?" Alistair said, prying at a loose thread on his shawl.

I hesitated. "You don't suppose…"

"Mr. Parker wasn't her friend; he was her patron."

I frowned. "But he *despises* that sort of conduct. When he speaks of England coming to ruin, he bemoans ribaldry above all else. Why, I have never told him my origin for that very reason."

"That doesn't mean that he has never indulged." Alistair closed his fan with a snap. "Come now, Mr. Bedford. You are no stranger to such hypocrisies."

With a sigh, I shook my head. "Very well, then I admit it is probable; but I don't blame him for it, lonely as he is. Besides, I could tell that he truly cared for her. He was near tears as he spoke to me. Such sincerity is not hypocrisy, only regret for her fate."

"Perhaps," Alistair conceded. "In knowing this man better than I, your more charitable sense may be correct. Nevertheless, I was making no judgment, only directing you towards your next place of inquiry."

"I also thought of it," I said, leaning forward to dab at the canvas. "He mentioned that she stayed at an old den."

"A brothel."

"Helmsley has no brothel, only one very tawdry inn."

"Then there you shall go," Alistair said with a warning smile. "Only take care to hide the reasons for your inquiry. The nearer you draw to the centre of it, the more you may risk. Go on any evening that suits you."

At that, I felt a pang of some unpleasant feeling. "But our early night tea…"

"Worry not. We have plenty of time for it after."

With that, he stood from the chaise lounge and stretched like a cat, before saying with a yawn:

"I shall help you with the painting before it begins to dry; but first, I must preserve this garment."

Alistair walked off, and returned shortly with the usual shirt that he had dedicated to being stained with paint. He inspected my work, praising what he deemed successful and elucidating what needed amendment.

Yet, as he leaned over my shoulder with a brush to demonstrate, he suddenly paused midway through a sentence.

Realizing this, I glanced up. "Sir?"

He was wearing a peculiar expression, as he stared at the painting and murmured: "What is that?"

"What is what?"

Alistair hesitated oddly. From his nearness, I could see the knot of his throat bob with a heavy swallow. "Orange of some sort."

I stared at the painting and could not see any orange. "Where?"

"Your new perfume."

"Ah, right!" I said, a little embarrassed. "I think there is orange blossom in it—but more bergamot, really. Mr. McKinley gave it to me."

"Bergamot," Alistair echoed oddly.

"If you find it unpleasant—"

"No, no. I was only trying to place the scent. It is very charming; let us carry on."

Though his words were agreeable, his voice seemed strained. Nevertheless, he went on with his corrections; but little by little, his focus seemed to wane, until he had been working over the same fold of fabric for an entire minute. His stance shifted, and at one point, his voice seemed to tremble.

I glanced back again. "Are you fainting, sir?"

Alistair was prone to fainting fits since childhood, he had explained to me; and indeed, aside from the one pitiable occurrence after I had shot him, he had swooned a few more times during our time together. Most were short and unremarkable spells, but others I remembered more keenly.

The first instance had been after finding a hare mauled half to death by some other animal. He had calmed it with his vampyric affinity, as I put it out of its misery; and he had professed to be fine, though appearing quite shaken, before collapsing not five minutes later.

The second instance had come during some heightened part of our reading of Hamlet, which I had cajoled him into acting out with me, and which I therefore felt quite badly about afterwards despite his reassurances.

But now, he merely shook his head. "I'm fine."

"Be honest," I chided. "At least sit down."

Though he shook his head stubbornly again, I would not have it; I brought him to the chaise, where he sank down with unusual lassitude, as I went to fetch him his fan.

CHAPTER XVII

Despite my urgency for investigating our poisoned lady's death, I felt no eagerness upon heading to town a few days later. In fact, I was feeling rather sore; the thought of trudging a long way through the cold, instead of sharing a warm pot of tea with Alistair, made me so sullen that I could hardly enjoy the walk. It seemed a waste to have an evening away.

Thus mired in my thoughts, I was relieved to finally arrive at the inn.

This was a worn old building without a sign, crouching in a dark street corner only visited by those who knew its purpose. The air was heavy with smoke when I stepped in, which mingled unpleasantly with bitter wood and the sting of liquor. A fireplace roared in the corner, casting an orange glow over the place; and near it, two weary-looking women hunched in weathered chairs. One smoked a pipe, while the other was busy pulling up her stockings. Farther from the hearth there was a large table with a number of men and women intermingled, engaged in uproarious chatter and laughter that filled the room. In the opposite corner, a pair whispered to each other. Upon hearing the door open, this pair gave a furtive glance and went quickly into another room.

This was a familiar scene to me, and I could only sigh upon seeing it.

As I closed the door behind me there was a murmur in the conversation at the table, and a few wine-softened eyes peered in my direction. At once, an older woman rose from the table and approached me.

"Welcome, sir," she said. Her ruddy countenance glowed, as she put a hand to my arm. "Do you fancy anything tonight?"

"I'm sorry," I said politely. "Not today; I have a few questions for you all."

At once, the conversation at the table stopped, and ten pairs of wary eyes were upon me.

"A few questions?" the woman asked.

I drew a few coins from my pocket and took her hand, pressing them in with a sly look. "A few questions."

At that, everyone at the table roared with laughter—"Let him ask me some questions too!" another cried out—and the woman bit one of the coins before brightening and giving a broad laugh.

"Well, you should have *said* so! Come, have a seat. Any wine?"

"No wine," I said as I sat down, setting my hat on the table. "I'm on business here, see; I'm the servant of a wealthy man, who wishes to know what became of a dear young lady here."

The entire table chimed in. "What lady?"

I feigned ignorance. "There was a lady that died here, wasn't there? Not long ago."

"Oh, yes! What a fright!"

"Nora, wasn't it?"

Over by the fireplace, the woman smoking the pipe raised her eyes. With an almost imperceptible movement she nudged the woman next to her, the one with long white stockings, whose eyes raised up in turn.

"Nora, poor Nora," another woman sighed.

One of the men nodded. "Aye, I remember her. Pity."

I lowered my voice to a conspirator's tone, though I gave a glance to the two by the fireplace. "Well? Is it true?"

The man put down his mug. "What's true?"

"Was it a murder, like they say?"

The table erupted in shouts:

"A *murder!*"

"Is there a murderer? Where?"

"Nowhere, you fool—"

"Don't be rude—"

"It very well may be! My cousin told me they *never* caught the wolf-man of Helmsley. Killed two folks!"

The woman next to the speaker of this last statement gave her a tart look. "Two hundred years ago."

The accused was offended. "Well, you *never know!*"

"No, no!" I interrupted with some dismay, seeing the conversation escape. "It was only a rumour that I heard. Did she not die here? Was there no one in her room at the time—an enemy—a rival?"

At that, the white-stockinged woman by the fireplace stood, letting her dress cover her legs. She was plain-faced, but her features were somewhat severe; her eyes glittered with suppressed ire beneath a set brow. "And who are you, to ask about her?" she said sharply.

"Now, don't ruin the mood, Ellie," an older woman called over.

"I mean it, who are you?"

Surprised to be met with such acerbity, I feigned casual disinterest. "A servant, that is all."

"Whose servant?"

I gave her a look. "What are you, a telltale?"

This led to an uproarious round of laughter. I had not intended such a reaction, and tried to quiet them:

"Please, all of you—"

At that, the woman, who the others had called by the name Ellie, flushed with fury and shook a fist.

"Then you go on and tell your busybody master, and all his *vile* friends, whoever they may be, to stop gawking at the death of my *sister!*"

In an instant, the table fell silent. A pall came over the room. The only sound remaining was the crackle of the fire.

Seeing all our eyes set on her, Ellie clenched her jaw and whirled to go, hissing through her teeth: "Forget it."

"Wait!" I cried out, standing quickly; but she had stormed up the stairs and disappeared.

A man muttered up in the silence. "Pity."

"Aye, a shame."

I stepped towards the stairs. "But I need to—"

"No use in laying chase," the other woman by the fireplace rumbled, giving a puff of her pipe. "You don't seem a bad sort, but if you follow her, she'll flay you."

I rubbed at my temple. "Will she flay me if I send her a letter?"

"She'll flay the letter," the woman said ominously, after divesting a cloud of smoke.

"Then I shall take my chances," I sighed. I took up my hat, nodding to the group. "Thank you all. I'm sorry for disturbing you; enjoy the rest of your night—"

"Wait," called the woman by the fireplace. She stood from her chair and beckoned for me to follow. "Perhaps I can answer something for you. Come with me."

A few from the table laughed and made vulgar remarks, but soon returned to their merriment.

Perplexed, I walked after her.

She led me to a stock room, where the guffaws from nearby faded behind the walls. There, among bottles and sacks of flour, she turned to me and said the last thing I could ever have expected.

"You're Adelaide's boy, aren't you?"

In an instant, I went pale.

But she only chuckled, waving a hand. "Oh, don't pull that face, I'm only asking. You were a sad little whelp when we met; I'm glad to see you've gained some foothold on life."

Flabbergasted as I was, it took me a moment to regain my wits. "When did we meet?" I stammered.

"Addy and I used to chat, when we worked on the old water lanes. When she fell ill, you came begging me for help to buy medicine."

For a moment, I could only stare. Then, I hesitated and spoke hoarsely:

"...Margaret?"

"Aye."

In an instant, I flushed with shock and desperation. Thrusting my hand into my pocket, I took all that remained of the ten pound from Alistair and pressed it into her hand with my trembling own. "Please."

She pressed it back. "Avery, keep it."

"Please, please—I beg of you—"

"Keep it, I said."

"I *never* forgot what you did," I strained, through a voice that shook violently. "I beg your forgiveness; I forgot your face, but *never* your deed, not for an instant. You were the only one who helped. Take it—"

"No."

"A crown, then, or even a shilling!"

"You know *she* would haunt me if I did, and lecture me until I followed her to the grave. I'm not apt to risk that sort of thing, if you don't mind."

I took the money back reluctantly, but pressed on with great urgency. "If I can help you in any way, you *must* tell me."

But she only sighed. "Just let me do you some good. I don't know what happened to Nora, but I know that your intentions, whatever they are, must be good. I can explain your background to Eleanor, and deliver a letter. You should expect no response, knowing her, but I can try. Let me give you my address."

I nodded, but my voice quavered as I replied:

"And I will give you mine—at least, the place I am staying for the year. You have done more than I could ever repay you for; should you ever need anything, you *must* write to me."

In reply, she shook her head as she dug a scrap of paper out of her pocket.

"I did nothing. Poor Addy still died."

*　*　*

Evening had turned to night by the time I reached the path out of Helmsley, led on through the dark by my altered sight. There was peace and silence, and the sweet scent of chilled earth. At times such as these, the night was not my enemy; it was water to a fish, and I was grateful for it.

Indeed, my mind was in a great tumult, and the cool darkness was a balm that soothed the burn of old memories. Yet, inevitably there came the familiar guilt that had always followed them.

I recalled the rowdy scene at the inn with profound unease. What had made me deserving to be borne up from places such as that? Now I was only a visitor in these lowest of places, where the simplest acts of human kindness were magnificent, and where the smallest of misfortunes could turn calamitous—these peculiar excesses, which could only come from scarcity.

Yet, the longer I walked from the town, the more I left the human world behind me, and with it all its ills. Night's safety afforded me the peace to see its beauty; and I looked up as I walked, reflecting the stars in my eyes, as I sought out the constellations that Alistair had taught me. I felt rather small.

It was then that a peculiar thought occurred to me. The scene before me was calm, and very beautiful; but I wished that Alistair could be with me. Surely he would have something amusing or intelligent to say, or he would lapse into a meaningful silence; and I would have the strange and soothing comfort of knowing that the one beside me, nearly three centuries old, was in that moment as small as I beneath the ancient sky.

I was lost in my thoughts to such a degree that I hardly cared when a coach rode up the path, until there was a snap of reins. It rolled abruptly to a stop beside me.

I looked up to find the shocked eyes of Henry, lit bright by the lanterns bolted to the sides.

How could I explain? I only called out in surprise: "Why—Henry!"

"Avery?" he cried in disbelief. "What are you doing, wandering about in the dark at this hour, in the middle of the *forest?!"*

"It was late, so I decided to walk—"

"Have you gone mad, my friend?"

Now thoroughly cheered, I laughed. "I'm just fine! Go on ahead. I thought you said you seldom travel along this road; what are you doing here?"

He ignored my question. "How are you even seeing in this blackness?"

"I know this road so well, I could walk it blind."

"No, no, that won't do. Come in at once, I would never *consider* leaving you here."

"But I cannot pay—"

"No charge!"

"Don't you have a passenger?"

"A generous one, I'm sure." Henry peered down to the coach. "Do you mind, doctor? One last stop along our way."

"Oh, no," a smooth voice said from inside, with the lilt of a slight accent. "Not at all."

"Then come in, Avery, do come in! This is the good Dr. Szilard with me. Doctor, this is Mr. Bedford."

With my peace crushed, I decided there was no other way to appease him; and so, I opened the door and clambered into the coach, sitting opposite from the man inside.

The doctor, as Henry had called him, was seated calmly.

He had the type of ambiguous visage that could have been belonged to someone anywhere from forty to fifty years of age, and wore a pair of spectacles which perched on quite an angular nose, behind which two stern eyes rested deeply-set in their hollows. His face was clean-shaven, and his hair was well-combed. In sum, he had rather the grave look of a professor,

"Good evening," I said politely, as the coach began to move

again. "Pardon me for the intrusion."

"No trouble. Do not worry," he said, in his particular accent. "It does well to have a companion on a journey."

"Oh, yes," I said absently.

"But you had no companion," he added with interest. "You were walking alone in the dark."

"Indeed I was."

"Why?"

"It gives me time to think, that's all. You can ask Henry; ever since I was young, I have rather enjoyed long walks." I cleared my throat, wishing to change the subject. "And you, Doctor? Are you on your way somewhere?"

"A simple errand."

"Is someone sick?"

"Hm," he said noncommittally.

We sat in silence for some time, until I looked up to him and said curiously:

"Say—since you are man of medicine, could I trouble you with a question?"

"Ask."

"It concerns arsenic. Do you know much of it?"

The doctor watched me curiously as the coach rumbled along. "Of course."

"I see!" I remarked. "Well, this may seem strange to you—forgive the suddenness of such a terrible subject—but I know of someone who met an unfortunate fate by poisoning, and am trying to find the truth of it. Tell me: if someone dies by arsenic, is there any way to know whether it was done by their hand, or by that of another?"

The doctor leaned back. "First, one question: how do you know it was arsenic?"

"I'm not certain," I lied, "But from the descriptions of those who witnessed it, all were in agreement that it was the most probable culprit."

"Fine," said the doctor. "Second question: how sudden was the death?"

From what Alistair had said of the amount in her blood, I answered surely: "Very sudden."

"Then the answer is simple."

"Yes?"

"I would assume this unfortunate victim took this poison with full knowledge. A cunning murderer would conceal it piece by piece in food and drink, and escape suspicion by passing it off as illness. A suicide would have no such concern."

"I see," I murmured, and thought it over.

"An interesting question to ask," the doctor said then, with a searching look.

"Ah—believe me, I ask it innocently!" I cried out at once, then called up jovially: "Henry, can you attest to my character?"

"Most assuredly!" he cried out. "The good Mr. Bedford is the last man on earth who would ever hurt a soul, believe me."

It struck me that he had been listening to the conversation in complete silence all the while; it was rather unlike him to do so.

But the doctor only shook his head calmly. "Oh, no. Don't misunderstand me; I never meant to imply guilt. I mean what I say genuinely. A sharp mind is one that searches for the best question to ask in all matters."

His words encouraged me, and for an instant, I wondered whether to ask something of vampirism; perhaps an experienced doctor such as this would have seen it. Yet, when the words had only just formed on my lips, I remembered Alistair's dire warnings on revealing any part of my nature, and the question died away ere it could be spoken.

Instead, I chatted pleasantly with the doctor on Helmsley and its history a while longer, for he explained that he had never visited; and this conversation went on for some time, until the coach slowed to a stop.

"Here we are, Avery!" Henry called back.

I stood, stooping awkwardly in the small space to shake the doctor's hand. "Take care of yourself, now. Come visit in the summer to see the heather bloom."

"Perhaps I shall," he replied.

With that, I stepped down, thanked Henry profusely with a promise to write, and headed eagerly towards the manor.

*   *   *

To my dismay, I found Alistair nearly all the way through a bottle of wine. It appeared that he had neither dressed, nor left his room; he had merely wrapped a banyan over his nightshirt, and sat at the table in his room with a glass held loosely in one hand.

It was therefore necessary to temper my eagerness upon seeing him by giving him a profound scolding.

"Sir!" I cried out, lifting the bottle to peer through it. "What are you doing, drinking so early in the morning?"

"'Tisn't morning," he sighed, leaning his cheek on his hand. With loose hair and flushed cheeks, he looked quite the pitiable picture, though somehow still graceful in his languor.

Looking him over, I sighed. "You know what I meant. Were we not planning to study natural philosophy tonight?"

"And we shall," Alistair replied. "The vampire's physiog—

378

physiology—shortens the strength and effect of wine."

"My goodness, you are drunk."

"Not as drunk as I should be," Alistair murmured.

I was perplexed. "Answer my question, sir. I have never seen you like this. Did something happen?"

Alistair shook his head.

"Are you absolutely certain?" I crossed my arms, unconvinced. "You woke, and then what transpired?"

"And then I went to the cellar," Alistair said, rubbing his forehead.

"Did you have a nightmare?"

"No. Mr. Bedford…"

"Were you having troubled thoughts upon awakening?"

"I thought you were once a butler," Alistair sighed. "Should you not have a taste for wine, and understand its draw?"

"Not at all," I said stoutly. "Indeed, that was why Mr. Crawford thought me fit for the position. I would never steal it, nor forgive any poor taste, having little value for the drink's other qualities."

Alistair gazed up at me curiously. "You never indulge in drink at all, Mr. Bedford?"

"Only as much as I need to distinguish taste, for my profession," I replied. "Otherwise, I prefer to keep all the faculties of my mind perfectly clear. To let myself sink into some torpid state would be abhorrent to me."

Regarding me with a peculiar softness, Alistair murmured: "How principled."

"Not principled, merely experienced. I have seen the worst of what it can do to a man."

I then glanced down at the bottle that I was holding, furrowing my brow.

"What is this, anyway?"

"Red."

"I know *that,* sir." I set down the bottle and picked up his glass. "Do you mind?"

Alistair seemed taken aback, and tilted his head. "You wish to appraise it?"

"Why not."

"Then I shall pour you a glass," Alistair replied; but before he could stand to fetch one, I waved him down.

"Now, now, don't bother. You have no more need for this one, anyhow."

With that, I swirled his glass briefly before having a sip from the edge.

Alistair seemed slightly startled, and stared up at me with some inscrutable feeling. His eyes fixed on the glass, then on me.

After a moment of thought, as I let the flavour diffuse over my tongue, I met his odd look. Though I could not understand its source, I found it rather amusing; and, assuming it was my judgment on the wine that he feared, I lifted the glass to my lips and took another long sip.

"How is it?" Alistair said then, a little hoarsely.

I shook my head. "Cheap."

"Ah, Josephine," he sighed, letting his head sink into his arms. "Far too scrupulous a guardian of my finances."

Then he looked up, hesitant, his gaze wavering as it met mine. After a moment, he extended his hand and added:

"What do you find cheap about it? I would like to learn. Let me have another taste."

"You only want your wine returned."

"I mean it truly."

Relenting, I handed it back. "Watery, and rather too sour. Try it again."

He took the glass with care. There was a trace of conflict in his countenance that almost seemed like guilt; but he raised his eyes to me and put his lips to the glass, then drank very delicately from the rim.

With my arms crossed, I waited. "Do you have a finer sense of it now?"

He shook his head and set it back down. "I find it sweet."

"Then if you are good, and I don't find you drunk on this swill again, I shall select a fine bottle for you from town on Christmas day. If *this* is good enough for you, then you will think *that* all the sweeter."

"Very well. I will remember that promise."

"And I shan't forget."

With that, he seemed both sated and uneasy, as he leaned back in his chair. "Sobriety should return within two hours' time. Until then, I beg your patience and your forgiveness."

Indeed, just as he promised, by the time I returned later the flush had gone and his speech had evened. He gave me an apologetic smile, restored to his usual elegant nonchalance, and gestured.

"Shall we?"

Thus we went to the library, and spent a pleasant day on the study of animals. This subject, Alistair seemed to know so keenly that he scarcely needed any book to describe it.

There was, however, one more peculiar moment later.

We were in the library with our late-night round of tea, as he explained some particulars on bats. For this purpose, he had found and called down the little bat Aeneas.

Unlike Dido, who had bitten me soundly at the start of our sojourn in the library, Aeneas was far more amicable. After

Alistair had held out the wings, showing me the delicate bones that stretched the skin, he released the bat to let it crawl onto the table; and when I held out my own hand, it came fluttering to me.

Seeing this small creature burrow willingly into my palm, I was once again beset by an excess of affection. Petting it, I cried out heedlessly:

"What a *fine* lad you are, warming yourself in my hand!"

At once, I heard raucous coughing, and looked up to find that Alistair had choked on his tea.

"Are you all right?" I said, quite startled.

Nodding, he dabbed at his lips with a handkerchief. "Fine."

"Is your throat dry from the wine?"

"I said I'm fine," Alistair replied, though he seemed a touch morose.

"All right," I said doubtfully.

CHAPTER XVIII

Alistair was most certainly not fine, and this matter began to claim my attention.

After having sent off my letter to Eleanor and receiving no reply, as I had been warned, I let the matter of our poisoned lady rest in favour of the more pressing issue: some dark thing was plaguing Alistair. Perhaps because of my fixation on the new mystery, I had failed to notice this change as it came on; but now that we were spending the days together as usual, it was impossible to ignore.

His manners towards me never changed—if anything, they were improved—but he was holding his distance, expressing his thoughts less and falling silent more. Before, he had exhibited familiar gestures regularly; he would occasionally touch my shoulder or my elbow, whenever he meant to reassure me or adjust my position as I painted. Now, he refrained entirely.

I could not fathom what was causing these alterations in his character. In my mind, we had carried on pleasantly for the past months, but now this notion seemed in doubt. There was a part of me, tactfully hidden, which felt hurt; I had placed a measure of faith in him, enough to tell him my history—which I had told nearly nobody in all my life!—so why did he withhold his own trust?

It was an old and childish feeling that I had, a kind of greed. How ardently I wanted him as a friend, and how frustrated I was to have no means of expressing it!

The most notable change came when I woke him in the mornings. Often, he would be weighed down in a heavy sleep, and I had to call his name many times before he roused. He remained tired throughout the day, and even fell asleep sometimes while I was with him.

On the first few occasions when it happened, I would call his name until he opened his eyes. "I was listening," he would murmur, with a wave of his hand. "I'm only resting my eyes. Do carry on."

After some time, I stopped waking him when it happened. He looked so tired that I pitied him. Instead I simply sighed and leaned back in my chair, watching his breath slow and his shoulders sink down.

My own sleep was not unaffected. As I tried to rest, I would think of one-thousand ways to win his trust, and this obsession lent itself to uneasy dreams.

This carried on for perhaps a week. Then, one night, I walked into his room to wake him and found him in the midst of a nightmare.

Usually Alistair slept soundly, with a grace and restfulness that made me envious. But now! I looked on in anguish; for his brow was tightened stormily—an alarming flush blotted his skin—his sleeping expression was all pained and resentful helplessness, which alarmed me greatly.

I set my tea tray down loudly. "Sir, wake up!"

But this did not wake him. Instead, he only shuddered and turned his head, still mired in whatever horror his mind had conjured.

All at once, my frustration flared within me. He had never trusted me, never let me help him in any way! What, then, was my purpose in staying? How was I meant to help him, without even the opportunity to know what plagued him? I could not help him, but I had to—and I would!

In a fit of desperation I flew to the wash stand, swept off a jug of water, and thrust it forward like a sling, sending forth a sea of water that drenched both Alistair and the bed in an instant.

Alistair opened his eyes.

For a few moments, as I stood panting with the jug held unsteady in my hands, Alistair stared up at the canopy. Then, he sat up, looked down, and lifted one soaked lock of his hair.

I swallowed, my face hot. "I…"

"Mr. Bedford," Alistair said, with slow incredulity, though he was still breathing somewhat heavily from the nightmare's exertion. "Did you *douse* me?"

I looked down at the jug, then back at him, at a loss for words. "Well, I—"

"Why?"

"You were having a nightmare, and I couldn't wake you!"

At that, he seemed to remember it. A troubled look passed his eyes, but he shook his head. "Fear not. A dream is fleeting." Then, he added archly: "A waterfall isn't."

I was red with shame. "My apologies, sir—ah, I don't know what came over me!" I set the jug back on the stand, upset at myself. Why had I done something so impulsive? "It was all I could think of to wake you quickly. Here!" Again I came to his side, and seized the edge of the sopping bedsheet that covered him. "I can take this—"

"Wait—"

"It will dry faster if I hang it up. Here—"

"Stop," Alistair said, and caught my wrist with his hand. He avoided my gaze. "I will do it. In fact, kindly leave me for a quarter hour. I have need to compose myself."

"At least let me help you with the sheet."

"I would prefer to compose myself first."

This frustrated me. "You never let me help you! If you tell me what is happening to you—"

"Mr. Bedford—"

"And in any case, the tea will grow cold, and—"

"Mr. Bedford!" he exclaimed suddenly. "I *implore* you."

I jumped in surprise. It was rare for him to raise his voice. "Well, all right, then!" Though I was offended, I took the tea tray. "I will return."

With that, I slipped back into the hall and closed the door.

Placing the tea tray gently on the floor, I took the time to walk through the halls. The sky was a beautiful colour, as the last of the setting sun caught golden across the clouds and gilded the night; but I was much too concerned to give it my full attention, half-sulking and half-worried. Alistair's distress had disconcerted me.

When I returned, however, the sight that greeted me was very different.

He was already sitting calmly on top of the bed, buttoning a waistcoat over his shirt. His hair streamed down his back, the ends coiling gently; and behind him, the soaked bedsheets were already set aside. His jug and basin had been moved to the bedside table. Most surprisingly, in contrast to his poor state earlier, Alistair now seemed to glow with health.

Upon hearing me enter, he looked up and gave a pleasant smile. "Good evening," said he. "I do apologize for being abrupt earlier; I have never taken nightmares with much grace."

Suspicious, I stared at him. "Are you feeling well?"

"Well enough. You ought not worry."

I sighed as I walked over, and set the tea tray down firmly.

"Sir, we need to talk."

"Ah."

"Oh, yes. We are going to have a—what did you call it once? A tea—a tet—" I bristled. "A conversation, then!"

Though his lips pressed with an urge to laugh, his eyes held subtle shame. "An interrogation, you mean."

"You trust my good intentions, don't you?"

"Of course," he said, folding his hands in his lap. "But this is a matter which has little to do with trust or intent."

"So there *is* something wrong, isn't there!"

Alistair only sighed and shook his head.

I handed him his cup. "At least tell me why it must be a secret. Do you suppose that I am so delicate, and will run at the mention of any trifle?"

"I know you won't, Mr. Bedford," Alistair said quietly, as I began to arrange his hair. "It is among the qualities I most admire in you."

This caught me off guard; I flushed, and then stuttered. "Well! Then what's the matter with telling me?"

Alistair hesitated, and had a sip of tea before answering reluctantly:

"Let us go out for firewood, and we can speak along the way."

*   *   *

A light snow drifted down, leaving a dusting on our shoulders as we tramped along.

The snowflakes spanned as far as the eye could see, bobbing and whirling agreeably in the wind, turning the night to a dance of one thousand specks. The day preceding it had left a blanket of white over the moor—not heavy enough to make passage difficult, but sufficient to dress the land in gossamer. Across this barren landscape, the only life was the single red fox we met along the way, which slunk silently across the woodland and vanished into some den.

We gathered our firewood separately, and only met again once we had found enough; so it was only after lashing our respective bundles, and starting back towards the manor with the wood on our backs, that Alistair finally made some effort towards answering me.

"You told me that you once wanted to be a clergyman."

This inquiry surprised me. "I did."

"Then you must understand what it feels like, to have a wish you can never fulfil."

Rather perplexed, I glanced over at him. With inky hair and dark cloak, he stood out starkly against the pale winter landscape; the pink of his cheeks in the cold shone brightly among these contrasts, giving him a wistful glow.

"Well, yes," I said, after a pause. "Sometimes."

"And did it not cause you great pain to lose it?" he mused, eyes dark with thought. "You found a wonderful dream, the dawning realization of what would give your existence meaning; but it was not to be. Had you been allowed it, you would have devoted yourself to it so wholly as to carve it into your soul and make it your heart. Without it, you were left with nothing but an overflowing cup of sweetness, which was destined to spoil away—bound to you forever, souring to regret."

He spoke these words with such sincerity, and such gentle pain beneath it, that I was glad to have the frigid wind to hide my flush of surprise. "So you're plagued by a dream of some sort?"

"I suppose," he murmured.

For a moment, I thought over his words as we treaded across the snow. The night was very quiet, and in the moonlight the snowflakes twinkled like drifting stars.

Finally, I scoffed. "You aren't wrong, and yet you are."

He gave me a weary smile. "How so?"

I adjusted the rope over my shoulder. "Well, of course I still carry my old dream with me, and ponder what could have been. It is a part of me, even if it was never realized; but it need *not* be realized."

Deciding that I would have to speak more openly than I was accustomed to, I cleared my throat and continued:

"I wished to be a clergyman because I hoped to help others find divinity, and to teach them compassion and grace. I thought I might spread goodness in the world, and sow hope; but I can do that outside the clergy, perhaps even better than from within." I coughed, embarrassed, but still went on. "That is why I have found satisfaction in being a servant. It isn't the profession itself that I dream of, but rather the pleasure of taking good care of something that holds value to the world—be that an illustrious family, or a fine set of dishes, or some other thing that I cherish dearly!"

At this point, I spared a glance towards Alistair, expecting to find mild curiosity or reluctant acquiescence. I found neither.

He was staring at me indecipherably.

I faltered, but then strengthened my voice. "I think…whatever you are *dreaming* about, sir, whatever impossible wish is causing you such pain, must be an *expression* of something that you already have, or something that you can already do. At the source of the dream—there, you shall find your remedy!"

As he listened to me speak this final phrase, a twinge of mirth entered his expression. When I finished, he tilted his head back and gave a lavish laugh, letting a cloud of chilled breath into the air.

"Ah, Mr. Bedford, you are right," he said merrily. "You always have such charming insights."

I felt startled at his sudden merriment, but ventured nonetheless: "Charming or not, are they helpful?"

There was a glimmer of mischief in his eye. "Yes. You have opened my eyes; I think I have everything I need, after all. I possess the nearest to my dream than anybody could ever hope to attain, and perhaps that is enough."

"Oh, sir, for God's sake!" I burst out; I could stand my curiosity no longer. "What on earth is this wish of yours?"

But Alistair only shook his head. "Forget my wish; it matters not. I am curious to hear more of yours."

My heart was suddenly beating quite hard, and not from the exertion of the walk. "Mine?"

"You said something compelling," he replied. "You said—"

But all of a sudden he froze, and held out an arm to stop me.

I stopped short. "What?"

"Hush. Do you hear that?"

I furrowed my brow and strained to hear; and then, very

faintly, I heard the high-pitched cry of an animal.

"What is that?" I said, but Alistair had already started towards it.

Surprised, I held tightly to the ropes over my shoulders and tramped off after him. When I finally caught up, he was crouched in front of a hollow log, staring deep into the jagged open end; and from inside this dark recess there came a faint bleating, which strained both ear and heart.

Approaching slowly, I tried to lean over and peer in. "What is it?"

"A fawn," Alistair murmured. Slowly, he let the wood off his shoulders, setting it down beside him. "I think it has lost its mother."

I clicked my tongue. "Poor thing. It must be frightened."

"Indeed," Alistair said, and continued to stare into the log. As I waited there and watched, he held so still that snow fell on his cloak unimpeded.

Then, gradually, the bleating faded away and stopped.

I shivered despite myself. "What's the matter with it?"

Alistair finally drew back, and settled on the ground. "Look down."

Though I was confused, I stared down at the fresh snow. Though it took me a moment, I finally cried out: "Fox tracks!"

"If the mother was merely out foraging, the fawn would not cry out. They were separated."

"Well, what should we do? Do you know where the mother is?"

"Nearby, I believe," said Alistair, tilting his head. "They may find each other soon without our interference, but I would prefer to make certain of it."

"All right," I said, setting down my own bundle of wood. "Do you need help?"

"No, no," Alistair murmured, then gave me a playful look. "I suppose this is as good a time as any to show you something new. Stand back."

I stepped back dutifully, allowing ample space. A few silent moments passed.

Then, slowly, from within the log, a small nose peered out and greeted the cold air. It was only after a few moments that the fawn stepped out gingerly, tottering on spindly legs through the snow.

Alistair received the animal into his lap as it came to him, letting it settle down. After petting the tawny fur for a few moments, and indeed looking quite pleased, Alistair glanced up at me. "Are you ready?"

I must admit to having been transfixed at the sight, and took a moment to respond. "For what?"

"This," Alistair murmured, and pulled a glove free from his hand with his teeth—and pressed his thumb to his fang, drawing blood!

I was a little startled. "Sir?"

"It only needs a trace," he said. "Come, now, Mr. Bedford. Do me a favour and guard my body for a moment."

"Guard your body?" I said, baffled, as I crouched down and settled beside him in the snow. "Where is the rest of you going?"

"On a brief journey," Alistair replied. In his lap, the fawn had begun to lick the wound.

"My goodness! What on earth are you doing?"

"I will show you," he said patiently. "Do me another favour, now, for I have need to concentrate. Count from ten to one— slowly, if you could."

And so, I gave him a quizzical look and began:

"All right, then. Ten, nine, eight…"

Alistair closed his eyes.

I swallowed. "Seven, six, five…"

The fawn in his lap grew still.

"Four…" I hesitated. "Three, two…"

A cold breeze blew across us, fluttering hair and fur alike, though not a muscle moved.

"One."

There was a moment of dead silence, as the snow fell around us.

Then Alistair's eyelids lifted and I gasped, nearly scrambling back; for his eyes had rolled back, showing only his whites—and yet, in his lap, the fawn had suddenly lifted its head and stirred!

"Sir!" I cried out.

But Alistair moved not. Only the fawn tottered up, and raised its head to meet my gaze.

I returned this stare, then gasped in realization:

"Sir?"

Seeming satisfied, the fawn then rose up from Alistair's lap. Steadily, with movements altered to peculiar gracefulness, it trotted off.

I watched it go for a long time, dumbfounded, until it had vanished into the landscape. After staring emptily into the trees for a few moments, I returned my attention to Alistair's listless body.

He was still sitting just as he had been, though his head had tilted and his shoulders loosened, somewhat like a resting marionette. Only one matter undid this illusion: after a particularly frigid wind, he began to shiver.

"Sir, hurry up," I urged, giving a shiver of my own, though I knew not whether he could hear me.

Alistair gave no reply.

Realizing that his body was senseless, I crawled up and took his one gloveless hand. After rubbing it between my own and blowing across it warmly, I slipped his glove back on.

Still, he shivered.

Growing frustrated, I tightened his cloak around him. "Oh, for goodness' sake, hurry! Can vampires freeze to death?"

But from the briskness of my movement, I upset the balance of his poise; and before I could do a thing, his weight spilled down into my arms.

"Fine, then," I sighed, and decided that it was for the best. Pulling him near, I bundled him to my chest and scolded him. "Now, don't make a fuss when you return, I had no choice."

Now certain that he could neither hear nor feel me, I warmed him briskly; I pulled off my own glove and rubbed his cheek, then the shell of his ear. Both were ice-cold, which only served to redouble my efforts.

Whenever my mother and I had run out of coal at the old inn, we had huddled precisely in this manner, and thus staved off the worst of the winter, so such efforts were not unusual to me; but upon gathering him near, I felt something quite unfamiliar. I thought it pleasant to hold him, and suddenly wished to hold him more tightly—much more so, as though I might even crush him.

A little startled at this thought, I searched within myself and found no trace of anger which would prompt such aggression. I only had the picture of pressing him near until he woke from his trance, and watching him give a surprised look from beneath frosted lashes, as he gasped for air from between cold-reddened lips—all the while, still burrowing close for warmth; and somehow, this thought was all the more appealing to me.

Though I was a little unsettled at the eagerness I felt, I took it to be a fierce and misplaced sort of endearment, as one might feel for a young animal or a childhood friend. Yet, just when I was beginning to question this sense—Alistair's eyes slid shut!

I held still, and waited with bated breath.

Then Alistair's lashes lifted, and he murmured with his sight still half-glazed:

"Bergamot."

Yet, at once, he realized where he was and gave a look so alarmed that it rivalled that of the fawn.

Seeing this, I decided to spare his dignity and announced:

"At last! You were freezing to death, sir, and your body would not stop shivering. Are you all right?"

"Mr. Bedford," he said numbly, then pulled himself upright just as quickly. Sweeping his hair back, he brushed the snow from his clothes. "My apologies for the length of my absence. I would not have had you trouble yourself for my sake."

"No trouble at all," I said casually, and stood to take up my bundle again. "More importantly, did you find the mother?"

"I did," he replied, though he still seemed addled by something, and took up his own bundle once more. "She was waiting by the beck."

"Were they happy to see each other?"

"Quite happy," Alistair replied, and finally appeared to regain his peace.

We began to walk again, heading towards the manor.

"Say," I said, suddenly curious, "How can you do that without living blood?"

"The animals? I suspect the vampire may maintain a trace of a single particular power in their corpse-fed state, though much diminished."

"Then—do you think I could do it, if I tried?"

"Not on corpse blood." He glanced back at me, and seemed almost wistful. "As much as I would like to teach you, I have the sense that your most essential ability may be another, which you have perhaps expressed without noticing."

"Without noticing! What could it be?"

"I know not," Alistair replied cordially. "You will tell me once you notice it, so that we may verify."

I thought over his words as we emerged at last from the trees, and started along the frosted heath.

"Well, if I were you, I would make more use of my powers," I said, as I clambered over tangled tree roots after him. "You should buy a horse."

He climbed a hill, then turned to wait. "On my income, Mr. Bedford, I should hope that a horse might buy *me.*"

"A cheap horse!"

"Even a fair Rocinante would put me in debt."

"You have no reason to live so scarcely, you know," I said, catching my breath as I reached him. "You have so much land! Why not take on a few tenants, and increase your income tenfold?"

He shook his head. "Because it would compromise my safety."

"Why, it would do the opposite! A fortune is safety and power intertwined, and may change your fate in an instant. I should know." I sighed. "Sometimes, sir, I do feel that you have no sense of what money could do for you."

But he only smiled. "Sometimes, Mr. Bedford, I feel that you think too highly of what it might do for *you.*"

"How so!"

"The more one has, the more others can take, and in their greed they may justify their hunt."

"Their *hunt?* Please, sir! Who would hunt you? A few grateful tenants?"

Waving me along, he strode on. "Then let me tell you what a few grateful tenants could do."

*   *   *

"Do you know what a deer park is, Mr. Bedford?"

The two of us sat opposite each other in the armchairs by the library fireplace. Our boots rested nearby, melting snow onto the hearth; and between us on the table, a pot of coffee sat steaming and fragrant.

I spoke slowly. "Why…an old hunting ground, I think."

"Old now," Alistair replied, "But not so old when I still walked these lands as a human—or rather rode them, on a horse just as you dream of. My father and I were sometimes invited to these parks, and I got a fine sense of it."

Then, leaning back comfortably, Alistair took a drink from his cup and went on:

"These were more than hunting grounds; they were the treasured playthings of the aristocracy. With permission from the king, a lucky noble could enclose one of these vast lands, sealing the fate of the animals within."

Despite the warmth of the cup in my hands, I shuddered. Nevertheless, Alistair proceeded, in a low and tenebrous voice:

"Sometimes, this land might be a paradise, lush and plentiful, where animals roam blissfully and rear their young. No deer could ever dream of a finer Eden—"

He leaned forward, with a gleam in his eye.

"—at least, until the baying of greyhounds came across the hills. What do you suppose happened then, Mr. Bedford?"

Though I already knew, I answered him in a whisper: "What?"

"Massacre," he said, meeting my gaze over the rim of his cup. "Slaughter, swift and inescapable. The quiet of summer turned to chaos, the fearful sounds of fawns. Bowers and nooks, green and lovely, painted with blood. Home turned to horror; hearth turned to grave."

I shrank back in my chair, but answered weakly. "It is grotesque and unfortunate—it is!—but animals do the same to each other, and it is no less natural for humans to seek sustenance—"

"Sustenance?" Alistair laughed coldly. "No. Remember who owned these parks, Mr. Bedford; these were men who had all they could ever want, except for the right to slaughter the innocent in hordes. Picture a man delighting in shooting you and your brethren in your beds, neither for sustenance nor safety—only for the amusement of killing something that flees."

I ventured again: "Then would you also consider the peasant cruel, for hunting to survive the winter?"

"Yes, but we can label that as an unfortunate fact of nature, if you wish. The deer park was different; this was cruel instinct engorged beyond the natural, beyond the human." He waved a hand. "Besides, if your concern was for the peasants, rest assured that even a single step into this plentiful land would secure them the same fate as the deer."

Chilled, I said nothing; and so at last, he settled back again and finished his point.

"That is why I will never take tenants, Mr. Bedford. In your time, it seems that many of these deer parks have turned to farmland, and humans tend to them peacefully; but somewhere, deep inside, I have no doubt that they still long for their former violent pleasures."

The firelight caught on his expression, making his eyes seem brilliantly aflame.

"They may not remember; but I do."

*   *   *

I could not sleep that night.

As I tossed and turned in bed, tangling the covers, two things plagued me.

The first matter: I wondered what Alistair's dream was, which had been so ardent as to put him in a state of distraction. Remembering the manner in which he had watched me as I spoke, I wondered whether it involved me. Was he dreading my leaving next autumn? Perhaps it was presumptuous to dare think that he might value my company so dearly; but for my part, even though it was many months away, I had begun to dread the same.

Would Alistair really be so affected by me, by my presence or the lack of it? I had known being wanted before; certainly, the Crawford children had wept when I left them, and Mrs. Crawford had told me over and over how much she regretted my departure. Yet, none of these attentions had awakened in me the odd feelings that this did.

The second matter: I could not stop recalling the sight of Alistair settled in the snow with his cloak pooled around him, holding the fawn in his lap and stroking it gently.

Realizing that an easy sleep would be hopeless, I went to my desk and tried to draw what I saw in my mind. Yet, the charcoal left me unsatisfied. Alistair's visage was very fine, and difficult for my unskilled hand to depict, especially if not drawn from life.

Pondering it for a moment, I suddenly remembered something.

I opened my door and crept out. It was morning, and I listened for Miss Josephine before finding my way to a storage room, where most of the painting materials were kept.

Here, on a small tray, there laid a few miniatures. Among them, the one Alistair had made of himself on my recommendation rested peacefully.

After a moment's hesitation, I took it.

When I returned to my room, I found that I was too tired to continue the attempt at my drawing. Instead, I went to bed and held the miniature overhead, gazing up half-asleep—staring at the slight smile on Alistair's face and his delicate hands on the lute, and remembering the music he had played for me that night when I had been so ill.

At last, resolving to finish my drawing some other time, I tucked the dear little painting into my night table's drawer and fell instantly asleep.

CHAPTER XIX

After our talk, whatever heaviness Alistair held in his heart seemed to ease; and he returned for the most part to his usual sound sleeping and calm spirit, which much assuaged my concerns. Though I still glimpsed traces of what plagued him, and he certainly behaved oddly at times, he seemed to be bearing his burden almost gladly, as though finding it fine and honourable to do so.

With this matter settled, I could have returned to pursuing my mystery. Yet, precisely at this time, there came an interruption far more pleasant.

Over a week had passed following my last sojourn into town, and November was coming to an end. With this, the winter holidays drew near; and though Alistair admitted to giving them no particular significance, he assured me he would be pleased to accompany me in any traditions that pleased me.

Thus, when Stir-Up Sunday came, I decided to make a fine plum pudding. Unwilling to be left bored as I worked, Alistair joined me in the kitchen. I directed him to gather and mix the ingredients, while I busied myself with candying orange peels; yet, at first he was determined to make mischief, and pretended to steal the brandy until I threatened to pour it all out.

I had made one change to my recipe, however. Remembering his distaste for the needless slaughter of animals, I used butter in place of suet; and when I cleared my throat and stiffly mentioned this alteration, he gave a soft laugh and placed his hand upon my shoulder.

"Mr. Bedford, we are scavengers. I would not have objected to using the remnants of an animal that a human has made fair use of."

Even so, I felt that he was very pleased with me after that, and he henceforth followed my instructions with such diligence that he could have made a fine kitchen maid. For this, I rewarded him with a few spare candied orange peels.

Yet, after we had put it all together, and I was tucking it into a pudding cloth, he surprised me with a question:

"Say," he said, as he reached for another peel with floured fingers, "What became of your charge?"

I stopped his hand, and handed him a rag. "My charge?"

"Your poisoned lady," he said, taking the rag and wiping off his fingers. "I was anticipating your next attempt."

Wrapping the pudding cloth carefully, I hesitated. "Nothing became of it."

"Nothing?"

"Why, for one so against the idea of investigating it, you certainly are curious!"

"That was before I found it interesting," he admitted. "I

cannot help it, Mr. Bedford; you make me feel young again, and full of vigour."

I flushed a little and scoffed, though I still passed him another handful of candied peels. "Scarcely a day over two hundred, I presume."

"Perhaps even one hundred," he replied, receiving them gladly.

I took advantage of his occupation with the peels to think over what to say, and at last sighed, settling for the truth.

"I decided to stop searching."

Alistair paused, and seemed mildly surprised. "Why?"

Meeting his stare, I set down the pudding and turned to him. "I was thinking it all over, and I simply…"

I hesitated, then went on with reluctance:

"If this was truly a self-murder, which seems quite likely now, searching further might sully her good name—or whatever remained of it, in any case. If her body was ever found, and could not be buried properly due to my meddling, I would never forgive myself. Perhaps the truth was hidden for a reason, and her sister at the inn was right to admonish me."

Alistair regarded me indecipherably as I spoke, and something dark crossed his expression. He seemed to hold back a thought until I had finished, then said evenly:

"Self-murder, Mr. Bedford?"

I felt a chill run through me, and returned my gaze to the pudding. "Well—yes."

"You mean a suicide."

Wishing to end the conversation, I shrugged. "Either way—"

"No, not either way. These terms are both meant to describe the indescribable, and to make rational that which defies all rationality. Thus, neither of them captures the true meaning of the act; but the one you used adds something that certainly has no place there."

"All right, then!" Now quite desperate to be free of the subject, I acquiesced. "A suicide."

"Why did you use the uglier term, if you have professed your sympathies for its victim?"

I was in a cold sweat. "Because I can have my sympathies, but self-murder is what it is! A terrible act, which both good moral conscience and the law would frown upon—oh, please, sir, why must you raise such an awful subject?"

"Because I disagree with you," he replied smoothly. "I have always thought it an injustice that a suicide should be regarded so cruelly. How vile is humankind, creating a hell and reviling those who seek to flee from it."

I shook my head. "No, sir, I *must* object. If the human world is hell, then a suicide is the wood that stokes its fires. It is a selfish and inexcusable thing, to take one's own life; it condemns to rot every kindness and sacrifice made in one's name, leaving only misery behind!"

"A suicide is someone overcome by unbearable suffering."

I turned on him, suddenly quivering. "It should *never* be done!"

"Did I say that it should be done?"

"You are certainly implying it!"

"When I was fifteen, my mother leapt to her death from her bedroom window."

I fell silent so abruptly that I nearly swallowed my own tongue.

But Alistair had said the words evenly, as though he had long ago made peace with the matter, and seemed neither upset at my callous words nor cognizant of my sudden pallor. "You're right that a suicide leaves misery behind. I was miserable for a very long time."

Then his gaze softened, and he finished quietly:

"But I never resented her. I only wished that she would have told me her burden before she leapt, so I could have found a way to save her. I would have done anything to save her."

For a few moments, I was stunned. When my voice at last returned to me, it was much diminished.

"I'm sorry," I said hoarsely.

"Trouble yourself not."

"I must—I'm truly sorry, sir. I spoke without thinking, and offended you severely."

"You were being honest with me, which I value. No offence was taken. I only ask of you two things."

Nearly trembling with shame, I nodded. "Anything."

"The first, that you never say *self-murder* again in my presence."

"I promise," I said ardently. "Neither in your presence, nor in that of anyone else."

"Excellent."

Then, he pointed to the stove and gave a pleasant smile.

"The second: that you please finish our hard work before the fire goes out."

"Right!" Remembering it, I turned quickly to the table, and continued tying the pudding cloth. Yet, as I did so, I began to face trouble. My vision blurred, and my movements turned clumsy.

Alistair finished his last orange peel before tilting his head. "Ah, wait, you said you wanted to put a sixpence in it; I shall go find one."

Without speaking, I pressed my lips together and nodded.

After that, he headed out the door and down the hall, and his steps soon faded into the distance.

Now left alone, I stopped.

Then, I took a spare rag, pressed it to my face, and wept.

By the time Alistair returned, I had settled myself. Still, I was in disbelief that he had accepted my rudeness so forgivingly; and so I was somewhat docile, and allowed him to tuck the little wrapped sixpence into the pudding wherever he pleased.

*　　*　　*

With the pudding stored away for Christmas day, I felt quite cheerful in anticipation of the holidays, and the month that followed was pleasant indeed.

Time passed quickly, as our studies resumed and gained in their vigour. Now that Alistair had helped me lay the foundation for various subjects, it became far easier to add to my knowledge. There were times when I became so lost in it all that I forgot everything—my own history, my strange situation, the world outside the moor—and lived my life knowing no personal past or future.

The only thought I devoted towards the future, particularly as the year's end approached, concerned the coming of Christmastide.

I woke on Christmas eve quite elated, to the point where I might have called it giddiness. I was a little embarrassed by myself—never had I greeted the holidays in such a manner!— but this was the first Christmas when I was neither a pauper nor a servant, but rather someone about to have a holiday of my own.

The snow had become thick and difficult to tread through, but I took an axe and headed outside upon awakening. Wrapped in a heavy coat and scarf, I was breathing with some effort by the time I reached the thicket of trees far behind the manor.

After circling a while, I finally settled on a tree that seemed thin enough to handle, and had a good bit of moss on it. Satisfied, I proceeded to shrug off my coat and unbutton my waistcoat, and folded them neatly by the old rope and tarpaulin I had brought; and after rolling up my sleeves, I finally braced my axe in hand and gave a few hearty strikes.

Yet, after a good while of working at it, I felt a shiver up my spine which came not from cold. Pausing, I glanced over my shoulder.

There was a deer standing nearby, unusually still and unaffected by the loudness of my work, watching me fixedly.

Wiping at my forehead, I turned to stare at it. "What?"

The deer stared back, then flicked an ear.

"Sleep a little longer, sir," I said, hefting up the axe again. "I shall return soon, and wake you properly."

After a moment longer of stillness, the deer seemed to suddenly come out of a daze, startle at my nearness, then leap off into the wintry landscape.

I had not been mistaken in my suspicions. Before long, I heard the crunch of footsteps through the snow, and glanced over to find a figure in a dark and billowing cloak treading towards me.

"Mr. Bedford, what are you doing?"

By now I was nearly through the trunk, and turned to Alistair with laboured breaths as he approached. "Don't you want a yule log?"

Alistair paused in his step. There was something peculiar in his regard, as though he was trying not to observe me too closely. "Are you not cold?"

"The work staves it off!" I called back. "This will be well worth the trouble, anyhow; it may not last us all twelve days, but it should give us a festive fire at least for a long while."

With that, I resumed my chopping

Alistair lingered a little longer, before calling out: "Do you need help?"

"No need; I am almost—" I grunted, as I gave another hard swing. "—through it!"

"Very well," Alistair said, but remained.

Noticing this, I gave him a quizzical look. "Go on inside and warm up. Put up the rosemary!"

But instead, after a moment's pause, he trudged up and held his hand out for the axe. "May I?"

"All right," I said curiously, and handed it to him. "But this might be the last few swings, so be careful and don't cut me in half."

With that, I propped my hands against the bough, nodding for him to begin; and he gave it a try, producing a muted thud with the blade.

I laughed. "Put more strength into it than *that*, sir."

His hair tossed as he gave it a heavier strike, and he let out a cloud of chilled breath. Whether from cold or exertion, his nose and his cheeks were both red. "I think you are stronger than I."

"Then take off your coat. It is far easier to move without it."

Alistair glanced briefly at my bared arms, then looked away and shook his head. "It would make little difference. You were probably strong in life as well, and have kept this trait."

"Perhaps!" I remarked.

Alistair gave a small smile. "From your more difficult days, I presume."

"Indeed," I said, and laughed wryly. "When I went to the old boarding school, the other boys were quite pleased to have a pauper to ridicule; but after a good round of fisticuffs, they never gave me trouble again."

To that, Alistair parted his lips as though about to say something, but held his silence.

Yet I was cheered somehow, and spoke boldly. "If you have never done it before, perhaps I can teach you to wrestle."

With an expression of either woe or helplessness, Alistair shook his head. "I would not think that wise."

This made me playful, and I decided to tease him. "Are you afraid?"

"No."

"I will be gentle with you, sir."

At that, Alistair clenched his jaw and gave a fierce swing to the axe, which struck the tree so soundly that it echoed.

I gave a cry of encouragement and propped my hands against the trunk again. "There! Just like that, go on, now!"

Panting and flushed, Alistair gave a few more swings of comparable force, until soon there came a tremendous crackle through the wood. After that, it only took one push to topple the tree, which came down with great force into the snow.

Seeing it fall, Alistair flung the axe aside and sat down in the snow, breathing heavily.

"See?" I cried out. "You have some brawn in you after all, sir!"

Alistair shook his head. "Not anymore. That was all of it."

"Well, I would hope you have more left," I said, gathering up the rope. "We still have to bring this back."

He sighed. "Can we burn it here?"

"Now, don't dally!" I began to tie the felled tree. "If you've tired yourself out, at least take yourself inside and get warm."

Hearing that, Alistair promptly pulled himself up, then

headed for my coat. "I will help, so long as you get yourself warm first."

We dragged the log along with rope and tarpaulin. Alistair struggled mightily, but refused to let me do it alone; so I roused him by making him join me in singing Oranges and Lemons, which I taught him through repetition until at last we reached the yard.

*　　*　　*

I lounged in my armchair in the library quite comfortably, watching the fire roar.

Christmas eve, though to us it was our Christmas day, had been so pleasant that I could hardly remember ever feeling so wholly at peace. We had decorated the great hall, and played music together, and finally shared the pudding we had stored away. My piece had the sixpence, though I suspected Alistair had spied it in his part and exchanged it for mine.

I had wanted to try playing snapdragon, but Alistair warned me that a vampire's innards might have less tolerance to fire, so I relented. Instead, we amused ourselves with a book of riddles, whereupon my inexperience drove me to beg for clues. The worse my answers were, the more delighted Alistair seemed; and seeing his mirth, I ceased to make any effort, and instead gave ever more outlandish answers. My wild justifications for these made Alistair laugh so heartily that the sound rang.

To finish the night, we took a basket of parkin and walked to the tallest hill on the estate, where we had a wonderful view of the moor. We remained there for hours, swapping amusing stories from our pasts and working our way through the gingerbread until dawn had begun to break.

Upon returning, we were both happy but a little ill, having eaten more than our physiology would prefer. Thus, we returned to our respective rooms. For my part, I slept like a stone.

We had decided to devote the next day to rest, and do nothing at all, waking at our own leisure; so I arose to a morning alone, and made myself tea. This left me restless, however, and I stared at a second cup for a while before sighing.

After milling about for some time, unsure of what to do with myself, I hauled a portion of our yule log to the fireplace and set it ablaze, before settling down to idly darn an old pair of stockings.

Now I gazed into the roaring fire and wondered what to make of the warmth in my heart, which still had no name by which I could confidently describe it.

I had been there perhaps an hour when I heard footsteps, and caught a hint of cloves and cardamom. At once, I was roused from my languid thoughtfulness, and scrambled up to look around. "Sir?"

It was indeed Alistair, striding up calmly. Yet, this time, the scent came not from his person, but rather from the tray in his hands.

"You made something?" I said in surprise. "Why, you were meant to be resting."

"I intend to rest," he said, setting it down on the table. "Do you mind if I join you?"

"Not at all," I said, then smiled fondly. "What have you made?"

"Have a guess."

"Mulled wine?"

Alistair shook his head. "Not quite."

"Do I have to answer a riddle?"

"No riddles today," Alistair replied, pouring a cup. "I had thought to mull wine, but remembered that you have a certain distaste for it, so I mulled chocolate instead."

I was startled, and felt suddenly very touched. To think that he had gone to the trouble of inventing something for my sake!

This had the effect of stirring my emotions from before, so as I received the cup from him, I could not help but give him a long and troubled stare.

Catching this look, he paused. "Would you prefer wine after all?"

"No, no, this is perfect," I said quickly. I took a drink, and felt the warmth of the spices all the way into my chest. "Quite perfect—thank you."

"Excellent," he said, pleased. "Then carry on with your work. Tell me if I am disturbing you."

After pouring his own cup and settling in his armchair, he took a book out from under his arm to read.

We sat there in silence for some time, as the fire crackled comfortably. Every so often, I heard the sound of him turning a page.

It was unusual for me to feel so calm, I thought to myself. Somehow, the mere presence of Alistair beside me was soothing. Perhaps lulled beneath the influence of this feeling, I dared to speak.

"Sir, would you mind a question?"

Alistair glanced up from his book.

Clearing my throat, I stared down at the cup in my hands. "It is about—well, the nature of the association between us."

In an instant, Alistair became so rigid that he seemed fashioned from stone. His stare grew fixed on the fire, as though he dared not look at me.

At once, I rushed to correct myself. "It's nothing bad! I was only curious about something."

But Alistair did not seem calmed, and if anything was all the more tense. In a strained voice, he answered: "Yes, Mr. Bedford?"

And so, at last, I took a deep breath and asked:

"Do you consider me your friend?"

Alistair stared into the fire a moment longer.

Then, with a sort of desperate helplessness, he put his forehead in his hand and began to laugh.

At once, I felt absurd, and flushed red. "Well! I—I suppose you might say that friendship is a human word, and you would be right, but—"

"Mr. Bedford," he interrupted gently, still laughing, "Of course I consider you my friend. I have done so for a very, very long time."

"All right," I mumbled, though I felt a swell of relief, and wished desperately to sink into the armchair and vanish.

He caught his breath, still giving that strange and tender smile. "Furthermore, your question troubles me. Have I given any sign to the contrary?"

"No!" I said quickly. "I simply—it might seem ridiculous to you, but naming this sort of thing matters to me."

Alistair shook his head. "It isn't ridiculous at all. Ah, this was my fault; knowing that you keep your life so orderly, I should have made myself clearer."

At this, I felt ashamed. "No, no, it really is fine; it is only my particular habit."

"Then I have a question for you as well," said he, with a twinkle in his eye, "Would you also name me as your friend?"

I stared red-faced into the fire. "Yes—I would."

"And is this the highest honour I can ever hope to have from you?"

I nodded solemnly. "It is."

With that, Alistair sank back into his chair; and though he smiled, there was something almost mournful in his regard.

"Very well," he murmured, so softly that it seemed meant for his ears alone.

I glanced over, still smouldering from embarrassment, and wondered what he meant by it.

Before I could ask, however, he gave a curious hum. "By the way, if you were uncertain of our friendship before, then how do you introduce yourself to others in town?"

"I call myself your servant. It is a convenient explanation, though no longer true."

He frowned. "I see."

Seeing that he was unsatisfied, I offered more. "Remember, they all knew me as the Crawfords' servant before. To see me suddenly without a profession, like some leisurely gentleman, would strain their belief or inflame their suspicions."

Alistair stared off, clearly still displeased.

"But," I ventured carefully, "If you would prefer, from now on, I can call myself your steward."

This piqued his interest. "My steward?"

"Perhaps."

"How cunning," he taunted. "Have you promoted yourself, Mr. Bedford?"

I had a sip of my chocolate. "As one must."

"You make a habit of it?"

"Of course," I replied, settling comfortably into my chair. "It is all I have ever done."

"Is that so."

"Quite." I closed my eyes for a moment. "Why, when I first arrived at the Crawfords' residence, it was the only matter on my mind. I began as the deputy to the valet—a glorified footman, you see."

"A difficult ladder to climb."

"Yes—but I worked hard at it!" I exclaimed. "For instance, when Mr. Crawford went hunting, I would always make sure to have loaded weapons at the ready; and every time he shot, I ran up and told him—'Jolly good shot, sir!'—before handing him a new one."

"What if it hadn't been a jolly good shot?"

"I still told him it was a jolly good shot."

This sent Alistair into mischievous laughter, which I was very pleased with. In fact, after the initial embarrassment had passed, I was glad to have asked him my question directly; for what a relief it was, to now have some natural way to describe my anxiety for his company, and the warmth I felt at his laugh!

After that, I was instantly in good spirits, and thought up an idea. "Speaking of servants, it is boxing day."

"So it is."

"Will you give something to Miss Josephine?"

Alistair paused for a moment, then shook his head slowly. "That would not be wise."

"Come now, sir! Why not?"

"Josephine is the most convenient maid who I have ever employed," Alistair replied, swirling his cup. "She mistrusts me enough to leave me alone, but tolerates me well enough to keep my secret. Any gift, no matter how well-intentioned, would be seen as some nefarious plot."

"Would she really be so rude?"

"It isn't entirely her fault." Alistair had a sheepish look about him. "I must admit to have contributed to this sentiment deliberately, in order to ensure her distance."

"But she isn't the traitorous sort. Now that you know her character, why not soften your relationship?"

"As I said, she would never accept it. Her judgments are chiselled from stone as well as any statue."

"Humour me and try."

Alistair gave me a sidelong look, mildly amused. "You truly want that?"

"Truly!"

And so, Alistair sighed; but he took the pot of mulled chocolate from the table, and poured another cup before rising from his chair. "Very well, then. I shall indulge you. Come."

Curious, I followed him.

We walked to the servant's hall and came to stand before Miss Josephine's closed door. It was early in the evening, but Alistair still listened carefully before giving a nod and knocking briskly.

"Josephine," he called.

There was silence.

He knocked again, this time more insistently. "Josephine."

A muffled voice came from inside, sounding rather annoyed. "What?"

"Come out a moment. Mr. Bedford is here with me."

I raised my brows at him, to which he replied by mouthing: *she trusts you more.*

In that instant, the door opened. Miss Josephine stood cautiously in the doorway.

Giving a cordial smile, Alistair held out the cup of chocolate. "For boxing day."

For a moment, Miss Josephine stared at him as though wondering whether he had gone mad, then slowly moved this dry regard towards me.

I returned a smile and a subtle nod.

Without a word, she took the cup from his hands.

At this, Alistair displayed a look of some surprise, and folded his empty hand politely behind his back before bowing. "I trust you will find it—"

"If it has any blood in it, I'll show you boxing," Miss Josephine snapped, and shut her door with a resounding blow.

"—pleasant," Alistair finished, then sighed. "Ah, Josephine, Josephine, what shall I do to earn your favour?"

When he was met with silence, his smile faded somewhat. Then, he went on in a tone somewhat quieter and more genuine:

"When have I ever done anything except what you have asked of me?"

That startled me, and I watched him curiously.

Then, slowly, and to my even greater shock, the door opened again.

This time, however, Miss Josephine did not appear. Instead, she merely thrust her hand through the opening and pushed something at Alistair, who took it more or less without a choice. Then, the door shut again, this time for good.

We both looked down into his hands, where a small pile of rounded black shapes had been piled.

Alistair hummed thoughtfully. "I have no idea what this is."

"Liquorice, sir."

"For what?"

"For eating," I replied. "It is popular in these parts. Try it."

And so, Alistair tried one curiously. Though he immediately made an expression of such wretched disgust that I had to seal my lips with both hands to impede my laughter, he swallowed down his grimace before turning to Miss Josephine's door and saying pleasantly:

"Thank you, Josephine, how generous of you. Please enjoy the rest yourself."

With that, Alistair handed the rest of the liquorice to me, and we returned to the fire. After pouring ourselves another hearty round of chocolate, we spent a long time in comfortable silence.

I could not help but look over to him every so often, half-asleep with comfort, and marvel at how arduous the journey to this point had been. How much had changed in three long months of cordial company! The one who I had once considered my bitterest enemy, and could barely tolerate out of fear and loathing, now came seeking my mere presence to read by the fire; and for my part, I was no less pleased by his company. Not only had I regained my peace, but found a rare friend.

At this thought, however, I frowned.

A peculiar feeling had come to me, when I conceived of that final word—as though something had tugged at the strings of my heart, which I had considered to be quite finely tuned, and instead produced a most discordant note.

CHAPTER XX

The peculiar feeling from our conversation at the fire lingered long into the night.

When I studied it closely, I found that this was no stubborn resentment, but rather another sentiment entirely: a sort of impatience, mingled with dissatisfaction—as though our talk had not put an end to my questions at all.

Yet, when I came to this realization, I was not unsettled. After all, it was only natural that a word such as friendship would never be sufficient to describe our relationship; and to believe that it could—what folly that would be! Alistair himself had always told me that to obstinately define something with an ill-fitting term was a human tendency, which had the effect of blinding one to a subject's true nature; and here, this was precisely the trouble. There remained complexities between us that could never be so neatly defined. We were certainly friends, but we were also many other things: two lone survivors of our kind, former enemies returned from the brink of murder, accomplices in our crimes at the chapel. It was reasonable to reach for more than one word.

When dawn came, I bid Alistair a good sleep, and decided to take our remaining gingerbread across the moor to Mr. Raleigh. It was on this brief sojourn, which I had meant to spend lost in my thoughts, that I was interrupted by a voice crying out:

"Help! Oh, mister, help!"

I turned in an instant, then spotted someone bent low over the ground. Hurrying to this fallen figure, I spoke briskly. "What's the matter? Are you hurt?"

It was then that I realized the person before me was a girl of perhaps sixteen years, who was perfectly unharmed, but engrossed in feeling her way frantically across the ground. Upon my approach, she spoke morosely, never removing her gaze from the withered grass.

"Mister, you *must* help me; I have lost my brooch!"

My worry vanished into wry amusement. "You were calling out for *that?*"

"Of course!" she pleaded. "It is my favourite brooch, and I have lost it. Won't you help?"

Heaving a sigh, I set down my basket and my hat, then searched all around. "What does it look like?"

"A flower!"

In the dim early morning, my vampire's sight still held a keen advantage, and I soon spotted a silvery glint among the grasses. Walking over, I picked up the brooch, which was indeed an ornate spray of flowers with a gem, and held it out to the frantically searching girl.

"Is this it?"

With a cry of joy, she leapt up and took it. "Thank you, oh, thank you, sir! I would have died of sadness, you have saved my life!"

Once she stood, I was able to see her outfit. She wore a periwinkle dress with a high and tailored waist, lengthening her figure to columnar dignity with its pleats; but a dense cloak, dyed a dark and noble blue, drew a wilder contrast. A few curls of hair escaped a shapely hat, which was decorated in a fine silk ribbon, and her cheeks were healthy and full. Simply put, this seemed to be a young lady from a family of good means, which left me with one crucial question:

"Young miss, what on earth are you doing in the middle of the moors at this hour? Are you lost?"

"Not at all!" she remarked brightly. "I came out for a very early walk, while everyone is still asleep."

"Everyone?" I said, bewildered. "Your family—where are they?"

She pointed off into some obviously feigned direction. "I came to visit my uncle's family for Christmastide. They have a farm over that-a-way, but I've really come to see the moors."

"Well, you've seen them now," I said, in as stern a voice as I could muster. "Come along! You shouldn't be wandering here on your own; when they wake and find you missing, they'll be worried sick. I'll help you find your way back."

"You will do no such thing!" she laughed, pinning her brooch back onto her cloak. "They know I wander. I came to explore the moors, as I have always wanted to, and that is what I intend to do."

"Young miss, it is dangerous here. There are wild animals—"

"My name is not *young miss.*"

I sighed. "Then what is it?"

"Mary!"

"And your family's name?"

With a cunning look, Mary lifted her chin. "That is my secret, which I shall not give up to you."

A little exasperated, I gathered up my basket and shook my head. "Fine then, Mary, I have done my duty and warned you. Should anything happen, I leave the rest to God."

With that, I began to walk again, but she followed me.

"Say, mister!" she said, bounding after me at my heels. "Are you headed to that old manor?"

"I am," I said shortly.

She cried out in elation. "So it *is* you!"

"Me?"

"You must be the earl who owns it!"

I shook my head. "The owner is neither I, nor any earl."

"Then why are *you* walking towards it?"

"Because I am the owner's steward," I said, stopping mid-stride. "And you really ought to keep far away from the manor. He abhors to be disturbed."

She ignored me. "May I visit? If you are his steward, can you invite me?"

"Absolutely not. Miss—"

"Mary!"

"Mary, your manners are quite shocking," I chided, desperate to find a reason for her to stay away. "If you want to see some quaint old place, go to Helmsley—or better yet, take a walk at the abbey ruins. Those places are far more interesting, and neither will get you run off an estate or in great trouble with your family."

Mary sighed sullenly, then at last relented.

"Fine, I will let you be—but would you at least answer a question, sir steward?"

Hearing this title from her mouth, I felt quite oddly, as though it did not describe my relation with Alistair after all; and so, I decided to amend it. "That is Mr. Bedford to you."

"Then, Mr. Bedford," said she, with a gleam in her eyes, "Could you tell me something about the old manor, and whoever owns it?"

Seeing this excitement in her, which I myself had once felt upon first arriving to the manor, I sighed and softened slightly.

"There are places on this moor where the past still lives," I said quietly, "But it wishes not to be disturbed. If you respect it, it may reveal its wisdom; if you bend it forcefully to your will, your own conceit will be your only reward."

This, she listened to with wide eyes and an interested disposition. Seeing that she was paying attention at last, I decided to return to my point.

"So run on back to your family!" I called, as I resumed my stride. "If you go now, you might steal your way inside before they wake."

This time, she did not follow me. She only watched me go for a while, wearing a distant look, before raising one hand to wave.

"Fine! Farewell—but I shall be waiting for my invitation!"

*　　*　　*

When I returned to my room that day, I did not go to sleep at once. Instead, I paced for a long while, unsure of anything, but knowing one matter for certain:

I was beginning to feel quite strangely, and not at all clear on my own thoughts.

To hear the word *steward* from my lips had not satisfied me; to hear the word *friend* from my lips had not satisfied me; and yet, surely, there must be some word for what I was suffering beneath! Yes—suffering, I could call it now, for it was truly beginning to plague me.

After a long while, realizing that I was wasting my sleeping hours, I went to bed. Still, even then, I could not rest. Instead, I took Alistair's miniature, which I had never returned, and turned onto my side to gaze at it. This was a habit which had begun since the day I took it; it had the effect of quieting my thoughts, reminding me of that engulfing peace which Alistair's presence afforded me, and lulling me to rest.

Yet, tonight it did its job rather too well, and I never returned the miniature to its place in my bedside drawer. Instead, I let my eyelids weigh heavy, and my hand grew limp with the object in hand.

As I drifted into rest, I had a dream.

*　*　*

I was trying to study, and something was disturbing me.

My attention was mired in a book, but I realized I could not read it. The harder I looked at it, the less I understood, and this put me in a state of great frustration. Yet, just as I was wondering why, I realized that I was being distracted—someone was distracting me, and preventing my work!

Behind me, two voices were whispering and laughing softly.

"Sir, I'm trying to study," I said stiffly, turning a page.

But the sounds behind me ceased not. Indeed, they only changed; whispers had turned to murmurs, and laughter to soft sighs, accompanied by the rustle of clothing.

Then, at once, there was the luscious and unmistakable sound of a kiss.

Feeling terrible frustration well up inside me, I turned in my chair almost furiously. "Would you *stop?*"

Alistair was settled on his bed, and somebody was there with him. It was a woman, wearing the olive-gold dress that Alistair had worn for my portrait of him; and the two of them were engrossed in each other, ignoring me entirely. As I watched, he embraced her and pressed another kiss to her lips, which she took with a soft sigh.

Then, his hand, which had formerly been engrossed in caressing her long and stockinged leg, slipped beneath the skirt of her dress.

I stared, wide-eyed, as an unfamiliar feeling sank through me. It was slow and thick as syrup, yet somehow potent. Though I could not look away, I did cry out, now quite incensed:

"For God's sake, sir! Would you go somewhere else? I'm trying to study—"

But he continued to ignore me. Now, his hand was sliding up further beneath her skirt, and his lips had found her neck; now she quivered, and a striking blush spread through her cheeks and coloured her face entire—until suddenly, she drew a sharp breath.

Hushing her gently, Alistair then began to move his arm in a steady rhythm. His elbow undulated gently, rustling the dress along with it, while I stared without moving an inch.

Frustration welled up, but I did nothing; indeed, I had entered a sort of dull-eyed trance. The pounding of my heart spread through my body entire, until even my skin seemed to thrill with it. I was so furious with him!—furious at the press of each finger forming shallow valleys in her thigh, the warm crush of his hold, the wine-like heaviness of his presence. I could almost feel it all myself, I thought with a certain revulsion—but soon, I realized something dire.

It was not a woman who Alistair held in his arms. It was I!

All along, I was the one being held, and it was my own plain self that was being pressed flush against Alistair's form. In the moment that I realized this, it was made real, and I looked up to the familiar face looming above mine.

I felt an unspeakable thrum across my skin, and was suffused with a certain expectant weakness. He could not—he would not—surely, I had made some mistake! In my shock, I made no move, only stared as he lifted my chin and coaxed my face nearer.

Feeling my head so gently guided, and my waist so securely seized, made me tremble with thrilling and visceral dread. My lips, which I had never thought much of, were suddenly being eagerly appraised. I remembered the luscious kiss I had watched him give the woman only a few moments ago; it had seemed so soft, and yet so vulgar and provoking in its intimacy! Realizing that this too would be my fate, I shuddered and closed my eyes.

Yet, when I could just barely feel the ghost of lips against mine, he stopped and smiled.

"Say, Mr. Bedford." He ran a thumb across my cheek. "Tell me something."

I opened my eyes slowly, as he went on with a murmur:

"What do you know about lust?"

"Lust?" I said hollowly, lost in his expression.

Then, all at once, I realized that his arm was still moving beneath me somewhere—it had never ceased!—and I gasped, clutching it desperately as it worked.

"Sir!"

Crying out, I embraced this arm madly, as though to lose it might kill me.

"Sir—mercy, mercy—*sir!*"

I woke with a start, bolting straight from the dream in a fit. For a moment I only sat still, panting madly.

But I soon became aware of the painful throb of my heart; and to my great embarrassment, its pulse had found its way through my veins, down through my body, and to the crucial place which inflamed with me such shameful frustration that I could barely stand it.

"Good God!" I exclaimed, and rubbed my eyes.

This problem, though not unfamiliar to me, had never presented itself in quite this manner.

I loathed to commit any act that would bring me shame, even if it would alleviate that excitement which I wanted no part of; but it seemed impossible to return to sleep in such a state. First I went to my basin, and splashed my face with cool water. Lingering over it breathlessly, I let droplets trickle down my face.

All the while, I was stricken with shock. Why on earth had I had such a dream about Alistair?

I tried to dispel it with uneasy amusement, deeming it one of the many absurd tricks of the mind, apt to reach for anything and concoct vulgar stories, willing to corrupt even the purest of friendships. The sleeping mind, I thought to myself, was like a lecherous old man whispering in one's ear; no part of it made up my true feelings.

But when I thought again about the position I had found myself in, the lazy heat of the embrace, the press of his hold and the promise of a kiss, I shivered; and upon this shiver I felt a renewed swell of wilder stirrings, which stoked my frustration further still. In vain I appealed to disgust to quell the urge, but found no answer.

For a moment I was awfully embarrassed; how would I look Alistair in the eye, knowing that my unconscious mind had produced such a strange thing?

Yet, though I did briefly entertain this worry, I soon shook it away and dismissed it. However powerful the effect had been, it had only been a dream, which would surely soon fade away and be forgotten. So long as I spoke nothing of it and left it to be lost, it would influence no part of our relationship; and since it represented no aspect of my true intentions, there was no reason to fret at all.

This reasonable thought eased my worries, but did nothing for my greater problem; the unfortunate excitement produced by my dream had not abated. At first I tried to sleep, but only managed to toss back and forth, trying in vain to ignore it. Then, I read from the book at my bedside; and finally, I stepped out into the daylight, letting the frigid air cool me. The latter eased my suffering at last, and in time I returned to bed and fell back into sleep.

I had been correct in my judgment. When I awoke, I barely spared a fleeting thought towards the entire event, and for a while forgot it entirely.

*　*　*

The rest of advent went wonderfully. We burnt our way through the rest of our yule log, which indeed lasted a few more days, and enjoyed the remaining holidays.

On New Year's Eve, I taught Alistair how to sing Auld Lang Syne, which I might even say that he adored. This time, I would have no respite; he made me sing it three times over as he accompanied me on the piano, only joining his voice with mine when I begged him to spare me the sound of my own unseemly warbling.

On Twelfth Night we had a lovely cake, which we decided to decorate with confectionery to look like a wintry landscape. Then, over our respective slices and cups of chocolate, we exchanged gifts. Neither of us had known that the other had prepared something, and so we ended in the amusing question of who should have a turn first, which we resolved by drawing cards.

Alistair's turn came first. He handed me a small wooden box, then held up a hand to prevent my opening it.

"First, I have a confession to make."

"All right," I said slowly.

"I opened your pocket watch, but could not reassemble it."

I sighed. "Well, don't fret, it was barely useful anyway."

Just as soon as I had spoken, I froze and looked down at the box in my hands, then helplessly back up to him.

"Oh, sir, *please* tell me you didn't."

Alistair gave a sly look. "What ever could you mean?"

"For heaven's sake, tell me you didn't!"

"You haven't even looked inside," he said patiently. "Before you plead with me, at least know what you're worrying over."

Consumed with dread, I set my jaw and opened the box with clammy hands, taking a single look. Then, immediately, I shut it and tried to thrust it back into his hold. "Absolutely not!"

He gave a resonant laugh, and would not take it. "Come now, Mr. Bedford—what was it you said? Don't fret."

I must admit to having been on the verge of tears. "How could I not fret?"

"You accepted the violin. Is this so different?"

"Only because you already *owned* it, and threatened to burn it otherwise; this is another matter entirely!" I paused, then added nervously: "Or did you already own this as well?"

"No. I sent Josephine—thrice, so you must thank her," he added pleasantly. "Once to describe the selection to me, once to deliver my miniatures for the enameller to copy, and once to collect it. It has been quite a trial to hide it from you for these past two months."

Now knowing for certain that it had been newly bought, I balked and cried out: "Sir, this is beyond your means! How much did you spend?

"That secret dies with me," Alistair replied, folding his hands in his lap. "But rest assured, it was not so terrible a cost. I had Josephine take in a few pieces of jewellery to offset it."

I put my head in my hand, unable to bear it.

"Come, now, Mr. Bedford," Alistair laughed, and placed a coaxing hand upon my shoulder. "I never meant to embarrass you. I only wish that you should keep a good count of your time, which ought always be as precious to you as it is to me."

"Not this precious," I said, through a voice that grew ever more unsteady. "You don't understand what you're saying."

Alistair gave no reply to that, and only waited patiently.

At last, seeing that I would not escape it, I braced myself and opened the box again.

Inside, laid out in silk, was a small golden pocket watch with its key laid out beside it. The watch-cover bore an enamel miniature, delicately framed; it was a deer curled beneath a bower.

I gave Alistair a despairing look, which made him laugh quietly and say: "Open it."

Still aghast, I then lifted it out of the box and opened the case to reveal the face.

A finely lettered dial laid beneath, set with filigree hands, which overlaid the painting gleaming in the very centre: it was a view of the manor from a high point on the moor, surrounded by greenery and blooming heather.

"Sir," I said hoarsely. "I really wouldn't know what to do with this."

"I already wound it for the day."

"That isn't what I mean."

"Then put it on your chain," Alistair went on patiently. "Do you have it still?"

I nodded listlessly.

And so, Alistair smiled as he leaned forward, searched in my pocket for the other end of the chain, and fastened both watch and key before tucking them back in.

All the while, I stared at him and was entirely overwhelmed. There was a wild urge in my chest, which swelled and crowded my heart; I wished to leap forward and embrace him. Knowing that this would be well beyond untoward, I instead spoke to him very softly.

"I don't know how to thank you."

Alistair gave a sigh as he settled back. "How about *my* gift?"

Hearing this, I flushed and suddenly felt terribly ashamed of my own effort, which could hardly compare to his. "You must give me more time. What I have now is so foolish—"

"Will you make me beg for it?"

For the second time that night, I put my face in my hand. "I'm so embarrassed."

"Mr. Bedford."

"I couldn't possibly."

"Please?"

And at last, I reached into my pocket and glumly held out my gift.

This was a square handkerchief, of the finest quality that I knew, which I had embroidered with a border of hawthorn branches. In the corner, however, was my neatest detail: I had added our two library bats, Dido and Aeneas, in the midst of flight. I considered myself skilled in embroidery, and had spent hours refining my work, but how could it compare to what I had just been given?

Yet, when Alistair took it and beheld these designs, his expression glowed; he was stunned. "Is this your work, Mr. Bedford?"

I managed to nod.

"You made it for my sake?"

"I did," I said quietly. "I thought you might—"

All of a sudden, my hand was being taken and enveloped, and was squeezed with such warmth that it would have put any embrace to shame. Astonished, I looked up.

Alistair regarded me with outright fondness, which seemed so genuinely fervent that it shocked me.

"Thank you, Mr. Bedford," he said in a strained voice, as though holding back much more. "I will keep it on my person."

Deep inside my chest, something dire began to ache.

It was something like the day I had woken up ill; I was roused to the fact that I was in terrible pain, though I knew not why. Watching him fold the handkerchief tenderly and tuck it into his pocket, I felt nearly ready to burst.

Indeed, I might have burst, had Alistair not distracted me with a question. "And the other object behind you?"

"Ah, right, I nearly forgot!" Grateful to have another topic, I reached over and handed him a bottle. "This isn't quite a gift, being paid by your pocketbook, but I thought you would like it. It is a good port wine—very sweet, which I know is to your taste. I did promise."

He was pleased. "Excellent. Thank you for your keen memory; I had forgotten."

Then, setting it aside, he paused. Something crossed his eyes, and he glanced back towards me.

"Now you have given two gifts, and I only one."

"Well! As I said, the wine was from your account, not mine."

Alistair shook his head. "But I, too, have something for you that was originally yours."

"Do you?"

With that, as though it pained him a little, Alistair reached into his pocket and drew something out.

In an instant, I recognized my silver pen knife, which at one point had been poised to deal him a final blow. "Why, that is…"

"Forgive me," Alistair murmured. "You asked for it when I gave you the option, but I could never find a good time to return it."

Then, as though he wanted to rid himself of it quickly, he reached forward and placed it in my hand.

For a moment, I stared at it with something like shock.

Then, I dropped it.

"Mr. Bedford?"

I could not answer him; I was beset by a sudden terror. I remembered that I could have killed him.

"Mr. Bedford."

Had I killed him, I realized, there would have been nothing: no learning in the library together, no bats named after an opera, no painting, no lute or harpsichord or flute, no tea and conversation every morning, no watching deer in the snow, no singing while dragging home a yule log, no clumsy confessions of friendship, no exchange of gifts over slices of cake, no warmth, no peace—none of it, not even the idea of it. Had I pushed in the blade, I would have been left with nothing but a silver pen knife dripping in blood, a corpse riddled with wounds and dead forever with all its wisdom, and nothing else in the whole of my life but endless night. The manor was a minuscule spot of warmth in an eternity of cold, and could have vanished at any moment.

"Mr. Bedford, breathe."

"I'm sorry," I gasped. The world around me seemed to spin. "Sorry—"

A steady hand rested on my back. "The fault is mine. I should have considered this."

"You were wearing something underneath your clothing, weren't you?" I said, still breathing shallowly. "Some metal plate, or leather—you wouldn't really have let me push in the knife, would you?"

Alistair watched me silently.

I swallowed, nearly choking on my own breaths. "How did you know that I wouldn't push in the knife?"

His voice was dark and quiet when he answered:

"I hoped you wouldn't."

This made me wild with panic. *"Never* trust me like that again, do you hear me?"

"Ah, Mr. Bedford," Alistair reassured me, and pressed my shoulder with his hand. "Worry not. You have given me no reason to doubt you." He picked up the pen knife. "Still, if you wish, I can keep this a while longer."

"Please," I burst out, then felt ashamed as I regained my wits.

"I know it's only a knife, but it reminds me so vividly…"

"It is no trouble at all," he replied, and smiled as he tucked it away. "When I have convinced you of your own trustworthiness, I shall return it."

After that, I left the awful memories behind gratefully, and we returned to our pleasant night, which was only interrupted by one more startling event: when Alistair opened the door of the library, Miss Josephine's vulgar book fell and struck him on the head.

"For the watch, I suppose," he sighed, as he leaned over and picked it up. For my part, I was consumed with laughter.

Time resumed its steady pace after the holidays, and the weather was bitterly cold. Snow came soon to coat the rolling lands in white, a colour most startling when awash in the pink of dawn. Alistair and I would watch the snowfall from the tall library windows, and the winter moon was very beautiful.

Then, there came a day in the middle of January.

CHAPTER XXI

Alistair and I trudged through the snow, heading towards the church.

The snowfall had made our regular path difficult to pass, so we took another. It was the dead of winter; the land was barren, and overcast by a dusty rolling of clouds which dampened the snow to an ill grey.

At one point, I fell into a snowdrift, and Alistair helped me stand. As I regained my footing, he gave an entertained little smile and said wickedly:

"Now imagine hunting for living blood in these conditions."

"I don't know how you could," I admitted, brushing the snow off my coat.

"You could," Alistair replied, as he ventured on, though breathless from exertion, "But you would live like primitive man, on the brink of starvation: always preoccupied by the thought of your next meal, and nothing else."

"Well, I feel rather preoccupied right now," I mumbled, as I nearly stumbled over a half-buried bough.

"We are nearly there."

True to his word, we arrived at last, and took a minute to rest behind the chapel. Alistair called down the barn owl, and we watched it for a while before sending it away.

Then, I climbed up the steps to the chapel, pulled open the door—and gasped!

All around the inside—arranged over the tables, along the floor and around the corpses, and even tucked into cracks along the windowless walls—an enormous amount of dried white flowers were arranged. They were beautiful, and yet there was a fearful quality about them that made me shiver.

I stepped in, utterly bewildered, and leaned over to pick one up. The small, pointed petals, which formed a neat bulb, bobbed as I lifted it.

"Sir?" I said, turning to Alistair.

I found him wearing a look of apprehension that I had seldom seen. He was entirely serious and alert, and the sight of that frightened me more than the flowers.

But his expression eased as he glanced at me, and I had the sense that he had muffled his worry for my sake. "There is nothing to fear."

"What are these?"

"Garlic flowers."

I started and dropped it with a gasp, but he shook his head.

"They cannot not harm you. Remember: if you haven't fed on living blood, you are invulnerable to remedies like this."

"Could this mean—!"

"Somebody is trying to ward vampires away."

My heart seized with fear, and the pit of my stomach plunged.

"It cannot be! They suspect us?"

"Be calm."

"How are *you* so calm?" I cried out. "Did you not once tell me that encountering a vampire hunter is the most terrifying trial one can face?"

"A *skilled* vampire hunter," he corrected, coming forward. "Whoever placed these here has no experience. To put garlic flowers in a mortuary is a fool's errand; a true hunter would know that a vampire feeding on corpse blood would be invulnerable. Someone must suspect there is a vampire, someone who has read too many old folk-tales and little else. Remember, you told me that the body of our poisoned lady was just stolen. Suspicions must be high."

"Oh, God!" I suddenly felt weak, as I came to a terrible realization. "This is my fault!"

"No, no."

"But it is! I asked the whole town about Nora—I led everyone to come here, and see our bites; there can be no other reason! Why else would they be thinking of vampires?"

"Similar things have happened before," Alistair offered. "It isn't unusual to find warding charms in a shroud."

"But this?" I said, gesturing frantically as I looked to him. "Is this not beyond that?"

"Yes," Alistair admitted. "It is."

"Then why aren't you worried?"

Alistair lifted off his heavy cloak, draping it around my shoulders. "I *am* worried, but worry will do us no good. Be calm, Mr. Bedford."

My knees were trembling. "What do we do?"

"Nothing," he replied, "For nothing has happened yet. We will feed, then take a few precautions upon our return to the manor. I have planned for this, and will explain upon our return. For now, however, we really must make haste to feed."

"And leave more traces of our bites?!"

"We have no better option."

"What if we cut across the imprints of our fangs, to conceal any evidence?"

"Then we reveal that we aren't merely bats or animals in the night, but rather thinking creatures, who are aware that we are being watched." Alistair went to a corpse and opened its shroud. "You must consider everything."

"What if they lock the door to the chapel?" I said in horror.

"They cannot. That is written in the original charter of the church; have I ever told you that I met the first priest of this parish?"

"Never."

"Then remind me to tell you that story one day." He leaned over his mark. "Feed quickly, now. Even though it is night, there could be someone listening in the dark. We must make haste."

This I did, though my heart pounded with worry and my mind spun with guilt. There was no doubt in my mind that this had been my doing; Alistair had been right from the beginning, when he warned me against meddling in human affairs! How foolish I had been!

I tried to offer him back his cloak before we set back across the moor, but he would not have it. Instead, he leaned down to fasten it more securely around my neck, and beckoned me to follow him. Before opening the door, he held a finger to his lips to bid my silence.

Consumed by shame, I walked out after him. The world seemed hostile now, and colder; I shivered despite the additional layer, and a profound dread overwhelmed me.

Alistair walked ahead of me, deep in thought.

*　　*　　*

When we arrived, I was still profoundly shaken; but there were matters to be taken care of, so I followed Alistair's directions numbly.

The first was to ensure that every window was shut, and every door locked. Though we knew not whether anyone suspected us, it was not out of the question for someone to come prying.

The second was to leave a note for Miss Josephine, advising her to be vigilant during the day, and to alert us of any strange character sighted near the manor. Whenever she went to town, she was to inform us so that one of us could remain awake and keep watch. We provided no account of why we were requesting this; Alistair explained that she would likely understand on her own, and would otherwise prefer to know as little as possible, as was her tendency.

Thirdly, we settled on a new schedule for our feedings.

"Weekly, rather than every fortnight," Alistair explained, as we settled finally in the library. "That way, if we face trouble with our supply, we are three weeks away from hunger rather than two."

Then he paused, and watched me carefully.

"How are you faring, Mr. Bedford?"

"Fine," I said briskly. "Very well, then. What now?"

Alistair tilted his head. "What now?"

"Yes—what more should we do?"

"Nothing," Alistair replied, with some amusement. "Now, we wait a week. Since we were interrupted, I thought we might return to our discussion on Carthage."

It took me a moment to understand his meaning, until I looked down and realized that our history books were still open where we had left them before going to feed.

"Carthage?" I said listlessly.

I made a valiant effort to return my attention to our studies, but it was useless; I was endlessly distracted, and constantly turning at every sound. Alistair called to me patiently, coaxing me back to our subject, but soon relented.

"You are distracted, understandably so. Perhaps some quiet reading would do you well."

He chose a text for me to read, before selecting a novel for himself and walking off to the chaise lounge. For a while, we both read in silence, with the flicker of the fire bathing us warmly.

My thoughts, however, strayed often from the words in front of me. The sounds of the fire gave me no peace; with every loud crackle from the fireplace, I startled and stared into it for a long while.

It was impossible to devote my attentions to anything, even in silence. Indeed, now that I had time to think, my mood was darkening swiftly, and I was overcome with anxious melancholy. After a while, I could take my own restlessness no longer, and stood to check the library windows again.

Alistair lifted his gaze and watched me over the edge of his book as I went, but said nothing.

I was terribly sad for the remainder of that night. Though I tried to act my normal self, it was nearly impossible; in truth, all I wanted was to be alone. Alistair's presence, which had previously been a great comfort to me, was now a reminder of my own ineptitude. It was because of my arrogance that he was in danger, though he was being careful not to show any worry.

Perhaps sensing that I needed time alone, Alistair bid me good dawn earlier than usual, and tried to reassure me before leaving me be.

That day, I barely slept a wink; I left my bed to check the doors twice and cleaned my pistols, before finally deciding that I would not rest at all. Instead, I left my room and climbed to the third floor, where the gallery streamed with sunlight, and paced around the windows to watch for interlopers.

In my solitude, however, I had ample time to ponder, and my thoughts grew ever more sorrowful.

My peace had been robbed from me; my illusions had been shattered. For a few months I had lived in a dream, coddled by new knowledge and new friendship, and truly came to believe myself to be capable of happiness. My disastrous fate had been dressed up in rosemary and snow, bathed in tea and music, until feedings at the chapel had seemed a natural thing. In my naiveté, I had even thought myself capable of giving something of value to the world I had fallen from—at least until now, when that very world had revealed its hostile nature.

All along, I had forgotten that I was condemned to be a vampire.

How deeply I had let myself fall into fantasy, and quickly it had been sundered, leaving me bare! The idea of being a scourge to the world, something to be hunted, sunk me in the lowest of spirits; and the bitterness of having been forced into such a fate was renewed and intensified, leaving me confused.

"Mr. Bedford."

I groaned quietly, moving away from the hand gently shaking my shoulder.

"Mr. Bedford, wake."

With a gasp, I sat up and looked all around. I had fallen asleep on the ancient old bed on the third floor, which had centuries ago belonged to Alistair!

"I'm sorry," I mumbled, rubbing my eyes and sitting up quickly. "How rude of me! I was only watching from the windows in the gallery. Has something happened?"

Alistair stood over me, peaceful as always, with his dark hair loose around his shoulders. "Worry not. You may sleep anywhere you find comfortable."

It was then that I realized night had fallen, and Alistair was already dressed. "I'm sorry, have I missed our breakfast?" I murmured, and checked my pocket watch. Upon seeing the time, I balked; it was already nine in the evening. "My goodness! I'm sorry—"

"No matter. I decided to make the tea for you this evening, and let you sleep a while longer."

It was then that I realized there was a tea tray on the table in the room, still steaming. Yet, whereas the sight of it might usually have inspired warmth and comfort, it now filled me with restless agitation.

"You can have it yourself," I said, as I stood. "I will go have a walk around the manor, and ensure that—"

Alistair held up a hand.

I stopped.

"Shall we go to the pianoforte?" he said. It was not a question.

What a horrible embarrassment it was, to know that I had failed so completely at maintaining my composure! I winced, feeling childish; but he said nothing of it yet, only beckoned.

"Come."

"We shouldn't waste the tea—"

"Leave it, Mr. Bedford. Come."

Too weary to argue, I followed him to the music room.

Outside, the wind whistled high and tenebrous through cracks, and seemed to be building towards a blizzard. In that wide, drafty room which had so often been filled with our merry music-making, I now stood feebly by the side of the piano.

Sinking gracefully down onto the bench, Alistair swept his hair over his shoulder. His sharp eyes glittered as he turned to me, and he even gave a placid smile.

"Do sit," said he.

I glanced down at his hands, poised delicately over the keys, and sat carefully next to him. My shoulder grazed his, and I could feel the warmth and weight of his body close to mine; but his face was too near to gaze upon with ease, so I set my hands upon my knees and stared down at the keys of the instrument instead. The pearly sheen of them was pleasant over the wood.

"A lovely instrument, isn't it?" he said.

I nodded. "I have always thought so."

"I bought it after years of reading about it," he went on. "A new instrument like a harpsichord, they said, which was simple to learn and pleasant to the ear—capable of being both loud or soft, just like a human voice."

I managed a weary smile. "Is that so?"

"Indeed. Some pieces for voice can even be spoken by an instrument like this." He glanced towards me. "One particular piece, I transformed from sung notes to an arrangement for the pianoforte. Dido's final lament—do you remember?"

"You said—" I hesitated. "You once told me that was the one you were playing, when I first heard you at the piano."

"Would you like to hear it again?"

For a moment, I wavered. After all, that piece carried with it painful memories, and I knew that having heard the piano on that fateful night had been my first step into the abyss. Yet, I also remembered the emotions that the piece had brought about. My curiosity overwhelmed me; I had to hear it once more.

I nodded.

"Very well," he said. There was the shift of his body, and his creeping fingers arranging themselves along the first keys.

I watched his hands and held my breath.

Then he eased into the first part, and my breath hitched. There they were—the hauntingly beautiful notes, the slow, simple tread of them down the piano, the desperation of their misery that I remembered. How the sound poured on, soaking the night in meaning, pulling it taut as a string! All the tragedies of the world seemed to be contained in it, rolling like thunder over the notes—oh, what a sound!

The thicker the music became, the more I forgot myself. It became nearly painful, filling my throat until I was drowning in it. My heart ached, oh, how it ached for relief; how I wanted relief from my own mind, and to flee instead into these notes that mourned along with me!

The emotions in my throat turned hard and pushed upwards. I pressed my lips together to keep them down; but my eyes began to well with tears. I tried to blink them back, but then came an especially poignant twist of notes, and they were suddenly dripping down my cheeks. As I tried to swallow, the floodgates opened, and at last I choked on a sob.

At the sound, the notes eased into silence, and I heard Alistair's voice next.

"What's the matter, Mr. Bedford?"

I began to wipe the tears away, responding with a trembling breath. "I have always been weak to music—"

"You know my meaning."

I tried to suppress my voice, for I knew it would betray me;

but eventually I drew in a breath, and let my expression twist with misery.

"How I *wish* I weren't a vampire!"

Alistair folded his hands in his lap and watched me patiently. "As do I."

That surprised me. I swallowed, dabbed at my cheek with my sleeve, and looked up at him.

"I miss my humanity," he said quietly to me. "I miss it terribly. I miss eating, and travel, and having many friends, even those who are untrue. I miss the company of strangers, rowdy celebrations and formal gatherings alike. I miss knowing that I am part of some grand society, and that I have a natural kinship with those all around the world who share my experience and sympathize with it; I miss the feeling that those who write in books are writing for me. I miss waking with the sun, and accomplishment, and the promise of change. I even miss petty scandal. I tell myself that it is better than being dead with all those from my time, whose bones have turned to dust; but I can never be certain. Those bones have danced happily through their years, and now rest peacefully. I remain."

That nearly set me off again, and I had to take a deep breath to keep from descending back into tears.

This was the time where he might usually have added a quip, and I expected it; but instead, he propped his elbow on the piano and waited for me to dry my face.

"Sir," I said, with a waver in my voice. "I know I made a promise to you—I told you that I wouldn't pry, that I wouldn't demand the reason why you turned me."

Alistair watched me silently.

"And I cannot *hate* you anymore," I went on, unsteady. "I haven't hated you for a very long time. I think of you as a dear friend, but—what you did to me! Oh, how I *despise* what you did to me! I cannot understand it at all. If you remember your pain—and you do—and if you are kind—and you *are*—and if you are rational—and you are, indeed, perhaps the most rational man I have ever known—then I cannot understand *how* you could have done something so cruel."

Then I wiped my eyes again, trembling with grief.

"But I was so happy to spend these months with you, and now I have put your entire life in jeopardy, and yet I have no inkling of who to blame. Do I blame you, for having put me in this position? Do I blame myself, for having been reckless?" I laid my head in my hand. "I'm sorry—I know that these words may very well cause you pain—but I know nobody else who could understand them. I'm so *terribly* confused."

Alistair watched me silently for a while, letting my thought linger, before responding.

"I have told you that I know two things about you," he said softly.

Shivering at the gentleness of his tone, I looked up.

He went on. "The first: that you are inclined take responsibility for all that you see, to think yourself in debt to the world, to take endless blame onto your shoulders and never forgive it; but here, where guilt is concerned, my answer to you is simple."

His voice grew so quiet that I had to strain to hear it, and he put his hand to his chest as he spoke.

"If you must blame someone, blame me. Always blame me. Let me take the weight from your shoulders; it was I who bit you, I who transformed you, and I who bear responsibility for any consequence that I face as a result, including this one. Never you."

Seldom had I ever been so shocked at his words. This was the first time that he had ever addressed his deed so directly, and the pain in his voice that accompanied it made the reason for his reticence obvious.

Still, displaying a gaze that now gleamed with vast hurt, he continued:

"As for my reasons, I regret that I cannot yet answer you. I wish I could."

"For goodness' sake, why not?" I said weakly.

Alistair shook his head, but replied in a gentle voice.

"The second thing that I have learned about you, I have likewise mentioned: I know that you are the type to search tirelessly for answers, and to never rest until you find them. It is in your nature to discern anything placed before you, and you are willing to chase understanding to its very end."

With a look that blazed suddenly, then, he faced me.

"Do you trust me, Mr. Bedford?"

"I want to," I said tearfully. "Believe me, I want to."

Hearing that, Alistair quivered; and all at once, he clasped my hands in his own, speaking now with a fiery and trembling conviction that had never hitherto left his lips:

"Then just this once, let me lead you blindly."

These words dealt the final blow to my composure. I was overwhelmed with exhaustion, and let my shoulders sink down. Gazing emptily into his hands, I replied quiet and drained.

"All right."

But Alistair shook his head, and pressed my hands tighter still. "No, Mr. Bedford; not as an act of destruction, but of faith. I want your will, not your resignation."

I gave a tearful laugh. "What good has my will ever done anyone?"

"More than you could know."

This gave me pause, and I looked up to find him wearing a look so earnestly beseeching that it pulled my heart taut.

In that moment, I realized that to know my own purpose had long ceased to be my most pressing concern. My wish to know the truth of my creation no longer came from such an urge; instead, it was *his* motive and soul that I longed to understand most of all. It was his regard of me that I ached for, not his penance.

And so, at last, I pressed his hands in return and raised my gaze to his.

"Then you have my faith, sir," I said, hoarse but steady. "Blind, if it must be, but no less firm. I only hope that you might one day trust my judgment well enough to remove my blindfold, and let me understand you completely."

Alistair was astounded. It was evident that he had not expected my assent; and when he answered, his look was almost wild with gratefulness. "You won't regret your trust in me, Mr. Bedford. I swear it."

Then, seeming to restrain something more, he pulled away and gave a regretful smile.

"Ah, but I never meant to make you weep."

I sighed, rubbing my eyes. "No matter. It seems tears come easily to me."

"Then we have that in common."

"You?" I said in surprise. "Why, but I have never seen you weep!"

"Only because you have kept me busy."

"I simply don't believe you."

"Watch," Alistair warned. "I have kept my composure, but one brick less will topple it. After that, Magdalene will have her equal."

Unable to picture it, I stared at him. "Really?"

"Yes, but enough of such things," said Alistair, tapping his fingers against the keys again. "It gives me no pleasure to see you sorrowful. May I play you a happier melody?"

Of course, I was all too glad to accept, and so he continued to play.

I listened and listened. The weight of my sleepless night replaced my anxiety, and my eyes grew heavy. Once or twice, I let them close, and jerked awake to find that my head had slumped to Alistair's shoulder, prompting him to pause.

Eventually, I felt that I was on the brink of falling from the bench; and when next I woke to find my head against his shoulder, I did not remove it. Instead, I let myself rest.

Alistair roused me some time later with murmurs and gentle touches.

"Mr. Bedford, you are falling asleep."

I stirred and mumbled against his shoulder: "Help me to the sofa, let me rest there a while."

"Come."

With my eyes nearly shut, I let him take my hand and lead me, though I barely knew where we went.

What happened beyond this point was dream-like, and scarcely remembered afterwards.

The place where he brought me was soft and cushioned, comfortable and pleasantly fragrant; upon stumbling onto it and settling my head on the pillow, I breathed in deeply and felt my worries loosen. The scent of cloves was all around, and soothed me to the point of lethargy.

"Sir?" I murmured, and stirred; but once I felt the weight of covers pulled up to my chin, I could move no more.

His voice was warm, as was his hand on my shoulder. "Rest easy. I will stay by your side."

"All right," I mumbled, then did something purely out of instinct.

During the time when my mother and I had lived in the old inn back in York, we had shared the same bed. When I wasn't hiding beneath it, waiting for her to finish with her work, we slept in it together. On such occasions, just before going to sleep, she always gave me a long embrace.

Without thinking, nor even opening my eyes, I raised my hands up.

In an instant, my arms were full, and I was being pressed very tightly, almost too tightly to breathe. The scent of cloves was redoubled.

Very distantly, I realized that the body against mine was trembling.

Then, I knew no more.

CHAPTER XXII

When I awoke at last, I knew not whether any of these last memories had been real, and truly thought them to be dreams. In any case, my first concern was another.

I sat upright in shock, and found Alistair half-asleep over a book at a nearby table

"Mr. Bedford," he said with a yawn. "Good morning. Did you sleep better now?"

I had indeed slept wonderfully, but upon realizing where I was, I was mortified in an instant.

"Sir!" I cried out, throwing off the covers. "By Jove! Did I fall asleep in your *bed?*"

Despite Alistair's amused reassurances that it had been his intent, and that it was a pleasure to have me as his guest, I was in agony at the thought that I had done something so boorish. When I tried to gather the sheets to wash them, he stopped me and led me away.

"Let me have a short sleep myself," he said, quite nearly dragging me to the door. "Go have a round of the manor, see whether you notice any sign of disturbance."

"I'm so terribly sorry—"

"I said it matters not, leave it be."

"In *your bed!*"

"If you want our ledgers equal, I can sleep in yours."

The thought of that somehow left me entirely speechless, and I let myself be pulled away.

*　　*　　*

I had slept through most of the night, and thus met the first rays of dawn upon venturing outside, which filtered through clouds and gave a gleam to the snow.

Filled with regret at having wasted the night, having essentially traded it with Alistair, I walked along morosely. How ardently I wished that I had the calm spirit to take a shock without stumbling, and to set fear aside with ease! Whenever I closed my eyes, I still saw the chapel with garlic flowers stuffed in every corner, warning us to stay away.

Yet, the events that transpired after that sorry event now filled my mind just as much. All around me, Alistair's fragrance still lingered.

He had fallen straight into the bed once I relented, and curled in the place where I had been, seeming very pleased to be there; and though I had fussed and begged for a while longer, pulling at the covers, he had gathered them to him and feigned sleep until I left.

To see him asleep in my place had stirred me oddly. I wondered why I felt flustered; in my strange embarrassment, I had even felt a childish urge to pounce on him and pull some mischief. Perhaps this was the more playful aspect of human nature, which would naturally arise from sharing an ever more casual friendship. Having seldom experienced such a thing, I could hardly know.

As I walked along, however, I remembered the other events of the night—the way he had grasped my hands at the pianoforte, and begged for my trust. Though no gust of wind blew, I shivered.

But in that moment, there suddenly came a voice, young and high:

"Mr. Bedford, Mr. Bedford!"

By this point, I had walked far enough that the manor was at some distance, and certainly hadn't expected to meet anyone along my way. Yet, I recognized this voice from a week prior, and raised my head.

"Mary?"

My guess had been correct; young Mary, with her cloak and scarves tossing in her stride, was dashing towards me across the moorland.

Prepared to meet with some unreasonable demand for an invitation, I stood firm and sighed; but as she drew nearer, I saw her stricken expression and grew worried.

"What is it?" I said, as she stopped before me and panted. "Have you lost your brooch again?"

She shook her head and straightened, still catching her breath. "I'm sorry—I've only been wandering here, I've not tried to intrude! But I when I saw you, I thought I should tell you—I found something so strange today."

My heart froze. "Found what?"

"Follow me!"

Waving me along, she then lifted her skirts and held onto her hat before hurrying off. Now entirely alert, I followed her.

After only a minute, she stopped and peered over, then pointed down a shallow incline. "Look!"

Striding up behind her, I followed the direction of her gesture with my gaze.

There, a great mass of fur rested in the snow. It was a deer, lying dead.

Mary shivered, wrapping her arms around each other. "I thought it was an ordinary deer, but there's something wrong with it. I think you have poachers; it's been shot, I believe—I dared not look closer."

Glancing all around, I held out a hand. "Wait here."

"What is it, Mr. Bedford? I have never seen a sight so strange."

"I don't know," I murmured, and slowly descended the slope for a closer look.

At first, my sight fixed on the matted fur stained with blood. These bloodied hairs shivered in the wind, and led back to a bullet hole; but that was not the strangest sight.

There was a cut along the animal's stomach, as though something had either been taken out or placed inside.

It took me a few moments to steady myself, as I raised the back of my wrist to my mouth and breathed against it. The frigid air burned my throat, and blooming terror replaced my shock. I stared, trembling, into the glazed-open jewels of the deer's eyes.

Then, I immediately turned to Mary.

"Go!" I called out. "Something is direly wrong. This is no simple poacher's gamble; go back to your family, come here no more!"

She made a move to follow me down. "But what is it?"

"Something dangerous, which you should play no part in. Go, I said, go! Quickly!"

"All right!" she called back. "But be careful!"

With that, she turned and ran off; and so did I, in the opposite direction towards the manor.

When I burst into Alistair's room, he was peacefully asleep in the bed, this time in earnest. In my panic, I roused him by shaking his shoulder, which made him wake with a start.

"Mr. Bedford?" he murmured.

Then, upon seeing my expression, his eyes grew sharp. He sat up.

"You found something."

I gave a garbled and trembling explanation as he stood, which nonetheless sufficed for him to understand. Upon hearing it, Alistair displayed a look of genuine worry, and began to walk without even donning his winter coat. "Show me."

"Do you know what it could be?"

With a dark look, Alistair only spoke one word:

"Hurry."

We rushed quickly out onto the moor, carrying a sheet and few coils of rope. Daybreak made the land bright, and full of birdsong; but this lively scene only made me feel terribly exposed, and I could not help but look all around, searching for someone crouched behind a bough or behind a tangle of grass.

Yet, when we reached the deer at last, it was Alistair's reaction which drew my attention.

The colour drained from his face. He gazed down with a terrible look upon the deer, as though seeing the calling card of some ancient enemy. One hand trembled.

Recognizing these ill-fated signs, I stepped forward. "Sir, do you feel faint?"

He shook his head. "We must take this at once."

And so, tying it up in the sheet, we dragged it all the way back to the manor.

The further we went, the more I felt Alistair's hold grow slack. I glanced at him often, watching for the tell-tale stumble that would foretell his fall; but he held steady until we reached the manor, and even helped hoist the carcass inside.

We took it to a seldom-used room by the kitchen, which had once been a larder. There, we laid it on a dusty old table, and pulled in a bucket of water.

Then at last, Alistair approached the animal, still awfully pale, and touched it gingerly, as though something about it might be painful.

I waited with bated breath. "Well? What do you make of it?"

Closing his eyes for a moment, Alistair seemed to gather his courage and make some silent, futile plea to nobody.

Then, he reached forward, carefully pried apart the cut along the deer's stomach, and lifted the skin by its fur—all at once, sharply, pulling it as far up as it would go.

In an instant, I gasped and stumbled back; for the sight within was unlike anything I had ever seen!

Silver skewers were stuck every which way through its gut, slick with congealed blood, fiercely pointed. The fold of meat seemed almost like a savage mouth, with fangs that protruded viciously; and as Alistair opened it, a few of these needles fell loose and tumbled noisily to the floor at his feet.

Alistair stared for a few seconds, then lowered the flap of skin and withdrew his bloodied hand. For a few moments, he gazed emptily down at it.

Then, he fell.

Luckily, I had the good sense to have recognized his state, and caught him as he swooned. The weight of him made me sink down, though I pulled him away from the skewers strewn across the floor.

"Pardon me," he murmured, with lashes fluttering. "I…"

Ordinarily, I might have felt terribly nervous; but somehow, having to mind him made me brave. Pulling him near, I reassured him:

"Rest easy, I am with you."

Still, his eyes were far away. "It cannot be."

"What cannot be?"

"Colden," he managed, then fell limp.

*　　*　　*

When Alistair awoke at last, and I helped him sit, he was quiet and pensive for a long while. I had loosed his hair from its ribbon; it hung around him, giving him a look both tenebrous and melancholic. He seemed immersed in a distant past.

Knowing he would need time, I brought him to the library and let him be, leaving to make a pot of tea. Upon my return, he appeared to have gathered his thoughts; and he turned to me, speaking with a reluctance seldom drawn from his lips.

"Mr. Bedford," he said at last. "In order to explain this to you, I will have to divulge some aspects of my past which you may find objectionable."

I set the tray down. "Your past?"

"My past as a vampire."

Despite his reticence, I already had a sense of what he was preparing to tell me. This was something that I had long suspected, though I had decided never to ask—in part out of fear of the answer, and in part out of understanding. The way Alistair spoke of humanity's hostility towards the vampire was too vivid to be drawn from imagination; and these hostilities must have been dispatched of in some manner, which he had hitherto avoided telling me.

Lifting the teapot, I filled the first cup of tea. As I did, I spoke plainly.

"You've killed, haven't you?"

There was a long and agonizing silence. Alistair turned to gaze out the window, then spoke nearly inaudibly.

"I have."

I swallowed. Despite a cold sweat washing over me, I questioned again:

"How many?"

"Two."

"How many intentionally?"

"One."

As I poured the second cup, Alistair offered quietly:

"If this alters anything in your perception of me, I would blame you not. You would be justified in revoking any association with me, whether your trust or your vow to remain until autumn; you knew not it was a murderer to whom you made your promises."

He paused, then fought with his next sentence.

"I regret having withheld—"

But I interrupted him, offering him his cup of tea.

Alistair blinked down at it, then looked up at me with some surprise.

"When I give my trust," I said, stalwart, "I give it completely, sir. It's no trivial matter to me. I doubt that you would murder in cold blood, and your countenance shows your true feelings; so tell me your story—tell it freely!—and know that I shall listen with no notions of your guilt, no accusations, no fears, unless you prove yourself to be entirely different from the person I know."

Speechlessly, Alistair stared at me.

"Which I doubt," I added, and thrust the cup towards him again. "So go on, now! Let us hear your dreadful little tale, and see what we can make of it."

With a look of mingled fondness and incredulity, Alistair took the cup. "I didn't expect that from you."

"Why not?"

"I underestimated your fealty, I suppose," Alistair murmured. "I thought your scruples might take precedent; perhaps I hoped they would."

"Who says it's about scruples? You err the same as many others, who mistake my principled nature for passivity. I would never fault you if you had to fight for your life."

Alistair watched me with some shame. "I appreciate your generosity, but I must admit that even I have my doubts about what I did."

"That is all the better. Think of me as your priest, who hears your confession!"

At last, Alistair nodded and leaned back in his chair. "Then hear it," said he, "And judge it with the full and honest weight of your virtue, that I might know at last whether I was wrong."

The air felt heavier as he regarded me, his eyes changing in the flicker of the candle on the bedside table; and all of a sudden, I had the sense that he had returned to a time long gone—that we in the room were slipping, back and back, receding into a distant time to which he was a native and I was a stranger. The cold wind whistled outside, but it could have been any year's winter. I felt a great and shuddering thrill.

He gazed off into the canopy of the bed and began, in a low and heavy voice, which seemed to carry the weight of centuries: "There are no more wolves in England."

CHAPTER XXIII: ALISTAIR'S FIRST STORY

There are no more wolves in England. They were hunted to extinction long ago, mercilessly, finally, and forgotten by all but those who pass their stories on. Yet, these lands, quiet as you see them now, were once among the last bastions where the English wolf survived. Their bitter howls came across the hills of the wolds; the imprints of their steps remained in the snow.

By the time I was born, the English wolf was so rare that it was seldom seen; but with great and morbid interest I listened to tales of wolves in Scotland, not terribly far, and wondered whether I might ever see one. You may think it strange that I wished for such a thing, but I longed for adventure and peril from the window of my life. It was never the danger of war that I desired, for that was too bound to gentry, and no less of a cage than the situation I found myself in; what I wanted was wilderness, the freedom to run with beasts and know no sovereign but the earth itself.

The irony is not lost on me, of course. I would come to regret this wish most profoundly.

After I was transformed, I slept for what I have surmised to be a month following my bite—quite unlike your sleep, which lasted only three days' time. I emerged starving, only barely clinging to any semblance of human consciousness; and as I have mentioned, I found three men engaged in ransacking the empty manor.

My first feeding was an agonizing event. I had not the strength nor the powers of living blood, and so it was by brute force and my sword that I subdued one of them and drank. It was very bloody, but he did not die; and even with the rush of power that flooded me from the taste of his living blood, I wanted for experience in using it, and was unable to purge the memory of the event from his mind. He fled with knowledge of me, calling after his fellows.

This proved to be a nightmare. Rumours spread about the demon of the moor; a few gatherings of people came in bands towards the manor, with fire and weapons aloft. With considerable effort, which weakened me greatly, I managed to bring a dense fog about the manor, and a devilish howling wind which deterred the bands for some time; but every night, they approached the abandoned manor with mounting proximity.

As for what my state was during this time, I can hardly describe it. This was a time of great confusion and frantic discovery. To some degree, I *understood* what had happened to me, for I remembered all the stories of revenants and werewolves that I had heard; but it was not until a century after, when the subject began to be printed, that I first read the word *vampire* and felt a shock of recognition.

That came later, far later. For the moment, assume that I

realized myself to be a daemon; that I was alone in the entire world; and that it would take every part of my being to survive. I had not the knowledge that I do now, nor the time for introspection, nor the courage gained from experience. Fear was my only guide, and hunger its footman.

For days on end I barricaded myself inside the manor, and drove myself half-mad from dearth of sleep. I knew that my time was short. Even amidst the uncertainty of knowing what precisely I was, I knew at least that I was still myself, and that in some manner I was finally free; and I yearned to live, even in such a state—indeed, it was the brink of annihilation that made life all the sweeter—and therefore, I was afraid to die. I was consumed with melancholy; I did nothing but linger anxiously at the windows, watching for the flicker of fire through the fog, and waiting for my hunger to stir again. Knowing that such an urge would force me from my safety, I was paralyzed with fear.

It was a fortnight later, when my hunger first began to rear its head, that the unexpected occurred.

At first, I thought I saw a dog from the window, coming over the crest of a hill. It was sundown, and I could only discern the black of its silhouette.

For a time I watched it, fearing it to be a hunting dog, and grasped my sword in hand; but more of them came, slinking over the hill and towards the manor. They had nobody with them. I believed at first that I was dreaming; but once they drew nearer, I rose at once and opened the window for a better look. It could not be, I thought, and yet I swept a cloak around my shoulders and hurried down to meet them, all weariness forgotten.

It was an entire pack of grey wolves, no less than thirteen of them, their eyes fixed upon me, their ears jaunted up in attention. From whence they came, I never knew—whether from the hidden depths of the forests nearby or from far away, almost impossibly far for them to have sensed me and travelled from Scotland, or from thin air, or perhaps hell—but they had come; and one of them, weak and with eyes already half-glazed, took two steps towards me through the grasses and fell down dead at my feet.

The wolves changed everything. The balance of fear was tipped in my favour; no more did any villagers attempt to cross the moor. In return, with my command over the pack, I let them settle around the manor in relative peace.

The usefulness of the wolves was twofold. The first use was protection, as I have described. Great alarm must have spread through the town at the first sighting of wolves, for villagers ceased to come so near. The forlorn howls echoing across the moor, returned after perhaps a century of absence, were a dire warning to all who would approach.

Now left alone, I managed to keep my small fortune and my estate by a deft collection of letters beneath the false name of a relative. Perhaps knowing the truth of these attempts, but being unwilling to challenge me, all involved parties accepted my excuses.

The second use of the wolves, of course, was in hunting.

I took the dead wolf and tanned its hide, made from it a cloak with a hood formed from the head, which would cast shadows over my features. When the time came to hunt, I would dress in it and summon the wolves about me, sometimes using my newly discovered powers of transformation to become one of them; and we would move swiftly across the moor, nearly in silence. The moon lit the sheen of fur that rippled along their backs as they prowled; it was a sight of great awe, which restored to me some sense of beauty in the world.

Whenever we found a human, I would bid the wolves to surround them, but not attack; and I would come forward, entrance the victim, then return to my human-like form. In this manner, I was able to feed as harmlessly as I could.

Upon finishing, I would command my mark to forget their experience. A vampire's sway over a human mind strengthens with the imbibing of their blood, and to feed them blood in turn deepens it further. At most, they would recall a vision of being accosted by a pack of wolves, but nothing more.

This approach was successful for a year. With great effort, I was able to escape notice.

The wolves, however, could not. I had hoped to use them as a shield, but they were also a beacon which invited unwanted attention. On occasion I would see villagers in the distance, watching with their weapons at the ready.

I began to grow paranoid at every sight. I agonized; I feared that the relative peace of my existence would be ruined.

In the grip of my terror, I made a fatal mistake.

Dimly, I remembered the name of a physician in Helmsley, who had often been summoned by my father to remedy my fainting fits. Though his efforts to cure me then had been futile, and I had often fought to escape his crueller and more reckless attempts—which resembled torture more than any healing effort—I wondered whether he might help me procure blood, and thus allow me to rejoin the human world.

Concealing my features with a cloak and a broad hat, I went into town for the first time in a year and found his shingle. Only once we had withdrawn into privacy did I remove my concealing garments and reveal myself.

I have never forgotten his look of shock, and the flinch of his hand towards his knife.

In my desperation I told him everything, and begged for his help. Out of sheer exhaustion and helplessness, I wept. He listened, and finally assured me that he would make every effort to bestow upon me what I needed.

When I departed that day, I was weary but full of hope. Yet, there still remained a drop of doubt; for when I had thanked him and moved forward to shake his hand, he had taken a step back and avoided me. Though I assured myself that his fears were only natural, I wondered whether my trust had been misplaced.

I was correct.

Within a month, the hunter came.

*   *   *

Colden was plain. I refer not to simplicity in the sense that he was ignorant or foolish; I mean that he neither embellished nor announced himself like a nobleman, and I had expected him to look very differently judging from the mighty degree of misery he brought upon me.

Yes, Sir Lawrence Colden was a simple man when I knew him, always dressing in an undecorated brown doublet and a matching set of breeches. His face was framed by a well-trimmed beard, and his eyes were clear. Here was a plain man with a plain, unclouded brow, and a plain heart set in its ideals. There was the terrifying austereness of the ascetic about him, the sense that life was quite clear to him, and that he would follow his beliefs to the grave. To him, you see, my entire ordeal was simple indeed: I was a servant of evil, and had to be killed at all costs.

At first I never saw him, for he was careful, experienced in avoiding notice while hunting. He tried to kill me as though he were hunting a rabbit, in the manner that a rabbit-hunter sets a fire at one escape of a den in order to catch prey fleeing from the other—all with the satisfied, easy consciousness of one who believes the rabbit is already his to consume, and that he was always meant to kill it.

First, he instructed the villagers wear silver crosses, and strings of garlic flowers about their necks. This was my first hint that someone who knew what I was, and how to kill me, had arrived; and though I was able to outsmart this tactic by entrancing my victims, compelling them to remove such measures of protection, I was still struck by fear to know that I was being hunted. He, too, must have known that these measures would not form a substantial obstacle—but it was a clear message to me: *You are known.*

This was but the first attempt. Oh, Colden made my life a misery, a new nightmare with every feeding. He bid the villagers stay inside at night, forcing me to venture nearer to settlements until I could bewitch a curious eye at a window, or find someone who knew not of his instructions. This always took substantial effort, which turned my feedings from the difficult obstacle of one or two days to the endless agony of several. He then told them to put garlic outside their houses, and stay inside in the evening; I was therefore forced to hunt in the day, in a state rather weakened, for the power of living blood is strongest beneath the moon.

His game grew more and more aggravating, carrying on relentlessly. He poisoned my grounds with garlic and other relics; with the help of my wolves, I removed them. He then turned his attention to killing my wolves, leaving carcasses to lure them—much like the one left on the moor today—though his were far more carefully arranged. Tainted with wolfsbane and run through with silver skewers, they were impossible for me to touch, and so they claimed the lives of two of my wolves while I could only watch. After that, I kept the pack nearer to me, commanding them to settle in the yard behind the manor.

This did not deter him. Finding where I had concealed them, Colden set fire to the grass. With great effort I brought a rainstorm, though it was too late. Another two wolves were killed, and both a pavilion and the stables burned irreparably.

After that fire, I was very much weakened by the exertion of my powers. Bringing the rain had been no small feat, and I knew that such a deed could not be easily repeated; if he set fire to the manor again while I slept, I would burn with it.

I therefore went to regain my strength at the only other place where I could pass freely: the cottage that once stood where the moor church is now built—a cottage precious to me, for reasons that I will one day explain to you, but which are not relevant now. To the cottage I fled, and though the night was restless, I managed to sleep.

I woke to thick smoke and the deadly crackle of flames.

Immediately I rose, and went to the door—I found it sealed— I went to a window, and found it boarded—I coughed and covered my mouth—the air was thick, and the heat unbearable. I was *furious* with myself for having been caught, with him for catching me, and with the world itself for allowing it all; and I would *not* die in such a way, I swore, burned alive in my awful inquisitor's grip.

In a frenzy, I sought a way out. With the last remnant of power from living blood that I contained, I transformed myself into a swift, and was able to escape through the chimney. It was when I regained my form again, half-fallen on the grass before the burning cottage, that I saw him at last.

He was watching, plainly dressed as I have described to you, and with an easy gaze that rested upon me for some time. He spoke not a word.

I, however, was still full to the brim with fury, and drew a dagger. "So this is the *insufferable* fly," I said through a snarl, "That drones about my head, refusing to die."

"A curious thing to call me," he said with ease, "Considering the fly's taste for blood."

"Then my blade must be such a creature, for I am quite certain it will drink thy blood ere long."

"Go ahead, then."

I tightened my grip on the hilt and narrowed my eyes.

"Well?" he said.

"I will spare thee if thou goest now from this land. Never return."

"This I cannot do."

"Thy preference is to die?"

"My preference is to prevent thee from consuming any lives, or spreading thy evil further in the world."

"My evil!" I barked a laugh. "In this, thou art mistaken. I have no desire to kill. The true murderer stands before me at this very moment."

"Thy intentions matter not to me. Thy nature is evil, and it is therefore my duty to end it, or to die trying."

"Thy *duty*? To whom? To the townspeople, who are in no danger?"

"To God."

"God created me."

"He has made thee as he has made the devil: to test the souls of men—to give the chance to prove one's honour."

"I have never known the devil," I said, "But if thou coms't

nearer, I shall give thee the chance to meet him."

"You are tired, demon," he said almost gently. "Exert thyself not with threats. I shall put thee to rest."

This enraged me. "Arrogant, fanatical man," I hissed. "So it is thy belief that God has created the world as a chess board, good against evil? If I am evil simply by *being*, what meaning does action have?"

He shook his head. "Waste not thy words; they cannot sway me. I know their source."

I stepped nearer, clenching the hilt of my dagger in rage. "Thou hast no right to take my life from me. God gave it to me, and it is *mine*. I deserve the chance to live harmlessly."

"Deserve?" he said. "Thou *art* deserving of peace; but this life brings thee pain. Art thou not in intolerable pain?"

He stepped forward, one hand outstretched, and spoke then so genuinely that I was terrified for my own soul.

"Lay your anguish down, demon; surrender to me, and I will ease your burden painlessly, as only I know how. I will give you peace. I mean you no harm."

"Ha! It is thy design to sweeten me until I seek death at thy hand?"

"Have you not died once already?"

I stepped back, and clenched my jaw; but then I lowered my weapon and regarded him with a type of wild hope.

"You spoke truly. My existence is painful; but it remains precious to me, and I intend to preserve it—yet, it need not be painful."

He watched me and waited.

I then stepped forward, feeling the heat of the smouldering fire at my back. "If you are so fixed on giving me peace, then help me."

"Help you?" he murmured.

"I only live in pain and anguish because I must hurt others to live, for I must take blood from the unwilling; but had I a willing person to give me blood, then I would never suffer again. Feed me, save me from this fate of hunting humans like beasts, and I shall be your slave for as long as you live. You can do anything you want with me, with my powers, with my body and soul. My only wish is to live."

After this, I fell silent; there was a tremor within my chest, at the gravity of the words I had just spoken.

But he laughed a pitying laugh.

"Oh, Count," he said. "You believe it is power that I desire?"

"All men do."

"I desire only holiness."

"If you reject my offer," I said—unsure of whether I was relieved or disappointed—"And if you continue to torment me as you have, then I must warn you that our next meeting will be our last."

"Of course."

"It is no personal grudge, of course," I said in mocking cordiality. "I will kill you with regret."

"I understand," he replied.

I was irritated but somehow impressed at how simply he took it all; but that was his nature, and he bid me a simple farewell with a bow before turning to venture back across the moor.

I looked back to the fire, still roaring. My precious cottage was ruined.

For a few minutes longer, I watched it burn. Then, I returned to the manor.

As he had promised, he did not relent, and the consequences would be dire.

After spreading word so far through the nearby towns, Colden had finally achieved his aim: he was starving me. I was left much weakened after our exchange, and then another week passed without adequate feeding, then two, then three. A month passed, and hunger began to claim me.

I tried to drink from an animal, which failed me severely, and caused me to lose even more of my reserve, weakened to the point of listlessness. The wolves bayed outside my window, but I could no longer feed them.

There came a point where I could do no more but lie in bed, filled with thoughts of blood, yet unable to gather the strength to search for it. I even began to feel the urge to drink my own blood, and nearly did so several times.

Delirious with hunger, I at last lost the ability to move entirely. Though I was surrounded by all the wealth of my human life, none of it could aid me. I lost all sense of time, and eventually, sleep overtook me.

I slept.

Then, I woke.

I was lying outside on a dirt road, facing the stars; and when I turned my head to the side I saw a human body lying on the street, gored past the point of recognition. Two horses laid dead and torn to pieces beside it, still tethered to a carriage which laid on its side; blood covered everything in sight. My clothing was steeped in it, still fresh.

I cannot describe that moment. It seemed to me that the sky had fallen. I could not understand what I had done, nor anything else. Trembling sickness and blinding terror overtook me.

Wild with disbelief, I transformed and flew to the manor. Wolf-howls rang in my ears as I went to the door; but upon reaching my it, I found it still locked. It was not until I went to the grass beneath the window that I understood.

There, now muddied, was a shower of glass shards. I looked up towards the window above, and found that the wind was whistling through a new hole broken through it.

With no memory, with no will, some instinct must have overwhelmed me and compelled me to escape through the window—in what form, I still know not—and hunt.

How can I describe the horror of that moment? It was beyond words; I could not believe what I had done. I barely managed to return to my room before fainting.

The torment of my deed overwhelmed me. I had never meant to kill anyone, had never even considered that I could make such a terrible mistake. I could feel the blood of the dead man coursing through me, and lost my mind in anguish.

It was then that I gazed upon the world and found it forever empty. All hope within me died. Before, I had been able to find fleeting joys and excitements in my existence, to experience a peculiar sort of liberation from which I could derive pleasure. I had been able to roam the wildest parts of the moor at night beneath a full moon, to watch the red and otherworldly sunrise from beneath a lone tree on a hill, to run and frolic with the wolves, dress in their fur and pretend for some time that I was one of them. But now—how could I justify such enjoyment, at such a terrible cost? All was lost.

This had been Colden's most cunning design all along. If he failed to hunt me directly, he would to strip my will to live; and knowing that I wished not to kill, he would drive me to it. Any sacrifice of a human life along the way would be incidental, and justified so long as it could be used to prove that I was a murderer by nature.

Herein, it may appear that a contradiction arises; if Colden claimed to have the interests of the townspeople at heart, why would he put them in danger by starving me?

This was his weakness, the pitfall of even the most loving souls—the sin of wrath. Humans love evil, even if it stokes rage, for it feeds their nature to hunt it. Ire is a catharsis; righteousness elevates it to moral ecstasy. If somebody can find a conduit to this feeling, it will consume them. This is what I believe happened to Colden: he was swept into his crusade against me, and in his plain single-mindedness, reason and compassion perished. If only some other subject had occupied him, he might have instead devoted himself just as feverishly to good.

Indeed—and this might seem to you the strangest part of it all—while I hated him, I also felt attachment to him, though I scarcely understood it. In some way, I suppose I envied what it was to be a simple human, inflamed with convictions of the pure and the profane. I yearned for him to understand me, and to have such a plain and stalwart conviction as his become my shield.

No such understanding came. Our dance continued for another year, bittering my every waking moment.

I grew tired; I realized that I could not beat him unless I waited for him to die; but he was young and full of life, and would never meet his end unless it was by my hand. I began to worry that I would have to flee the manor; but where would I go, and how would I flee?

It could not go on. At last I appealed to his sense of honour and wrote him a letter, in which I challenged him to a formal battle. To my surprise, he agreed.

There was a pitched battle. We fought amid the howl of wolves, fog and storm; fire, arrows, and bullets flew. It seemed that it would never end, and I was weakening quickly.

But Sir Lawrence Colden, bold as he was, was also mortal. After hours of the stalemate, he grew tired; and it was thus that I managed to corner him within the walls of the ruined courtyard, surrounded by my wolves; only seven of them now remained. I climbed to the top of the remaining pavilion and stood there on the tall stone, gazing far down at him as the ring of wolves gathered. They snapped and snarled at him, furious, but I ordered them to hold back. A bitter wind howled, and the quarter moon was high in the heavens.

"Sir Lawrence," I said to him.

He lifted his eyes up to mine. "Count."

The wolves bared their teeth and snarled. From my perch I looked down upon them, and allowed them to close in nearer to him.

"Surrender," I said, "And I shall spare you. Flee—go far— never return."

In response, he gave a soft laugh.

I grew agitated. "Why do you laugh?" I barked. "Do you not see that you are on the brink of death? You agreed to fight me; take your loss with dignity!"

"I agreed to fight you to the death," he replied, "And that is what I intend to do."

"From whence comes this *obsession* of yours with death? You irritate me—you *vex* me."

"Death is where you and I differ," he said quietly. "Your being may shun it, but Death is precious to me; it is natural and holy."

"So you *wish* to die? Why did you not tell me upon our first meeting? I could have saved myself this trouble."

"You and I cannot both live on this earth together."

"You fool!" I roared; I had reached my limit. "You ignorant, *obstinate* wretch! Together is the *only* way that we can both live!"

"Are you referring to your proposal?" he said, amused—I could not believe how calm he was, with an entire pack of wolves surrounding him. "That I would feed you like Lilith, with her beasts to her breast, so you could live to perpetuate your evil?"

I was exhausted. "Lawrence, on my soul, by God and the heavens and the devil himself, *listen* to me. Whatever your ideas are, this petty game ends tonight. You are leaving here either dead or alive, and it is your choice which of the two it is."

"Then kill me," he said patiently.

"I *will!*" I exclaimed, straightening as tall as I could muster atop that crumbling roof upon which I stood. The wolves felt my anguish; they bayed and pawed at the ground. "I will kill you, I *must* kill you—" I sank down. "I must—"

But my knees began to tremble. On the cusp of a sudden fainting fit, I could barely stand, and my words ended with a high and throaty whisper which betrayed me.

"Good God, I don't want to kill you."

For a long and moved moment, he watched me.

Then, he sank to his knees in the grass, took up his snaplock from where he had dropped it, and loaded a single silver bullet into its muzzle. With both his hands he brought it up; my breath stopped, and I held the wolves on the brink of attack.

"Then I shall make this easy for you, demon," he said softly.

He cocked the musket and aimed.

*　　*　　*

I watched Alistair with bated breath as he paused, his gaze fixed in the far distance.

"What happened then?" I burst out.

He turned his head to me slightly. "I didn't see the precise moment he died. He did manage to fire before the wolves claimed him, and his silver bullet struck my side. Luckily it was only a graze, but it still burned like the blazes, and I stumbled and nearly fell from the pavilion."

In rapt silence, I waited for him to continue.

His eyes slid towards me. "Then, I collected him—what was left of him, at least, that the wolves had not claimed."

I shivered. "What did you do with him?"

"I drank the rest of his blood, then burned him," he murmured. "I built a pyre…but before I set fire to it, I decided to feign my own demise; so I went to the crypt, and drew out my father's bones to mingle with Colden's remains. To complete my deceit, I drank myself into a stupor and pulled out my fangs, adding them to my father's skull. The pain of them growing back in was the nearest I have been to abject madness."

I stared in horror.

"Then," he said with a sigh, "I dressed myself finely, powdered my hair to give it age, and altered the appearance of my face with a case of old paints from the manor. After placing the mingled remains in a box, I went to the inn at Helmsley. There, meeting the inn owner and Colden's sinewy porter, who had not seen his 'good sire' for a few days, I opened the box and displayed it, then said…"

Miming the opening of a lid, Alistair spoke with a flourish:

"Gentlemen, I believe there has been a grave misdeed done, though there remains nobody to pay for it."

I gave a cry of surprise. "You showed it to them?"

"Indeed. The innkeeper was startled, but the porter only seemed sad, as though he had long suspected his master would meet such a fate."

Putting aside his teacup, Alistair continued.

"I pretended to be the steward of the estate's true owner, and assured the porter that I would seek no compensation from Colden's family for the fire's damages—though I made it *eminently* clear that any further trespass on the estate would prompt swift action on that front."

"And what of the physician who accused you?"

"That, I know not. I rather hoped he thought me dead."

I was pensive for a long while. How the story had stirred me—how it would haunt me in the days to come! I could scarcely imagine having to weather such things, to have awoken as a vampire with nobody's guidance. It dwarfed the agony of my own awakening and terrified me.

"That is all," Alistair concluded, brushing one long hair from his face. His eyes eluded mine, and gloom crept into his voice. "I regret not having told you sooner. It was easier to let you assume that my hands were clean."

"So you've dreaded telling me this, for all of the time we've spent together?"

Either too afraid or too unsure to respond, Alistair regarded me silently, his dark eyes searching my face.

Seeing this, I sighed. "Do you truly consider me so harsh in my judgments?"

A glow of relief suffused him at this reply, but he still lowered his voice and spoke quietly. "It would not be harsh to condemn the killing of at least one innocent man."

"That was not your kill, sir, it was your hunter's. You tried to do what was right, but the circumstances were against you. I fail to see what else you could have done, other than to sacrifice your own life!" I softened my voice, and met his gaze with the steadiest look I could muster. "I know you did the best you could. Nobody could ask more of you than that—certainly not

I.”

Alistair gave a wistful smile at my words, but shook his head. “Ah, Mr. Bedford; though you may be right, I still wish I had a more courageous tale with a better ending. I don’t want your pity, but your esteem.”

This statement surprised me; I suppose I hadn’t realized that Alistair cared so much about his appearance in my eyes. Emboldened, I therefore pressed on with my honest thoughts.

“Absolute virtue is the domain of the wealthy, sir,” I said stoutly. “It is impossible to chase such a thing when fighting for food and life; you and I have that experience in common. You went beyond your duty by trying to spare your hunter, and taking pains to keep the townspeople from undue harm. That, I esteem *most* greatly.”

Hesitating, then, I went on.

“Though I know guilt might always weigh heavy in your chest.”

“Indeed,” Alistair mused. “The guilt remains, even after centuries have passed. Yet, somehow, the worst guilt of all...”

His voice trailed off; he fell silent.

“What is it?” I said.

He sighed, lifting his gaze towards the ceiling. “I suppose I haven’t finished my story.”

I watched him and waited.

“The wolves.” His voice now dipped so low that I felt it in my chest. “After Colden was dead, after the church was built over the ruins of the cottage, after I gained easy access to corpse blood—that story, I shall leave for another time—I began to feed from the dead, lost my power, and soon realized that I had a dire problem.”

“You would lose your control of the wolves,” I realized

suddenly, "Without the power of living blood."

Alistair nodded.

"So if you had lost control of them…"

"By the time that I realized it, I was already losing control of them." His voice dipped lower still. "They would only heed my broadest commands, and began to chase after the livestock nearby, rousing the townspeople into taking up their weapons. My dear wolves could not help themselves, for it was their nature; they were guiltless, blameless, and dependent upon me, as I had once been upon them; but I…"

There, he paused. A hideous moan of wind went through the cracks in the room, and I shivered despite myself, but my curiosity was not extinguished.

"What happened to the wolves, sir?"

He was silent, gazing off into the distance.

I spoke again. "What did you do?"

There was the faint gleam of a tear in his eye.

"I did nothing," he said softly. "I watched them die."

CHAPTER XXIV

Once Alistair had gathered himself and risen once more from his past, he stood from the chair and paced.

"A carcass prepared thus, full of silver, which so resembles what I remember, may have some relation to my old hunter; it certainly seems devised with wolves in mind, though I have none with me now. Either Colden once took inspiration from an earlier text, which our current nuisance is now referencing—or, more likely, Colden invented the method himself and left some type of document describing it. We must be vigilant."

But as one week passed and turned to two, nothing transpired.

We went to feed every few days now, without even waiting a week, to the point where I felt my complexion grow ruddy; but no more did we find garlic flowers, nor any felled deer along our path. No interlopers tried to enter the manor, and no other sign of danger made itself known.

By the time another week passed, and February began, our

guard had loosened. We surmised that these two attempts at warding us away had occurred simultaneously, and that whoever performed them had likely given up upon seeing no result—or perhaps it had all been a trick for twelfth night, done in very poor taste.

I thought I might ask Mr. Parker whether he had sold any sinister old journals, but Alistair warned me against it, reasoning that it was best not to draw attention to anything at all. If the danger had truly passed, it was best to leave it be.

With our peace regained, at least for the moment, we were able to renew our studies, and spent the frigid beginning of February in good spirits.

In the meantime, something more pleasantly intriguing presented itself.

Alistair informed me of it one day, when I visited his room towards the end of the night. We had taken a short break while he washed his hair, which always took him quite some time, and so I knocked before calling out:

"Hurry up!"

"I am nearly finished."

"Are you mopping the floor with your head?"

"Yes, and I am nearly finished."

By this point, we had become quite informal with each other. Having passed danger together, which has the effect of drawing souls together, we had lost any sense of propriety which had formerly governed our interactions; but Alistair still seemed reticent to show himself in any state of undress, or to see me doing the same.

"Well, of course," I had replied quizzically, when he mentioned it once, "If that is your preference, I shall be glad to accept; but really, you needn't be so shy!"

He seemed a touch aggrieved. "I'm not shy, Mr. Bedford."

"Then why fret? I was a valet, you know. I have seen all manner of things."

"I'm sure you have."

"Then elaborate."

"No."

Knowing that a stubborn Alistair was like a rock, sitting unmoved for centuries, I relented. Though I found his shame amusing—and I must admit, I was curious to know what he hid!—I would have loathed to pry him from his comfort, and let him be.

It was therefore only once he called out for me that I entered. He had dressed again, though with a rich shawl draped about his shoulders to prevent his locks from dampening his clothes.

"Well, Mr. Bedford?" he said, as he strode to the table in the study. "You said you had something to show me."

I had wanted to show Alistair a bird's nest I had found; but seeing his sodden hair, I suddenly thought better of it. "It was outside, but never mind—you will catch a chill."

"A vampire can take a chill."

"But you will be cold."

"Then you owe me some other sort of entertainment," said he, giving his hair another wring. Then, he paused. "Ah, I have remembered something."

"Yes?"

He gestured languidly to his desk. "Speaking of entertainment, have a look."

There was a letter lying open; I picked it up and skimmed it. "What is this?"

"The manor has been hired for a celebration. Not tomorrow night, nor the next—we will have those to do as we please—but the following night."

"Oh!" I cried out in surprise. "You should have told me earlier, so that we could prepare the manor properly!"

He shook his head. "They prepare their own matters, and Josephine aids them; we only wait. Unfortunately, it will impede our freedom that night."

"I see." I frowned. "So what shall we do?"

"Remain in our respective rooms, and listen to the music."

I was a little glum. "For the entire night?"

Noticing my mood, Alistair placed his hand on my shoulder. "Only one night. Now, may I beg for you to show me what you found earlier?"

And so, after fastidiously helping him dry his hair, I took him outside to show him the nest. It was tucked in a furrow between two branches of a thick old tree, which spread so far as to make a little clearing over the frosted grass.

Though I was puzzled to find bird's eggs in winter, Alistair explained to me that it was a crossbill's brood. "A brave and resourceful bird, which can pry seeds from crevices in the dead of winter—though perhaps not so commonly from this variety of tree."

"And what variety would that be?"

"A yew tree—long-lived. I do like them. It is agreeable to find something that has seen so many more years than I."

Touching the weathered old bough as though it were his own kindred, he smiled and turned towards me.

"Come. I will show you a poem about an old seat settled in a yew, which I love very much. It is by Wordsworth, I believe, far nearer to your time than mine; in fact, I may have some of it memorized."

And so, in a low and serene voice, he recited a portion of it as we made our way back towards the manor:

*   *   *

I placed my book aside and rubbed my face wearily.

At first, it was the din of the celebration in the great hall that had woken me, but I had been having an uneasy rest all the same.

Though days had passed, the sound of Alistair's murmur as he stepped down from the yew tree's roots still rang like a bell in my head, and stirred me an ache so strong that I nearly felt ill.

Indeed, if I was ill, then something was worsening in my condition. Perhaps loosened by the short danger we had passed, the unfamiliar swell of feelings that accompanied my friendship with Alistair was growing ever stronger and more difficult to contain, to the point where I truly thought it to be some sort of madness.

After that evening when we returned from seeing the nest, I had nearly told him. I had wondered what he would make of it, in all his wisdom; but I only got as far as a flimsy attempt.

"Sir," I had said, as we stepped into the manor. "I must confess something."

"Yes, Mr. Bedford?" he said, as we walked.

But the moment was not yet ripe, and I was suddenly embarrassed. Losing all my courage at once, I mumbled: "I'm feeling a little ill."

He paused in his step and turned at once. "What is it?"

486

"I don't know." I stopped alongside him. "I feel cold."

His expression eased. "Come. We can light a fire."

"Not so cold as that," I said sullenly, and was frustrated with myself.

Alistair then seemed to grasp that something was amiss, and spoke slowly. "Where do you feel cold?"

Seeing his fine and erudite mind trying in vain to make sense of my nonsensical complaint, I felt hideously stupid. At last, I gave the first answer that came to mind.

"My hands."

Then, at once, I realized I was still wearing my new gloves, which he had furnished me with. Cursing myself for my rudeness, I quickly amended:

"I took my gloves off for a moment, when we were outside."

Alistair tilted his head. "Did you?"

By this point, I had no sense of what I was saying. "Oh—forget it, never mind."

Now with a touch of amusement, Alistair held out his hand. "Perhaps you have some small wound, which the cold has provoked. Let me see."

Despite knowing that it was all a farce, I removed my glove and held out my hand. He took it in his, inspecting it carefully.

At once, I felt my shoulders slacken and my soul rest. How warm and delicate was his hold, how soothing! He had a rare talent for calming touch, which I could never inform him of, lest it complicate matters; but indeed, were he to be a valet, or a physician, or any other who made his living by laying hands on others, I thought to myself that he would be greatly sought after.

Yet, this touch was not the height of what he offered, nor what I secretly sought. Whenever Alistair was beset by a rare and sudden passion, I had noticed that he had the habit of tightly clasping my hand in his. He had done so upon receiving my gift of embroidery, upon reassuring me at the flower-laden chapel, and finally upon my promise of trust; I sometimes found myself reminiscing on this grasp, puzzled at the warmth it inspired in me, and wishing to have it again to better understand it.

This time, I had no such chance; after reassuring me that nothing was amiss, Alistair had asked me whether I still felt ill, whereupon I could only shake my head mutely. After that, he had let my hand fall away.

I had managed to put it all out of mind until now, when I was stranded in my room with nothing to do but ponder it.

Raising my pocket watch, I gazed for a while at the deer on the cover before opening it. The hour was half past nine.

"Very well!" I muttered to myself; I would have to find some way to occupy my time until peace returned to the manor.

Or, indeed, that was what I settled upon doing; but by the time the clock read ten, I had crushed every last grey drop of entertainment that my room contained, and was reduced to pacing in my room, feeling trapped. The colourful warbling from upstairs, laced with the occasional bout of drunken shouting, was beginning to grate on my nerves; and inevitably, no matter what I did, my thoughts returned again and again to Alistair.

Wayward fragments of my conversation with Miss Josephine from many months prior whispered quietly to me through my boredom. I remembered her description of Alistair listening to a dance just like this one, alone in his room, and her words chilled me even now.

A most mournful coat of night, he wears.

Was he in such a state at present, I wondered?

A curious frustration ruffled me, and I finally could restrain myself no longer. He would not remain alone, I resolved; and so, I dressed myself well enough that I might meld with the crowd, and stepped out of the room.

The noise swelled incredibly once I reached the grand hall, and the amount of people was suffocating. How peculiar it was, I thought, to see the hall so full, whereas it had once been the quiet place where Alistair and I spent our nights!

I suddenly felt a deep distaste for it all, and a longing for the return of quiet darkness.

But I had to cross the chaos in order to find my way to the stairs, and so I steadied myself and began to manoeuvre through the chattering masses. At one point I had the misfortune of pushing past one particularly drunk gentleman, who immediately peeled off his poor companion and stuck to me. "My good sir!" he slurred joyfully, leaning off my arm.

"Excuse me," I said, wincing. "Pardon—"

"Be happy!" he blurted loudly, leaning over my shoulder. "Be happy, my friend! You look sour—"

"Yes, well, excuse me—"

"Over here, gentlemen! This poor fellow needs a drink!"

There was a chorus of agreements, and the trickle of wine being poured. Somebody pushed a glass into my reluctant hand.

"Thank you," I said to them, elbowing past. "Now, if you'll excuse me—"

Without thinking to set down the glass, I turned and fled from them, and in a few short steps reached the merciful rise of the stairs. With a sigh of relief I climbed, sparing a glance back over the balustrade at the lit scene below as I crossed the gallery.

Soon, I reached the door to Alistair's quarters. To my surprise, I found that it was ever-so-slightly open; and so, raising my unoccupied hand, I slowly pushed the door open and slipped inside.

"Sir?"

Alistair was poised precisely as Miss Josephine had described him: draped over the desk in his study, his back curved away from his chair. His hair streamed down around him, the ends curling like black roots onto the wood.

He was wearing one of my favourite outfits that he owned, a coat of earthy olive-brown with a small cape about the shoulders, the whole ensemble rich with folds of fabric and given charm by a black bow on the cravat. It was magnificent on him due to his stature, and I had always been a little awed to see him walk about in it, as though he were some grand old aristocrat of yore.

Now the very same Alistair was silent, statue-like enough that dust motes turned slowly overhead, fearless to approach him.

Upon my entrance, however, he raised his head. At once, his countenance brightened. His sharp brows rose, and he straightened his back.

"Mr. Bedford?"

I closed the door behind me, already embarrassed. "I, er—" How could I explain such a thing? "I grew tired of waiting."

Amusement spanned his face. "Did you?"

"Well, yes!" I stammered. "It is also very loud, on that lower level—but forget that! What were you doing?"

Leaning back, Alistair stretched lightly. "Listening."

"To the music?"

"Of course." Something wistful touched his countenance, as he glanced towards the door. "It is such a rare pleasure."

There was a brief silence, while his gaze lingered there. Then, the moment was broken; he laughed quietly, leaning on his palm. "Well, you're here now. What do you propose we do, to alleviate your boredom?”

Realizing that I had not thought of anything, I fumbled for an idea. “I do have this glass of wine. Would you like to try it?”

Alistair smiled wider. “Why, Mr. Bedford, how cunning. You stole from our guests?”

“I stole nothing!” I rebutted, holding it out to him. “It was nearly forced upon me, I will have you know.”

Carefully, he took it from my hand. “Then I shall relieve you of this burden.” Lifting it gently to his lips, he nearly took a drink; but first, he raised his gaze to mine, then held it out.

“Could you tell me first whether you consider it good?”

Though I gave him a look, I took the glass and had a short drink. Then, with a noncommittal hum, I returned it to him.

“Champagne. Passable, if you wish to try it.”

Alistair took a short drink, then immediately grimaced and covered his mouth.

I laughed. “What’s the matter?”

He swallowed, then regarded the glass with startled curiosity. “What is in this?”

“Champagne, sir.”

“Is it meant to froth like that?”

“Indeed; that is its most particular quality.”

“How novel,” he mused, and tried it again.

For a moment, I merely watched him, as the music from downstairs went on. At the sound of it, something occurred to me, and I cleared my throat.

“Well, since there *is* music, would you like to dance?”

At once, he set down his glass and seemed mellowly surprised. “To dance?”

“Why not? We may have no other chance like this, after all.”

For a few moments, his gaze lingered on me, and he echoed

with an odd look:

"No other chance like this."

"Yes—we cannot dance to our own music."

"I suppose not," Alistair said, and stood with a fond smile. "But I must warn you, I know only the dances from my time."

"And I only know the dances from mine," I said immediately, with mounting eagerness. "So teach me yours!"

To see a dance from three centuries ago—what an idea!

We pushed all the furniture aside in his study, and tucked away the rugs in our way, until the familiar study was all neatly bare. Then, Alistair approached me.

As I watched his graceful movements, I began to regret my recommendation. I was certainly not as limber as he, and knew that I was set to be embarrassed; but my curiosity overwhelmed me, so I faced him bravely. "Show me your dance first."

Listening to the music for a moment, he tilted his head. "The speed isn't right."

"Then hum, and we shall heed the music later, when I show you mine."

"Very well." He extended his arm with a smile. "Your right hand, Mr. Bedford."

After a moment's hesitation, I lifted my hand and placed it in his. Now, we faced the same way, his fine hand holding mine aloft.

"Are you ready?"

"Yes."

"Good. Then I will show you a little volta. Mimic my steps; we will start slowly."

And so, Alistair led me in a curious little dance, humming his tune. With every stride, he swung his leg forward and gave delicate, lively steps; and I tried my best to do the same, though at first I was quite out of rhythm.

"Move one leg forward—" he demonstrated—"Then the other, like so. One, two, three, four; one, two, three—ah. That is my foot, Mr. Bedford."

"Sorry—"

"No matter. Keep going."

He led me patiently on with mounting speed, until we were making lively work of it. Then, he stopped and faced me.

"Now for the volta itself—the turn." He took my hand, and placed it up on his own shoulder. "Jump lightly, and I shall lift you."

"Lift me?!"

Alistair laughed. "Trust me, Mr. Bedford. Steady yourself here, at my shoulder."

I grasped it, finding it warm and sure, and grew a little flustered. "All right,"

Then, I felt his hands press my waist gently.

I froze still as an odd sensation sank through me. I had remembered my dream, and barely heard what he said next.

"Follow my count. Step on one, leap on two, land on three. One *two...*"

Though I was nearly too addled to comply, I quickly followed his step and leapt up; yet, I could not help but gasp in surprise— for his knee had pressed against my side, and thrust me far higher into the air than I had anticipated!

But he steadied my waist as I dropped, and I landed very softly, with barely a sound. "Just like that," he said. "How was it?"

An urge to laugh swelled up inside me, quivering in my chest and brightening my gaze. I looked up at him, delighted. "One more time!"

And so, seeming rather delighted at my enthusiasm, he gave me more practice until at last I could do it fearlessly. It was then that I gained the courage to ask:

"Could I try lifting you as well, sir?"

With some surprise, which seemed almost demure, he nodded. "If you think you can take my weight, go on." Then, he watched me dryly. "Only take care not to drop me, Mr. Bedford."

I placed his hand on my shoulder and faced him with confidence, stating plainly:

"Trust me."

His answer was a look of soft surprise, mingled with something that was almost tenderness.

"Of course."

The startled look that he gave when I hoisted him up high and swung him around, framed by the toss of his hair and his sharp intake of breath, seemed to me so perfect that I committed it to memory. When I brought him down, his cheeks were flushed, and they remained so as we danced on.

After we had mastered the volta, taking turns with the leaps, he stopped me and said with great interest:

"Now your time has come, Mr. Bedford. Show me your dance."

And so, gathering my wits, I moved closer towards him, though a rush of nerves suffused me. With a steadying breath, I reached up to gingerly take hold of his waist, while I fumbled for his other hand.

He understood and soon met it with his, but then twined his fingers through mine. At that, I had to suppress a shudder.

"Not quite like that," I said with some strain, and pulled my hand away, hoping desperately that he could not feel the clamminess of my skin. "Here. Copy this position, sir."

I felt odd to instruct him, but he did as I said, though he murmured with mild surprise:

"This close?"

"This close," I replied, though I stammered. "It is a common sort of waltz."

Then, very carefully, I began to lead him.

We started slowly, turning over the floor, one pair of our arms forming a bower overhead. I could feel the steadiness of his grasp around my waist, as I too could feel his waist in mine; he was so very graceful!

Though at first our movements were stilted, he soon grasped the rhythm of the dance; and then he was off, sweeping me along with him. How peculiar it was, to be one with his elegant movements, which had so often pleased me to watch! In some manner, I felt that I understood him through them, and for a moment knew what it was to have his long and elegant body. Piqued, I wondered whether he, too, was living for an instant through mine. Our small, shuffling steps widened into great, loping strides, and we spun—how we spun!

When I looked up and met his eyes, I found that he was watching me intently. My chest was somehow shivering as we turned again and again, and the music might as well have been playing beside us for the way it filled my head. I was overwhelmed, and could make no sense of it.

In my confusion, I stumbled; but a look of excitement lit Alistair's features, and he clasped me more securely in response. "Are you well, Mr. Bedford?" he said, as we narrowly avoided a chair. "Am I moving too quickly?"

Dizzy with the feeling of spinning, I laughed. "I am very well!"

He was pleased. "I must admit, the people of your time have fine taste."

We alternated between the dances of his time and mine, teaching each other different styles, dancing on and on into the night. Whenever we rested, we related stories of festivities from our human lives, and shared a great deal of laughter before standing once more to go on. One hour passed in this manner, then two.

Yet, slowly, something was building in my chest—something burning and dire, which swelled up whenever I faced him. To frolic with him like this felt like catharsis, but catharsis of what? I had seldom ever been interested in dance, and yet I was filled with a ruinous joy so powerful that it frightened me; only the safety of our mutual grasp held me from bursting.

How I ached for relief, yet knew nothing of where to find it!

Eventually, the music began to slow, and we slowed with it. Yet, my frenzied heartbeat would not rest, and my eyes remained boring into his.

Finally, the music ceased entirely, dying away on the night. The last song of the celebration had ended.

With our breaths still laboured, we stood still. Sweat clung like dew to my forehead.

What was Alistair thinking? I looked up at him, feeling confused and expectant. I finally had the courage to ask him whether he knew what was wrong with me; but my own questions were now so many that I could no longer distinguish them.

Alistair, for his part, seemed equally affected—though by what, I knew not. His eyes shone strangely, and he seemed to finally come down to rest from some dream.

His hand slid slowly from my waist.

"Thank you for the dance," he said quietly.

Then, he lifted my hand, bent down, and pressed his lips gently to the skin just above my knuckles.

My breath caught. I immediately assumed it to be either a jest, or some old Spaniard custom. Still, I was startled.

"And to you," I blundered out.

But Alistair did not release my hand. Instead, he turned it over slowly, exposing the softer, inner part of my wrist.

For a moment, gazing down at it, he held still. There was a heavy and trance-like gleam in his eye.

Then, all at once, he bowed his head again; and before I could fathom his intent, he had pressed a kiss to that sensitive spread of veins, which thrummed with my quickened pulse.

A spark of thrill went down my back, and my heart clenched. Something indescribable dropped through me.

Alistair paused for a moment, as though waiting for something.

But once a few seconds of my dead silence had passed, his shoulders loosened. He gave a smile which, though fond, also held some finality in it; and with that, he released my hand at last and pulled away, saying pleasantly:

"Come, let us put the furniture back."

Yet, in the instant that he spoke, a shattering thought came to me with sudden clarity:

I was being dragged from the brink of my relief—*I could not let him go!*

In a frenzy, I pitched forward and clutched his arms tightly.

The effect this produced was immediate. In a single swift movement, Alistair seized me and drew me in. One hand encircled my waist, while the other raised my chin; but he brought my face up gently, trembling as he did, and with an expression that burned with ardour.

My instincts all cried out to me discordantly, each pulling me in a different direction. I ignored them all.

Surging up in his arms as he sank down, I met him in a torrid kiss.

CHAPTER XXV

At first, I was overwhelmed with relief.

I closed my eyes and gripped him, nearly wild with it. There was a thrill through my entire being, which coursed from the place where our lips were pressed flush against each other's in loving comfort, and seemed to sob: at last—at last!

But just as quickly, I recognized what I was doing, and opened my eyes in shock. Then, with a surge of wild panic, I broke free and stumbled back!

Alistair was left standing alone, his arms still outstretched where he had held me. He stared at me in surprise for a moment, then opened his mouth to speak; but I backed away, entirely distraught.

At once, upon seeing my expression, his look changed. "Mr. Bedford—"

"What was that?" I said, in quiet horror.

"Nothing," he said, trying to soothe me, though a slight

tremble betrayed it. "We were taken by a passionate moment, and acted on impulse—"

Hearing it spoken so openly, I was seized with frantic disbelief. "By God! What have I done?"

"Nothing!" he insisted again, more adamantly, then stepped forward. "You did nothing. It was all my doing—"

"But you *never* do anything on impulse!" My knees were weak, as I took another step back. "If that was *my* reason, then what was *yours?*"

At that, his expression verged on desperation. "I thought…"

"You thought what?"

"I'm sorry."

"Sorry for *what?*" In the tumult of my emotions, my rationality was annihilated, and I was suddenly gripped with doubt. "Did you intend to do this from the start?"

"Never!—this was never my intention," he pleaded. "It was my fault. I was never going to speak a word of my feelings for you—"

"Your *feelings* for me?" I cried out. "What do you mean? What in God's name do you mean by that?"

"Please listen, I beg of you." His voice grew in intensity as he spoke. "It was my fault, for mistaking your gesture; it was my own foolish heart that wronged you, forgive me—ah, forgive me!"

But that was the crux of it: he had mistaken nothing!

With a trembling breath, I looked back at him, and found to my horror that his eyes shone with the beginnings of tears. The guilt that followed nearly crushed me; my heart was pounding, and my mouth grew dry. Mired in shame and confusion alike, I backed away towards the door.

"Wait," he called after me breathlessly. "Mr. Bedford!"

It was then that I suddenly saw a tremble run through his hand. This cleared my head, and I found the steadiness to approach him. "All right, calm down."

But when I reached for him, he flinched away, and yet begged me: "I won't touch you, but don't go—"

"I won't go!" I cried out. "But sit first, don't faint."

Though he stiffened when I touched his arm, he let me guide him to an armchair and sank down listlessly, seeming on the very brink of delirium.

Once I ensured he was settled, I hurried for the door again. "I need a moment to think," I said hoarsely. "I'm not upset with you. Stay here, don't do anything rash; I swear I'll return!"

My guilt and bewilderment had flooded me; I needed silence, I needed time to think, I needed air!

But as I went, Alistair called out after me with a plea so soft and heartsick that it made me tremble:

"Avery."

My hand froze on the door handle. There was a long and dreadful silence.

Then, I choked out the only thing I could think to say:

"That is Mr. Bedford to you, sir!'

With that, I left him and fled.

*　　*　　*

I rushed, barely thinking, down the hall towards my room.

With the music finished, guests were beginning to leave, and servants were busy with tidying; but I barely paid them any attention at all. My mind was elsewhere.

I could still feel the soft and ravenous touch of Alistair's lips pressed to mine, and the shameful swell of passion that had risen to meet it.

Having had to reckon with Alistair's bite, and made peace with setting it aside for the moment, I thought that I might have gained experience in facing great and shattering events; but this! This had been thrust before me with no warning, and I was not entirely blameless; but blameless in what, precisely? What was the entire affair, and who was most responsible for it?

Though my thoughts spun madly, my steps carried me by instinct to my room in the servants' hall; but I was not alone. Miss Josephine, just arriving from the grand hall, looked up from her keys.

I stopped, and we stared at each other. Then, her eyes narrowed.

"What happened?"

"Nothing," I managed, trying in vain to hide my stricken look, before fumbling with my door. "Nothing—good night, Miss Josephine."

With that, I entered my room, and the familiar surroundings began to calm me; but the calm lasted little. The door opened behind me, and I heard Miss Josephine's steps shuffling in.

With a sigh, I turned. "I said good night."

But I found the furrows of her face deep with suspicion, and her brow knitted stormily. She spoke with stubborn harshness. "What did he do?"

I faltered. "Why—nothing!"

She glared, unconvinced. "You are a pitiful liar."

"Truly, nothing, I said! I'm only tired, and we had a small argument. That is all."

"Your countenance tells a different story."

"He did nothing," I insisted, then sighed. "Nothing important."

Her stare did not abate. Uneasy as I looked away from her, I noticed suddenly that a long, black hair clung to my waistcoat. With a morose look, I pulled it off and let it fall.

"All right," she said, and walked out.

I looked wearily after her, as she shuffled across the hall and entered her room. Indeed—nothing important, I thought to myself. This changed nothing, and could perhaps be settled with enough careful thought.

Yet, suddenly, I heard a particular rattling, and recognized it as the unmistakable sound of a firearm being loaded. With a gasp, I rushed across the hall into her room. "Miss Josephine! What on earth are you doing?"

She was saddling up her musket. "What I should have done a long time ago."

With a strange and horrified laugh, I hurried forward and seized the end of the barrel. "You can't kill him with this, I assure you—"

"Then I will give the blackguard a face full of gunpowder before he kills me."

"Now, just wait a minute!" I pleaded, now genuinely concerned, and pressed the musket down. "Please believe me, this is nothing so dire as to end in death! It was something that transpired between us, where the blame lies on both our shoulders."

"I hardly believe that," she snapped, "I sensed his little forays, though I never thought he would dare to go any further than—"

"Miss Josephine," I interrupted, flushing deeply red. "We didn't."

She searched my eyes with suspicion. "Didn't *what?*"

"It isn't what you think," I strained out, though I was

becoming very flustered. "Only something very small, which happened on impulse, and which I…"

I trailed off as my courage wavered, but managed to finish weakly:

"Which I did not wholeheartedly discourage."

"Stop being vague. What was it?"

"Well," I said gingerly, as I rubbed the back of my neck, "Where decency is concerned, I would hesitate to—"

"I have three times your age and one-third of your patience. Tell me what it was, or he eats my bullet."

"It was a kiss," I strained finally, and felt that I would die of shame.

But she regarded me dryly. "That was all?"

At once, I was anxious, and hurried to add: "Yes! And at least there was nothing further, so we have done nothing that the law would frown upon, but—"

She gave a sardonic laugh. "The *law*, Mr. Bedford? Are you a lawful vampire?"

"Apart from the obvious matter, yes!" Then, I hesitated. "The law itself isn't the point, but rather the moral issue of it."

"Oh, don't be ridiculous." Taking the musket, she shuffled to a drawer. "Have you not heard? In France, now, they do whatever they please, and not even the law can touch them."

I was shocked that she would react with such indifference. "Well, no wonder we went to war with them!"

"You cannot be so naive as to think nothing of the sort happens in England."

"I'm not naive," I said sullenly. "I have seen *plenty*, believe me! But *that* is the very reason that I cannot stand for this. Why, this sort of licentious conduct is borne of the unbridled lust of men— useless other than slaking perverted desires, and therefore corrupting! I will have you know, I was raised in a brothel; so where lust is concerned, I have seen the very worst of it, and it is the ugliest, most repulsive…”

I suddenly saw Alistair's face in my mind's eye—the almost feverish glow that had suffused him when I handed him my embroidery, and the way he had pressed my hand between his to thank me. In the light of the fire, the reserved fondness in his gaze had burned hot enough to melt sugar.

“Unbridled lust?” Miss Josephine sneered, now mocking me openly. “What unbridled lust? One chaste kiss after months of tormenting himself like a fool?”

This returned me from my thoughts. “What do you mean, months?”

“Are you blind, Mr. Bedford?”

Indeed, I was not; and upon even the most cursory review of the time we had spent together, it was suddenly obvious what he had been struggling with. Yet, I had long discarded this possibility for one very simple reason.

“But why *me?*” I burst out, suddenly upset. “He cannot *possibly* desire me, that is preposterous—and if he has indeed been restraining himself for months, then it must be I who has imposed something upon him, and subjected us both to this!”

Miss Josephine stared in disbelief.

Quickly, I became flustered, and then deeply embarrassed. “But I shouldn't have burdened you with these thoughts, nor come into your room uninvited.” I began to step back. “Excuse me; you caught me in a moment of weakness. Good night—”

“Stop.”

I stopped, and she went on with even greater amusement.

“Are you implying that you *seduced* him?”

“No! No, but I have made him desire something that isn't

real—made myself appear grander than I am, and therefore pushed him to where he might not otherwise have gone. He has always been patient and proper; it must be something in my own sordid nature that has altered him, not his."

At that, she did something that surprised me greatly; she gave a low chuckle, a true one, and sighed. "You're very young. I will give you a piece of advice."

Meeting her eyes, I hesitated. "Yes?"

"Go and speak to him," she scoffed. "Sort out your little *kiss*. You yourself said that you have done nothing untoward. If *he* did, my bullet would answer."

Though I shuddered a little, I gave a weary smile. "Very well. I suppose I shall."

I was suddenly grateful for her presence. It had eased my soul and settled my thoughts to speak with her, and the moment of panic now seemed distant and excessive.

"But there is one more matter," she said suddenly.

"Oh—yes?"

She raised her brows at me. "What sordid nature might *you* have?"

I remembered the dream that I had about Alistair, the closeness of his body, the firmness of his touch as it crept up my leg. Then, I smiled tightly.

"I'm not sure; forgive me. Good night, Miss Josephine."

CHAPTER XXVI

I paced and paced in my room, agonizing over the best course of action.

Miss Josephine's words echoed in my mind. I could not deceive myself, not any more than I could deceive her; I had grown to feel something for Alistair more intricate than ordinary friendship.

But could there not simply be some extraordinarily close companionship? Was it so unusual to wish for an embrace from a friend? Even between man and woman, that most crucial line between cordial acquaintance and true affection was subject to much deliberation; and so, perhaps an unusually familiar friendship between men could produce the same confusion.

That, however, held true only without considering the matter of my own unusual feelings. Though I had never pursued a woman in my life, this was by design; I had long promised myself that I would never participate in the sort of dissolute conduct that had always surrounded me, and thus be worthy of leaving it behind.

Curiously, I had never found such abstinence difficult; repulsion had been my greatest ally until now, when it had suddenly abandoned me.

Never had I thought that I would find myself unprepared in such a situation!

But more than anything, the longer I thought to myself and calmed my worries, I was overcome by guilt over the manner in which I had left Alistair, and haunted by the heartbroken pleas for patience that he had called after me.

If anyone could help me reason through it all, it was him. There was no escaping my shame; I had to face Alistair again.

Bracing my wits, I fixed myself in the mirror and left the room.

My heart beat frantically in my ears as I climbed the stairs, and grew deafening as I reached his door. With a deep breath, I cleared my throat and knocked; but instead of waiting for his response, I lifted my head and spoke.

"Sir, I've returned. May I come in?"

For a moment, there was utter silence, and I feared that he was not there at all; but soon, his voice rose up.

"Of course."

My palms were clammy with nerves, but my mind was clear and numb as ice. I went to his bedroom door, then stepped in and faced him.

Alistair was sitting up in his bed. I noticed immediately that he was terribly pale, his expression taut and struggling for calm, though it betrayed a flare of anxiety at the sight of me.

As though he could bear his own thoughts no longer, he broke the silence first.

"Mr. Bedford," he said, with urgent earnestness. "Before you say anything, I must express my deepest apologies for the misery I brought upon you tonight. It was a profound failure of my judgment, and an insult to the trust that you have—"

"Sir," I said quietly. "Would you stop for a moment?"

This, he did, though there was a spark of worry in his eyes.

I went on. "I don't need your apology."

This was unexpected; I could tell, by the stillness of his shoulders. Still, with enviable poise, he replied at once. "Then tell me what you need."

"First, I apologize for having left you as I did. I regret to have caused you anguish."

"Ask what you must."

With that, he made a movement as though he meant to stand, but I shook my head. "Rest easy," I sighed, pulling an armchair to the bedside. "We will have a proper conversation."

Alistair glanced at the chair. Then, he nodded mutely.

I sat, then raised my gaze to his with burning honesty. "I would like to understand you, sir; that has never changed. Neither has the fact that you are my friend, and that I trust you."

At a loss for words, he stared down at the blanket over his lap before answering quietly. "Thank you, Mr. Bedford."

This demure gratitude nearly made me shiver, but I went on stolidly.

"Before I left, you made reference to some feeling that you had. I wish to know *precisely* what you meant by that."

Alistair's eyes drifted downward, with a troubled and delicate look; but a reverie of fondness soon came into his expression. Raising this tender look to me, he folded his hands in his lap.

"I have come to love you," he said softly.

Immediately, I was seized with shock, and the hairs on the

back of my neck and arms stood on end; I had not expected him to speak so directly. "Now, now, don't be hasty; let us put that word aside for a moment!"

"But I have."

"You mean to say that you feel a strong *friendly* affection for me."

"No," he said steadily, though not without shame. "Amorous love."

How can I describe the effect those words had upon me? It was as though some force had gripped my chest from within. Still, I rebuffed him.

"All right, sir," I said hurriedly, with some relief. "Worry no more. I understand *precisely* what has happened here, and it isn't your fault in the slightest."

Alistair tilted his head, ever patient, though softness pervaded his gaze. "And what is that, Mr. Bedford?"

Settling myself, I said firmly:

"In all your centuries of seclusion, you have lost your sense of what is natural. Having passed so long apart from the company of men and women, dressing according to your whims, you have come to think of them as indistinguishable; and having spent so long without—" I coughed politely. "Without a means to express the natural impulse which lives inside man, you have built up an excess of it, and have thus mistaken intimate friendship for amorous affection!"

Taking on the tone of a schoolteacher, I then leaned forward and reassured him:

"There can be great *friendly* love between men, and that is what you feel for me, and I for you."

Alistair looked silently down at his hands for a moment, before saying reticently:

"When I was in the most defiant phase of my human life, did you think that I had *only* women?"

I stared at him, dumbfounded.

Then, I felt my face flush, and wrung my hands. "Well, I—I assumed that—all right, how many?"

Alistair seemed surprised at that. "How many men?"

"One or two, or…?"

Alistair watched me helplessly for a moment, then shook his head.

"Three?" I said hoarsely.

With that, he began to count reluctantly on his fingers; but at that point, I waved my hand. "All right! All right, don't tell me." I took a deep breath. "Very well. You have had men, and that is that, I will leave it alone. That is *your* business; but such things are the result of misguided *lust*, not love."

Hearing that, he at last took on a firmer tone. "Mr. Bedford, I could never be mistaken on this matter. I'm sorry; I know what love feels like to me, and I feel it most profoundly for you now. I never intended to feel such a thing, and much less to trouble you with it; but now my worst nightmare is upon me. Had I not mistaken your gestures for mutual desire—"

"That wasn't your fault!" I said quickly. "It was also pure and thoughtless impulse on my part, which is why I don't blame you; and I myself must apologize for—"

"But you kept my miniature," Alistair murmured.

I nearly swallowed my tongue. "What?"

"I saw it go missing," he whispered. "I thought…"

Realizing how that would have looked, I rushed to correct him. "That was for—"

For my reference, I was set to say, then realized that I had never tried to use it for that purpose.

"—for some other reason," I finished clumsily. "But forget me; I have already told you my side! You never finished with yours."

Alistair paused, then said gently:

"You seem determined to persuade me that it does not exist."

Sensing the very faintest trace of hurt, and realizing that I had caused it, I stumbled over my words. "It isn't that. I only thought that if I could easily resolve your problem…"

Alistair shook his head. "This is not some repulsive problem to me; I would not wish to have it explained away, even if it were possible. I ask not for your reciprocity, Mr. Bedford; you have nothing to be wary of. I am only trying to give you the understanding you asked for."

He then watched me with a hint of sorrowful amusement.

"You trust my knowledge in most other matters; why do you doubt it here, where it concerns my own feelings, which I undoubtedly know better than any other?"

I felt sweat gather on my palms. "Because—oh, let us be honest with each other; I am most certainly *not* the type of person to inspire the type of desire you describe!"

"In what manner are you not?"

"In—well, everything, but first and foremost, in looks."

Alistair stared, faintly surprised, and opened his mouth to speak; but I interrupted him.

"And before you flatter me—"

"No flattery," he interrupted in turn, with mingled hopelessness and urgency. "Only candour. You are very beautiful, Mr. Bedford."

I had never heard such a thing from anyone's lips, and promptly lost the calm air I had feigned. "Oh, don't be ridiculous!"

"It's true."

Unable to bear it, I looked away from him. "For God's sake—
"

"I cannot forget the day when you became ill from animal blood," he whispered. "When you were lulled by my music, the sight of you sleeping in your nightshirt—"

"That is enough!" I cried out, pale with shock and embarrassment. "Sir, I'm very sorry, but that is not love; that is *lust!*"

"Not crude lust," he urged. "It is your heart that I want most of all; but your spirit lives through all of you, and sweetens your allure. My desire is no base instinct; it is a wish to bring physical form to my emotions, which could find no other escape."

"Sir," I said, with mounting disbelief, "Perhaps you have forgotten, having lived away from humanity for so long, but such desires *do* have a method of escape, which sometimes has the effect of clearing the mind; though it is bad for the health, and I would not necessarily recommend it—"

"I've tried," Alistair said, with some strain. "It hasn't helped."

I balked at the thought of it, and nearly scrambled back in my seat. "You mean to say you—!"

With a pained, polite smile, he folded his hands. "I would never have told you, but you asked."

The thought of him performing such deeds with me in mind struck me rather like a stone, and left me dumbfounded.

Taking my silence as offense, Alistair continued with low remorse. "Forgive me. It was all I could do, to nurse my suffering; I would find bliss in your company, and pay for it with heartsickness later—which I would try to relieve by letting my mind stray to the occasional liberty, which I hoped your soul might forgive me for."

"How long has this been weighing on you?" I said faintly.

"I have always enjoyed your company, and felt a budding love, which I tried in vain to ascribe to profound friendship; but it was not until I played the lute for you that day in November when I knew that affection had blossomed full-fledged, and could no longer be quelled."

"You have been in this state for *months* without telling me?"

"I wished to pour out my soul and confess, but feared a result such as this." After a pause, he added quietly: "And lest you worry, it wasn't any part of why I bit you."

Realizing that he had never trusted me enough to disclose his feelings—and had, indeed, been justified in his fears—I was suddenly awash with shame, and said with a heavy heart:

"Regardless of what I think of this, I wish I had given you enough reason to trust me with your confession. If I have hurt you in any way—"

"You haven't," he said, quiet but firm. "This has never been bitter to me—always sweet. I would rather carve out my heart than rid myself of what I feel. Furthermore, I never mistrusted you; I merely never wished to burden you, and was content to let you nourish my affections with the vigour of your kindness. My only regret..."

He seemed to lose his breath, then regained it before saying in anguish:

"Mr. Bedford, if I could take back what I have done tonight, and regain innocence of the friendship we shared—" His jaw trembled, and his hands curled into his bedsheets. "I would sell my soul for it."

At that, I could restrain my voice no longer. "Regain it? Why, who said that it was lost?"

He hesitated. "But you—"

"You have not broken my trust, nor done anything that I did not allow. Though it was done entirely on impulse, I *did* meet your kiss, and was not repulsed by it in any way!"

Alistair regarded me with some surprise. "By that, you mean to say—"

"Listen closely!" I said, meeting his gaze. "I am glad that my company inspires such lofty feelings as you describe—indeed, I almost understand them myself. I, too, have been a little thrown by the nearness of our friendship, and have at times wondered what to do with it. Why, had my upbringing not tainted love and lust for me irrevocably, perhaps I would have been equally inclined as you!"

Clearing my throat, I then looked down with some embarrassment and went on:

"Lest that give you false hope, I must tell you honestly that I don't think I can bring any resolution to your passions; but I will trust your testimony that they are real. So long as you are content with letting them go unsatisfied, as you have done so most patiently and selflessly thus far, I can remain your friend with no qualms."

His expression was tense, nearly dying of hope. "Even if I have upset you so severely?"

"You have not upset me, only surprised me—here, I shall prove it!"

With that, I rose up and leaned forward, hardly believing my own actions, and clasped his hands warmly in mine. How my heart sped when I did! I was filled suddenly with a fear that he would push me away; but instead, I felt a tremble pass through him.

"You are an angel of mercy," Alistair said breathlessly, with relief loosening his expression. "Ah, I could never deserve you."

I scoffed. "Enough of that."

He began to draw his hands away. "Neither would I compel you to touch me—"

But I only reached forward, and gripped his graceful hands tighter. "Why not? To want for touch is a very human thing, and I would not withhold it from you." Realizing that such a reason would not suffice, I braced myself and went on. "Indeed, I myself am no stranger to friendly affection either, and I—I *do* find your touch very comforting."

Spellbound, Alistair stared.

"On the whole..." I met his regard again, and found that amazement was fading into his expression. "I think that you are the closest friend that I have ever known, and when I leave, I know that I will miss you terribly. I am truly dreading it!"

He was choked with some nameless feeling. "As am I."

"Then let us enjoy the time we have together without worrying overmuch about little matters like these, shall we?"

His eyes shone so brightly that I nearly had to look away. "Mr. Bedford—"

"You have already used my name once, haven't you? Go on, we are near enough that it makes no difference. I will allow it."

For a moment, he struggled, and then spoke with a softness that made me ache:

"Avery."

I answered stiffly. "Quite."

"You will not regret the trust you have placed in me. You have my word."

"Well, I certainly hope not," I said good-naturedly, as I slipped back.

Finally wearing his usual impish smile, Alistair leaned back against his pillows. "Ah, I was so worried."

I straightened my clothes. "Were you?"

"I thought you would cast me straight through the window."

At that, I laughed. "Well, it isn't out of the question." Then, I turned to him again. "But so long as you are *entirely* honest with me from now on, and tell me whenever something troubles you, then we can leave the window shut."

"I have no choice, then."

"And we are *not* finished discussing this," I added. "I would like to better understand your perspective on this subject."

"On love?"

The word still made a shock go through me, but I steadied. "Indeed."

"The Greek had much to say on it. We can make it our study for today."

"Then I will make us tea, and we can meet in the library."

"Very well," he murmured, before pausing. "Avery…"

I stiffened, still unused to the use of my name upon his lips, as well as the flutter in my chest at the sound of it. "Yes, sir?"

His regard, though steady, held a touch of shyness that I had never seen him wear.

"Make haste."

*   *   *

With that, I left the room, and almost instantly felt as though a weight had been lifted from my chest. My heart pounded wildly and freely; I pressed a hand to my chest and shivered. Overtaken by wonder and bewilderment, my mind reeled, and I sensed a tremble from deep beneath my ribs.

This sensation was so powerful that I sank down, sitting on a step.

Despite the steady way I had presented my answer to Alistair, the reality was another. What chaos reigned within me! There was a part of me that balked with fear at the prospect of being loved, a part that smouldered with guilt, and a part that pulsed with the desire to tear myself wide-open to whatever returning his feelings would give to me.

I had always promised myself that I would never love amorously, that I would live a chaste life and bring ruin on nobody. Love could be terrible and filthy; lust was worse. But this! What was this?

Lost in my thoughts, I went to the kitchen and brewed a pot of tea, struggling between caution and excitement. I was terrified of where my thoughts might lead, but somehow still expectant.

When all was prepared, I left the kitchen and walked through the now deserted grand hall, heading for the library.

It was then that the sound of heavy knocking on the door pierced the night.

I froze at the sound at first, then startled when it came again. It was far too late for anyone to visit; but I then remembered the celebration that had just passed, and reasoned that it must be some servant coming to retrieve something they had left behind.

With my mind still occupied, I set down my tray and went to the door, pulling it ajar. A cold wind swelled up, and blew past me. I looked up; an instant passed.

Then there was the violent flutter of a cloak, a tremendous crack through the silence, and a sudden force that made me stumble back. At first, I understood nothing in my shock, coughing amid an acrid cloud of smoke; what had happened?

Bewildered, I looked down to see blood streaming from a bullet-hole in my stomach.

End of Volume I